*The power of the mind to imagine is
humankind's greatest gift.*

Year's
Best
SF
13

Praise for previous volumes

"An impressive roster of authors."
Locus

"The finest modern science fiction writing."
Pittsburgh Tribune

Edited by David G. Hartwell

YEAR'S BEST SF
YEAR'S BEST SF 2
YEAR'S BEST SF 3
YEAR'S BEST SF 4
YEAR'S BEST SF 5
YEAR'S BEST SF 6

Edited by David G. Hartwell & Kathryn Cramer

YEAR'S BEST SF 7
YEAR'S BEST SF 8
YEAR'S BEST SF 9
YEAR'S BEST SF 10
YEAR'S BEST SF 11
YEAR'S BEST SF 12
YEAR'S BEST SF 13
YEAR'S BEST FANTASY
YEAR'S BEST FANTASY 2
YEAR'S BEST FANTASY 3
YEAR'S BEST FANTASY 4
YEAR'S BEST FANTASY 5

YEAR'S BEST SF 13

EDITED BY
DAVID G. HARTWELL
and KATHRYN CRAMER

An Imprint of HarperCollinsPublishers

Additional copyright information appears on pages 495–496.

EOS

An Imprint of HarperCollins*Publishers*
10 East 53rd Street
New York, New York 10022-5299

Copyright © 2008 by David G. Hartwell and Kathryn Cramer
Cover art by Paul Youll
ISBN 978-0-06-125209-9
www.eosbooks.com

First Eos paperback printing: June 2008

HarperCollins® and Eos® are registered trademarks of Harper-Collins Publishers.

Printed in the U. S. A.

10 9 8 7 6 5 4 3 2 1

We would like to dedicate this volume to the ambitious anthologists who this year in particular made our job pleasant and just a bit easier than usual. Keep up the good work.

Contents

x   Acknowledgments

xi   Introduction

1   Johanna Sinisalo
Baby Doll

27   Tony Ballantyne
Aristotle OS

41   John Kessel
The Last American

60   Gene Wolfe
Memorare

143   Kage Baker
Plotters and Shooters

164   Peter Watts
Repeating the Past

168   Stephen Baxter
No More Stories

185   Robyn Hitchcock
They Came from the Future

189   Gwyneth Jones
       The Tomb Wife

207   Marc Laidlaw
       An Evening's Honest Peril

229   Nancy Kress
       End Game

244   Greg Egan
       Induction

261   Bernhard Ribbeck
       A Blue and Cloudless Sky

299   Gregory Benford
       Reasons Not to Publish

304   William Shunn
       **Objective Impermeability in a
       Closed System**

319   Karen Joy Fowler
       Always

334   Ken MacLeod
       Who's Afraid of Wolf 359?

349   Tim Pratt
       Artifice and Intelligence

359   Terry Bisson
       Pirates of the Somali Coast

375   Ian McDonald
       Sanjeev and Robotwallah

395   Tony Ballantyne
       Third Person

413 Kathleen Ann Goonan
The Bridge

443 John Hemry
As You Know, Bob

453 Bruce Sterling
The Lustration

474 James Van Pelt
How Music Begins

Acknowledgments

We would like to acknowledge the hindrance of the unknown forger who deposited a fake $46,000.00 check drawn on our account a month before this book was due, and created time-consuming havoc for weeks until it was completely resolved in our favor. He or she made this book infinitely more difficult to complete. We would further like to acknowledge the sympathy and support of our publisher under these awkward circumstances.

Introduction

The year 2007 in SF was a year in which average mass market sales decreased, and bestseller sales increased—a few books sold a lot of copies and fewer copies were sold of a lot of books. Generally hardcover sales were good. The SF magazines hung on. A publisher that did a lot of edgy SF, Thunder's Mouth, closed its doors and ceased to exist, the Orbit line was launched in the U.S. by Hachette, and the military and economic news in the real world was not good.

One of SF's standard scenarios, global warming, long accepted as science by scientists, was accepted by some politicians when it was suddenly discovered that the Arctic ice cap was melting very fast and might well be disappearing. Other politicians continued to maintain that science is just a matter of opinion. Still, I suppose we could say there was progress. The last volume of Kim Stanley Robinson's major trilogy on global warming was published.

Tens of millions of computer games were sold. As the year progressed, it was announced again that the electronic book is just about to replace the printed book—we are not holding our breath until it happens, though everyone in publishing would like to be able to make more money on electronic books. The money isn't there yet. There was a World SF convention in Japan, and a conference in China.

The rhetoric of fear was invoked by politicians fairly steadily to shut off debate about freedom, individual rights, and moral and ethical responsibilites, never mind objective reality. Much government corruption was exposed in the U.S. and elsewhere, and a truly enormous amount of debt heretofore hidden was noticed by the world economy. The assumptions of the quality of daily life granted as permanent in the twentieth century were rapidly disappearing.

And a lot of SF short fiction was published in magazines, anthologies, online, in pamphlets and printed zines, and by small presses of all descriptions. Much of the best of it was concerned with how we will deal with the world of the future that has replaced the assumptions of the present (now past) we have been clinging to, progressively more uncomfortably. And as in 2006, the highest concentrations of excellence were still in the professional publications, including the regular short short stories in the great science journal, *Nature*; in the anthologies from the large and small presses; and in the highest paying online markets, though the small press zines and little magazines were significant contributors as well. The small press really expanded in recent years and was a major force in short fiction this past year, both in book form and in a proliferation of ambitious little magazines, in the U.S. and the rest of the world. The difference in 2007 was that this was the year of the ambitious original anthology, in both fantasy and SF. Aside from the usual pretty good and partly good anthologies, there were several outstanding ones, including *Fast Forward 1*, *The New Space Opera*, *Eclipse 1*, and *The Solaris Book of New SF*.

Jim Baen's Universe and Strange Horizons remained the leading online SF publications, with Subterranean changing at the end of the year from print to online, and looking to join them at the top. And Aeon, Revolution SF, Eidolon online, Fantastic Magnitude, Clarkesworld, and Challenging Destiny, for instance, continued to show real promise.

This is a book about what's going on now in SF. We try in each volume of this series to represent the varieties of tones and voices and attitudes that keep the genre vigorous and responsive to the changing realities out of which it emerges, in science and daily life. It is supposed to be fun to read, a special kind of fun you cannot find elsewhere. The stories that follow show, and the story notes point out, the strengths of the evolving genre in the year 2007.

This book is full of science fiction—every story in the

book is clearly that and not something else. It is our opinion that it is a good thing to have genre boundaries. If we didn't, young writers would probably feel compelled to find something else, perhaps less interesting, to transgress or attack to draw attention to themselves. We have a high regard for horror, fantasy, speculative fiction, and slipstream, and postmodern literature. We (Kathryn Cramer and David G. Hartwell) edit the *Year's Best Fantasy* as well, a companion volume to this one—look for it if you enjoy short fantasy fiction, too. But here, we choose science fiction.

We make a lot of additional comments about the writers and the stories, and what's happening in SF, in the individual introductions accompanying the stories in this book. Welcome to the *Year's Best SF* in 2007.

Baby Doll

JOHANNA SINISALO

Translated from the Finnish by David Hackston

Johanna Sinisalo lives in the city of Tampere, in southern Finland, and is a contemporary Finnish SF and Fantasy writer. She is also a reviewer, columnist, comics writer, and screenwriter. She worked in advertising for fifteen years before turning to writing full time. Her first novel, published in the U.S. as Troll: A Love Story, *was awarded Finland's most important literary prize. Her first collection came out in Finnish in 2005,* Kädettömät kuninkaat ja muita häiritseviä tarinoita *["Handless Kings and Other Disturbing Stories"]. She has edited* The Dedalus Book of Finnish Fantasy.

"Baby Doll," which appeared for the first time in English in 2007, in The SFWA European Hall of Fame, *edited by James Morrow and Kathryn Morrow, was previously collected in the 2002 Finnish anthology* Intohimosta rikokseen; *it has also appeared in French, and in several other languages. It is a dark story which extrapolates on all-too-familiar social trends. Bruce Sterling singled out this story as one of the highlights of* The SFWA European Hall of Fame, *describing it as a "Finnish denunciation of materialistic exploitation of children." James Morrow calls it "a nightmare world of assembly-line Lolitas." Cutting-edge Finnish SF apparently has much to offer the world SF readership.*

Annette comes home from school and shrugs her bag onto the floor in the hall. The bag is made of clear vinyl speckled with metal glitter, all in rainbow colors that swirl around the iridescent pink hearts and full kissy lips. The vinyl reveals the contents of the bag: Annette's schoolbooks, exercise books, and a plastic pencil box featuring the hottest boy band of 2015, Stick That Dick. The boys wear open leather jackets across their rippling bare torsos, and their jockstraps all feature the head of some animal with a large beak or a long trunk. Craig has an elephant on his jockstrap. Craig's the cutest of them all.

Annette slings her bright red spandex jacket across a chair and starts to remove her matching stretch boots. They're tight around the shins, but she can't be bothered to bend down and wrench them off. Instead she tries to pry one heel free with the opposite toe, but succeeds only in tearing her fishnet stockings.

"Oh, for fuck's sake!"

Mumps walks in from the kitchen, still wearing her work clothes. "What was that, darling?"

"I said, 'Golly, I've wrecked my tights.' "

"Oh, dear, not again. And they were so expensive. Well, you'll just have to wear the plain ones tomorrow."

"I'm so *not* wearing anything like that!"

"Darling, you don't really have a choice."

"Then I'm not going to school at *all*!" Annette snatches up her bag and stomps off toward her room, but the TV is on

2

in the den, and it's time for her favorite show, *Suburban Heat and Hate.* "I'd look like a total dork!" she continues, half to herself, half to her mother, who can no longer hear her, as she throws herself on the couch.

The show begins. The plot's as thick as it gets. Jake has just been discovered in bed with Melissa, but Bella doesn't know that Jake knows she's having an affair with his twin brother Tom. Jake meanwhile doesn't know that Melissa is in fact his daughter, because years ago he helped a lesbian couple get pregnant.

"Let's make a deal, darling." Mum has come in from the kitchen and is standing by the couch.

"Quiet! I can't hear a thing." Just then Bella pulls Jake off Melissa, screaming a barrage of abuse, leaving Melissa's enormous boobs and Jake's white butt in full view. At school today Annette heard Ninotska telling everyone to watch this afternoon's episode because Jake's got such a fantastic butt. Annette doesn't see what's so fantastic about it. It's paler than the rest of his brown skin, and it isn't as hairy as other men's butts. Still, tomorrow she'll find an opportunity to tell Ninotska she got a glimpse of Jake's butt, and of course she'll say she thought it was totally hypersmart, and give a low giggle the way you're supposed to when you talk about these things.

Mum waits till the commercials come on. "I have to go back to work the minute Dad gets home."

"I'll be fine."

"Lulu's at a shoot. Dad'll pick her up around nine or ten, and then it's your bedtime."

"Tell me something I don't know."

"One more thing, darling. I'm going on a business trip tomorrow, and I'll be away for two days."

"You're always going off somewhere."

"Dad can help you with your homework."

"Yeah, right, I bet he makes me watch Otso so he can play squash."

"That's what I mean by the deal. Promise me you'll help Dad and all you kids will behave yourselves."

Annette is pissed off—big time. Whenever Mumps goes

away, they end up eating all sorts of weird meals that Dumps cooks himself, instead of pizza or deli sushi or toasted sandwiches like Mumps gives them. You need to tell Dumps at least a hundred times what stuff to buy at the store, and why you need it. Once when Mumps was away Annette spent an hour explaining to Dumps why she categorically had to have a new eyelash-lengthening mascara and a bottle of golden body-spray.

"On one condition," Annette says.

"What's that?"

"Can I go to a sleepover at Ninotska's Thursday night?"

Although Annette hasn't actually been invited, rumor has it Ninotska's still deciding on the final guest list. Annette has noticed Ninotska checking out the Stick That Dick pencil box that Mum and Dad brought back from London. Annette could give Ninotska the pencil box, then later ask Mum for money to buy another—she could always say she cracked the old one.

Just in case she gets invited, she has to make sure she has permission to go. If you get invited you have to be able to say "Sí, sí, gracias" without worrying about it. *Nobody* is tragic enough to say they need to ask permission, and if you say "Sí, sí, gracias" and don't turn up, you can pretty much forget about being invited anywhere again.

"Who's Ninotska?"

"Ninotska Lahtinen from our year, stupid! She lives on Vuorikatu."

"And why do you have to go over there?"

"She's having her nine-yo party. And I'll need to take a present. I can catch a bus if Dad can't take me."

Mumps sighs, and with that Annette knows she won't have to sweat it anymore. The commercials finally end, and Annette turns back to the tube. Melissa's a professional stripper. She's wearing a bikini with golden frills. It's so mega.

The apartment door opens, and Dumps comes in, having picked up Otso at the nursery. Otso is five-yo.

Mumps has laid the table with pasta salad from the deli.

It's all right except for the capers; Annette doesn't like them and shoves the awful things aside. Dumps starts raving on about how they're the most delicious bits, then spears a caper off Annette's plate and stuffs it in his mouth, loudly smacking his lips. Otso only ever eats the pasta twists, but wouldn't you know—nobody gives him a lecture about it.

"So Otso, how was nursery today?" Mumps asks, all treacly like a TV kiddie host. Did she really use that twittery voice on Annette when she was five?

"I'm going on a date! With my girlfriend!" Otso can't say his *f*'s properly, and his speech therapist has her work cut out with his *r*'s too. The word "girlfriend" sounds like Otso's trying to spit something out between his front teeth.

Mumps and Dumps exchange one of their grown-up looks. "Well, our big boy's going on a date!" says Dad in the same cringe-o-matic voice as Mum. "When is your date, and who is it with?"

"Tomorrow, with Pamela. Her Mum's picking us up."

Mum and Dad simper at one another again, pretending to swoon, then shake their heads in the phoniest way, meanwhile smiling like split sausages.

"Pamela's my main squeeze," says Otso, shoveling down different colored pasta swirls.

Once Mum has gone back to the office, Annette flops down to watch the reality show *Between the Sheets,* in which the contestants try to find the perfect sex partner. "What first comes to mind when I look down your cleavage: (a) lemons, (b) apples, or (c) melons?" a male contestant asks a woman sprawled behind the curtain on a canopy bed when the door opens and Dad and Lulu walk in.

Lulu's only two years older than Annette, but looking at her you'd never believe it.

She's still wearing her photo-session makeup, a pair of giant false eyelashes, with so much black and gray around her eyes it no longer looks like makeup at all; the eyeshadow just gave her a tired and hungry look. Her lips feature a dark crimson pencil-line to straighten her Cupid's bow, the puffy parts filled with a lighter plum-red, and there's so much lip-gloss involved that her mouth appears bruised and swollen. Her hair has been curled in tiny ringlets and tied in a deliberately careless bun.

Not long ago Lulu got calls from photographers in Milan and Tokyo, and she burst into tears when they later told Mum and Dad not to bring her because she was too short after all. Before that disaster she'd been weighing herself twice a day, but now she's checking her height three or four times a week. She has a special chart on the wall for marking her growth. The pencil lines are so close together they form a gray smudge.

Lulu's face recently landed on the cover of the Finnish *Cosmopolitan,* a very big deal, so now her agent says she has to stop posing for the catalogs. Being associated with Monoprix and Wal-Mart won't help her image. She's far too sensual.

Lulu heads upstairs to rinse off her sensual makeup. Annette's stomach twists and churns. She goes to her room and stands before the mirror and tries to stare herself down, as if she could make her face look more sensual by gazing at it angrily enough. She sucks her belly in, but she still resembles a flat squash.

"Annette! Bedtime!" comes Dumps's voice from downstairs.

"Yes yes YESYES!"

"Annette's a slut!" the boys start shouting as she walks onto the playground, pretending not to hear them. It's fairly normal and not worth worrying about; anybody they're not trying to pull they call a slut—and they're not trying to pull Annette.

There are far worse things they could shout out.

Ninotska and Veronika are standing by the main entrance, whispering to each other. Veli and Juho walk past. Veli attempts to grope Ninotska, and Juho tries shoving his hand up Veronika's black leather miniskirt. Ninotska giggles, squirms, and pushes him away, and Veronika dashes to hide behind her. Veli and Juho swagger toward the door, and on their way each boy sticks his index finger through the looped thumb and finger of the other hand. Ninotska and Veronika giggle until the boys are out of earshot.

Annette approaches the two girls. "Hi," she says awkwardly.

Veronika and Ninotska toss their fountains of permed hair and look at her disdainfully. Ninotska's skimpy shirt allows a wide strip of skin to show between her golden shiny hipsters and her spaghetti-strap top. She has a silver ring in her bellybutton.

"Ninotska, can you come over here for a minute?" says Annette, backing toward the Dumpster. "We need to talk."

Ninotska glances at Veronika, a scowl on her face, then joins Annette. "Well, what's the big deal?" she asks suspiciously.

Annette reaches into her bag and brings out the Stick That Dick pencil box. "You know, I'm really bored with this. You want it?"

Ninotska's eyes light up, and Annette realizes her offer's having the desired effect. "What makes you think I'd want your old crap?" Ninotska bluntly replies, but it's all part of the script.

Annette shrugs. "Okay, fine then," she says and starts to throw the thing in the Dumpster.

Ninotska's hand shoots out, grabbing the box before it can join the rubbish. "Easy pleasy. I believe in recycling."

Annette smiles as Ninotska slips the pencil box into her golden bag printed with the words EAT ME. "Hey, what're you doing Thursday night?" she asks finally, and Annette's heart leaps with excitement.

On the bed Annette has spread out everything she'll need: best lace-chiffon nightie, makeup kit, perfume—plus books and stuff for the next day at school. Her nine-yo present for Ninotska is wrapped in silver paper, three shades of nail polish that Annette picked out herself because Mumps would've gotten something tragic. It should all fit in the flight bag borrowed from Mumps. Now Annette must decide what to wear for the evening. She plumps for a pair of lizard-scale leggings and a skirt with a slit up the side. She hasn't got any swank-tanks like Ninotska, but her green top is fray-proof, so she takes a pair of scissors and cuts a good ten centimeters off the bottom, making it stop well short of her bellybutton. The ragged cut is totally glam; it looks a bit like those TV shows where the jungle women's clothes are so tattered they reveal lots of skin.

Annette studies the nightie and the matching thong underwear. Then she looks in the mirror.

She slips off her skirt, leggings, and panties. She opens her makeup kit and removes a black eyeliner. With her pink plastic sharpener she gives the pencil a serious point.

She sits spread-eagled before the mirror and with careful pencil strokes draws thin wavy lines between her legs.

Ninotska's Mum and Dad are away somewhere for the evening. In addition to Ninotska and Annette, Veronika and Janika and Evita and Carmen and Vanessa are all naturally at the pajama party. The sleepover boasts buckets of pizza-flavored popcorn and big bottles of high-energy soda, "so we can last through the night," squeals Ninotska.

Once Ninotska has opened her presents everybody gets ready for the fashion show. Back home Annette thought her nightie was fantastic, but now it looks like an old woman's shirt. It's too long, reaching almost to the knees, and totally unrevealing. Everybody agrees that Evita's nightie is the best. It's slightly see-through, like violet blue mist, and it's so short it barely covers her ass. Ninotska's is nice, too, with wide frilly shoulder straps and loose laces on the front so it's open almost all the way down, and it's made of red silk. But because it's her party Ninotska decides to be generous and votes for Evita's nightie.

Around ten o'clock everybody gets all excited and snickery when Ninotska takes a stepladder and goes into her Mum and Dad's room and comes back cradling a stack of DVDs. "Let's watch a film." The girls sort through the pile. Each DVD has naked men and women on the cover, sharing the space with titles like *Hot Pussies* and *Grand Slam Gang Bang*. All the girls start giggling, hiding their mouths with their hands, and Ninotska puts a DVD in the player.

The pounding music and the script with its endless shouts of "Give it to me, baby" and "Meats to the sweet" are all very monotonous, but they still stare at the screen—nobody dares not watch. Annette feels twitchy and uncomfortable, and sometimes it's like there's a second little heart beating under her stomach, and that makes her uncomfortable, too. She knows you're supposed to stay the distance with this stuff, and you're also supposed to pretend it doesn't bother you in the slightest, the way boys watch slasher movies—if you let on you're scared, everybody laughs and takes the piss. Even though the whole point of horror flicks is to upset you, and that's why they get made in the first place, you're still not allowed to be scared. And so they have to watch these grand slam hot pussies as if it didn't mean anything.

Once the second flick is halfway over, and two black dudes simultaneously pumping a woman with gigantic boobs, Ninotska gives a loud yawn, and this is a sign that the guests are no longer expected to be interested in the film. She switches the machine off, slipcases the disc, and drops it on the stack.

"Who wants to check out my Mum and Dad's room?" she asks, and everybody wants to, of course. The girls jostle behind Ninotska and make their way into a lovely bedroom with an enormous four-poster and a gold-framed mirror on the wall. Ninotska climbs the stepladder to the top shelf of the closet. She returns the stack of DVDs, then takes down a big cardboard box and jumps back onto the rug. She opens the box and spreads the contents across the bed. Red-and-black underwear that's nothing but a belt with bits of fabric on the sides: in the middle they're completely open. A pair of man-acles with fur on the cuffs. Ninotska grabs a pinkish zucchini and gives the end a twist, and the thing starts shaking in her hand. "Brrrrr!" she says, trying to imitate the noise of the zucchini, then waves it in each girl's face, and they all move away giggling hysterically.

"Has anybody ever tried one of these?" she asks slowly, challenging them, and Annette feels like Ninotska is looking straight at her.

"I'll bet none of you would *dare*." Ninotska glances across the group of girls. Somebody attempts a giggle, and then they all fall silent.

"I dare you. I dare you."

The silence rings in Annette's ears, her mouth is dry with anticipation, and she feels that any second now Ninotska's eyes will stop at her.

Lulu's chewing gum and trying to look mega, but every now and then she gives a quick laugh, her straightened, whitened teeth flashing between her dark red lips while the tabloid photographer takes her picture, over and over. Occasionally the female reporter glances at the LED screen to see how the photos are coming out. Annette is sulking in the den. She can look into the living room, but the people from the newspaper can't see her, and she would refuse to be photographed next to Lulu even if they begged her.

In any case, they haven't asked.

"So tell me, how does it feel being the new face of Sexy Secrets Underwear?" the reporter asks.

Lulu lowers her false eyelashes, so overlong they almost reach her boobs, and smiles. Annette knows that Lulu uses this posture so she'll have time to think without seeming like a dork. Finally Lulu looks up.

"Okay."

"People say you're about to become the object of a national fantasy. Do you agree?"

The eyelashes tilt down, then rise again. "I guess."

The reporter smiles and switches off her digital recorder. "Thanks, Lulu. That'll be all."

Annette simply has to walk out of the den before the tabloid people leave. She's got her makeup on, and she's wearing her shiny black dress—plus of course her high-heeled ankle boots, even though Mumps has told her not to use them on the parquet.

"Well, lookee here," the photographer says, squinting at Annette, "there's *another* stunning woman on the premises," and he almost sounds sincere, but she can't be sure.

"That's my little sister," Lulu says before blowing a bubble gum bubble. "She's eight."

Annette could kill Lulu. Annette thinks she looks at least ten-yo, but by now the tabloid people are already in the hall, telling Lulu the article will run on Friday.

Naturally Mumps has bought three copies of Friday's paper. On the front page of the fashion section is a picture of Lulu, her head thrown back, a gush of curls cascading down her shoulders, her teeth showing between pouty lips and her eyes half shut. MODEL SENSATION LULU: I LOVE BEING THE STAR OF GUYS' WET DREAMS! screams the headline.

Lippe from the next apartment has come over to share a glass of wine with Mum. Lippe admires Lulu's picture, and then they gab about the contract. Though Mum whispers, Annette, sitting in front of the TV, can still hear her. With her hand to her lips, Mum says, "A hundred and twenty thousand euros." At least they'll get back all the money they sank into Lulu's career, Annette thinks. A year ago Lulu took some modeling courses that cost ultrabucks, but thanks to that move a fancy agent saw Lulu at the graduation show and signed her up on the spot. Lulu doesn't go to regular school anymore; she's supposed to be studying with a private tutor and taking the odd exam, but Annette hasn't noticed much evidence of this. There have been no reported sightings of Lulu reading a schoolbook.

Annette once applied to the modeling school, but you have to get through the preliminary round. They looked at her for about half a second and didn't bother asking her any questions. A month later a letter came saying that she didn't have "sufficient camera presence."

Mum explains to Lippe that originally another girl had been tapped for the Sexy Secrets campaign, a seventeen-year-old from Turku called Ramona who'd already done a lot of modeling and was a runner-up for Miss Finland.

"Hasn't her face been used to death?" asks Lippe.

"She's well past her prime," Mum says, nodding, "so Lulu got the contract."

The door rattles, and Dad comes in with Otso. Otso's cheeks are red, and he's wearing a smart jacket, a white shirt, and a bow tie. He's been on another date with Pamela: Dad took them to a film or something. Both Mum and Dad prattle about what a handsome little boy they have. Otso runs into Mum's arms shouting "Guess what! Guess what! Me and Pamela got engaged!" which of course starts off such a wave of fawning and gushing that Annette feels like throwing up.

Annette is on the school bus. The journey is less than a kilometer, only a few blocks, but the law states that all school-aged children must ride to school in their parents' cars or on a supervised bus. "For the protection of our children," ran the ads a few years ago when the law went into effect. Annette is standing in the aisle, but her new platform shoes cause her feet to slide down toward the point, and she keeps losing her balance. Once the bus stops at the traffic light she raises her eyes, and the view out the window hits her like a punch in the face.

From a gigantic roadside billboard Lulu stares back at her, ten times larger than normal, her eyes dark, her lips shining cherry red, a wind machine billowing her hair.

When Annette finally gets off the bus, as if to further taunt her, another billboard appears, a startling three-panel display this time, looming near the school gates. And of course the star is Lulu, modeling three different lines of underwear—Naughty Red, Sinful Black, and Seductive Green, according to the words.

Each image bears the same caption: BABY DOLL.

Trussed in a bright red string, Lulu's ass practically bursts from the first panel; with half-closed eyes she twists her head toward the camera, brushing her hands against her bare shoulders so that her false nails, painted the same color as her panties, gleam against her skin like drops of blood.

Then comes Lulu crouching, shiny black-laced boots matching her underwear, holding a ridiculous toy snake and making like she's kissing the thing, its orange velveteen head sliding between her lips.

And finally there's a shot of Lulu from the side, hugging a beige teddy bear. Her back is arched, and her boobs, wrapped in jade-green lace, thrust defiantly upward.

Lulu's priceless tits.

But a few days later a miracle occurs.

Annette arrives on the playground for recess, and instantly her stomach starts tightening, her chest pounding, just like every other time she has to walk past the gangs of boys. She hunches her shoulders, lowers her head, and wonders where the mockery will come from today, the cries of slut and dwarf-butt, and of course the comments about her tits—bee-stings, milkduds.

One gang mutters something indistinct, but Annette manages to reach the pavilion without her face blushing bright red. All of a sudden he's standing right next to her. His name's Timppa, she knows that. He's two years ahead of her and plays ice hockey with the F Juniors, and many times she's heard Ninotska and Veronika whispering that Timppa is absolutely *shagtastic*. He's still standing right next to her, looking at her, and Annette is so startled she almost runs away for fear of yet another insult, but Timppa gives her a friendly smile and doesn't look a bit like all he wants to do is shove his hand down her top.

"You're Annette, right?" he asks. Annette is so taken aback that all she can manage is a nod. She's utterly speechless. Timppa must think she's a total dork because she doesn't know how to respond with something quick and sassy the way Ninotska and Veronika always do when boys talk to them. But Timppa doesn't seem to care; he looks Annette up and down, and his eyes stop at the sight of her platform shoes.

"Awesome boots."

"Thanks," Annette stammers as Timppa reaches into his leather jacket and produces a packet of SuperKiss, which he holds out to Annette. "Gum?"

Annette takes one, fumbles off the wrapper, and pops the

stick in her mouth just as the bell rings, saving her. Timppa backs away, smirks, and waves at her. "Catch you later, Annette."

Annette stands there and forgets to chew her gum, her mouth half open. Her heart is about to burst out of her chest.

During the next lesson Annette writes TIMPPA TIMPPA TIMPPA on her arm with a sharp pencil, scratching so hard the skin almost breaks.

Ninotska and Veronika have of course noticed that Annette was talking to Timppa during recess, and they'll be sure to catch up with her at their first opportunity, instead of Annette nonchalantly trying to hang around their gang.

"Well, well, our little Annette's got a *boyfriend*," Ninotska says, her eyes burning, and for the first time Annette feels like she's *somebody*, not just that girl whose Mum and Dad brought her a Stick That Dick pencil box from London; suddenly there's something a little bit glam about Annette.

"He's not my boyfriend. We're just . . . friends."

"Then it must be the first time ever that Timppa Kujala is *just friends* with a girl."

Veronika gives a hollow chortle. "He's the horniest stud in the school."

"Careful you don't get burned, Annette, darling."

Ninotska and Veronika shuffle off, their curls gushing, their little bottoms bouncing contemptuously, and Annette looks at them and says under her breath, "They're just *jealous*."

And with that a great warmth fills her.

Timppa is loitering near the gates when Annette leaves school. He asks her where she's off to, and when she says she's going home he says he's headed the same way and suggests they walk together, fuck the bus law. Timppa spits on the ground and says the whole rule is a load of crapola; he walks to school whenever he wants to. Annette wants to sound mega and says she thinks it's a dumb-ass rule, too, and for some reason she feels safe walking with Timppa.

Annette sees that Veronika notices her leaving with Timppa, and her sense of triumph is so great she's able to chat almost normally with Timppa, even though the silences are long, and she ends up asking him the same questions over and over; but he doesn't seem to mind, and he talks practically the whole way home about which hockey players he admires the most, the ones that have the fastest cars and the juiciest babes with the hottest knockers.

When they arrive at Annette's building, Timppa shuffles awkwardly for a moment and stares at the ground. "Can I come in for a bit?"

Annette is about to faint. Even though Ninotska and Veronika have kissed lots of boys at parties, and while Carmen spent a whole semester walking around hand-in-hand with Pasi, nobody has ever had a boyfriend who wanted to *visit*. It could mean almost anything. Annette can hardly breathe.

"Sure, come on in."

They enter the elevator, and Annette presses the button for the sixth floor. Inside the car they don't say a word, and for Annette this is quite a relief. Finally they arrive; she opens her apartment door, shows Timppa in, and gives him a hanger for his leather jacket. This time she doesn't drop her bag on the floor but carries it down the hall past the living room and the den, Timppa at her heels, then stops outside her bedroom door, on which there's a large Stick That Dick poster and a piece of cardboard with thick red lettering: ANNETTEZ ROOM PRIVATE NO ENTRY!

Annette steps toward Timppa so she's almost right up against him. "Want to see my room?"

Timppa doesn't appear to be listening, he's inspecting the other doors in the vicinity. One features a full-color poster of the world's most glamorous supermodel, Marinette Mankiewicz. Her moist skin sparkles with hundreds of little pearly beads for a major wetness effect; her bikini looks wet, too, clamped tight against her tits and almost see-through. Lulu once told Annette it's all done with oil instead of water, because oil is shinier and doesn't dry out under the studio lights.

"Is that your sister's room?"

"Lulu's? I guess."

"When's she coming home?"

At first Annette doesn't understand, but then it strikes her, and her stomach feels like it's about to spill out around her heels, and her head starts to spin.

"Around four o'clock," she mutters almost inaudibly.

"I can hang out and wait, huh?" Timppa asks, his eyes fixed on Marinette Mankiewicz, and Annette realizes that Lulu and the photographer have ripped off the idea behind this poster for their three-panel billboard—the Seductive Green Lulu with her tits pointing skyward.

"Make yourself at home," she says and goes into her room, and only vast amounts of self-control prevent her from slamming the door shut much louder than normal.

After that Timppa visits almost every day. He comes around at the same time as Lulu and often doesn't leave till late at night, after Mumps and Dumps have stood next to the Marinette Mankiewicz poster coughing or clearing their throats or knocking on the door, and Mumps says, pretending to be all thoughtful and considerate, "Right, I think it's time for our Lulu's beauty sleep!"

Ninotska and Veronika have been giggling to themselves and tossing their curls around and whispering so much that Annette can feel it in her stomach. They ask her, real smarmy, "How's your *boyfriend* doing nowadays?" then burst into a hyperly loud chortle as if the joke gets funnier every time. At first Annette can't understand how exactly Ninotska and Veronika learned that Timppa and Lulu have been hanging together, but it all becomes clear during morning recess when she's walking behind a group of boys who haven't noticed her, and she overhears one of them chattering about what a hottie Timppa has pulled; he then describes Lulu at great length and brags that Timppa's on the verge of scoring. Timppa, naturally, has told the entire school.

Annette runs straight to the girls' toilet and throws up, filling the bowl with globules of meat and potatoes. The ketchup makes it look like she's been vomiting blood, and she decides that vomiting blood probably feels like this. A moment later, her puke-tears having dried, she feels slightly dizzy, but her thoughts are surprisingly clear.

As she leaves the stall, she bumps into Nana, one of the girls in her year, loitering by the sinks. She must have heard Annette barfing. Nana gives her a conspiratorial smile.

"Have you just started?"

Annette doesn't understand. Nana pulls a bottle of Evian from her schoolbag and hands it to her. "If you want to stay fit while you're on the program, remember to drink enough water. Don't let yourself dry out. No calories in water, you see."

Annette gulps down a mouthful of Evian and mumbles her thanks. Nana slips the bottle back in her bag. "One good tip: get yourself some xylitol chewing gum and use it after you've barfed. That way the stomach acids won't take the shine off your teeth."

Annette nods. Nana slings her bag across her shoulder and looks Annette up and down. "Yeah, you could do with losing a few kilos." Nana moves toward the door, her little ass snugged tightly in her jeans. "Good luck."

Mum and Dad are watching a movie on late-night TV. Timppa is around again.

Annette has a walk-in closet that runs along the wall she shares with Lulu's room. When they were little, they used to play telephone. Every time Annette held the rim of a drinking glass against the back wall of her closet and pressed her ear to the bottom, she could hear what her sister was saying even if Lulu used a normal voice.

Annette visits the bathroom and dumps the toothbrushes out of the glass. She returns to her room, slides back the closet door, and makes her way through the hanging clothes. Chiffon, fake leather and the hems of her black and brightly colored miniskirts brush her face, and the heels of her shoes clatter as she pushes them out of the way. The closet smells of fabric conditioner, sweaty sneakers, and lavender sachet.

Annette holds the glass against the plaster. She knows that Lulu's bed is on the other side, right up against the wall.

At first all she picks up is a lot of mumbling, moaning, whispering, and creaking bedsprings. Then comes a thump as though somebody's arm or leg has hit the wall. The sound shoots right into Annette's ear, and she almost jumps out of the closet.

"For Christ's sake, what's your problem? We've been together a whole month." She can hear Timppa clearly now, sounding all shrill since his voice hasn't yet broken. Lulu responds with a murmur Annette can't quite make out.

"What're you saving it for?" Timppa chirps. "I'll bet you've already been screwed every which way, at least that's what the guys are saying."

Again Annette can't hear Lulu's reply—is she talking into her pillow or what?—but Timppa understands her, and he answers immediately.

"Don't you know this town's full of chicks just begging for it?" he scoffs. "Why should I waste my time on some snooty tight-twat? Shit, are you like planning to hold out till you're fourteen or something?"

"No," Lulu says. "I don't know."

"Then what's your problem? Aren't you on the pill?"

Lulu hesitates. "Well, not exactly." Her voice is all raspy and apologetic, the way it gets when she's embarrassed. "I haven't quite got mine yet."

"Your pills?"

"My . . . periods."

"Bingo! Then there's no need to mess with rubbers!"

Again Lulu says something Annette can't quite hear.

"I just think it's time our relationship took a step forward." Timppa's words sound like he's reading them from a book.

Another loud thump, followed by a rustling sound, probably Lulu's sheets. She whimpers a little.

"Stop it."

"Stop it? You're like a walking invitation, ass and jalookies on billboards all over town, and you have the balls to say *stop it*?"

Again the rustling of Lulu's sheets. She mumbles something, and then comes Timppa's voice, and this time it's more of a whine. "When you lead a guy on like that, you've got to see it through."

Annette stands upright, and her head hits the metal rod, but she doesn't give it a second thought. She crawls out of the closet, sending her shoes clattering into the room. An instant later she's in the hall banging on Lulu's door.

"Lulu!"

A moment's silence, then Lulu's voice, trying to sound calm and normal. "Now what?"

"Mum says your guest has to go!"

From behind the door comes a stifled curse, still more rustling; the bed creaks. There follows a lot of low harsh muttering, and Annette hears a zipper being pulled up. Timppa comes out of the door, his hair messed up and his face all red. He glowers at Annette, who's leaning against the wall minding her own business, and she stares back at him with a shrug and an innocent, slightly apologetic smile that says, *Parents will be parents.*

Lulu's door stays closed, and after a short while the sound of soft sweet music floats out into the hall.

Timppa has stopped coming round and Annette is ferociously happy about it. But her triumph starts falling apart, cracking and flaking and blowing away with the wind when she realizes that Lulu hasn't changed; she's still always giggling and yawning and stuffing herself with laxative licorice candy. It's the same Lulu who smiles mysteriously from beneath her false eyelashes, and for some reason she doesn't seem to pine for the lost Timppa in the least.

The worst of it is the way Lulu had the nerve simply to forget Timppa, whose name still throbs where Annette scratched it on her forearm, TIMPPA TIMPPA TIMPPA.

He was Annette's first chance to be the way everyone expected her to be, and Lulu acts like she took up with him just for the hell of it, then let him go for the same reason. As if Annette wasn't the one who split them up in the first place.

Would it kill Lulu to show, even for the tiniest instant, that she knows what it feels like to be Annette?

In fairness, ever since the night with the drinking glass Lulu has acted almost friendly toward Annette, chatting with her and giving her stuff from her makeup kit that's hardly been used at all. Sometimes Lulu looks at her with big wet spaniel eyes, which is actually pretty maddening, and Annette almost breaks a tooth trying to stay calm when Lulu gets all palsy-walsy. Annette knows Lulu's just pretending, her way of covering up the wound Annette caused in coming between her and Timppa. And with that phony chumminess Lulu in snatching away the last precious thing Annette has, her pissy little victory.

And on top of it all Mumps keeps simpering, "It's so nice to see you sisters getting along so well."

Annette is vegging out before the television, the big noisy climax of some dopey rock show. Stick That Dick has dropped to number six on the charts, and now in the number one slot there's the girl band Jugzapoppin' who perform topless. After that there's nothing on; even the trash channels are boring once you get used to them. Annette visits a chat room using the remote, but soon gives up. You can barely write two answers before somebody asks about your cup-size and what color panties you're wearing. She surfs the net, then skips through different TV channels, but all she can find are unfunny sitcoms and grotty old movies.

One of them catches her attention.

The title of the flick is *Welcome to the Dollhouse*. At first Annette is only interested because the star is so unbelievably ugly. Why would they let anybody who looks like that be in a movie? The girl must be about eight-yo, Annette's age, and she's not even making an effort to appear older. She wears glasses, of all things, which tells you right off the film is ancient, because nowadays nobody, no girl that is, would be that insane; you either have an operation or at the very least get contacts. Annette follows the film for a few minutes, occasionally flipping through the other channels, but she keeps coming back to *Welcome to the Dollhouse* as though drawn by a rubber band.

The girl's name is Dawn, and everyone at school hates her and calls her a dork and a dog and a dyke. She has a little sister named Missy who does ballet. Missy's about six-yo. She wears a pink tutu and a pink leotard—a pink angel— her hair tied back in a bun, with flowers, cute as a doll. Dawn's Mum and Dad spend all day fawning over Missy and neglect Dawn really badly, and Dawn hates Missy so much her stomach hurts. Okay, sure, Dawn never actually *says* Missy makes her stomach hurt, but Annette knows what it means when Dawn wraps her arms around herself, clenches her teeth, and shuts her eyes tight.

Then one day Dawn's Mum asks her to tell Missy, who's about to leave for a ballet class, that she can't pick her up today, so Missy should ask the teacher for a ride home.

But Dawn doesn't tell her.

And Missy is left standing alone outside the ballet school and gets kidnapped. Goodbye Missy.

Annette feels a devilish red glow of satisfaction, and yet at the same time terribly guilty, as if *she* were the one who'd gotten rid of Miss Goody Two-Shoes Sugar-Plum-Fairy Missy for good.

She changes the channel and doesn't watch the end of the *Dollhouse* flick, but still the mood of the thing follows Annette for days, and she can't quite shake that sickly-prickly thrill she felt when, with the police cars flashing their red and blue lights outside Dawn and Missy's house, it became clear that Dawn had succeeded.

Lulu has a shoot somewhere on the other side of town. Mumps is in Gothenburg, and Dumps is supposed to pick her up after the session. Annette has of course been asked to babysit Otso. Surprised that the little Casanova's not at Pamela's place, she wonders, nastily, has Pamela found herself a more mega stud and finished with Otso just like that? Annette is lounging on the couch watching the celebs on *Junior Pop Idol*. Otso sits a meter from the TV, staring at the screen, and tries to sing along except when Annette hisses at him to be quiet. Four-year-old Jussi does a rendition of "I Want Your Sex," then Kylie comes on, the same age, singing "Like a Virgin." Kylie wears a shiny sequined dress and a pink ostrich-feather boa with matching lipstick. Halfway through the performance the telephone rings. Annette's in a pretty ticked-off mood when she answers, interruptions being just about her least favorite thing.

It's Dad, and there's a lot of noise in the background. He's had to borrow somebody else's phone to call her. Some idiot smashed into his car, and on impact his headset phone flew out the window and broke. Dad's got to take the car to the garage and get himself a new headset, and that will take some time. He says Lulu probably switched off her phone for the shoot, so could Annette send her a voice mail or a text message saying Dad can't pick her up and she should take a taxi? He explains this over and over like it's the most difficult assignment ever.

"Yes yes YESYES!" Annette screams and ends the call, but still she's missed two more potential Junior Pop Idols; now a five-yo boy is singing "Hit Me Baby One More Time." Otso joins in whenever Annette doesn't try to stop him.

Annette picks up her mobile and has already selected Lulu from the quick menu when her hand goes limp.

This can't be just a coincidence.

Annette stares at the phone.

"Welcome to the dollhouse, Baby Doll," she says, then switches off the phone entirely.

Hours later the apartment phone rings for the sixth time, and each time the caller-name on the screen is Lulu.

The fact that nobody's answering isn't exactly unusual. Otso's a light sleeper, so Dad often unplugs the phone after he's put Otso to bed, and all the headsets or mobiles in the apartment are in a drawer or under a pillow or turned off altogether.

The phone rings for a seventh time.

The police car is parked in front of the building, but the lights on its roof aren't pulsing red and blue like in the film; the car is totally dark and totally silent.

Dad carries Lulu inside, wrapped in a gray blanket. Her mascara has dribbled down her face, and one of her cheeks is red and scratched and bleeding. Her right eye is almost swollen shut, and her lower lip is split. Dad carefully lays her on the living room couch and staggers into the kitchen like he's gone blind. He returns with a dish towel soaked in warm water and tries to wipe the mascara streaks off Lulu's face, but she gently pushes his hand away.

"Remppu," she whispers. Dad looks at Lulu; he doesn't know what she means—but Annette knows, so she goes to Lulu's room and pulls a drawer out from under the bed. Remppu is lying among the other junk with his spindly legs in a knot: a stuffed terry-cloth monkey whose long dangling arms have little orange mittens sewn at the ends. The terry-cloth loops have worn away on those places where Lulu used to suck on Remppu when she was a baby.

Annette walks up to Lulu and places Remppu in her arms. Lulu squeezes him against her chest and places her lips to his battered old head, near where Annette once tore off the eyes and Mum had to sew on a pair of blue buttons instead. Lulu closes her own eyes and lies there perfectly still.

The two policemen wander around the living room like flickering shadows. It's as though Annette is not really in the same place where all this is happening; instead she's standing outside somebody's else's apartment watching these events through the window. Her stomach's filled with a heavy sweetness, as if her breath has turned to syrup.

"Messages sometimes disappear when the operators are busy," says one officer. Dad nods blindly; he clearly doesn't even hear.

"We've got some possible sightings of the four men, and

of course we'll try our best, but, sad to say, cases like this are getting more common all the time, so who knows?"

Dad bobs his head like an automaton. Annette stands there silently and doesn't know what to do; she feels totally stunned. Now she realizes how stupid she was. She didn't mean for this to happen. She thought Lulu would just disappear, would get lost somewhere in town and, like a child in a fairy tale, never find her way home.

Now Annette is annoyed that she didn't watch *Welcome to the Dollhouse* all the way through; she doesn't know what finally became of Missy.

Would Dawn have made such a dumb-ass mistake?

"Are you sure you'll be okay?" an officer says.

Dad nods for a third time, then takes Lulu and Remppu in a single bundle in his arms and walks off toward Lulu's room; beneath the blanket Lulu's feet dangle as limply as Remppu's terry-cloth limbs.

Mum and Dad are in the den talking all hushed and low, thinking nobody will hear them, but the walls are thin and Annette has sharp ears; she can easily sort out both their voices, almost every word, from the noise of the TV in the background.

Not that she wants to hear them, because her stomach is aching, and she'd much rather swat the voices away like flies and pretend they don't exist, but she also feels compelled to listen, like that time at Ninotska's nine-yo party when Annette kept her eyes on the screen even though she didn't want to see any more grand slam hot pussies.

"The insurance will cover Lulu's plastic surgery," Dad says. "If we can believe the doctors, there won't be any scarring. She can probably start modeling again in a couple of months. Thank God they finished the Sexy Secrets shoot in time."

"The men who did this, if they ever get caught—should we try to get . . . restitution?" Mum asks indistinctly.

Dad sighs. "Caught? Not too likely. Wouldn't matter anyway. The whole problem is that she never changed her clothes—she thought I was picking her up—so they'll just say she was asking for it. Their lawyers will argue that Lulu brought it on herself."

"Then we won't see a penny?"

" 'Fraid not," Dad says.

Annette's head and stomach start aching again. What could that mean, *Lulu brought it on herself*? No, no, *she* did it—she, Annette, caused all this just as surely as if she'd bought a gun and shot herself in the foot. Annette would give almost anything for this, of all things, never to have happened.

Word has circulated around the school.

The boys' hand signals have become grosser than ever, and naturally Ninotska and Veronika keep trying to get all chatty with Annette. Annette vows to act hypernormal, a bit indifferent, even slightly chipper. She won't show those dopes how much she's really hurting.

"Four," Ninotska trills. "Four horny dudes!"

"Was it one after another, or did they all do it together?" Veronika carries on.

Annette shrugs. "I couldn't care less." She walks off, and the hallway echoes with shouts of *lulululululululululululu.*

Mum has brought home burritos from the deli. She cuts one into small pieces for Otso and squeezes ketchup over them from a plastic bottle. Otso would eat Styrofoam if it was covered in ketchup. Lulu won't come down to eat. She won't even leave her room, and that infuriates Annette, too—Lulu always has to make herself special somehow. Annette pokes at her burrito with a fork. She normally likes them, but now her throat feels blocked. Lately nothing tickles her fancy.

"I want implants."

The words bubble abruptly out of Annette's mouth, almost like vomit. Mum stops in mid-squeeze, the bottle gives a little fart, and Otso has a laughing fit.

"Implants? For you?" Mum looks confused, as though she'd never heard the word before.

"Everybody's got them!"

"At your age?"

"Ninotska's getting them, Sarietta's already stopped being a milkdud, and today I heard Veronika's shopping around!" Annette bangs her fork rhythmically against the table. "Anyway, Lulu's got them. You gave her implants the minute the agent told you to!"

Everything freezes. Mum stares at her, eyes like saucers, and even Otso stops eating. The silence gets so intense that Annette's ears almost hurt, and then Mum clears her throat.

"But . . . we don't want the same thing happening to you that happened to Lulu," she says, her voice all hoarse.

"You never want *anything* to happen to me, do you?" says Annette, giving Mum big saucer-eyes in return.

Mum doesn't answer. All the doors and windows of her face are shut tight.

Annette slams her fork so hard it springs out of her hand and somersaults to the floor, clanging like a bell.

"I knew it! I knew you never wanted anything to happen to me!"

Mum looks at her, the side of her mouth twitching. This is a sign.

"Everybody thinks I'm just a child!" Annette screams. She upends her plate, sending chicken pieces and veggie bits flying out of the tortilla all over the tablecloth and onto the floor. "Nothing real is ever supposed to happen to me!"

Mum stands there frozen, and Annette picks up a knife and starts banging it against the table. Mum moves quickly and grabs Annette's arm. "There, there, dear, we can ask Dad when he gets home," she says, then carefully takes the knife away.

Aristotle OS

TONY BALLANTYNE

Tony Ballantyne (www.tonyballantyne.com) is a British writer, living in Oldham, England, with his wife and children, whose works tend to focus on the subject of Artificial Intelligence and robotics. In college he studied mathematics and later became a teacher, first teaching math and, later, Internet technology. He began publishing SF short stories in 1998, mostly in Interzone, *and has since published three idea-rich novels:* Recursion *(2004),* Capacity *(2005), and* Divergence *(2007), which comprise the Recursion trilogy. If there is such a thing as post-cyberpunk hard SF, that's what he writes. He had such a good year in 2007 that we include another story by him later in this book.*

"Aristotle OS" appeared in Fast Forward 1, *edited by Lou Anders, one of the best anthologies of the year, from which we have taken several stories for this book. Claude Lalumiere described the story as "a biting satire of our computer-dominated lifestyles." It's about operating systems and belief systems. Here Ballantyne writes in the mode of Rudy Rucker—painting not merely with broad brushstrokes but with a broom, in order to get at the essential weirdness of computer operating systems.*

Turning on a computer has a whole different feel nowadays, but I had to write this somehow.

I'm running CP/M now. If that doesn't mean anything to you, then it soon will. It's an old operating system from the seventies: A *Platonic* OS. Lots of people are installing it.

It's only a few months since I heard the term *Platonic Operating System*.

I wish I hadn't. I wish I'd never listened to my brother.

"Can you fix it?" I asked. Ken was gazing at the screen with that half smile on his face he always has when he's doing me a favour.

"It's not broken," he snorted. "You just had the security settings turned up high. The computer must have detected unsuitable words in your files."

"What are you implying?"

Ken gave a laugh. "Don't be so sensitive. They're there to stop children accessing inappropriate stuff on the Internet. Of course, most children would have no problems turning them off. Don't worry. I'll soon have things sorted."

"Oh good."

He tapped away, the clacking of the keys the only sound in my half-empty flat. So much space to fill with half the furniture gone . . .

There seemed to be empty spaces in the conversations between Ken and me too, lately. Just like this one.

"Do you want some more coffee?" I asked, breaking the silence.

"Yes please." He held out a flowered mug, one that Jenny must have overlooked when she disengaged her possessions from mine. "And how about a spot of brandy in it?" he added. "It's cold out there."

He leant back in the elderly chair and gave a dramatic sigh. "Of course," he declared, "the *big* problem here is that you are still using a *Platonic* operating system."

Ken has this way of dropping conversational hooks then sitting back and looking smug whilst he waits for you to bite on them. Normally I'd just ignore him, even say something sarcastic, but—just like when you speak to the tax office—you're always polite to the person who is fixing your computer.

"Platonic operating system?" I asked. "I thought it was just Windows, like everyone uses."

He laughed at that.

"Windows, Linux, Mac OS. They're all the same. They model the real world inside your computer. Whether you're running a spreadsheet to do your household accounts, or playing a car racing game, you're just running an imperfect model of the real world."

He looked at me again, another one of those little pregnant pauses. I was the one who went to university, he was saying. I was the one who studied philosophy; he had left school to become an electrician.

"Okay," I said. "Plato said that humans experienced the world like a group of people sitting inside a cave, watching the shadows of reality that dance on the walls before them. Are you saying that my computer just does the same? Models shadows on a wall?"

"You got it," said Ken sliding a plastic case from his pocket and holding it up for me to see. "This is something new. It dispenses with the paradigm that the computer only *models* the real world. This operating system makes the assumption that everything input is real."

I took the case from him and turned it over in my hands. There was a shiny CD-ROM inside, half hidden by a torn piece of paper on which were scrawled the words "Aristotle OS."

"What's the point of that?" I asked.

"You'll see." He pressed a button and the DVD tray on my computer slid smoothly open.

"Ken," I began, "I'm perfectly happy with my computer the way it is. All I want to be able to do is write articles and lesson plans. Maybe try to keep track of my spending—"

It was too late. He had already dropped the disc into the tray and was beginning to type at the keyboard.

"Now," he said. "Where's my coffee?"

Ken eventually left two hours later with a promise to meet at our mother's house for dinner the following Sunday. I didn't hold out much hope. Something would come up; an old acquaintance would buttonhole him in a pub somewhere. Either that or he would lose track of time, busy downloading more illegal stuff from the net. It had been a long time since he had made a family meal. I looked across at my guitar, gathering dust in a lonely corner. It was longer still since Ken had come around on a Wednesday night so we could rehearse together. I couldn't remember the last time we had played a gig. . . .

I busied myself with tidying up the kitchen. I had an article to write, but, truth be told, I was putting off starting it. I didn't want to see what Ken had done to my poor computer. His modifications tended to complicate my life, not simplify it. They were all done in good faith, of course, but sometimes I longed for the days of my old AMSTRAD word processor with its green screen and simple commands. I groaned as I saw my PC, its screen, once a familiar pale blue, now shining at me in bright orange.

Maybe I should mark a set of essays ready for tomorrow's lessons.

Still the orange screen seemed to be staring at me.

"Okay," I said, seating myself before it. "Let's see what Ken has done this time."

The screen looked pretty much the same as before, apart from the bright orange background. I clicked START and launched my accounts spreadsheet.

It was exactly as I had left it. Neat columns showing my monthly income and expenditure. Ken had been hassling me to use a copy of the Money Management software he had installed, but I preferred this. I could understand it. I had control. I could spot mistakes. Just like that one there.

I was saving up for a car. Each month I transferred what I could into my savings account. That month I had mistyped an entry. £10 instead of £100. That was easily rectified. I clicked in the cell and made the change. An error message flashed up on the screen.

Reality dysfunction. £10 is not £100

"I know that," I muttered. "I made a mistake." I tried the correction again and received the same error message.

"Bloody Ken."

I picked up the plastic disc case, still lying by the keyboard and read the scrawled insert. *Aristotle OS*. That was a clue, of course.

"Come on now, Jon," I said to myself. "You can figure this out. Ken said that this was not a Platonic OS. This does not model reality. . . ."

It made a certain sort of sense, when you thought about it. Aristotle believed that Plato had got it wrong. Reality wasn't something that existed "behind" us and could only be seen as shadows; it wasn't something that could only be modeled with our reason. Aristotle believed reality was that which we perceived through our senses.

What senses did a computer have? Inputs. Keyboard presses and mouse clicks. Digital samples of sounds and images played into their memories a byte at a time. If the keyboard had said there was £10 in the savings account this month, then £10 there was. If the keyboard later on said there was £100, then the computer would want to know which was right. It would be like me opening my wallet and finding £100 in crisp notes there, when minutes before there had only been £10. I'd want to explain the change.

I gazed at the screen. What was the point of my computer

acting like this? Well, it was easily fixed. I entered another £90 in the cell below the £10. There. Now I had £100 in my savings account.

If only mistakes in life could be remedied so easily.

I grew to like the Aristotle OS. It came into its own when I was typing up long articles. I came to rely on the little messages that flashed up as a piece of work took shape.

> J Davies cannot have published
> *An Introduction to Existentialism*
> in 1982 *and* 1984

or

> Grumman cannot have been born
> both French and German

It had other uses too. Ways of making you think; of confronting you with your own assumptions.

> Why do you begin so many sentences
> with the word "Hopefully"?

or

> Why give £40 to *Feed the Homeless* when this month
> you threw out food to the value of £45?

Why indeed? I resolved to be more careful with my shopping. I would eat everything that I bought. There was half a lettuce going brown in the bottom of the fridge. I boiled a couple of eggs and made a salad with it.

My first inkling that something was not quite right came when Ken phoned late one night, maybe three weeks after he had installed Aristotle.

"Hey, Jon . . ." His speaking was slurred. I could hear the

clink of glasses in the background, the muffled sound of laughter made by men drinking in a pub after hours.

"Ken," I said. "It's two o'clock in the bloody morning. Can't it wait?"

"Jon, have you been using your computer?"

"Of course I've been using my computer. Why have you rung me in the middle of the night to ask me that?"

"No. No. I don't want another pint. No. Whisky." His voice was muffled. I could picture him standing there, that way he did, phone cradled at his neck, shaking his hand in a "drink" gesture at the barman. "No. No Jon. That should be okay. Of course you should use your computer. Just don't connect it to the Internet."

"What? Why not? How am I supposed to read my mail? Look Ken, what's the matter with you?"

The line went dead.

I went back to bed and stared at the ceiling. I couldn't go back to sleep. My mind drifted inexorably to Jenny. What was she doing now, I wondered? After half an hour of torturing myself I got up and went into the lounge and picked up my guitar, blew the dust off it. I tried to play something, but the strings were old and I couldn't tune them.

The picture on my computer screen was of Ken and me, standing on the summit of Ben Nevis. It was a cold scene, gray cloud swirled over the lifeless vista: rocks and rubble and the remains of a building. A man in a yellow waterproof and thick woollen hat could be seen squatting there, stirring a pan on a portable stove. Steam from hot soup rose into the air.

Ken was dressed in a thin jumper and coat; on his feet was a pair of old training shoes. He looked as if he had wandered out of a pub in Fort William with a couple of his mates and decided to climb the mountain for a laugh.

That's exactly what he had done.

He was holding up a can of Tennants Super Lager for the camera to see. I stood by him, in my old Craghoppers jacket, looking seriously concerned for my brother's well being.

A picture paints a thousand words . . . This one captured

the moment perfectly. It told the viewer everything they needed to know about my relationship with my brother.

Just one thing. I've never been to Ben Nevis.

How had the computer managed to superimpose me onto that picture?

Ken almost looked embarrassed when he came around.

"Look," I said. "Look!"

I clicked the mouse, flicking through picture after picture on the screen. Me in front of the Taj Mahal; a strange city of silver towers, the Houses of Parliament clearly visible nestling amongst them; an aeroplane the like of which I'd never seen, flying over a blasted plain.

"Where have they come from?" I asked. "I certainly didn't put them there."

"No," said Ken. "It's Aristotle. It's trying to make sense of contradictory data. Let me explain." He looked around for inspiration. "I know; it's better if you close your eyes. . . ."

I stared at him. He looked a mess.

"You stink of beer," I said. "When are you going to sort yourself out?"

He looked angry.

"I've got nothing to sort out. Look, close your eyes. I'm trying to explain it to you. Do you want me to fix your computer or not?"

That threat was always there. I closed my eyes. "Now what?"

"Now imagine an orange. Are you doing that? Imagine the feel of its skin, that slightly waxy, warm sensation. Imagine pressing your thumbs into it, forcing a hole, juice squirting over your hands, that sharp citrus smell in your nose—"

"Is there a point to this?" I said, my eyes tightly closed.

"Yes. Open your eyes. Look at me. Now, tell me. How do you know what you just experienced was imagination and not the real thing?"

"Is this some sort of philosophical question. 'Am I a butterfly dreaming I am an Emperor?'"

"No. I'm dealing with facts, not some philosophical bollocks. Listen, I'll tell you how you know the difference: the signals in the neurons in your brain that fired when you imagined the orange were not as strong as they would have been if you had *really* handled one. The same neurons fired, but there was a difference in the magnitude of the signal."

"If you say so. . . ."

"I do say so. Well, your computer can't do that. For a computer, a memory location is either on or off. It holds something in memory, it accepts an input, it has no way of knowing if what it has stored is real or imaginary. You connected your computer to the Internet. It has encountered all sorts of data out there. Games, models, jokes—some things that are just plain wrong. But it has no way of knowing what is real and what is made up. It tries to resolve what it sees as contradictory realities. Your pictures are an example of your computer doing just that."

"Oh. So what are you going to do about it?"

He held out another disc. This one read "Kant 2.0" "This'll sort it out."

"Why don't I just go back to Windows?"

"You can't. Aristotle won't let go. It refuses to accept a Platonic OS as valid. It will upgrade to Kant, though. Don't ask me why."

I gave a grim smile. "I know why." It wasn't often I managed to put one over on my brother where computers were concerned. "Kant built on Aristotle's materialism. He distinguished between the thing in itself, and the way it appears to an observer. He said that we only experience the world through the forms of time and causality. I'm guessing that the upgrade on that disk will give my computer just enough of a context to make sense of the world."

Ken swayed as he looked from me to the computer. His clothes smelled of stale cigarette smoke.

"Whoever thought that philosophy could be useful?" he said sarcastically.

"Whoever designed the program on that disk, I imagine," I replied sweetly.

Kant 2.0 seemed to do the trick. The composite picture of me and Ken at the top of Ben Nevis was efficiently separated into its component parts and placed in a query folder, along with other files with ambiguous dates. I went through the folder at my leisure, assigning the files to their correct context.

> Picture files "Jon Paris.jpg" and "Ken Eiffel Tower.jpg"
> have the same date. Merge Yes No ?

They had the same date because both files would have been newly created when I copied them across from my old computer. Piece by piece I separated my life back out, disentangling it from the imaginary web in which it had become entangled.

I found it quite therapeutic. Like playing my guitar.

All seemed to return to normal. Until I came home late one evening from college and found a message on the screen.

> hi jon gone to mallons with charlotte and najam
> back late don't wait up jen xxx

It was from Jenny. There was no doubt about it. She regarded ignoring punctuation or the shift key as a way of demonstrating her refusal to take my work seriously. It was "only writing" after all.

But what was she playing at, e-mailing me now?

Her number was still on my mobile. I dialed her. She answered on the third ring.

"Jon. What do you want?"

The sound of her voice still hurt, especially when it was twisted into something so suspicious and hostile.

"Me?" I replied. "What do you want? What do you mean; you've gone to Mallon's?"

"Why shouldn't I go to Mallon's?" she said. "It's Charlotte's birthday." I could hear the sound of a jukebox playing in the background: wine bar jazz, bland saxophones over a Latin clave. The sort of MOR crap I hate. "Anyway," she snapped, "what's it got to do with you? Are you spying on me?"

"What?" I looked at the computer screen again, just to

confirm that I wasn't seeing things. "Spying on *you*? No. I got your message."

"What message? Jon, stop pissing me around."

And at that the line went dead.

I stared at the screen for a while, then I went to close the message down. A prompt appeared on the screen.

Save changes to file? Yes No

After a long moment, I clicked on the Yes Button.

I don't think I could name the exact moment I realised I was not living my real life. It was a slow process of comprehension, a picture that gradually took form as the different pieces slotted into place. It was like watching an image downloading from the Internet on a slow connection.

Here there was an e-mail from Jenny telling me that she would meet me at the Tate at seven that night.

Here was confirmation of two tickets to see Chris Smither at the Half Moon in Putney. Two tickets, one for me, one for Ken.

Here was a picture of Jenny and me riding on a boat down the dark stripe of the Thames, late on a warm July evening. London rose up on either bank outlined in red and yellow and white lights. What a delightful scene for a wedding reception. I could see Charlotte in the background, looking beautiful as the bride.

Here was confirmation of a flight to Geneva, and later on there was picture of Ken and me sitting on the terrace of a refuge high in the Italian Alps. Ken was holding up a glass of water to the camera to say "cheers!" His nose was burned red by the sun; he looked happy and healthy and utterly relaxed and I felt suddenly stifled by the half empty room in which I sat. South Street was so dull and lifeless compared to the world on my screen. I stared again at Ken, looking so peaceful. When was the last time I had seen him so happy with nothing but a glass of water in his hand?

That was my computer. That was Kant 2.0. It viewed the world through keyboards and scanners and microphones, and built up a pattern of life through causality and time that was as optimised and validated and free from illogicality as was anything else on my computer. My new OS didn't understand about repression and self destruction and pride and all those other human traits in which Ken and I had steeped our lives. On the screen I could see my PC living out my life for me as it should have been lived, if only I had the courage and the sense to have seized my opportunities as they came along.

And it made me feel sick to my soul to see it, because there, dancing in the pixel light of my dim room, there was no room for excuses or dreams or might-have-beens. That was a picture of my failure in negative, a successful life painted for all to see in twenty-four-bit glory.

Ken rolled up at my house two nights later. It was half past ten, there was still forty minutes worth of drinking time left in the pubs, but I guess his money had run out. I offered him a coffee; he accepted it with a decent measure of brandy poured in for luck.

"Ken," I said. "Why didn't we go and see Chris Smither?"

He sat back on my old sofa, knocking yesterday's newspaper onto the floor, and took a big drink.

"Chris Smither?" His eyes lit up for a moment. "Yeah—he did that cool arrangement of Statesboro Blues. How did that go again?"

He put his mug down on the carpet and began to play air guitar. "Doo dn doo dn dah dah . . . Wake up Mama, turn your lamp down low . . . doo dnn . . ." He shook his head. "I don't know. We just didn't have the time, I suppose."

He mimed some more, singing to himself. Ken used to play the guitar a lot: he was very good. Way better than me. I pulled my computer chair up so that I was sitting closer to him.

"Why not?" I asked. "Why didn't we have time? It's not like we ever do anything. I spend my evenings sitting here at a computer typing out lesson notes and articles that are never published. What about you?"

"I don't know. I guess I was busy. You know how it is. . . ."

"Busy doing what? Ken, we used to go to a concert at least once a week. You used to love listening to live music."

"I still do."

"No you don't. Ken, we'd have been at the concert if you hadn't been 'too busy.'"

I tapped at the keyboard and brought up the picture of Ken sitting outside the refuge in the Alps, glass of water in his hand.

"Looks good, doesn't it?" I said. He didn't seem surprised to see it. I pressed home my point.

"We'd have taken that holiday if you hadn't decided to stay in the pub and have another drink. That"—I pointed to the PC—"knows the logical thing would have been to put down your beer and come with me to the travel agents."

"What does it know?" said Ken dismissively.

"That you're an alcoholic."

The words were out before I could stop them. Ken held my gaze for a lengthening time, and then both our eyes slid back to the computer screen.

"Have you been on the Internet lately?" he asked, changing the subject.

"Just for e-mail. Research, that sort of thing."

"Have you looked at the news sites?" There was an edge of danger in his voice.

"I prefer to read the papers." I looked at the tangled mess of yesterdays *Guardian* being ground into the floor by his restless feet. He stood up suddenly.

"Come here," he said, walking to my computer.

He opened the web browser and typed in an address at the top: news.bbc.co.uk.

My Internet connection is slow. The words and pictures dropped into place piece by piece, slowly revealing the picture of the world as understood by Kant 2.0.

There were pictures of cities full of gleaming towers.

A classroom full of beaming black children.

A field of tanks, painted in rainbow colors, flowers growing amongst their tracks.

A spaceship sitting on the red rocky surface of Mars.

I turned to Ken.

"That's not true, is it?" I said. "None of it is real."

"No," said Ken. "But it could be. If we really wanted it."

There was another of those deepening silences that seemed to have infected our lives. Eventually, he held out his mug.

"More coffee?" I said.

"Yes. Don't forget the brandy."

The Last American

JOHN KESSEL

John Kessel (www4.ncsu.edu/~tenshi/index2.html) lives in Raleigh, North Carolina, with his wife, Sue Hall, and their daughter, Emma. He is a literature professor at North Carolina State University, where he is currently the Director of Creative Writing. He began publishing fiction in 1978. He has published a number of novels, short story collections, and anthologies. In 2007 his anthology Rewired: The Post-Cyberpunk Anthology, *co-edited with his longtime collaborator James Patrick Kelly, appeared from Tachyon Publishing. A new collection of his short fiction,* The Baum Plan for Financial Independence and Other Stories, *is due out from Small Beer Press in 2008.*

"The Last American" appeared in Foundation 100 *in the special fiction issue in the summer of 2007, and in the February 2008 issue of* Asimov's. *This story is a satirical political biography concerned with what it is to be human and what it is to be an American, once both experiences have become post-human forms of entertainment. A hundred years from now, after the imperial regime of President Steele, the AI civilization triumphs. This is an artificial PBS history program as a future art form, about the twenty-first century.*

The Life of Andrew Steele
Re-created by Fiona 13

Reviewed by The OldGuy

"I don't blame my father for beating me. I don't blame him for tearing the book I was reading from my hands, and I don't blame him for locking me in the basement. When I was a child, I did blame him. I was angry, and I hated my father. But as I grew older I came to understand that he did what was right for me, and now I look upon him with respect and love, the respect and love he always deserved, but that I was unable to give him because I was too young and self-centered to grasp it."

—Andrew Steele, 2077
Conversation with Hagiographer

During the thirty-three years Andrew Steele occupied the Oval Office of what was then called the White House, in what was then called the United States of America (not to be confused with the current United State of Americans), on the corner of his desk he kept an antiquated device of the early 21st century called a taser. Typically used by law enforcement officers, it functioned by shooting out a thin wire that, once in contact with its target, delivered an electric shock of up to 300,000 volts. The victim was immediately incapacitated by muscle spasms and intense pain. This crude weapon was used for crowd control or to subdue suspects of crimes.

When Ambassador for the New Humanity Mona Vaidya-nathan first visited Steele, she asked what the queer black object was. Steele told her that it had been the most frequent means of communication between his father and himself. "When I was ten years old," he told her, "within a single month my father used that on me sixteen times."

"That's horrible," she said.

"Not for a person with a moral imagination," Steele re-plied.

In this new biography of Steele, Fiona 13, the Grand Lady of Reproductions, presents the crowning achievement of her long career re-creating lives for the Cognosphere. Andrew Steele, when he died in 2100, had come to exemplify the 21st century, and his people, in a way that goes beyond the metaphorical. Drawing on every resource of the posthuman biographer, from heuristic modeling to reconstructive DNA sampling to forensic dreaming, Ms. 13 has produced this labor of, if not love, then obsession, and I for one, am grate-ful for it.

Fiona presents her new work in a hybrid form. Compara-tively little of this biography is subjectively rendered. In-stead, harking back to a bygone era, Fiona breaks up the narrative with long passages of *text*—strings of printed code that must be read with the eyes. Of course this adds the bur-den of learning the code to anyone seeking to experience her re-creation, but an accelerated prefrontal intervention is packaged with the biography. Fiona maintains that *text*, since it forces an artificial linearity on experience, stimu-lates portions of the left brain that seldom function in con-ventional experiential biographies. The result is that the person undergoing the life of Andrew Steele both lives through significant moments in Steele's subjectivity, and is drawn out of the stream of sensory and emotional reaction to contemplate the significance of that experience from the point of view of a wise commentator.

I trust I do not have to explain the charms of this form to those of you reading this review, but I recommend the experience to all cognizant entities who still maintain elements of curiosity in their affect repertoire.

Childhood

Appropriately for a man who was to so personify the 21st century, Dwight Andrew Steele was born on January 1, 2001. His mother, Rosamund Sanchez Steele, originally from Mexico, was a lab technician at the forestry school at North Carolina State University; his father, Herbert Matthew Steele, was a land developer and on the board of the Planter's Bank and Trust. Both of Steele's parents were devout Baptists and attended one of the new "big box" churches that had sprung up in the late 20th century in response to growing millennialist beliefs in the United States and elsewhere.

The young Steele was "home schooled." This meant that Steele's mother devoted a portion of every day to teaching her son herself. The public school system was distrusted by large numbers of religious believers, who considered education by the state to be a form of indoctrination in moral error. Home schoolers operated from the premise that the less contact their children had with the larger world, the better.

Unfortunately, in the case of Andrew this did not prevent him from meeting other children. Andrew was a small, serious boy, sensitive, and an easy target for bullies. This led to his first killing. Fiona 13 realizes this event for us through extrapolative genetic mapping.

We are in the playground, on a bright May morning. We are running across the crowded asphalt toward a climbing structure of wood and metal, when suddenly we are falling! A nine-year-old boy named Jason Terry has tripped us and, when we regain our feet, he tries to pull our pants down. We feel the sting of our elbows where they scraped the pavement; feel surprise and dismay, fear, anger. As Terry leans forward to grab the waistband of our trousers, we suddenly bring our knee

up into Terry's face. Terry falls back, sits down awk-
wardly. The other children gathered laugh. The sound
of the laughter in our ears only enrages us more—are
they laughing at us? The look of dismay turns to rage
on Terry's face. He is going to beat us up, now, he is a
deadly threat. We step forward, and before Terry can
stand, kick him full in the face. Terry's head snaps
back and strikes the asphalt, and he is still.

The children gasp. A trickle of blood flows from be-
neath Terry's ear. From across the playground comes
the monitor's voice: "Andrew? Andrew Steele?"

I have never experienced a more vivid moment in biography. There it all is: the complete assumption by Steele that he
is the victim. The fear and rage. The horror, quickly repressed.
The later remorse, swamped by desperate justifications.

It was only through his father's political connections and
acquiescence in private counseling (that the Steeles did not
believe in, taking psychology as a particularly pernicious
form of modern mumbo jumbo) that Andrew was kept out of
the legal system. He withdrew into the family, his father's
discipline and his mother's teaching.

More trouble was to follow. Keeping it secret from his
family, Herbert Steele had invested heavily in real estate in
the late oughts; he had leveraged properties he purchased to
borrow money to invest in several hedge funds, hoping to
put the family into a position of such fundamental wealth
that they would be beyond the reach of economic vagaries.

When the Friends of the American League set off the At-
lanta nuclear blast in 2012, pushing the first domino of the
Global Economic Meltdown, Steele senior's financial house
of cards collapsed. The U.S. government, having spent itself
into bankruptcy and dependence on Asian debt support
through ill-advised imperial schemes and paranoid reactions
to global terrorist threats, had no resources to deal with the
collapse of private finances. Herbert Steele struggled to deal
with the reversal, fell into a depression, and died when he
crashed a borrowed private plane into a golf course in Southern Pines.

Andrew was twelve years old. His mother, finding part time work as a data entry clerk, made barely enough money to keep them alive. Andrew was forced into the public schools. He did surprisingly well there. Andrew always seemed mature for his years, deferential to his elders, responsible, trustworthy, and able to see others' viewpoint. He was slightly aloof from his classmates, and seemed more at home in the presence of adults.

Unknown to his overstressed mother, Andrew was living a secret life. On the Internet, under a half dozen false IP addresses, he maintained political websites. Through them he became one of the world's most influential "bloggers."

A blog was a personal web log, a site on the worldwide computer system where individuals, either anonymously or in their own names, commented on current affairs or their own lives. Some of these weblogs had become prominent, and their organizers and authors politically important.

Andrew had a fiction writer's gift for inventing consistent personalities, investing them with brilliant argument and sharp observation. On the "Political Theater" weblog, as Sacré True, he argued for the impeachment of President Harrison; on "Reason Season," as Tom Pain, he demonstrated why Harrison's impeachment would prove disastrous. Fiona sees this phase of Steele's life as his education in manipulating others' sensibilities. His emotion-laden arguments were astonishingly successful at twisting his interlocutors into rhetorical knots. To unravel and respond to one of Steele's arguments rationally would take four times his space, and carry none of his propagandistic force. Steele's argument against the designated hitter rule even found its way into the platform of the resurgent Republican Party.

Interrogator

"You don't know why I acted, but I know why. I acted because it is necessary for me to act, because that's what, whether you like it or not, you require me to do. And I don't mind doing it because it's what I have to

do. It's what I was born to do. I've never been appreciated for it but that's okay too because, frankly, no one is ever appreciated for what they do.

"But before you presume to judge me realize that you are responsible. I am simply your instrument. I took on the burden of your desires when I didn't want to—I would just as gladly have had that cup pass me by—but I did it, and I have never complained. And I have never felt less than proud of what I have done. I did what was necessary, for the benefit of others. If it had been up to me I would never have touched a single human being, but I am not complaining.

"I do however ask you, humbly, if you have any scrap of decency left, if you have any integrity whatsoever, not to judge me. You do not have that right.

"Ask Carlo Sanchez, ask Alfonso Garadiana, ask Sayid Ramachandran, ask Billy Chen. Ask them what was the right thing to do. And then, when you've got the answer from their bleeding corpses, then, and only then, come to me."

—Andrew Steele, 2020
Statement before Board of Inquiry

Contemporary readers must remember the vast demographic and other circumstantial differences that make the early 21st century an alien land to us. When Steele was sixteen years old, the population of the world was an astonishing 6.8 billion, fully half of whom were under the age of 25, the overwhelming majority of those young and striving individuals living in poverty, but with access, through the technologies that had spread widely over the previous twenty years, to unprecedented unregulated information. Few of them could be said to have been adequately acculturated. The history of the next forty years, including Steele's part in that history, was shaped by this fact.

In 2017 Steele was conscripted into the U.S. army pursuing the Oil War on two continents. Because he was fluent in Spanish, he served as an interrogator with the 71st infantry division stationed in Venezuela. His history as an interrogator included the debriefing of the rightfully elected president of that nation in 2019. Fiona puts us there:

> We are standing in the back of a small room with concrete walls, banks of fluorescent lights above, a HVAC vent and exposed ducts hanging from the ceiling. The room is cold. We have been standing for a long time and our back is stiff. We have seen many of these sessions, and all we can think about right now is getting out of here, getting a beer and getting some sleep.
>
> In the center of the room Lieutenant Haslop and a civilian contractor are interrogating a small brown man with jet-black shoulder length hair. Haslop is very tall and stoop shouldered, probably from a lifetime of ducking responsibility. The men call him "Slop" behind his back.
>
> The prisoner's name is Alfonso Garadiana. His wrists are tied together behind him, and the same rope stretches down to his ankles, also tied together. The rope is too short, so that the only way he can stand is with his knees flexed painfully. But every time he sways, as if to fall, the contractor signals Haslop, who pokes him with an electric prod. Flecks of blood spot Garadiana's once brilliant white shirt. A cut over his eyebrow is crusted with dried blood, and the eye below it is half-closed.
>
> The contractor, Mr. Gray, is neat and shaved and in control. "So," he says in Spanish, "where are the Jacaranda virus stores?"
>
> Garadiana does not answer. It's unclear whether he has even understood.
>
> Gray nods to Haslop again.
>
> Haslop blinks his eyes, swallows. He slumps into a chair, rests his brow in one hand. "I can't do this anymore," he mutters, only apparently to himself. He wouldn't say it aloud if he didn't want us to hear it, even if he doesn't know that himself. We are sick to death of his weakness.
>
> We step forward and take the prod from his hand.

*"Let me take care of this, sir." We swing the back of
our hand against Garadiana's face, exactly the same
motion we once used to hit a backhand in high school
tennis. The man's head snaps back, and he falls to the
floor. We move in with the prod.*

Upon the failure of the Oil War and the defeat of the government that pursued it, a reaction took place, including war crimes investigations that led to Steele's imprisonment from 2020 to 2025. Fiona gives us a glimpse of Steele's sensorium in his third year in maximum-security prison:

*We're hungry. Above us the air rattles from the ventilator. On the table before us in our jail cell is a notebook. We are writing our testament. It's a distillation
of everything we know to be absolutely true about the
human race and its future. There are things we know
in our DNA that cannot be understood by strict rationality, though reason is a powerful tool and can help
us to communicate these truths to those who do not,
because of incapacity or lack of experience, grasp
them instinctively.*

*The blogs back when we were fourteen were just
practice. Here, thanks to the isolation, we are able to
go deep, to find the roots of human truth and put them
down in words.*

*We examine the last sentence we have written: "It
is the hero's fate to be misunderstood."*

*A guard comes by and raps the bars of our cell.
"Still working on the great opus, Andy?"*

*We ignore him, close the manuscript, move from
the table and begin to do push-ups in the narrow
space beside the cot.*

*The guard raps again on the bars. "How about an
answer, killer?" His voice is testy.*

*We concentrate on doing the push-ups correctly.
Eleven. Twelve. Thirteen. Fourteen . . .*

*When we get out of here, all this work will make a
difference.*

This was indeed the case, Fiona shows us, but not in the way that Steele intended. As a work of philosophy his testament was rejected by all publishers. He struggled to make a living in the Long Emergency that was the result of the oil decline and the global warming-spawned environmental disasters that hit with full force in the 2020s. These changes were asymmetric, but though some regions felt them more than others, none were unaffected. The flipping of the Atlantic current turned 2022 into the first Year Without a Summer in Europe. Torrential rains in North Africa, the desertification of the North American Great Plains, mass wildlife migrations, drastic drops in grains production, die-offs of marine life and decimated global fish stocks were among only the most obvious problems with which worldwide civilization struggled. And Andrew Steele was out of prison, without a connection in the world.

Artist

"The great artist is a rapist. It is his job to plant a seed, an idea or an emotion, in the viewer's mind. He uses every tool available to enforce his will. The audience doesn't know what it wants, but he knows what it wants, and needs, and he gives it to them.

"To the degree I am capable of it, I strive to be a great artist."

—Andrew Steele, 2037
"Man of Steele"
Interview on *VarietyNet*

At this moment of distress, Steele saw an opportunity, and turned his political testament into a best-selling novel, *What's Wrong with Heroes?* A film deal followed immediately. Steele insisted on being allowed to write the screenplay, and against its better judgment, the studio relented. Upon its release, *What's Wrong with Heroes?* became the highest grossing film in the history of cinema. In the character of Roark McMaster, Steele created a virile philosopher king who spoke to the desperate hopes of millions. With the money he made, Steele conquered the entertainment world. A series of blockbuster films, television series, and virtual adventures followed. This photo link shows him on the set of *The Betrayal,* his historical epic of the late 20th century. The series, conflating the Vietnam with two Iraq wars, presents the fiascoes of the early 21st as the result of Machiavellian subversives and their bad-faith followers taking advantage of the innocence of the American populace, undermining what was once a strong and pure-minded nation.

Fiona gives us a key scene from the series:

INT. AMERICAN AIRLINES FLIGHT 11

Two of the hijackers, wearing green camo, are gathered around a large man seated in the otherwise empty first class cabin of the 757. The big man, unshaven, wears a shabby Detroit Tigers baseball cap.

> WALEED
> *(frantic)*
> What shall we do now?

> MOORE
> Keep the passengers back in coach. Is Mohammad on course? How long?

> ABDULAZIZ
> *(calling back from cockpit)*
> Allah willing—three minutes.

Moore glances out the plane window.

MOORE'S P.O.V.—through window, an aerial view of Manhattan on a beautiful clear day

CLOSE ON MOORE

Smirks.

MOORE

Time to go.

Moore hefts his bulk from the first class seat, moves toward the on-board baggage closet near the front of the plane.

ABDULAZIZ

What are you doing?

From out of a hanging suit bag, Moore pulls a parachute, and straps it on.

WALEED

Is this part of the plan?

Moore jerks up the lever on the plane's exterior door and yanks on it. It does not budge.

MOORE

Don't just stand there, Waleed! Help me!

Waleed moves to help Moore, and reluctantly, Abdulaziz joins them.

ATTA
(from cockpit)

There it is! Allah akbar!

Moore and the other two hijackers break the seal and the door flies open. A blast of wind sucks Abdulaziz and Waleed forward; they fall back onto the plane's deck. Moore braces himself against the edge of the door with his hands.

MOORE

In the name of the Democratic Party, the compassionate, the merciful—so long, boys!

Moore leaps out of the plane.

The Betrayal was the highest rated series ever to run on American television, and cemented Steele's position as the most bankable mass-appeal Hollywood producer since Spielberg. At the age of thirty-eight, Steele married the actress Esme Napoli, leading lady in three of his most popular films.

Religious Leader

The next section of Fiona's biography begins with this heart-rending experience from Steele's middle years:

We are in a sumptuous hotel suite with a blonde, not wearing much of anything. We are chasing her around the bed.

"You can't catch me!"

We snag her around the waist, and pull her onto the bed. "I've already caught you. You belong to me." We hold up her ring finger, with its platinum band. "You see?"

"I'm full of nanomachines," she says breathlessly. "If you catch me you'll catch them."

The Scarlet Plague has broken out in Los Angeles, after raging for a month in Brazil. We have fled the city with Esme and are holed up in this remote hotel in Mexico.

"When are we going to have these children?" we ask her. "We need children. Six at least."

"You're going to have to work harder than this to deserve six children," Esme says. "The world is a mess. Do we want to bring children into it?"

"The world has always been a mess. We need to bring children into it because it's a mess." We kiss her perfect cheek.

But a minute later, as we make love, we spot the growing rash along the inside of Esme's thigh.

The death of Steele's wife came near the beginning of the plague decade, followed by the Sudden War and the Collapse. Fiona cites the best estimates of historiographers that, between 2040 and 2062 the human population of the earth went from 8.2 to somewhat less than two billion. The toll was slightly higher in the less developed nations; on the other hand, resistance to the plagues was higher among humans of the tropical regions. This situation in the middle years of the century transformed the Long Emergency of 2020 to 2040— a condition in which civilization, although stressed, might still be said to function, and with which Steele and his generation had coped, into the Die Off, in which the only aspect of civilization that, even in the least affected regions, might be said to function was a desperate triage.

One of the results of the Long Emergency had been to spark widespread religious fervor. Social and political disruptions had left millions searching for certitudes. Longevity breakthroughs, new medicine, genetic engineering, cyborging and AI pushed in one direction, while widespread climactic change, fights against deteriorating civil and environmental conditions, and economic disruptions pushed in another. The young warred against the old, the rich against the poor. Reactionary religious movements raged on four continents. Interpreting the chaos of the 21st century in terms of eschatology was a winning business. Terrorism in the attempt to bring on utopia or the end of the world was a common reality. Steele, despite his grief, rapidly grasped that art, even popular art, had no role in this world. So he turned, readily, to religion.

> *"Human evolution is a process of moral evolution. The thing that makes us different from animals is our understanding of the ethical implications of every action that we perform: those that we must perform, those that we choose. Some actions are matters of contingency, and some are matters of free will.*
>
> *"Evolution means we will eventually come to fill the universe. To have our seed spread far and wide. That is what we are here for. To engender those chil-*

dren, to bear them, to raise them properly, to have them extend their—and our—thought, creativity, joy, understanding, to every particle of the visible universe."

—Andrew Steele, 2052
Sermon in the Cascades

Steele's Church of Humanity grew rapidly in the 2040s; while the population died and cities burned, its membership more than doubled every year, reaching tens of millions by 2050. Steele's credo of the Hero transferred easily to religious terms; his brilliantly orchestrated ceremonies sparked ecstatic responses; he fed the poor and comforted the afflicted, and using every rhetorical device at his command, persuaded his followers that the current troubles were the birth of a new utopian age, that every loss had its compensation, that sacrifice was noble, that reward was coming, that from their loins would spring a new and better race, destined to conquer the stars. Love was the answer.

His creed crossed every ethnic, racial, sexual, gender preference, class, and age barrier. Everyone was human, and all equal.

The Church of Humanity was undeniably successful in helping millions of people, not just in the United States but across the bleeding globe, deal with the horrors of the Die Off. It helped them to rally in the face of unimaginable psychological and material losses. But it was not the only foundation for the recovery. By the time some semblance of order was restored to world affairs in the 2060s, genetically modified humans, the superbrights, were attempting to figure a way out of the numerous dead ends of capitalism, antiquated belief systems, and a dysfunctional system of nation states. This was a period of unexampled experimentation, and the blossoming of many technologies that had been only potentialities prior to the collapse, among them the uploading of human identities, neurological breakthroughs on the origins of altruism and violence, grafted information capacities, and free quantum energy.

Most of these developments presented challenges to religion. Steele came to see such changes as a threat to fundamental humanity. So began his monstrous political career.

Politician

"The greatest joy in life is putting yourself in the circumstance of another person. To see the world through his eyes, to feel the air on her skin, to breathe in deeply the spirit of their souls. To have his joy and trouble be equally real to you. To know that others are fully and completely human, just as you are. To get outside of your own subjectivity, and to see the world from a completely different and equally valid perspective, to come fully to understand them. When that point of understanding is reached, there is no other word for the feeling that you have than love. Just as much as you love yourself, as you love your children, you love this other.

"And at that point, you must exterminate them."

—Andrew Steele, 2071
What I Believe

Steele was swept into office as President of the reconstituted United States in the election of 2064, with his Humanity Party in complete control of the Congress. In his first hundred days, Steele signed a raft of legislation comprising his Humanity Initiative. Included were The Repopulation Act that forced all women of childbearing age to have no fewer than four children, a bold space colonization program, restrictions on genetic alterations and technological body modifications, the wiping clean of all uploaded personalities from private and public databases, the Turing Limit on AI, the Neurological Protection Act of 2065, and the establishment of a legal "standard human being."

In Steele's first term, "non-standard" humans were allowed to maintain their civil rights, but were identified by injected markers, their movements and employment restricted by the newly established Humanity Agency. Through diplomatic efforts and the international efforts of the Church of Humanity, similar policies were adapted, with notable areas of resistance, throughout much of the world.

In Steele's second term, the HA was given police powers and the non-standard gradually stripped of civil and property rights. By his third term, those who had not managed to escape the country lost all legal rights and were confined to posthuman reservations, popularly known as "Freak Towns." The establishment of the Protectorate over all of North and South America stiffened resistance elsewhere, and resulted in the uneasy Global Standoff. Eventually, inevitably, came the First and Second Human Wars.

Fiona includes a never-before-experienced moment from the 23rd year of Steele's presidency.

We are in a command bunker, a large, splendidly appointed room one whole wall of which is a breathtaking view of the Grand Tetons. We sit at a table with our closest advisors, listening to General Jinjur describe their latest defeat by the New Humans. There are tears in her eyes as she recounts the loss of the Fifth Army on the assault on Madrid.

We do not speak. Our cat, Socrates, sits on our lap, and we scratch him behind his ears. He purrs.

"How many dead?" Chief of Command Taggart asks.

"Very few, sir," reports Jinjur. "But over ninety percent converted. It's their new amygdalic bomb. It destroys our troops' will to fight. The soldiers just lay down their arms and go off looking for something to eat. You try organizing an autistic army."

"At least they're good at math," says Secretary Bloom.

"How can these posthumans persist?" Dexter asks.

"We've exterminated millions. How many of them are left?"

"We can't know, sir. They keep making more."

"But they don't even fight," says Taggart. "They must be on the point of extinction."

"It has never been about fighting, sir."

"It's this damned subversion," says Taggart. "We have traitors among us. They seed genetic changes among the people. They turn our own against us. How can we combat that?"

General Jinjur gathers herself. She is quite a striking woman, the flower of the humanity we have fought to preserve for so many years. "If I may be permitted to say so, we are fighting ourselves. We are trying to conquer our own human élan. Do you want to live longer? Anyone who wants to live longer will eventually become posthuman. Do you want to understand the universe? Anyone who wants to understand the universe will eventually become posthuman. Do you want peace of mind? Anyone who wants peace of mind will eventually become posthuman."

Something in her tone catches us, and we are finally moved to speak. "You are one of them, aren't you."

"Yes," she says.

The contemporary citizen need not be troubled with, and Fiona does not provide, any detailed recounting of the war's progress, or how it ended in the Peace that Passeth All Understanding of 2096. The treatment of the remaining humans, the choices offered them, the removal of those few persisting to Mars, and their continued existence there under quarantine, are all the material for another work.

Similarly, the circumstances surrounding Steele's death—the cross, the taser, the Shetland pony—so much a subject of debate, speculation and conspiracy theory, surely do not need rehearsing here. We know what happened to him. He destroyed himself.

Awaiting Further Instruction

> *"The highest impulse of which a human being is capable is to sacrifice himself in the service of the community of which he is a part, even when that community does not recognize him, and heaps opprobrium upon him for that sacrifice. In fact, such scorn is more often than not to be expected. The true savior of his fellows is not deterred by the prospect of rejection, though carrying the burden of his unappreciated gift is a trial that he can never, but for a few moments, escape. It is the hero's fate to be misunderstood."*
> *What's Wrong with Heroes?* (unpublished version)

Fiona 13 ends her biography with a simple accounting of the number of beings, human and posthuman, who died as a result of Steele's life. She speculates that many of these same beings might not have lived had he not lived as well, and comes to no formal conclusion, utilitarian or otherwise, as to the moral consequences of the life of Dwight Andrew Steele.

Certainly few tears are shed for Andrew Steele, and few for the ultimate decline of the human race. I marvel at that remnant of humans who, using technologies that he abhorred, have incorporated into their minds a slice of Steele's personality in the attempt to make themselves into the image of the man they see as their savior. Indeed, I must confess to more than a passing interest in their poignant delusions, their comic, mystifying pastimes, their habitual conflicts, their simple loves and hates, their inability to control themselves, their sudden and tragic enthusiasms.

Bootlegged Steele personalities circulate in the Cognosphere, and it may be that those of you who, like me, on occasion edit their capacities in order to spend recreational time being human, will avail themselves of this unique and terrifying experience.

Memorare

GENE WOLFE

Gene Wolfe (fan site: http://mysite.verizon.net/~vze2tmhh/
wolfe.html) *lives in Barrington, Illinois, with his wife Rose-
mary. He is perhaps the most highly regarded of science
fiction writers, and we rarely publish a* Year's Best *volume
without at least one Gene Wolfe story. He grew up in Hous-
ton, Texas, which like most of Wolfe's settings was a stranger
place than one might expect. Of his neighborhood in Hous-
ton, he says, "Our house stood midway between two mad
scientists. Miller Porter in the house behind us was my own
age but much tougher and cleverer, and built Tesla coils
and other electric marvels. Across the street Mr. Fellows, a
chemist, maintained a private laboratory over his garage.
He blew himself up once in true comic-book style." His
most recent novel is* Pirate Freedom (2007), *the tale of a
priest and pirate, and his next,* An Evil Guest, *a Lovecraf-
tian novel of cosmic supernatural horror, is out in 2008.*

"Memorare," which appeared in F&SF's *special Gene
Wolfe issue, is a complicated hard SF space opera on the
high aesthetic level of Wolfe's classic novella "Seven American Nights." In the future, some people will build tombs in
space, but they will be vulnerable to robbery, and so some
of them will have complex traps. This is possibly the best
science fiction story of the year.*

The moment March Wildspring spotted the corpses, he launched himself across the shadowy mortuary chamber. He had aimed for the first, but with suit jets wide open he missed it and caught the third, flattening himself against it and rolling over with it so that it lay upon him.

Bullets would have gotten him; but this was a serrated blade pivoting from a crevice in the wall. Had it hit, it would have shredded his suit somewhere near the waist.

He would have suffocated before he froze. The thought failed to comfort him as he huddled under the freeze-dried corpse and strove not to look into its eyes.

How much had his digicorder gotten? He wanted to rub his jaw, but was frustrated by his helmet. Not enough, surely. He would have to make a dummy good enough to fool the mechanism, return with it, and. . . .

Or use one of these corpses.

"Remember, O most gracious Virgin Mary, that never was it known. . . ."

The half-recalled words came slowly, limping.

"That anyone who fled to your protection, implored your help, or sought your intercession, was left unaided."

There was more, but he had forgotten it. He sighed, cleared his throat, and touched the sound switch. "These memorials can be dangerous, like this one. As I've told you, this isn't the big one. The big one we call Number Nineteen is an asteroid ten times the diameter of this, which means it could have a thousand times the interior volume. Frankly, I'm scared of it. We may save it for last."

He had a harsh, unpleasant speaking voice. He knew it; but it was the only voice he had, and the software that might have smoothed and sweetened it cost more than he could afford. Back on his hopper, he would edit what he had said into a script for Kit. She had a voice. . . .

"There are at least five sects and cults whose members believe the deceased will be served through all eternity by those who lose their lives at his or her memorial. Some claim to be offshoots of major faiths. Some are openly satanic. We haven't seen enough to identify the bunch that built this one, and frankly I doubt we will."

If the show sold, if it made one hell of a lot of money, it might—it just might—be possible to buy or build a robotic probe. Of course, if that probe were destroyed. . . .

He began wiggling out from under the corpse and sliding under the next.

Nothing happened.

"Memorare. . . ." He had read the Latin twice, perhaps. It was as lost as the English now. No, more lost.

The blade was set to rupture the suit of anyone who came in. That much was plain. What about going out?

When he had the first corpse steady and vertical, a gentle shove sent it across the chamber in a position that looked practically lifelike.

Nothing. No blade, no reaction of any kind as far as he could see.

Possibly, the system (whatever it was) had detected the imposture. He tried to make the second corpse more lifelike even than the first.

Still nothing.

What if a corpse appeared to be entering? A few determined pulls on his lifeline got him plenty of slack. Hooking it to the third corpse, he held the thin orange line with one hand while he launched the corpse with the other. When it had left the memorial, a gentle tug brought it in again.

The blade flashed from its crevice, savaged the corpse's already-ruined suit, and flung the corpse toward him.

"You've got a new servant," March muttered, "whoever you were." Playing it safe, he went out the way he had come in—fast and high.

Outside, he switched on his mike. "We just saw how dangerous a small percentage of these memorials are, a danger that poisons all the rest, both for mourners and for harmless tourists who might like to visit them. A program for identifying and destroying the few dangerous ones is badly needed."

Propelled by his suit jets, he circled the memorial, getting a little more footage he would probably never use. His digicorder had room for more images than he would ever need. Those millions upon millions of images were the one thing with which he could be generous, even profligate.

"Someone perished here," he told the mike, "far beyond the orbit of Mars. Other someones, employees or followers, family or friends, built his memorial—and built it as a trap, so that their revered dead might be served. . . . Where? In the spirit world? In Paradise? Nirvana? Heaven?

"Or Hell. Hell is possible, too."

Flowing letters, beautiful and alien, danced upon the curving walls. Arabic, perhaps, or Sanskrit. It would be well, March thought, to show enough of it that people would recognize it and stay away. For the present, the corpses floating outside it might be warning enough. His digicorder zoomed in before he switched it off and returned to his scarred olive-drab hopper.

There was an Ethermail from Kit when he woke. He washed, shaved, and dressed before bringing her onto his screen.

"Hi there, Windy! Gettin' lonely out there in the grave-yard?"

She was being jaunty, but even a jaunty Kit could make his palms sweat.

"Well, listen up. Have I got a deal for you! You get me to em-cee this terminal travelogue you're makin'. As an added bonus, you get a gal-pal of mine. Her name's Robin Redd, and she's a sound tech who can double in makeup.

"What's more, we come free! Absolutely free, Windy,

unless you can peddle your turkey. In which case we'll expect a tiny little small cut. And residuals.

"So whadda you say? Gimme the nod quick, 'cause Bad Bill's pushin' me to come back. Corner office, park my hopper on the roof with the big boys, and the money ain't hopscotch 'n' hairballs either. So lemme know."

Abruptly, the jauntiness vanished. "Either way, you've got to be quick, Windy. Word is that Pubnet's shooting something similar out around Mars."

He said, "Reply," and took a deep breath. It was always hard to breathe when he tried to talk to Kit. Yes, even when she was three hundred million miles away.

"Kit, darling, you know how much I'd love to have you out here with me, even if it were just one day. I want you and I want to make you a superstar. You know that, too."

He paused, wishing he dared cough. "I couldn't help noticing that you didn't mention what Bad Bill wanted you *for*. Knowing you and knowing that there isn't a smarter woman in the business, I know you've found out. It's his pet cooking show again, isn't it? He wouldn't give you a corner office for those kiddy shows, or I don't think he would.

"So get yourself one of the new semitransparents, okay? 'Vaults in the Void' is just about roughed out, everybody in the world is going to want to see it by the time we're finished with it, and nobody who sees it will ever forget you, darling.

"God knows I won't."

He moved his mouse and the screen went dark, leaving only the faint reflection of an ugly middle-aged man with a crooked nose and a lantern jaw.

The on-board had found three interesting blips strung out toward the orbit of Saturn, but Jupiter—specifically the mini-solar system surrounding it—was closer, and every hop took its toll of his wallet. He put the Jovian moons on screen and began speaking, just winging it so as to have something to work over for Kit later.

"Mightiest of all the worlds, Jupiter has drawn travelers ever since hoppers became a consumer necessity. When the first satellite was launched in nineteen fifty-seven, the men and women who put it into orbit could hardly have dreamed that Luna and Mars would be popular tourist destinations in less than a hundred years. Nor could the pioneers who built the first hotels and resorts there have anticipated that as soon as translunar travel became popular, travelers seeking more exotic locales would come here to the monarch's court.

"You've got to throw a lot of money in the hopper. That's for sure. But that only makes it that much more attractive to those who've got that money and want to flaunt it. It's dangerous, too—transmissions from tourists whose icoms go abruptly silent make that only too clear, and every edition of the *Solar Traveler's Guide* strives to make the danger a little plainer.

"Unfortunately, the striving doesn't seem to do much good. People keep coming, alone or in company. Sometimes they even bring children. Every year, five, or ten, or twenty don't make it back. Do all of them get memorials in space, *memoria in aeterna*? No, of course not. But many do, and such memorials are becoming more popular all the time. Some are simple stones. Others—well, we'll be showing you a few. In an age in which the hope of a life after death gutters like a candle burned too long, in a century that has seen Arlington National Cemetery bulldozed to make room for more government offices, the desire to be remembered leaps up with a bright new flame.

"If not remembered, at least not totally forgotten. We wish it for our loved ones, too. We'd like some spark of them to remain until the sun grows dim. And who can blame us?"

Now to make the hop. Perhaps he would learn, soon, just what had happened to that poor girl who had tried, for so short a time, to raise her sweetheart and his friends.

The first memorial he checked was a beautiful little thing. Someone with taste had taken a design intended for the desert and reworked it for space, with no up and no down, a lonely little mission shrine not too near Jupiter that reached up for God in every direction.

The bright flames inside belonged to votive candles, candles that burned in vacuum, apparently because their wax had been mixed with a chemical that liberated oxygen when heated. They made a glorious ring of white wax and fire around the shrine, burning in nothingness with fat little spherical flames.

"A shrine sacred to the memory of Alberto Villaseñor, Edita Villaseñor, and Simplicia Hernandez," he told his digicorder, "placed here, deep in space, by the children and grandchildren of the Villaseñors and the grandchildren and great-grandchildren of Simplicia Hernandez."

How many thousands of hours had Al Villaseñor labored under a broiling sun before he could buy the hopper that had carried him, with his wife and the very elderly woman who had probably been his mother-in-law, to a death somewhere near Jupiter? Their 3Ds were in the shrine; and the mark of those hours, of that sun, was on Al's face.

Turning off the audio, March murmured a prayer for all three.

· Back on his hopper, clicking Ethermail got him Kit's blue eyes and bright smile. "What's this 'semitransparent' bull, Windy? Transparent's only a couple thou more. I've got a good one, and I've been posing for the mirror. No picky-picky underclothes underneath. Wait till you see the pix! You're gonna love 'em.

"But Windy, you didn't say a thing about my li'l pal Robin Redd. Can she come, too? I gotta bring her, Windy, or not come myself. She's on the lam from a ex who beats hell out of her. She's got an Order of Protection and all that crud, which he doesn't give a rat's ass about. I know he doesn't, Windy. I was with her on Wednesday when he kicked her door down. Scout's honor! I grabbed the carving knife and screamed my cute li'l head off.

"Windy, honeybear, I can't leave Robin high and dry. I won't! Not after what we went through Wednesday night. So can she come? It's me, Windy. This is Kit, and I'm begging."

March sighed and leaned back in the control chair, collecting his thoughts before he spoke.

"Gee, Kit, here I thought you were longing for the sight of my manly profile. Okay, I've got it now. Bring your friend. I trust she's too well-mannered to push back the curtain when she hears funny noises from a bunk. Trust me, I'll wash the sheets this time.

"But Kit, you're going to have to wear something under that see-through suit. Get used to the idea if you want me to show you below the neck."

As March edged his hopper just a little nearer Number Nineteen, he turned up a new memorial, an asteroid circling Jupiter well outside the orbit of Sinope. Earlier he had thought it *only* a rock, a piece of pocked debris too small to hold even the chips knocked loose by meteorites.

Now he could see the entrance of the tomb. It was closed, though most such entrances gaped open, and square, though most were rough circles. As he zoomed in on the tumbling asteroid, the neat lettering before that entrance grew clear: PLEASE WIPE YOUR FEET. This was one he wanted.

His own suit, orange and strictly opaque, was starting to show signs of wear. Nothing dangerous yet, but it would have to be watched. A military suit. . . .

Well, a military suit wore pretty much like armor. A military suit got rid of built-up heat and kept the wearer warm no matter what. The wearer could relieve himself right there in his suit, and eat and drink whenever eating and drinking seemed necessary or advisable. Three kinds of lights, a score of tools, and half a dozen weapons were built into the suit; so was a mini computer with enough capacity for a whole lot of AI. That little on-board could and would offer warnings and advice. It would watch the wearer's back and even stand guard while he slept.

A soldier in a military suit could reach up into his helmet and pick his nose, or even take a suitless comrade—wounded or otherwise—into the suit with him.

A military suit. . . .

Cost more than March Wildspring had been worth before his divorce, and twenty times more than he was worth at the moment. His own space suit, this dull orange suit that was beginning to show wear, provided propulsion, communication, and breathable air for four hours plus. Little more beyond a fishbowl helmet that would darken when hit with a whole lot of ultraviolet light—Twentieth Century tech, and he was lucky to have even that. Shrugging, he closed his suit and buckled on his utility belt.

Spaceboots over the feet of the suit were not strictly necessary, but were (as March reminded himself) a damned good idea. Suits tore. Cheap civilian suits tore pretty easily, and tore most often at the feet. Small permanent magnets in the boots would keep him on the sheet-metal body of his hopper without holding him there so tightly that he would have trouble kicking off.

With the second boot strapped tight, he hooked his lifeline to his belt and put on his helmet. On Earth, his suit weighed fifty-seven pounds. Here it weighed exactly nothing; even so, his irritated struggles against its frequently pigheaded mass provided a good deal of useful exercise. People tended to get soft in space.

Kit would be another source of salutary exercise, he reflected, if things went as well as he hoped.

The airlock was big enough for one person in a pinch, if that one person was mercifully free of claustrophobia. March shut the inner door and spun the wheel, listening to his precious air being pumped back into the hopper, to its whispering, whimpering departure. Then to silence.

Fifteen seconds passed. Half a minute, and the outer door swung back. He kicked off from the inner door and turned on the suit's main jet. Steering jets and seat-of-the-pants flying kept him on course for the asteroid into which some unlucky tourist's tomb had been carved, and enabled him to match the asteroid's rotation.

The inscribed welcome mat before the door was, on closer inspection, wrought iron. His boots stuck to the iron nicely. Was he to knock? He did, but there was no response. Presumably there was no atmosphere inside the tomb, but it would have been possible—even easy—for a mike to pick up sound waves transmitted through the stone walls. Checking a third time to make certain his digicorder was running, he searched the doorframe for a bell button and found one.

The wood-grained steel door opened at once, apparently held by a bald, pleasant-looking man of about sixty. "Come in," the bald man said. He wore an old white shirt and faded jeans supported by red suspenders. "It was darned nice of you to come way out here to see me, son. If you'll just come inside and sit down, we can have a good chat."

March switched on his speaker. "I'll be happy to, sir. I know you're really a holographic projection, but it's very hard not to treat you as a living person. So I'll come in and chat, and thank you for your hospitality."

The bald man nodded, still smiling. "You're right, son. I'm dead, and I'd like to tell you about it. About my life and how I came to die. I'd like to, but if you don't want to hear it, I can't keep you. Will you stay and make a poor old dead guy happy?"

"I certainly will," March said, "and half the world with me." He indicated his digicorder.

"Why that's wonderful! Sit down. Sit down, please. I hate to keep my guests standing."

It was just possible that there were knives that would slash his suit concealed in the fluffy pillows of the sofa behind the long coffee table. March chose what appeared to be a high-backed walnut rocker instead, tying its cord so that he floated a few inches above its seat.

The bald man dropped into an easy chair that showed signs of long use. "I'd make you some iced tea if you could drink it, but I know you can't. It doesn't seem right not to offer a guest something, though. I've got some little boxes of candy you could take back to your hopper. Maybe give to the missus, if she's in there? You like one?"

March shook his head. "She's not, sir. It's very kind of you, but what I'd really like is to hear about you. Won't you tell us?"

"Happy to, son. Glad to recite my little adventures, at home and out here in space. Frank Welton's my name, and I was born in Carbon Hill, Ohio, U.S.A., one of a pair of twin boys. Probably you never heard of Carbon Hill, it's just a little place, but that's where it was. I was a pretty good ball player, so I played ball for eight years after high school. See my picture? The kid with the glove and bat?" The bald man pointed, and March swung his digicorder to get it.

"That was taken when I played for the Saint Louis Cardinals. I played left field, mostly, but I could play all three outfield positions and I generally hit pretty close to three hundred. The money was good, and I meant to stay in baseball as long as I could. That turned out to be eight seasons, but for that last season I was a pinch hitter, mostly. An outfielder has to have a good strong throwing arm, and my shoulder blew out on me."

March said, "I'm sorry to hear that, sir."

"Well, I got out of baseball and went home to Carbon Hill. A friend of my dad's was in the sand and gravel business in a small way. He was getting on and wanted a younger partner with some money they could use to expand the business. I threw in with him, and when he died I bought his widow out. Pretty soon I was making more in sand and gravel than I ever had playing ball. I got married. . . ." The bald man took out a handkerchief and dabbed at his eyes.

March cleared his throat. "If this is too painful for you, sir, I'll go."

"You stay, son." The bald man swallowed audibly and wiped his nose. "There's things I got to tell you. Only I got to thinking about Fran. She died, and I didn't have the heart anymore. Business is like baseball, son. If you got nothing but heart, you can still win on heart. Not all the time, mind, but now and then. That's what they say and it's the truth. But if you don't have heart, you're done for."

March nodded. "I understand you, believe me."

"That's good. I turned the business over to our kids. That's Johnny, Jerry, and Joanie, and they're the ones who built this memorial for me. They owed me a lot, and they still do. But they paid off a little part of what they owed with this. Like it?"

"One of the best I've seen, sir, and I've seen quite a few."

"That's good. I bought me a hopper when I retired. I told everybody I wanted to see Mars because of all the sand and gravel they had there. I thought it was true, but what I really wanted was to get away from Earth. Maybe you know how that is."

March nodded.

"So I did. Spent a little time on Mars and a few days on the moon, then I thought I'd have a look at Ganymede, Callisto, Titan, and so forth. The big satellites of the outer worlds, in other words. People don't realize how many there are, or how big they are, either.

"It was Io that did me in. Not the li'l gal herself, but trying to get there. Oh, I knew all about old Jupiter. How far out his atmosphere goes, and the radio bursts. All that stuff. What I hadn't figured on was just what all the gravity meant. Just how quick it grabs you, and how quick a hopper heats up when it hits ol' Jupiter's atmosphere. I guess I've 'bout talked your ears off now."

March shook his head. "If you've got more to say, sir, I'll listen."

"Then I'll say this. My dad was a good man and a hard worker, but he was a day laborer all his life, and he died at fifty-four. Go back a few generations, and my folks were slaves. I had a better life than my dad did, and one hell of a lot better life than they did. I'd like a prayer or two, son, and I'd like to be remembered. But I'm not complaining. I got a fair shake, and I had a lot of luck. Want to see how I looked when I was dead, son?"

"I don't understand how that's possible, sir." March hesitated before adding, "You were pulled down to Jupiter, and your hopper must have been burned away completely before it hit the planetary surface."

"Well, son, I can show you just the same. This is pretty slick, so have a look." Leaning forward the bald man touched the top of the coffee table, and it became as transparent as glass.

A dead man lay just below the transparent surface, his eyes shut and his hands folded. His white shirt and casual jacket were well-tailored and looked expensive. After studying his features, March said, "That's you all right, sir. Computer modeling?"

"Nope." The bald man had turned serious. "It's an actual

tridee, son, taken at the funeral. That's my twin brother, Hank. He died forty-six days after I did. That happens a lot with twins. One gets killed and the other dies. Identical twins I mean. Which is what we were. Nobody knows why it happens but it does. Hank turned in for the night like usual. Barbara went to get him up in the morning, and he was dead. You want to be dead, son?"

March shook his head. "No, sir. I don't."

"Then you take a lesson from me and watch out for that ol' Jupiter."

Back in his hopper, his on-board signaled Ethermail. He touched the keyboard, and Kit's arresting eyes and perfect complexion filled the screen. "Hi, Windy! If you don't want us, say so. One more should get us there, so this's your last chance.

"But first, stop worrying about what I'm going to have on under the suit. I am going to wear a bra. Guaranteed. Haven't you seen what zero-g does with boobs the size of mine? I have. They go all over, and believe me it's not a pretty sight. So I've got this wonderful little pink bra. You're gonna love it! The saleswoman got out a needle and pulled the whole, entire thing through the eye."

Kit had a charming laugh, and she used it. "Don't look at me like that, Windy. Put down that fatal eyebrow. Okay, it was a big needle like you might use on denim or leather. So it had a big eye. But she pulled it through, exactly like I said. I'll show it to you—by golly and geewhillikers, I'll model it for you. So if you don't want us you've gotta be quick."

March clicked REPLY. "Kit, darling, you know I want you more than life itself. Please hurry! Now don't get mad, but I'm a little bit curious. Why didn't I see your pal Robin Redd in the background. Is she really that ugly?"

He had hardly resumed his search for memorials when his on-board signaled a fresh Ethermail.

"She's in the can, Windy. That's all. She'll be out in a minute. Not bad-looking, either, if you dig redheads with bruised faces. So if you're all hot to fantasize, go right ahead. Just don't try to make 'em real, 'cause you know damn well there ain't space enough in your hopper for three bare-ass bodies playin' games.

"Speakin' of space, I got a li'l surprise. Have a look out your driver's-side window. Wanna couple?"

It was Kit's hopper, as he knew it would be, a new one gleaming with chrome and unscarred maroon paint and roughly the size of one of the compact pre-fabs older people still called mobile homes. Twice the size of his own hopper, in other words.

Suiting up again, he grabbed his line launcher and went out onto the hull.

A tiny figure emerged from the big maroon hopper, and the icom in his helmet buzzed and clicked. "You got a launcher, Windy? I didn't bring mine, but I can go back in and get one."

"Right here." He aimed his launcher, activated its laser guide, and launched, the solid-fuel rocket trailing a slender but strong Kevlar line.

"You got us, Windy. Want me to pull?"

March started his winch. "We'll just get it tangled. I'll reel you in."

"You gotta wench winch. Ever think of that?"

"Saying things like that cost you 'Building People for Kids.'"

"I didn't care. I'd already done the parts I liked. Got anything to eat in that tin can?"

"Self heats. Stuff like that."

"We've got that beat hands-down. Robin can't cook worth a damn. I, upon the other well-washed hand, am an internationally famous cheffettej. One who—"

March said, "There's no such word and you know it."

"There is now. One who, I was saying, knows there's nothing for getting the ol' pencil sharp like a real, authentic Caribbean pepper pot. Be ready in an hour or so, but if you'd like to come over now for a long-time-no-see kiss. . . ."

With their hoppers grappled, it was not necessary to turn on his suit jets to go from his own to hers. He kicked off, somersaulted in space, and landed feet-first next to her airlock.

"Nicely done, Windy," she said as he was taking off his helmet and just beginning to appreciate her flowery perfume. The long-time-no-see kiss followed, and lasted a good two minutes. When they separated, she added, "If you weren't wearing all that machinery, I think I might've raped you."

He leered. "Men aren't supposed to make jokes about rape. You told me that—"

"I'm not a man. You failed to notice."

"Therefore, madam, I will say quite seriously that if I had not been swaddled in all this gear, I believe I might have ravished you."

She had put her finger to her lips; he lowered his voice as he said, "You escaped by merest chance."

"Rape's a sensitive topic with Robin," Kit whispered. "I shouldn't have shot off my mouth. Only when a man does it, it's ten times worse. I think her ex raped her. Maybe a couple times."

"I see."

"Okay, she'll cramp our style verbally. Not in bed. I'll see to that."

"So will I," March said. "Marry me, Kit. I mean it. How the hell do you kneel without gravity?"

"You meant it last time. I know that."

"And I mean it this time."

"I turned you down." Kit's face was somber. "Did I say why?"

"No. Just that you weren't ready."

"Then I'll say it now. I love you to pieces, but I've got a career and they print your name on the toilet paper in the executive washroom. You think I'm kidding?"

"Damn right I do." March opened his suit. "You've never set foot in the executive washroom."

"Wrong. When I was talking to Bad Bill about the cooking show I had to powder my nose, and he loaned me his key. It's on the paper."

March scowled, then chuckled. "And you used it."

It got him the sidelong glance and sly smile he loved. "I'm taking the Fifth, Windy."

"It wasn't a question. Speaking of washrooms, when are we going to see what's-her-name?"

"Robin. How would I know? She's been in there forever. Do you understand why I said no, Windy? You don't have to agree with it. Just understand it."

He shrugged. "Does it mean you'll be wearing a fake mustache when you narrate for me?"

"That's not the same thing, and you know it. I'm not with the network right now. Not officially. My contract's run out. It'll probably be renewed, but it might not be. Nobody's going to raise hell because I took a stop-gap job narrating a documentary. Besides. . . ." Her sudden silence betrayed the thought.

"Besides," March rasped, "'Vaults in the Void' may never be broadcast. Go ahead and say it. You'll be saying something I've thought a thousand times."

"There's not much market for documentaries, Windy," Kit was trying to make her voice kind, something she was not particularly good at. "Yours is sure to be a complete downer, even with me in it acting all respectful. So if—"

A latch clicked five steps away, and one of the flimsy doors opened and—very softly—shut. He turned.

And froze.

"Hello, Marchy." The woman with her hand on the latch was a head shorter than Kit. The small face beneath the mop of blazing red hair looked pinched and white. One eye was bruised and swollen nearly shut; there was a second bruise on the cheek below it.

"Sue." March did not realize that he had spoken aloud until he heard his own voice.

"That isn't my name now."

Shrugging was difficult, but he managed it. "You've sued me so often that I don't see how I can call you anything else."

She drew herself up. "My name is Robin Redd."

"So I've heard."

"Hold it!" Kit edged (most enjoyably) around March to stand between them. "You owe me. Both of you do. Windy, I bought this hopper and came way the hell out here into

God-forsaken outermost space just because you needed me. Tell me that's not right, and I'll head back home as soon as you clear the airlock."

"It's right," March said.

"Robin, you had to get away. I'd seen what Jim could do, and I stepped up like a Girl Scout. I never ran your card or asked a favor. I said why don't you come with me, I'll be glad to have the company. If you say that's not how it was, I'm hustling you back to Earth and shoving you out. Wasn't that how it was?"

Robin nodded.

"Okay. It's a mess. Even I, good-hearted dumb li'l Kit, can see that. But I don't know what kind of mess I've made, and I'm going to raise holy hell till you two fill me in. You know each other. How?"

March sighed. "We made the mess, Kit. Sue here did, and I did. Not you."

Robin whispered, "He's my ex, Kit."

"Jim?" Kit goggled at her. "I saw Jim. It was Wednesday night."

"Not Jim. Oh, God! I hate this!"

March said, "It's been years since the final decree, Kit, and the proceedings dragged on for a couple of years before that. I had abused her—verbally. I had said things that injured her delicate feelings. Things that were quoted in court, mostly inaccurately and always out of context. I had persecuted her—"

"Don't! Just don't! Don't say those things."

"Why not?" March was grim. "You said them to a judge."

"I had to!"

Kit threw up her hands. "Hold it. Stop right there. I'm making a new rule. You don't talk to each other. Each of you talks only to me."

She glared at March, then turned to Robin. "How many times have you been married?"

"T-twice." Her eyes were overflowing, their tears detached by minute motions of her head to float in the air of the hopper, tiny spheres of purest crystal.

"Windy was your first husband?"

Studying her without hearing her, March was besieged by memories. How beautiful she had been in the days when she still smiled, the days when her hair was long, soft, and brown. In his mind's eye, she was poised on the high board, poised for a second or two that had somehow become forever, poised above the clear blue water of some hotel's swimming pool.

"Windy? Did you hear me?" It was Kit.

He shook his head. "I was remembering, I'm afraid. Thinking how it used to be before it went bad."

Robin shouted, "Before you stopped paying attention!"

"Shut up!" Kit snapped. "Windy, she said you never hit her, but you abused her verbally and psychologically. Threats and put-downs. All that stuff. True or false?"

"True," March said.

"Is that all you've got to say?"

He nodded.

"Did you ever love her?"

He felt as though his feet had been kicked from under him. "Oh, my God!" He groped for words. "I was crazy about her, Kit. Sometimes she wouldn't speak to me for weeks and it just about killed me. She left me over and over. I'd come home from work, and instead of being there spoiling for a fight she'd be gone. She'd live with some boyfriend or other for a few days, maybe a week, and then—"

"Jim!" Robin cocked her head, her smile a challenge. "It was always Jim, Marchy."

"Shut up!" Kit turned to glare at her.

"That isn't what she said. Do we have to talk about this?"

Kit studied him. "You look like you've lost a quart of blood."

"I feel like it, too."

"My pepper pot ought to help. And I've made Cuban bread. That's easy. You ever eat stew out here?"

He shook his head.

"Me neither. I've got it simmering in hopsacks. Those clear plastic thingies. That's why you don't smell it."

"Sure." It was wonderful to speak of something else. Of anything else. "I've got some, too."

"So I figure we can drink the liquid, and there'll be little chunks of crayfish and pork and so forth in there too. When it's gone, we can open the hopsacks and eat the solids."

"Should work."

"Do you still love her, Windy?"

He shook his head.

Kit in her transparent suit was simply incredible, lush curves that changed and changed again as the suit flexed, but in that light were never more than half seen. He shot her from the waist up, not quite always, knowing it would keep five hundred million men watching, waiting, and wondering.

"Hi. It's me again, Kit Carlsen. When I do a cooking show, I tell you—sometimes—about the chef who developed a recipe, or the person the dish was named after. Peaches Melba for Nellie Melba the opera singer. You know. Well, today we're going to visit the tomb of a lady who was her town's best, and best known, cook. I plan to ask her about her cooking as well as her life and death. You may think it's tasteless, but March Wildspring and I think you'll find it interesting if you'll just stick with us. March is our producer, so what he says goes."

With a wave and a beckoning smile, Kit entered the tomb. March grinned. After a moment he followed her, watching her image in the digicorder screen more closely than Kit herself.

That's me, there. The woman in the gray dress on the red chair.

The voice was without even the semblance of a living speaker, the picture calm, serious, and motionless.

My name was Sarah-Jane Applefield. I was sixty-three at the time of my demise. My parents were McAlister Rodney Applefield and Elizabeth Warren Weyerhaeuser. I bore three fine children in my time, Clara, Sheryl, and Charles. All were much loved. Would you like to hear about my early life?

"No, Sarah." Kit's voice was soft, coaxing. "We'd like to hear about your cooking. It made you famous all over Southton. Can you tell our audience something about that?"

Certainly. Would you like recipes, or the secrets of good cooking?

Kit smiled in her plastic bubble. "Your secrets, please."

I call them secrets because so few women seem to know them. They're secrets I tell freely to anyone, but they stay secret just the same. Do you cook?

"I do," Kit said. "I cook a lot, and so do a lot of busy women and men in our audience."

Good. The first is to release the inner self. We're all a little bit psychic, but we've been taught to pretend we're not. Let that go. Feel the dish. Sense what it feels. In the storybook, Alice talks to the food, and the food talks back to her. I read it to my children. Lewis Carroll wrote it, and he was an old bachelor. He cooked for himself, you see, so he knew.

Kit smiled again. "I need to read that book, and I will."

The second is to use your nose. Cooking would be difficult for a woman who was blind, but if she learned, she would be a better cook than a seeing woman who would not use her nose. Food may look very nice when it's really quite awful, but food that smells good is good, just about always.

The third is to taste. Spices lose their flavor. Two pieces of beef may be from different animals, even though both are beef. There are breeds of cattle just like there are breeds of cats, or one animal may be old and the next young. If you buy your beef at the store you have no way of telling. What it comes down to is that recipes can't be exact. The cook must taste, and taste again.

"That's very wise, I'm sure."

It is. Your name is Kit. Your husband told me when he was here before.

"He's not my husband." Kit's smile was warm. "But close enough."

If you were wise yourself, Kit, you would ask me what I should tell you. Whether it concerns food or not.

Kit glanced at March for guidance, and he nodded.

"Then I do, please. What is it I ought to ask? Pretend I did."

There is nothing close enough to marriage, Kit. I bore three children to the man who stands behind me in my picture. We were never wed. As time wears on, that will grow easier and easier for the man, Kit, and harder and harder for you. Look closely at my picture, and you'll see I wear a ring.

March zoomed in on it.

I bought that ring for myself, Kit, in a little shop that sold old jewelry. He begged me to take it off once, when we were going to bed. I did, and while we slept he hid it.

Kit looked stricken, but her voice remained smoothly professional. "I'm glad for your sake, Ms. Applefield, that he didn't keep it."

Don't you see? He would've had to give it to me if he had—would've had to give it back to me. Make the gesture he would never make.

"I've got it." Kit shook her head as if a blow had left her dizzy.

I like you. If I didn't, I wouldn't have spoken to you as I did just now. This will be easier for you to hear, but you must not discount it for that reason. There is another flying grave, like my own but larger than my own. It's on the other side of Jupiter today.

"One you think we ought to visit?" March sensed that Kit was breathing normally again. "Can you tell us what's there?"

I can't. Your man asked the same question. That's why I'm mentioning it now. I can look outside this grave. Did you know?

"No, Ms. Applefield, I certainly didn't."

I can. Hoppers park at that grave sometimes. I see them. People—live people like you—go inside. Pay attention now, Kit. They don't come out again, and pretty soon their hoppers drift away.

Kit was doing deep-space aerobics, throwing herself from floor to ceiling and from ceiling to floor, her lush body enveloped in a fine mist of sweat that her hopper's air system stripped away only sluggishly. "I say we gotta go in," she gasped. "Round-file that sweet old lady giving us her warning? Over my dead body."

"If you go in," Robin said, "I might go in it, too—only I wish you wouldn't."

"I'm going." Kit grunted. "If Windy won't go, I'll go in by myself. You can shoot me."

Watching her, March thought of all the things he would do—or try to—if Robin were not present. Aloud he said, "You'd better stop. You're wearing yourself out."

"Just landed a little wrong and hit my knee. I do a hundred of these." Kit sprang from the floor, twisting like a gymnast in air that smelled of shampoo. "I've been counting to myself. This's eighty-seven."

"Then I'll count the rest for you. Eighty-eight. Eighty-nine. Ninety. . . ."

"You're the only friend I'd got," Robin told Kit. "The only good friend. If you die, it'd be just me and Jim, and he'll kill me."

"Ninety-two. Kit, doesn't that tell you something about your little pal here? She's thirty-five, and she's got exactly one good friend. You. One good friend, and a second husband she thinks may kill her."

"Thirty-one, dammit!"

Kit snatched at breath. "How many?"

"Ninety-six. And I know how old Sue is. She's eight years younger than I am, and her birthday's October thirty-first. That ought to tell you something, too. Ninety-nine." He watched Kit throw herself, with obvious effort, back to the crimson carpet. "One hundred."

She straightened up, and Robin handed her a towel. "Thanks for giving me an honest count, Windy. I kind of thought you'd cheat."

He nodded. "That's what Robin thought, too. She had me followed for a couple months."

"Did you?"

He shook his head.

Robin threw a pepper mill at him. "You were too smart for them!" Missing his head by at least a foot, it slammed against the wall.

March's eyes had never left Kit. "I was under the impression that Sue and I weren't speaking. Apparently I was wrong. I, however, am not speaking to her. It may spare your hopper a few scars."

"She can throw my stuff at me," Kit told him. "Robin, you're a guest in this hopper. Windy's another guest in my hopper. I asked him to dinner. If you two want to rip open old wounds, I can't stop you. No violence, though. I mean real violence, like throwing stuff. Or hitting. Do it again, and you go out."

"Into *his* hopper?" Robin's contempt was palpable. "I'd rather die!"

"I doubt that he'd let you in. I'll just get you suited up and shove you out the airlock. Tourists come to Jupiter pretty often. Somebody will probably pick you up before your air runs out."

March sighed. "You want me to say I'd take her in. And if I don't. . . ."

"I'll think a lot less of you, Windy."

"All right, I will. I only hope I won't have to. If I do, I'll probably kill her before I can get her back to terra firma."

"I'm not from there, smart-ass." Robin cocked her head. "Terror whatever you said."

Kit giggled as she joined Robin at the tiny table. "I'm not going to touch that straight line. Don't you touch it either, Windy."

She tied the soft cord that would keep her from floating out of her chair. "Bulbs are hot. Windy, get over here and sit down. I know you always like coffee with your meals. How about you, Robin? Coffee? Tea?"

"Tea, please." Robin's voice was one breath above a whisper.

"Here you go. And here's your coffee, Windy. Now before you start gobbling my *Truite Farcie aux Epinards*, we've got to talk seriously about the next shoot. Do you remember when I said I'd go into that damned mausoleum or whatever it is alone if you wouldn't come with me? I meant every word of it."

March sat. "You may change your mind when you've had time to think it over. I hope you will."

Kit looked as grim as a pleasant blonde can look. "I change my mind before I've told anybody. Never after. If you won't go in, I'm going in alone tomorrow."

So close to March that their elbows touched, Robin raised a beverage bulb to her lips and put it down. "Do either of you actually know where this awful place is?" Her perfume, musky and hinting of cinnamon, crept into his nostrils.

Kit shook her head. "I'll find it. The dead lady can probably tell me, just to start with."

"I call it Number Nineteen," March told her. "I've known about it awhile, but I haven't gone inside."

"Then I won't have to ask her—I'll get it out of you. Shameless prostitution, right? Are you going in, too? Yes or no."

"Then it's yes. I'll go in there with you on one condition."

Robin said, "I'd go in with Kit if she was going in there alone. Not if you'll be with us."

"That would have sounded better," Kit told her, "if you'd said it before Windy said he'd go. We call that bad timing in show biz." She turned to March. "What's your condition? Maybe I won't agree."

"You'll have no reason not to. There's another one, not as big. I haven't gone into it either, but I've every reason to think it's dangerous. I want you to go into that one with me first. If I'm right, you'll get a little seasoning there. When we tackle Number Nineteen you're going to need some."

"So you think," Robin said.

Kit motioned her to silence. "I'm all for seasoning. Have you got any reason for thinking this one's not quite so hairy? Besides its being smaller?"

March shook his head.

"Then I'll go. When do we do it?"

Robin said, "I'd like to know what reasons he's got for thinking it's dangerous at all."

"Tomorrow," March said. The oven buzzed as he spoke.

"Sounds good." Kit untied her cord. "Everybody ready for food?"

The trout was served in Pyrex-topped dishes with tiny hatches that slid away at the touch of a fork. Kit demonstrated, thrusting her own fork in, and pulling it out laden with fish and spinach. March tried it, and a wisp of spinach floated away before his fork was halfway to his mouth. "Chopsticks might be better," he suggested.

Robin giggled.

"You've got 'em," Kit told him. "There's a trigger at the front of the handle. Feel it? Pull that, and the chow bar flips over to hold your stuff on. Loosen up when it's in your mouth, and you can get your food out.

"Robin, can you clean up that spinach for me? Make yourself useful?"

"You betcha."

The *Truite Farcie aux Epinards* was delicious. March took another bite before he said, "Ever hear of the Thugs?"

Kit chewed reverently and swallowed. "Like muggers, Windy?"

"Not quite. There was a cult called Thuggee, and the members were the original Thugs. They worshipped Death and sacrificed people to her."

Robin muttered, "Why do we always get blamed?"

"Mostly they strangled them, although I believe they also stabbed a few. They offered the deaths of their victims to their goddess, and kept the victims' possessions to cover operating expenses. The Brits wiped them out two hundred years back."

"Why are you telling us this, Windy?" Kit's hand hovered over the clip that would hold her fork when she had no need of it.

"Because it seems like they're with us again, in a new and improved Westernized form. And I'm not telling you and Sue. Just you."

"You mean they gave up the goddess business?"

March shook his head. "The West has never abandoned religion, Kit. You just think it has because you and your friends have. Okay, I'm your friend and I'd like to be more. But you know what I mean."

"We'll talk about that other thing sometime when we're alone." For a moment, Kit looked a trifle stunned. "You—

You said they were Westernized, Windy. If you didn't mean no goddess, what did you mean?"

"Computers, secure lines of electronic communication, and hoppers just to start with. Guns. Poisons. Ever been in an abattoir?"

"A slaughterhouse? No, and I don't want to go."

"You're going." March sighed. "Or I think you are. You said you'd go into this one—into Number Thirteen—with me if I'd go into Number Nineteen with you. Something like that. That's what it came down to."

"This is good." Robin paused to sniff the fish on her fork. "Has anybody told you so yet? It's really luscious, and you'd better finish yours before it gets cold."

Obediently, Kit ate. "Food doesn't taste as good when you're scared."

"Then I wish I weren't," March told her, "and you won't be in Number Thirteen. Or I don't think so. If you'd been in a modern abattoir, you'd know the cattle aren't frightened. Fear makes them noisy and hard to control, so it's been eliminated. They get on a slow belt that doesn't shake at all, or make any kind of sound. It moves them down a narrow chute, and by that time they're used to chutes. This one seems less frightening than most. But when they get to the bottom and start back up, they're dead."

"You're not eating," Kit said.

"I thought you'd have another question." March took a forkful of trout and chewed it with appreciation. It was still delicious. Firm, fresh trout and tender, young spinach. Onions, shallots, cream, and something else. No, he corrected himself, several somethings else.

"Well, I do," Robin said. "You told us you hadn't been in there. Or implied it anyway."

Seeing that March intended to ignore her, Kit asked, "Is that right, Windy? You've never been inside?"

"Correct."

"Then how did you know I wouldn't be scared?"

"Because the others weren't. When I was still poking around the asteroid belt, I picked up the traffic of a party

going in there. Or at least, I think that's where they were going. They weren't afraid. When the first stopped transmitting, the rest just tried to raise him. The last one thought her
icom had gone out. About a minute later, she went silent,
too."

Robin said, "He may fool you, Kit, but he's not fooling
me. I know him too well. They went into the big one, the one
he's so scared of. Not the little one he's been talking about."

"Did they, Windy? Was it really Number Whatchacallit
and not the one you want us to shoot next?"

"Number Nineteen," March said. "The one I'm hoping
will give you a little experience without killing us is Number Thirteen."

"Thirteen?" Robin grinned. "Oooh! That's scary!"

"Shut up," March told her.

The grin widened. "You betcha. But I thought you weren't
talking to me, Marchy darling."

"I wasn't. It didn't work, and I should have known it
wouldn't. You always chipped away until I said something
you could throw back at me in court. You haven't changed,
and neither have I."

He paused to collect his thoughts. When neither woman
spoke, he said, "Sue doesn't really care, Kit, but you may. If
I'd been assigning numbers to the memorials I found for
advertising purposes, Number Nineteen would have gotten
thirteen. I wasn't doing that. Number Thirteen was the thir-
teenth I found. That's all. Number Nineteen was the nine-
teenth. I could take you to Number Fourteen or Number
Twenty. Both those look pretty safe. Just say the word if
you'd like to go."

Kit said, "I've finished my trout, Windy. So has Robin.
Finish yours, so I can serve dessert."

"No salad? That's not like you."

"You're right. I forgot. Eat your trout."

"In a moment. Sue had—"

"It's Robin, dammit!" She was untying her cord.

"It wasn't Robin when Sue and I were married," March
told Kit, "and if she tries to live up to that red dye-job, I'll
have to defend myself. I hope you understand."

"I'm bigger and stronger than she is," Kit said levelly. "She may not know it, but I am. If she cuts up rough she'll find out fast."

"I'm a black belt!" Robin screamed.

"Sure you are—a black belt in Bad Sock Hop. You needed me when Jim kicked down your door, remember?"

March cleared his throat. "Right now I want to grab you and kiss you, Kit. I want it as much as I've ever wanted anything in my life. What do you say?"

"I think it had better wait. You know what we did last time."

"All right." March sighed. "Your friend Sue had a legitimate question. Could the people whose transmissions I caught have been going into Number Nineteen? There were three empty hoppers near Number Thirteen, so I think that's where they went. I could be wrong."

He took a bite of trout. As he had expected, it was still quite hot. "What's in this, Kit? What's the taste I can't label?"

"Could be the fresh tarragon. Or the cider." Kit grinned. "Or my secret ingredient."

Robin muttered, "Watch for bones."

They met a mile plus from Number Thirteen, he in his worn orange suit, she looking like a lingerie model wrapped in cellophane. "We're alone now," he said, and gestured. "This is interplanetary space, so we're as alone as two people can be. Will you marry me, Kit?"

"Robin's listening, Windy. I told her to listen in, and call the network for help if we stopped transmitting."

"Kit—"

"It's just common sense. After what you'd told me, I thought we ought to take a few precautions. I told her to ask for Bad Bill, or Phil Inglis if she couldn't get hold of Bill. Tell them we're in trouble and ask for help."

March did not know what to say, and if Kit did, she did not say it. Silence closed around them, the menacing silence of the giant planet above them and the cool and watchful silence of the stars.

At last Kit said, "Are you there, Robin? Speak up."

"She probably doesn't know how to work the set."

"I showed her. Robin?"

"Maybe she'd rather listen than talk. That would be a first for her, but it's possible."

"Poor Robin." Kit's face, distorted only slightly by the plastic bubble of her helmet, looked as though she meant it. "You don't want to admit that she might have a single shred of human decency."

"All right, I admit it. She's probably got one, even if I couldn't find it."

"You think she's listening in." From her expression, Kit thought it was at least possible.

"I don't think it or not think it. I don't care one way or another. But I'll tell you this. If she is, she'll let us know when she hears what I'm going to say next."

He took a deep breath of far-from-odorless suit air. "I know I'm not handsome, Kit, and thanks to your friend Sue, I'm just about broke. You're a star, and I'm a washed-up producer who was never terribly big anyway. Knowing all that—because I know you know it, too—will you marry me? Please? As soon as we get back to New York?"

Kit listened for a moment. "You're right. She'd be screaming at me not to do it. She's not there. Come on, let's have a look at this mugger tomb."

"You didn't say no." Suddenly March felt at least ten years younger.

"I didn't say yes, either. The guy who sold me my suit said to lock arms."

He complied, and she switched on her jets; a moment later he turned on his own as well.

"Looks pretty dark in there, Windy. You got a helmet light?"

"If you'd like to think it over, that's fine." For a moment he wrestled with his feelings. "All right, it isn't really fine but I'll wait. I'll wait till tomorrow or next week or next month."

"Thanks."

"Or next year. I—I don't know how to say this, but I'll wait for as long as you ask me to, just as long as you don't say no. And if you should change your mind after that, I'll probably come running. Hell, I know I will. I love you. I love you, and I know I'll never stop loving you. You're . . . I can't put it into words, Kit, but I'll never get over it."

Her hand tightened on his, and her smile shone through her plastic helmet bubble. "You've got a lovely voice, Windy. Anybody ever tell you so?"

He shook his head. "I've got a lousy voice and I know it. It sets people's teeth on edge. No resonance, no overtones."

"Handsome is as handsome does, Windy, and you've got a voice that says beautiful things. You just proved it."

"Is that why you didn't say no?"

"That and a whole lot of other reasons." Kit pointed. "This fake lintel they carved out of the rock—what are those things pretending to hold it up? Is that a bird?"

"You didn't say yes, either. Is it the money?"

"I've got enough for both of us. Tell me about the bird."

"It's an adjutant stork. The other animal is a jackal, I think. They're symbols of death."

"Don't storks bring babies?"

"Not this kind. Those are nice storks. Won't you tell me why you didn't say yes, Kit?"

"Well, for one thing, you don't say you love me often enough."

"I just did." When she did not reply, March added. "We'd better slow up."

"Okay, I'm turning 'em down. Are you good with these controls?"

"Fair. Yours are probably a little different."

"Then look at this and tell me why it's not working." Kit held out her left arm.

For a moment, he studied the buttons and the tiny screen. "You don't have Jets up." He pushed three buttons in rapid succession. The looming asteroid still rushed toward them, but it rushed no faster. "You've got to hit Control, select Jets, and press the Down key."

"We're still going awfully fast, Windy."

"Of course we are. There's no air resistance. Why didn't you say yes? You said there were a lot of reasons. Give me two or three."

"I gave you one already. I know you said it just now, but you don't say it often. Bad Bill's another. I want to get dramatic roles, not just kids shows and cooking shows, all that crap. Marrying you would hurt my career—or it would just now, anyway."

"If he found out, yes. What are you going to say if Bad Bill asks you to marry him?"

"That he'll have to dump Loretta." Kit was grinning.

"And if he does?"

"It'll take a while. I know her, and she'll put up a fight. You could give lessons on that stuff, Windy. Why are you asking me?"

"And meanwhile—?"

"Meanwhile, I'll get some roles I want. Can we slow down? I'm getting scared."

"Wait till we get inside, Kit. Be scared then." March spun them both until their reduced jets were braking.

"Can I give you another reason? One more."

"That's enough."

"I want to. I didn't say yes—yet—because it would hurt you. Bad Bill hates your guts already for showing him up. If we get married and he finds out, he's going to hate you worse than poop on his birthday cake. It'll be twenty times rougher than it is now."

March chuckled. "It couldn't be."

"He could hire a hit. He's got the contacts and the money won't mean a thing to him. You can hire a good pro to smoke somebody for the price of a really nice hopper. Did you know that?"

"I'd heard." March nodded.

"So how many nice hoppers could Bad Bill afford? I'd say a hundred. At least that many."

Kit's helmet LEDs stabbed invisibly at the entrance, which glared as though under a spotlight. "There! I got it on. Only it's not as dark in there as it was."

"Turn it off," March told her. "Turn it off, and get your digicorder rolling. We want both digicorders for this one."

They entered cautiously, he keeping them six feet above the stone floor.

"It looks safe enough, Windy."

He glanced at her; the blue-green light of the tomb had robbed her face of rouge as well as blood. "Did Ms. Applefield say it was?"

Here lies the founder of our faith and prophet of the goddess. The voice might have been that of the blue-green illumination. *Jayashankar the Great here reposes in his house of Eternity, as he wished. We, his disciples, have laid him here. Would you learn Truth, O visitors? Our faith is truth, and truth is joy. Like us, you are the subjects of the goddess. Know it. To know it, to rejoice in it, is paradise. Enter with—*

"Kit!" March grabbed her arm, his fingers flying across her keyboard.

"What's up, Windy!"

"Air! They're flooding the place with air. Look behind you."

She did, and saw what he had known she would see: a steel door blocking the entrance and pinning their lifelines to the floor. "Are . . . Are we locked in?"

You are free. There are switches to left and right, switch pads we have made large for you, so there can be no mistaking them. Black shuts, for black is the color of the goddess. Yellow opens. It will return you to the world of illusion. To open, you need only press the yellow pad to your right.

"You're saying there's air in here, Windy? That we could live in here without the suits?"

"There's air in here, and you'll die if you take off your helmet." He unhooked her lifeline. "It's poisoned—I don't know what with."

A new voice said, "If it were poisoned, we'd be dead." It was a man's voice, a resonant baritone.

A woman who was not Kit added, "We'll die if you break the hermetic seal now. We've no suits, so we'll suffocate. Please don't."

A naked man and a naked woman had emerged from hidden entrances on either side of the tomb, he tall and muscled like a bodybuilder, she sleek and big breasted, walking on her toes though she wore neither shoes nor boots. They crossed the stone floor as if subject to gravity, and smiled as they looked up at Kit and March. The man said, "For as long as you're strangers in the paradise of the goddess, we shall guide you."

"Holograms, Windy?" Kit looked as if she were about to cry. "I know they aren't real. Are they holograms?"

The naked man reached up and grasped her boot at the ankle. "Come here, my lovely, lovely friend. Kiss me but once, and you may call me false thereafter."

"They're droids!" Kit's other boot caught the naked man full in the face.

"Get up!" March unhooked his own lifeline. "Get out of reach."

Scooping up the naked woman, he jetted toward the steel door and flung her at the right-hand switch. The arc that burned and melted her plastic skin half-blinded him.

"Up here, Windy!" Kit waved as a stone flung by the male droid struck his thigh.

He rose to meet her, and she hugged him. "We're trapped. How can we get out?"

"Pray," he said, and the Latin of an ancient prayer chanted in deep corridors of his mind.

"That won't help!"

"It'll keep us calm and let us think, Kit. Pretty often, that's all it has to do."

Another stone whizzed past them, a near miss.

"He's breaking them loose," Kit whispered. "My God, but he's strong!"

"Nuclear powered?"

"Do you really think so, Windy? I—watch out! I didn't think they could make them that little."

"They can't. It could be a fuel cell, but it's most likely batteries, and they'll have to be pretty small. The power draw he needs to bust that rock will be pulling him down fast. Have you noticed what happens to the ones he's thrown?"

"They keep bouncing around. There's no gravity."

March nodded. "Just air resistance. It slows them a little, but it will take a long time to stop them. Suppose we catch a couple and—"

The steel door was sliding up, not quite soundlessly now that the interior of the tomb was filled with air. He shot toward it with all jets at one hundred percent and Kit trailing after him like a kite; Kit's free arm caught Robin as she crossed the threshold.

Back in Kit's hopper, with beverage bulbs bubbling in the microwave, March took a seat at the little table and tied himself down. "Grab a chair, Sue. I won't bite."

"It was dangerous in there, wasn't it? That's why you and Kit came out so fast."

"We just about got killed," Kit told her. "Windy saved us."

"Sue saved us," March said dryly. "She didn't intend to, but she did."

"Yes, I did! Not you, March, but Kit. She wanted me to listen on the icom and call for help if you two got in trouble, but I knew it would be too late. So I watched you instead and put on my Star-Chick Number Nine as soon as you had gone inside."

Kit handed her a steaming beverage bulb. "We'd have been trapped in there and died if it hadn't been for you."

"I'd have gotten us out," March said.

"Sure, Windy. Here's your coffee." Kit laid her vacuum tray on the table and sat down, groping for the cords that would hold her in her chair. "Now it's Answer Time. Know what I mean? The last five minutes of the show, when Mike Wanitsky fiddles with his gun—"

Robin tittered.

"And tells us how he knew the cocker spaniel was the real murderer. You, Windy, are Mike Wanitsky."

"Thanks. I've always wanted to be a really good-looking cop."

"You just said you'd have gotten us out. How would you have done it?"

"I don't know." March sipped his coffee and jiggled the

bulb to stir the sugar. "I just know that it could be done, and I could do it. Did you think there were people in there lying to us through the droids and running things? There weren't."

"I never even thought about it."

"Nobody wants to spend weeks or months sitting around in a tomb waiting for somebody to come in. They build those things—the great majority of them were never meant to be traps for human beings—and go back to America or the E.U. or whatever. So what you're dealing with when you go into one of the bad ones is a machine. It can be a sophisticated machine, which that one was. But it's still just a machine, built by someone who didn't have all the time in the world to plan it or all the money in the world to spend on it."

Robin said, "So you'd have gotten out."

"Correct. Maybe I'd have found the circuitry that controlled the door. Maybe something else. But I'd have gotten us out."

"I want to go back to the beginning, Windy. You told us about overhearing some people's transmissions from in there. Remember?"

"Sure. I believe I can remember something else, too." March scratched his head. "Weren't you the one who began at the end? That's how I seem to remember it. I don't think it was Sue, and I know damned well it wasn't me."

"Right. It was, and it was a mistake. You said the woman you overheard—it was a woman, wasn't it?"

"That last one?" March nodded.

"You said she thought her icom had gone out and kept trying to talk to the others until she went dead herself. What happened to her?"

"Strictly speaking, I don't know. I wasn't there. I might make a pretty good guess, though, now that I've been inside. What happens when you're wearing a suit and you get into your hopper, where there's air?"

Kit looked puzzled. "I take it off."

"I know!" Robin waved both hands. "The salesman told me when I bought mine. It stops using the air in the tank and takes in air from outside."

"Correct. You can disable that if you know the codes. If you do, you have to switch the system over manually when you want it switched. When you go into that Thuggee tomb, it shuts the door and fills the tomb with air to turn your suit air off. There's something in that air to kill or disable you, something that has to be pretty dilute because the tomb's big. The woman I heard may have been in an area where the air was relatively pure. Or maybe she wasn't a deep breather or had a slow suit. Whatever."

"Wouldn't she have seen the others fall down?"

"Sure, if they'd fallen." March grinned. "How do you fall without gravity? My guess is that they seemed to be moving around pretty normally. It probably makes you dopey at first. Later it may kill you, or the droids may do it. The idea of their machine offering lives to Death—real throats really cut on an altar—would tickle the kind of people who build things like that." He sipped his coffee.

Kit said, "He grabbed my arm and reprogrammed my suit, Robin. As soon as the air started, he knew what was up."

"Hooray."

"Don't be like that. Windy saved my life, and if he hadn't I wouldn't have been around to save yours. Besides we got some great footage. Only I wish you'd waited until we'd thrown rocks back at the droids."

"We can go in there again," March said.

"After Number Nineteen maybe. Not now. I've got one more question."

"Fine with me, as long as I get to ask one after I've answered yours."

"Yes, if you promise to be nice. Robin won't bother us. Okay, here's my last question. The floor was stone, right? But the droids walked on it, and stayed down there like there was gravity. Only there wasn't any. How did they do it?"

March smiled. "That's a good one, and I hadn't even thought of it. You've got rare-earth magnets in your boots. You probably know that. It's why you stick to the floor of this hopper till you take them off. They let you walk on the outside if you want to, stand on the roof and so on. Those droids had rare-earth magnets in the soles of their feet."

Robin objected. "But it was a *stone* floor."

"That's right, Windy. Cut right out of the asteroid or whatever you call it."

"A lot of asteroids and meteorites contain a lot of iron. Ever heard of Excalibur, King Arthur's sword?"

Kit nodded.

"Now you know where the legend came from." Pausing, March sipped his coffee. "Here's my question for you. You knew right away that the droids weren't real people. How?"

"I looked at the woman, that's all. So did you. I know you did—she was naked and you're not gay."

"All right, I did."

"She had a perfect figure, didn't she? No figure flaws. None. Real women always do. Big feet or thick ankles. No calves, like Robin. Bony knees. Thunder thighs. There's always something wrong. Women on vid can look perfect. So can women in magazines. But they look perfect because the cameramen and directors know just how not to shoot them. Watch the tabloids and you'll see the other thing, the flaws that some paparazzi shot through the fence."

There was another hopper not far from their own when March left Kit's. Curious, he jetted a few miles, tapped the airlock politely with a wrench from his utility belt, and pressed his helmet to the hatch.

After half a minute, there had been no sound from inside. By law, airlocks could not be locked or barred; he was tempted to go inside and take a look around. He contented himself with a tour of the exterior.

It was, he decided, the oldest hopper he had ever seen, one that had actually begun life as an RV. Its pressure-bulged sides and top were battered, and had been holed more than once and patched with epoxy. Peering through its tinted windshield and windows revealed an interior to match—an unmade bunk, worn seats, cigarette butts and trash everywhere.

What it did not reveal was a human being. No one awake, asleep, or dead. When his inspection was complete, he jetted over to his own hopper—to the pre-owned hopper he had considered ready for the scrap heap before he had seen the one he was leaving.

He had taken off his helmet and was pulling off his boots when he smelled cigarette smoke.

"I hope you don't mind me coming in like this," the smoker said; he was young, with a face a quarter of an inch too long to be handsome. "Okay if I smoke in here? You've got a good air system. It's taking care of it."

"Sure." March opened his suit. "What's up?"

"I need to talk to you, that's all. I need a little info, and it seemed like this was the place to get it. You were over in the big hopper you're grappled to? The new maroon job?"

"Uh huh."

"Okay. Listen, I just want one little piece of info. Just one, and I don't think there's anything secret about it. I could go over and pound on the lock, and somebody would tell me, okay? So who does that big hopper belong to?"

"I want some info, too," March said, "and the info I want had better not be secret either. Let's start with an easy one. Is this a friendly visit?"

"Absolutely. I know you must be ticked off because I came in the way I did." The smoker ran slender fingers through glossy, coal-black hair. "But my jetsuit's pretty uncomfortable, and to tell the truth I'm not sure how far I can trust it."

"Besides," March said, "you couldn't smoke in there."

"Right. I realize I'm using up some extra oxy that way, but it doesn't amount to much."

"That's good to know. Here's question number two. Want some coffee?"

"Sure, if you do."

"I do." March climbed out of his suit and stowed it in the locker. "I'm kind of bushed, and I've got the feeling you're not somebody I ought to deal with unless I'm fresh." He went to his hopper's tiny microwave.

"You don't have to deal with me." The smoker bent to grind out his cigarette on March's floor. "Tell me what I want to know—that one thing—and I'm out of here. You can go to bed."

"Wondering whether you'll come back inside once I'm asleep."

"Yeah." The smoker looked thoughtful. "There's that. I won't, but you can't know it. You could hop somewhere else. Take a long hop. I wouldn't know where you'd gone."

March shook his head. "I've got another question. What's my name?"

"What's *your* name? I thought you'd want to know mine."

"You can ask your own questions. I'll ask mine. You heard it. Who am I?"

"I've got no frigging—I don't know. You want to tell me?"

"No. I want you to tell me. Tell me who I am, so I'll know where we stand."

"I can't. I don't know."

"You don't know who owns the big red hopper, either." March reached past the locker to his tool box, flipped it open, and pulled out a two-pound dead-blow hammer.

"You're not going to need that."

"I hope not. Think you could take me?"

The smoker shook his head. "Not as long as you're holding that I couldn't."

"Good." The tool box snapped shut. "If you answer every question I ask, fast, I won't have to use it. Did you snoop around my hopper?"

"A little bit, yes."

"Fine." The microwave beeped, but March ignored it. "What were you looking for?"

"An ashtrap and cigarettes. I don't have many. If I found any, I was going to bum one."

"There are at least twenty books in this hopper. Maybe more. Did you look at them? Any of them?"

The smoker shook his head. "Just for an ashtrap and cigarettes. I told you."

"I asked you that because my name's written in the front of most of them. I'm March Wildspring. Ever heard of me?"

The smoker's grin took March by surprise.

"You have," March said. "Tell me about it."

"I've just heard you mentioned a couple dozen times. You're a real dyed-in-the-wool son of a bitch. That's what she says. I've been wanting to meet you."

"Congratulations. You have. Who said it?"

"My wife. Her name's Robin Redd."

March nodded to himself, recalling Robin's swollen eye and bruised cheek. "I should have seen that coming, and I didn't. You're Jim."

"Right." The smoker extended his hand. "Jim Redd. Glad to meet you."

March ignored it. "You bought that old hopper—the cheapest one you could find—and came out here looking for your ex-wife."

"Hell, no." Redd shook a cigarette from a vacpack, crumpled the pack, and stuffed it into his pocket. "I'm looking for my wife, Robin Redd."

"She says you're divorced."

"Bullshit. Me and Robin aren't divorced till it's final, and that hasn't happened. No final decree, capeesh? I'm fighting to save my marriage, and I'm going to keep on fighting as long as there's a marriage to save."

March sighed. "You've come way the hell out here, millions of miles, looking for her?"

"Right."

"So you can beat hell out of her and save your marriage."

Redd lit his cigarette. "I wouldn't put it like that."

"How would you put it?"

"I want to talk to her, that's all. I want to sit her down and make her listen to what I've got to say. If she'll just shut up for a minute and hear my side of it, she'll come home with me. I know that. The trick is to get her to shut up and listen. Out here, I thought maybe she would."

"Would you care to tell me what you plan to say to her?"

Redd inhaled and allowed the smoke to trickle from his nostrils before answering. "What I want or don't want doesn't matter. I can't tell you, because you're not her."

"I see. Sue and I—I call her Sue. She was Sue Morton

when we were married, and Sue Morton afterward, too. She kept her own name."

"I wouldn't have let her do that."

March's shoulders rose and fell. "I did. I let her do anything she wanted."

"She dumped you anyhow? That's what she says—that she dumped you. Maybe you dumped her."

"No. She dumped me."

"It makes you crazy, just thinking about it. I can see that."

March nodded.

"Okay, that's how it is for you. I don't want it to be like that for me, capeesh? I'd like to have you on my team. But if you're on her team, that's okay, too. I only want what's good for her, which is staying married and making this one work."

"She says you hit her." March struggled to remember. Had anyone really said that Jim had done it? Or had it only been implied?

"A few times. Yeah. She got me so damned mad. Ask me if I'd break her arms to save our marriage."

"Would you?" March sighed again.

"Hell, yes. Can I tell you about the names? I'll feel better."

"If you like."

"I picked her up for a date one time, and she showed me a paper. A legal paper, you know? It said she'd changed her name. You have to have a lawyer and pay a couple thou, but you can do that. Her new name was Robin Redd. I go what the fuck, we're not even engaged. And she said when we got married she didn't want to change her name. It would be putting herself down—she had a fancy word, but that was what it meant. So this way she could tell everybody she was keeping her old name."

March glanced at his wristwatch. It was twenty-four hundred. Midnight. Aloud, he said, "I guess that meant a lot to her."

"Then after we were married, she told people we had the same last name because I'd changed mine to match hers.

She said my real name was Rosso. That was my grandfather's name, and I'd told her one time. My dad changed it. You see where I'm coming from, March?"

"Not as well as you do yourself." How could he be this tired without gravity? "I need sleep. I'm going to offer you a bargain. You can accept it or reject it, but you have to leave this hopper promptly either way. Is that clear?"

"I got it."

"Fine. You promise not to go to the big maroon hopper tonight. Everybody in there's asleep anyway, and I don't want you waking them up. In the morning—let's say ten o'clock—I'll go there with you and introduce you."

"I get to go inside? To see them?"

Wearily, March nodded.

"Then it's a deal." Redd extended his hand again; this time March accepted it and they shook.

When Redd had gone, March got some coffee, icommed Kit, and stayed on until she answered. "This better be important, Windy. I was sound asleep."

"I don't think it is, but you will. You were the one who hauled Sue out here. Have you been looking out your windows lately?"

"No. Tell me."

"There's an old beat-up hopper out there. Blue originally, but showing a lot of gray primer and rust. It's Jim's, and he was ready to pay you a little visit tonight."

"Can he do that?"

"Legally, yes. All he has to do is claim he has some kind of emergency. If he does, you've got to let him in. He may not know that, but it's the law."

"Or he might."

"Bingo. I got him calmed down and promised I'd bring him over myself tomorrow at ten. That's today now. This morning."

"I see. . . . Does he know Robin's here?"

"No. But he suspects it pretty strongly. Strongly enough for him to turn your hopper inside out looking for her."

"Unless you're around to stop him."

"Unless we both are. He's at least ten years younger than

I am, and he may have a gun or a knife—he's the type. The thing for you to do is hop back to Kennedy, and I mean right now. Shove Sue out of your hopper as soon as you get there and tell her that her trip's over. In a day or two you can come back here if you want. Or not."

Slowly, Kit said, "I won't do it, Windy." In the screen, her face looked troubled.

"You'd better change your mind. I told Jim I'd bring him over at ten. I like to keep my word."

"I know you do, Windy. It's one of the things I love about you. Have I said that?"

He shook his head. "I don't think so."

"I don't go back on mine, either. We're a couple of old-fashioned people, Windy. We belong together. Don't worry about Robin or me. We'll think of something."

"I hope so." He felt he was about to choke. "I love you, Kit. The two of us can handle him. I can handle him alone if I have to."

A sad nod and a blown kiss, and she was gone. He muttered "out," switching the icom function back to Standby.

Next morning, over coffee and a single-pouch self-heating breakfast, March pondered strategy. Would it be better to arrive promptly, or to give Kit more time to prepare?

Prepare what? What preparations were possible? She might try to coach Robin on ways of dealing with men, but Robin had been as unteachable as anyone he had ever known. Granted, Kit was probably a better teacher, and Kit was certainly better positioned to teach.

If he waited for Redd to come and get him, he could achieve the maximum possible delay—but only if Redd actually came. What if Redd waited until ten, then jetted over to Kit's hopper alone? What if Redd didn't wait, for that matter? It might be best if he went to Kit's hopper now and waited for Redd there.

He glanced at his watch. It was already nine fifteen; he suited up and jetted to Redd's hopper. Three raps on Redd's airlock elicited three answering raps from inside. He opened the airlock, entered the tiny chamber, and shut the hatch behind him. In half a minute, the second hatch opened. "You're early," Redd told him.

March nodded. "I thought we ought to talk about what we're going to do when we get there."

"If you mean discuss it, there's nothing to discuss. I can tell you straight out. Want some coffee?"

It would have to be found and microwaved. March said he did.

"Sit down. Espresso? Cappuccino?"

"Just coffee, thanks. Whatever you have."

"One espresso doppio and one caffè Americano. I'm a coffee snob. I bet you'd never have guessed."

"You'd win."

"My family's in ice cream. One of these days I want to open a coffee shop. There's a hell of a lot of coffee shops, and the coffee stinks." Redd put two bulbs into a microwave that looked older than he did and shut the door. "Ready before you can fart. I'll sell coffee and Dad's ice cream. Con him into putting some money into it. I could make it go."

"I'm sure you could," March told him.

"Damn right. Arabica, the real thing, roasted and ground in my kitchen that morning. Made right, in clean equipment. Most guys have never had a decent cup of coffee."

"What are you doing now? Got a good job?"

"Pretty good. I'm a sound man at UDN. Or I was, before I quit to look for her. Same place Robin works. You used to work there, too."

The microwave buzzed.

"I'll get it. Sit tight."

It was good coffee just as Redd had promised. March sipped and sipped again, finding that the flavor improved with repetition.

"That's arabica. I filled the bulbs before I left and froze them. Robusta's what you've been drinking. Arabica's better, smoother, more complex. Less caffeine, but you can't have everything."

March smiled. "It takes a long time for some of us to learn that."

"Her, you mean. Robin. You're right, she hasn't. Nobody's good enough for her. You weren't and I'm not either."

"But you can bring her around just by talking?"

"You watch. You wanted to know what we'd do when we got there. Only last night you wouldn't say she was there. She is and I know it. You wouldn't be acting like you are if she wasn't."

"I never refused to tell you that." March set his bulb on the wheezing old vacuum table. "I wouldn't tell you who owns the big hopper. You never asked about your wife."

"I'm asking now."

"And I'm answering. Yes. She's in there, staying with the owner."

"You out here trying to get her back?"

"Hell no." March rubbed his big jaw. "I'd spit on your floor, but you'd try to break my nose for it and it's been broken twice already. You can have her. Anybody can have her as far as I'm concerned. And if you'll just take her to a town that I've never heard of on some God-forsaken island, I'll go dancing down the street."

Redd tossed his empty bulb to the table surface. "That's good. I'd fight you for her, and I'd beat you. Only I like you and don't want to. Couple more questions before we go? These might help me."

March glanced at his watch. "Sure."

"Why wouldn't you tell me who owns the big hopper?"

"Because she's a woman and I was afraid you'd go over there and push her around when I wasn't looking."

"But I wouldn't push around a guy? Hey, I've pushed around quite a few."

"I believe you. I thought you might be more careful, just the same. Wait for me to take you over this morning."

Redd grinned. "Okay, I've waited. Finish your coffee and let's go."

March was still in his suit when Redd stepped from Kit's airlock and took off his helmet. "Here he is," March said. "Kit, this is Sue's husband, Jim Redd. Jim, this is Kit Carlsen. You've probably seen her at work."

"Other places, too." Redd hesitated, then smiled. "The lady with the big knife."

"That's me," Kit told him. "Back then, we hadn't been properly introduced, Jim. Now we have. Shake?"

"Sure." He opened his suit and pushed it toward his knees. "Pleased to meet you properly, Kit. Only I want to say Ms. Carlsen, because that's what we had to call you while you were hosting *Kids' Klassics*."

"You worked on that?" Kit tilted her head.

"Great body language, Ms. Carlsen. Nobody in the business does it better."

"Thanks, but I still don't remember you."

"I filled in for Don Ayres when he was on vacation or sick, Ms. Carlsen."

"He's a sound tech," March explained.

"Like Robin?"

Redd nodded. "I taught her while we were together. I thought she could get a job at the network and make us a little extra. She waited till she got on there and dumped me. She's a good dumper. Ask March."

Kit nodded. "He's told me already. She dumped you, but you've come way out here where people don't belong to get her and take her back to New York."

"To talk to her so she'll come back with me willingly. Right. I'm not a kidnapper, Ms. Carlsen, no matter what Robin's told you. With a couple of witnesses, I'm sure as shit not a kidnapper."

"You wouldn't hit her?"

Redd kicked off his suit and stowed it in a locker with his helmet.

"Would you hit her?" Kit repeated. "I'd like to know."

"I know you would, and I had to think it over so I could give you an honest answer. I want to be honest with you, Ms. Carlsen. I don't want to lie to somebody I admire so much. I want her to sit down and listen to me. No jumping up screaming. No yelling about cops or bad things she said I did. Things I really didn't do, by the way. You won't believe that, but it's the truth. They're lies she made up so she could dump me, and she's said them over and over to me and everybody she's ever talked to until she practically believes them herself."

"I hear you."

"Only if I had to bat her a couple of times to get her to sit down and shut up, I'd do it. Nothing she wouldn't get over in a day or two. So will I smack her? I don't want to, but I will if I have to. You want to tell her to come out, Ms. Carlsen? If you don't, I'm going to go looking for her."

March said, "She's not here. I know you won't believe me, but she's not. Tell him, Kit."

Kit shook her head. "He won't believe me."

"Yes, I will, Ms. Carlsen. Tell me."

March picked up his helmet, replaced it, and began to screw it back on.

"Windy—that's Mr. Wildspring to you—told me you were here looking for Robin and that the two of you would come here this morning. I woke her up and told her about it. I said we wouldn't let you force her to do anything she didn't want to do. She wanted me to go to the tomb Windy calls Number Nineteen with her. She said we could hide in there until you went away. I told her hell no, Robin, you're out of your mind. We talked about it for a while before we went back to bed. When I got up this morning, she was gone."

"Merda! La fica stupida!" Redd slammed his fist into his palm. "If that isn't just like her."

March added, "Her suit's gone, too. She may actually have gone into Nineteen. If so, she's probably dead. You'll want to search this hopper before you do anything else. I know the memorials. You and Kit don't. Give me your word you won't hurt Kit, and I'll try to find Robin."

Kit said, "You can look anywhere you want. I already have. Just don't make a mess."

"To hell with that!" Redd jerked open the fiberglass locker door. "I'm going with March."

"You mean you trust me?" Kit looked—and sounded—slightly stunned.

"If she's here, she's safe." Redd was climbing back into his suit. "She's safe, and I'll catch up to her sooner or later.

If she's in some crazy graveyard out in space, she could die. She doesn't have sense enough. . . ."

March closed the airlock behind him and heard no more.

Had Number Nineteen been on the farther side of Jupiter, it would have been necessary to hop, making certain that the speed of the hopper was sufficient to keep it in or near its new orbit when the hop was completed. Number Nineteen was not, but close by—threateningly close to someone who suspected it as deeply as March did.

Back on his own hopper, he cast off from Kit's. Once inside, he hooked up his lifeline, edged the hopper within a hundred feet, and looked down at his utility belt. Its adjustable wrench, its long black flashlight, and its multi-tool had gotten him out of danger . . . ? He tried to count them. Three times? No, five. Five at least.

"One more," he whispered. "Just once more, please. After this I'll go home and never come out here again. I swear to God."

God was everywhere, or so they said. If so, God was on his utility belt just now. Certainly he was praying to his utility belt. He smiled at the thought.

And God was in Number Nineteen. A dark and vengeful God, perhaps.

There were multiple entrances to Number Nineteen. Six that he could recall, although he had never counted them. His orange lifeline would show Jim Redd which he had taken, if it did nothing else.

Would show Redd, that is, if Redd actually came.

No trailing lifeline revealed the way Robin had gone; she had used none, obviously. One entrance was as good as another; and she might have chosen another memorial in preference to this, no matter what she had said to Kit. She might actually be hiding in Kit's hopper, for that matter.

Passing through his airlock, he stood alone with God in the inhuman desolation of space. Overhead, where he had to crane his neck to see it, spun the huge, semi-spherical rock that might be Hell.

The entrance he chose conformed to no architecture with

which he was familiar, a wide, circular port whose smooth black sides might have been metal or polished stone. With his digicorder rolling, he jetted cautiously into it.

"Welcome to paradise." The voice was female, warm, and friendly; it seemed to come from nowhere in particular.

"Thanks." March spoke into his mike. "I've always wanted to go there."

"You're here." The voice giggled. "Well, just about here, anyway. You have to go through our airlock. I'll bet you never thought paradise would have an airlock."

"Or an angel to greet me." March was looking for the airlock and for the source of the female voice.

"It's got both. I'm a watcher. That's what we call people like me. My name's Penny."

"Shouldn't it be Angela?"

"Nope. Penny the Angel. Angela's the blonde. We take turns, us angels. It's my turn, so you're mine. What's your name?"

He told her, and she said, "Well, you're looking too close, March Wildspring."

He switched on his helmet light. The airlock was deeper in and several steps up, by far the largest he had ever seen. "That looks like a whole room in there."

"It is—we've got gravity here. Did you notice?"

"I've noticed I settled to the floor."

"Right. And you can walk to our airlock, if you're careful not to bounce. Part of our gravity really is gravity like you get on Earth. This rock's real big. It's bigger than the moons of Mars and dense. There's lots of iron in the rock, and that makes it heavy. There's a lot of something else, too, that's heavier. Come in and I'll show you."

March had not moved. "You could tell me now."

"No, I can't. It's against the rules. There's other things—a whole lot of them—you have to see first. The rest of our gravity's turning, only it's not real gravity. It just feels like it. When you were outside you must have seen how fast this rock turns."

Certain by now that she could see him, March nodded.

"He turns it. So it doesn't feel exactly like Earth, but

there's enough to keep our bones strong. You know what happens to people who spend too much time in hoppers."

"Sure."

"It's called osteopor'sis. Your bones lose calcium and break easy. Only it won't happen here. Won't you come in? It's paradise, and you don't have to stay."

"That's good, assuming it's true."

"Only everybody does. Everybody wants to stay. I did. You will, too."

March cleared his throat. "Before I come in, I want to ask one question. Just one. Answer it, and I'll come in. Did a girl calling herself Robin come in a few hours ago?"

"Ouch." The young woman sounded genuinely unhappy. "I wish I could tell you, only I can't. There's seven gates. Each gate gets a watcher—we take turns. When somebody comes like you just did, the watcher goes around with them to show them, and the new watcher takes over. I've been on this gate for three sleeps, so she didn't come in through Number Four. But she could have come in through one of the others. I wouldn't know."

"Is there any way to find out?"

"Of course." The young woman's voice was serious. "You can come inside and look. You know what she looks like, don't you?"

"Yes. Would you like me to describe her?"

"It wouldn't do any good. I can't leave this gate till somebody comes, and she'll look different anyway. Better. Everybody looks better in here."

"Are you saying I wouldn't recognize her if I saw her?" March found he was walking toward the airlock. He wondered just when he had begun, but kept going.

"No. No, I'm not. Not really. Only it might be a while before you knew it was her. Everybody looks better. Sometimes a whole bunch better. We still look like us, but older if we're young and younger if we're old. Prettier, too. You know."

"No," he said. "I don't."

"You will. Come in and you'll see."

"So you can leave your gate." He had stopped in front of the airlock.

"No, not a bit. It's nice here. You'll see that, too. Besides, my friends come around to talk and bring me stuff. Nobody minds being watcher. Nobody minds anything here."

"That's good."

"Except one thing. I'll tell you about that later, after you've seen. I've never done it, but I guess it can be icky."

"I can leave whenever I want to?"

"You won't want to. Just climb in, and I'll shut the big door for you."

"But I can?"

"Naturally you can. Only the people who leave don't want to. That's the thing I said could be bad. Leaving. I'll tell you all about it later."

He mounted the few steps, and the hatch swung swiftly shut behind him. This airlock was the size of a small room. There were chairs, pictures on the walls, and a fireplace, complete with fire. He walked toward it for a better look, and discovered that the hatch had severed his lifeline. "Hey!" he said.

Then, "Penny? Are you still there?"

There was no reply.

The fireplace was real and so was the fire. The logs, however, were not. Some flammable gas with a small feed of oxygen, March decided.

He heard his air supply switch over, and thought of returning it to suit air but did not. The new air he breathed smelled better, a clean fresh smell as though it had known a windswept meadow by the sea. Walking around the airlock quickly, he found that he was not dizzy and was not blacking out.

"This," he told his mike, "is surely the strangest of all the memorials, as well as the biggest. If Penny's not a real and living person, her voice certainly conveys that impression."

A wall of the room swung back. "Welcome," the girl standing a foot beyond its arc told him. She sketched a curtsy, lifting a diaphanous scarlet skirt. "Welcome to paradise, Mr. March Wildspring. May you remain long and return soon."

"Thank you." He stepped down from the airlock, and discovered that he was smiling. "Okay if I take off my helmet?"

"Oh, yes! Aren't you sure there's air here? If there wasn't, I'd die."

"I know there is." He unscrewed his helmet. "You'd die if you're real. Are you?"

"You betcha!" She giggled. "Want to touch?"

"Sure. Give me your hand."

"You can't feel much through that glove. I know. I used to have a suit like that, only mine was white and not so big. I kept wanting to take the gloves off."

"Your hand."

She held it out. "It doesn't have to be there. You could touch other places. I wouldn't mind."

Leaving the airlock, he took her hand. "You're not a hologram."

"Of course not. I'm a real live person. Not exactly like you because of the sex thing. Only real close. How do you like me up top?"

"Good." He nodded thoughtfully. "Nice molding."

"I'm not molded! I grew up. I'm a real person, too. Kissing would prove it. Want to kiss?"

"Later, maybe. Right now I'd like to see paradise."

"That's good. Take off your suit. I'll put it in one of these box things for you."

"I'll keep it on. I'm holding onto my helmet, too."

"That way everybody will know you're new, March. It'll be a lot of trouble. You'll see."

"But I can keep it if I want to?"

"I guess so." She sounded doubtful. "I've never done this before. Watched a gate. This is my first time and they never said anything about suits. So I guess you can. Or if you can't, somebody will tell us. Only I'll be in trouble."

"I'll explain that it was my fault."

"Thanks." She led him past the wall-mounted lockers and the benches on which newcomers presumably sat to take off their boots, and into a wide and apparently sunlit room. A well-remembered face pontificated about politics on a digivid there, too proud to notice the incomplete jigsaw puzzle on the floor before him. A dozen plates held half-finished food, and dolls and a teddy bear occupied comfortable-looking chairs; on the farther side of the room a wide arch opened out onto what appeared to be a sunlit garden on Earth.

He hurried to it, then stopped to stare.

"Isn't it pretty?"

Slowly he nodded.

"How about me? You can see me better in this light. Aren't I pretty, too?"

Turning, he studied her. "You are. You're really quite beautiful." It was the truth.

She laughed, delighted, and smoothed her lustrous coppery hair with both hands.

"Is it all right if I jump?"

"You better not. People turn around funny sometimes. Come down on their heads."

"I'll risk it." Gathering all his strength, he sprang into the air, rising to a height of twenty feet or more. The garden spread as far as he could see, its low hills dotted with little sunlit lakes, trees, tents, airy cottages, and fountains. A quick sweep of his digicorder took it all in—or so he hoped. Skillful manipulation of his suit jets landed him on his feet.

"You're good at it," the young woman told him.

"Not really." He grinned. "I'm wearing a lot of heavy gear and not as young as I used to be. In a way that was an advantage. I knew I wouldn't come down any faster than I had gone up."

"Want something to eat? Or just walk around?"

"Just walk around. I'd like to talk to some other people."

"In your orange clothes?" She giggled. "You will."

They had not gone more than a thousand yards when they were surrounded by a crowd. More than once, he had found himself in crowds of actors at parties, and the feeling was much the same. Not all the men were tall, but most were handsome; those who were not, were attractive without being handsome, with kind, honest faces suggestive of good humor or sparkling wit.

The women were cute. Or pretty. Or beautiful. All of them.

He raised his hands for silence. "I'm looking for a missing woman. Her name's Robin Redd, and I think she ran in here because she thought a man named Jim was going to kill her. I'm not Jim. I'm a friend. . . ." He let his arms drop.

"Not a friend." The speaker was a silver-maned man who looked as though he might once have been a judge—or played one on vid. "Who are you, then?"

"I used to be her husband, sir."

"If she's in here she's safe, son. Perfectly safe."

A score of voices seconded him.

"Why do you want to take her back to a place of danger?"

March drew a deep breath—air so clean and pure it might have come from a mountain top. "I'll take her back only if she wants to go, sir. If she wants to stay here, that's fine. But I want to know where she is, because she may need help if she's not here. Do you know?"

The silver mane was shaken. "I do not, but I'll try to find out. What's your name, son?"

"March Wildspring."

The young woman said, "Marchy hasn't decided to stay yet, Barney. How can I talk him into it?"

Someone in the crowd asked, "Just talk?" and there was laughter.

The silver-maned man joined it with a throaty chuckle. "When he's seen a few more like you—"

Quickly, the young woman raised an admonitory hand. "That's enough of that. Please! He'll think I'm easy. I'm not, Mr. Wildspring. Don't let this dress fool you. Nobody wears much in the way of clothes in here."

A beefy man with a likable grin pointed to March. "Nobody but you, that is."

It got another laugh.

"Folks!" March raised his voice. "I'm looking for Robin Redd. I don't want to hurt her." He scanned the crowd through the viewfinder of his digicorder. "If any of you know her, will you please tell her March is looking for her? She can stay here if she wants to, or I'll take her back if she'd prefer to go."

That raised the biggest laugh of all.

A rustic bridge crossed one of several small lakes. The young woman paused halfway across to point out their reflections in the water. "Look there, Mr. Wildspring. See how good-looking you are?"

He did, seeing a grimly handsome man with abundant brown hair and finely chiseled features; this flattering reflection wore what appeared to be a Day-Glo orange military spacesuit. The young woman beside him was clearly the young woman with him. He raised an arm; the reflection raised an arm as well.

"Aren't we an attractive couple?"

"Yes," he said, "we certainly are."

"If you were to take off all those clothes, would you just throw them away?"

"No. No, Penny, I certainly wouldn't want to do that. If I were to take them off, I'd want a safe place to put them, a place I could find again without much trouble. I'd want to be able to get them back in a hurry if I needed them."

"That's good." The young woman looked thoughtful. "He might want to send you out. He does that sometimes. They can come back later, I think. But they have to go if he says so."

"He runs this? What's his name?"

"I don't know, but there's a big statue of him in a park. We could probably find out there. Everybody just says 'he.' Everybody knows what it means."

"I'd like to see that statue and take some pictures." March indicated his digicorder. "But first I'd like to go on across and get a few of you posing in the middle of this bridge. It should be a lovely shot. Can I do that?"

"It sounds like fun." She smiled. "Just tell me what poses you'd like."

"I will. You're not afraid I'll run off on my own?"

She cocked her head, looking more charming than ever. "Are you going to?"

"No."

"That's good. Strangers need somebody. A guide. That's why we do it. But you wouldn't have to trick me. Anytime you want to go, you can do it. I'll go back to the gate and wait for you."

"All right, I'll remember that. But wouldn't he have sent somebody else to watch the gate by now?"

"I suppose. I guess so. How'd you like me to pose?"

"Sitting on the railing, I think."

"So you can get my legs. You're right, I've got good legs. How's this?"

It was fine, her long, smooth legs out over the water, one delicately rounded calf resting on the rail, the foot of the other leg hooked around one of the supports, and her gossamer skirt hiked halfway up her thighs. He backed down the bridge, passing a sleeping man and shooting as he went, stopped his digicorder briefly to note the precise number on its whirling dial, and shot more from the bank.

When he rejoined her, he said, "That was beautiful. I've got a couple of questions now. No, three questions. All right if I ask them?"

Her smile would have melted stone. "If I can't answer, we'll find somebody who can."

"First question. If this were Earth, people would've cut their names into this rail. Hearts, with MW plus KC. All that kind of stuff. Nobody's carved anything in this one. Why is that?"

"On Earth we do it so people will remember." The young woman said slowly, "and so we'll remember ourselves. We think maybe it will never happen, he'll dump me or I'll dump him. But years from now when I've almost forgotten, maybe I'll see this. I'll think, oh yeah, he wasn't good-looking or talented, but he had the best heart. If things had gone a little differently. . . ."

March said, "I didn't mean to hurt you."

"You didn't. I was just thinking. It's all different now. Different here. That's what I think. We know we're going to remember this place and the people we love here. Remember everything about it forever and ever. What's hard is remembering how it was before we got here. Like, I used to have a little apartment back on Earth. It was just two rooms and a bath, and nothing in it could be very big at all. There was a cabinet I couldn't open that had been built into a corner a long time ago and painted white. The white paint had stuck the doors shut."

"I understand." He laid a hand on her shoulder.

"I was pretty sure there was nothing in there, but I always wondered. Now I'm here, and it feels like it happened a long, long time ago to somebody else. Somebody in a show I saw one time, and I wish she'd broken that cabinet open."

The young woman slid from the railing, cocked her head, and smiled. "That wasn't a good answer, but I don't think I can answer any better. You said three questions."

"I did." March sighed. "Here's the next. There's no litter on the lakeshore and no junk floating in the water. There aren't even any cans for garbage. Why not?"

"Because it's ours. This whole place is ours. He gave it to us. We're his, and we own this. It's where we live. On Earth everything belongs to the government, really. In America it does, anyway. They pretend it's yours, but do something they don't like and you'll find out. This really is ours. We can cut down the trees and pick the flowers, but we don't want to. Not mostly. If there were more people, it might be different."

"He sends some away, you said."

Looking pensive, the young woman nodded. "He might send me away someday. I hope not."

"They go back to Earth?"

She nodded again.

"What do they do there?"

"I don't know, and that's more than three. All right, I do. They do whatever he's asked them to, and when they get it all done they get to come back."

"Those weren't my third question," March said, "just follow-ups. Here's the third. When I jumped and looked around, I could see little houses, and when we were up on the bridge I could see two and a tent. Do they have vids in there? Any of them? You had a vid in your room at the gate."

"I'm not sure, but I think that anybody who wants one gets one. Some people don't. Is there something you want to watch?"

"Yes. I used to work for UDN, and—well, it's kind of complicated. But there are things I want to see. Maybe even things I want to show you. There's no hurry, though. Let's go look at his statue."

It was large and imposing, but not at all what March had expected. An elderly man, bald and rather fat, knelt. His enormous bronze hands were held out to those who had followed a narrow and seemingly aimless path through a wilderness of flowers. They seemed to shelter a sleeper at his feet.

"He looks like my father," March murmured.

"Like my grandfather," the young woman said. "I've never been here. I'm new, and I hadn't gotten around to it. If I'd known how beautiful it was, I'd have come sooner."

March retreated to the path. "I'm going to pan the gardens and stop on you, looking at the statue. Look up at it while you count to ten, normal speed, then turn and look at me and smile."

She did. When he appeared to have stopped recording, she said, "I've found a little notice that tells you about it. The statue's twelve feet high, and the figure of the Founder would be twenty-three feet high if he were standing up. The bronze is eight inches thick. Most statues like this are thin, it said, but they could make this one almost solid because its base sits right on the solid rock of this asteroid. Is it an asteroid? That's what they said."

"I suppose. Does it give his name?"

"Let me see. 'It is composed of copper, tin, and gold, the proportions being fifty, forty, and ten; all three metals were mined during the excavation of the perfect world in which you stand. The sculptors worked from photographs and digivid recordings made during the last years of the Founder's life. The ancient lost wax method was employed to create the statue, although it required wax brought from Earth. His body has perished, but his mind lives on and is your god.' No name. It doesn't name the artists, either."

"It would be an interesting thing to know," March said. "I'm going to keep trying to find out. How many people are there in here?"

The young woman shook her head. "I have no idea."

"Guess."

She hesitated. "I'm going to say five hundred. About that."

"I would have said fewer. Half that, maybe. Even if you're right, it should be possible to ask all of them."

"About this girl Robin Redd?"

"No. I know where she is, Penny. The name of the Founder's going to be harder, I think."

"I don't, because I don't believe you know where that girl is. You couldn't."

"I do." March sounded as tired as he felt. "You—"

The statue spoke, surprising them both. Its voice was deep, resonant, and kind. "I am pleased—oh, wonderfully pleased—to announce that we have been joined by four this wake. That is the highest total since the five of December twentieth and surpasses the three of February third. Our newest lovers are Robin Redd, Katarina 'Kit' Carlsen, March Wildspring, and James Frankie Redd. Welcome, all!"

March could only stare.

"My dear children," the statue continued, "this wake has wound to a pleasing end. The time of rest is upon us. Repose with me in your humble homes, and repose with whom you like. Sleep, and I promise you that all your dreams will be pleasant ones.

"Though nightmares stalk the dark, if you sleep they cannot trouble you."

"Nightmares?"

The young woman said, "I don't know about them. I guess I've been asleep."

"If they can't hurt sleeping people, how bad can they be?" March was conscious of a slight dimming of the light; the meter built into his digicorder confirmed it.

"Just sleeping people who are inside somewhere." The young woman looked frightened. "That's what I think. We need to get inside."

"You don't know?"

"No! Let's go. These people are nice. Somebody will take us in."

The light had dimmed again, very slightly.

"Can you jog, Mr. Wildspring? I can, and I think we ought to jog until we find someplace that will take us in."

March shook his head. "Not wearing this. No, I can't jog and won't try."

"Well, take it off." The young woman's fear was almost palpable.

"I won't." March caught her arm. "In a minute I'm going to let you run if you want to, but I need to say something first. If you decide you want out, just look me up. I'll get you out if I can. Understand?"

The young woman nodded and tried to smile. The smile was a pathetic failure.

"Fine." March released her. "You jog ahead and find a place to hide."

His suit felt heavy now even in the slight gravity of Number Nineteen. His wristwatch told him that only six and a half hours of the day had passed for him. The knowledge did nothing to relieve his aching shoulders; he was hot and tired.

"We have seen the founder's statue," he told his mike, "and learned that this asteroid contains copper, tin, and gold. Those metals—the last, particularly—no doubt financed much of the building of this memorial. We have learned two other things of considerable interest. I have, at least, in the course of walking over several miles of it." Some time ago, he had removed his gloves and pushed them under his utility belt. Now he employed a forefinger to wipe his sweating forehead.

"First, this is the only memorial I am aware of that actually enlists visitors to serve its agenda, which we may assume was that of the Founder. As you have heard, some of them are returned to Earth. We can only speculate as to their purpose.

"Second, it seems at least possible that the Founder's accomplishments included one of the holy grails of physics, the creation of artificial gravity. You may recall that our guide told us the gravity here was a combination of mass and spin. Real gravity—gravity from mass—pulls us inward. Spin forces us outward. The two are antithetical, in other words, and cannot be made to act in concert. I would estimate the gravity I feel here to be about one quarter that of Earth. I doubt that a core of heavy metals could provide that much gravity to an asteroid this small, and this asteroid is certainly not spinning fast enough. If it had been, it would have thrown me back into space when I landed."

Beyond the flowery border, a rolling green landscape displayed two neat white cottages some distance apart. The light had diminished twice before March reached the first.

His knocks brought a remarkably handsome, angry, and suspicious man who answered all March's arguments with "We don't let anybody into our home."

Total darkness came before March reached the second cottage. It was a night without stars, and without the least attempt to counterfeit them. The day sky had been a passable imitation of Earth's: a blue dome traversed by a single bright light, wispy clouds that might, perhaps, have been steam. By night, the cavern was plainly that. The air was cool, and soon grew cooler still.

"March? March?" The voice was plaintive, sad, and old.

"That's me," he said. "Who are you?"

"You left me to die, March. You left me alone in that hospital so you could go off to some meeting. And I died, March. I died alone, abandoned."

"Mom?" His free hand was fumbling with the flashlight on his utility belt.

A child's voice said, "You don't know me. You'll never know me, March. You'll never know me because I was never born. I'm March Wildspring, Jr. I'm the son you never got."

"Uh huh." March's fingers had found the switch. "I'm going to turn this on now, son. You might want to cover your eyes. It's a lot brighter than a helmet light."

He did, and there was no one there. For two minutes and more, the glaring beam probed the darkness in search of the other white cottage he had seen; there was no such cottage, and it began to rain.

Sighing, he returned the flashlight to his belt, resumed his helmet, and switched on his helmet light.

"I sat beside you, March. Beside you in home room, and behind you in history. You let me copy your answers once, March, and I thought you liked me. I liked you and tried to show you I was yours for the asking. You were in all my daydreams, March. Other things changed, but you were always there."

He said nothing, plodding wearily forward. His helmet light showed no one.

"Remember the time I touched your hand? You pulled away. I loved you, and you pulled away."

"You scared me," he told the disembodied voice. "I was one of the biggest boys in the class, and you were bigger than I was. You had those hungry eyes."

The old voice said, "You left me alone, March. You left me alone to die."

"You weren't supposed to die." His helmet light revealed no speaker. "There was a meeting I had to attend, a planning meeting for next year's schedule. They said you'd be home in a week."

A dog barked. It was a soft and friendly bark, and though it did not bark again he could hear its panting. "I'm sorry," he told the dog. "I didn't know how sick you were."

By the time he reached the second cottage, he was determined to get in at any cost. "I'm a new arrival," he told the handsome young man who answered his knock. For a moment he paused, sniffing.

"So are we." The young man made no attempt to conceal his naked body. "Get your own dump."

The air March's suit was utilizing now carried a whiff of tobacco smoke. "I'm out here with the nightmares, and I don't like it. I need a place to sleep, and something to eat, if you've got it."

The muscular (and very naked) young man tried to close the door, but March had stuck the toe of his boot into it. "I'll behave myself, and I'll be eternally grateful."

"You get the hell out!"

From behind the muscular young man, Kit's well-remembered voice called, "Let him in, Jim!"

The muscular young man snarled, "Shut the fuck up!"

March's shoulder forced the door open, throwing Jim backward. A split second later, March's left took him in the pit of the stomach. It was followed at once (perhaps unnecessarily) by March's right, which caught the side of Jim's neck.

He went down, March unhooked the flashlight from his belt, and Kit said, "Windy! Thank God." She was wearing the pink brassiere he remembered so well.

He had never tried to kiss anyone through his helmet before. Both laughed, he unscrewed the helmet, they kissed properly, and he picked Kit up and swung her around like a child.

"You shouldn't do that," she told him breathlessly. "I'm too fat. You'll hurt yourself."

"You're not fat, and there isn't much gravity here."

"I should lose ten pounds and you know it. Twenty would be better."

"You look great." It was difficult to keep his eyes on her face.

"Everybody looks great here. You look great, too."

"How did you know it was me? I didn't know you were in there until I heard your voice."

"I didn't, at first." She grinned. "I couldn't see you because Jim was in the way, and I didn't recognize your voice because you sound better here. It was just that you were a stranger, and maybe you'd protect me from him. He tore my clothes off, and I think I'm going to get a black eye."

By that time, Jim had picked up the flashlight and was trying to stand. March took it from him and hit him with it. Twice.

"Shove him out the door," Kit suggested.

March shook his head. "Not yet. I've got something to show you. If it's what I think it's going to be, I want him to see it, too. Hell, he's entitled to see it. Turn on that vid, will you? You can keep the sound off."

She did, and dancers as naked as Jim Redd capered across the projection area.

"I didn't know it was you," she told March, "until I saw the orange suit. The lights in here aren't very good."

"I've noticed, and I think I may understand that. Another thing I've noticed is that though whatever the Founder's got makes everybody else look different—"

"Better," Kit said.

"You look just the way you always did. You're still the most beautiful woman in the world."

"I look different, Windy, and you know it. You just won't admit it."

He shook his head. "You look exactly the same. You sound the same, too. When you couldn't see me, I couldn't see you, either. I heard your voice, and it was the most beautiful voice in the business. No different."

"I don't think I understand."

"Neither do I. That's how it was, and that's all I know." He was sweeping the room with his digicorder. When he finished, he found the remote and changed channels.

"Vid looks just the same as at home," Kit said. "I don't understand that either. Do you?"

"If you mean how the system here does that, no. If you mean why it does it, it ought to be pretty obvious. The people get reminded of how it really was back home every time they look at it. This place is the carrot. What they see on vid is the stick. It's what they'll be going back to if they try to leave. So they don't. Wait a minute. Is there a hand-mirror around here?"

"Probably. I can look."

"Do that," March told her.

Redd groaned. After a minute or two, he groped the contusions on his head.

"Stay flat on the floor," March told him, "or you'll have another one." He had opened his suit and taken out his wallet.

Kit returned with a mirror. "You know, this is really a pretty place. It's not big, but it's awfully nice. Our watcher explained that the couple that had it before had gone back to Earth. The Founder'd sent them there, she said. They might come back eventually, but we could have it until they did. All this was before Jim jumped me."

March nodded.

"She said she'd go back to her gate and sleep there, but she'd come by for us in the morning. I thought I could handle Jim—that was a big mistake—and this looked nice. It would give us a base to operate out of while I looked for you and Jim looked for Robin. So I said okay, fine."

"You saw my lifeline."

"That's right. So we knew where you'd gone, Windy. Only it had been cut in front of the airlock, and that worried the hell out of me."

"The door did it," he said absently. "The airlock door. When you look into that mirror, do you see a new, improved you?"

"That's right, and I look great."

"Now look at this." March held up his wallet. "Which you is this?"

There was a long pause before Kit said, "That's the old me. This isn't real, is it? I never thought it was."

"But it was fun to pretend."

Kit nodded.

"Besides, philosophers have argued for centuries over what we mean by 'real' and what we ought to mean. When I look at you, the physical body I see is composed of atoms that form molecules. That's what it really is, but I see a person. Which one's real?"

"Both of them," Kit said promptly.

"I agree, but not everyone does. I used to know a man whose wife cheated on him and bragged about it. He told himself it wasn't real because it didn't matter. What was real was the love he had for her, and the love he thought she had for him."

"I think I know him, too."

"Nothing mattered but that love, so only that love was real. It wasn't a lie he was telling himself, because he thought it was the truth. He'd convinced himself."

With an almost inaudible grunt, Redd sat up. Though still handsome, he looked sick; a few seconds later he spat onto the intricately beautiful Persian carpet.

March switched off his digicorder and took out the disk. "I want to play this. Let's see what we see."

What they saw first was a blue screen dotted with instructions and cautions printed in yellow. He pressed fast forward, stopped at a shot of Kit, and turned up the sound.

"No, Sarah. We'd like to hear about your cooking. It made you famous all over Southton."

The real Kit said, "That's the way, Windy. Hide those hips."

March hit fast forward again. "If only you knew what I feel every time I see them. Is Jim watching?"

He was, still sitting and looking only a little the worse for wear.

"Let's see if we can find Sue."

Robin appeared, simpering. Soon, March's voice said, *"You are. You're really quite beautiful."*

She laughed.

March's voice continued, *"Is it all right if I jump?"*

Kit asked, "Is that how she looked to you then?"

March shook his head and killed the sound. "She was lovely, and looked like nineteen or twenty. Did you notice the dolls behind her?"

"And the mess. There was a teddy bear, too."

"She wanted me to think she was a kid, twelve maybe, who looked older here. She tried to talk like that at first, but after a while she forgot and I noticed. She'd seen me coming, somehow, and gotten to the gate in time to talk the real kid into going out for coffee or something while Sue subbed for her. Presumably there's a place where you can watch like that, and Sue had found out about it fast, because she thought Jim here might come after her. So I came and was met by a gorgeous redhead who told me her name was Penny. Look at the screen."

It showed a vast cavern, with a floor of mud and water. Here and there grass struggled to live, its sallow blades ill-nourished by sunlamps high overhead.

"That isn't what I saw when I jumped," March said wryly.

"It isn't even what I saw in the viewfinder. It's what the digicorder saw, just the same."

"You mean . . . ?"

"I mean it's where we are. Right now."

Redd snarled, "You got me into this."

"If you're talking to me," March said, "I agree. I did. If you're talking to Kit, you and I are going to have words again."

"Without the flashlight?"

"Try it and see."

"That's what I want," Kit said. "I want to see. You were shooting when you came in here. I know you were. I want to see Jim and me, and I want to see what this place really looks like."

They did.

The three of them left together the next morning, after eating what they now knew was a paste of ground grain.

"I'm going to make you a deal," Redd told them.

"Think you can outrun me? Either one of you?"

Kit shook her head, but March said, "I'd be willing to try. Want to find out?"

"In that suit?"

"You're a smoker, and I'm willing to try."

"You may get the chance. Look, I could just take off and look for Robin. When I found her—and I would—I'd take her to my hopper and we'd be back in New York before you knew we were gone. Capeesh?"

March nodded.

"That's got one big hole in it." Redd paused, looking thoughtful. "Are they going to let us go without a fight? Maybe they will. Maybe they won't."

"They won't," Kit said.

"I don't think so either," March told her, "but I'd like to hear your reason."

"Simple. We've seen through this place. They'll know we have, because nobody who hasn't would want to leave. If we get out we'll tell other people. So we don't get out."

Redd grinned. "Smart lady. How about you, March? You thinking the same as she is?"

"Close enough. What about you?"

"I'm not as sure as she is." Redd picked his teeth with a fingernail.

"But you think so, too. Why?"

"Everything's easier to get into than to get out of, that's all. You probably think I'm a goodfella."

March shook his head. "You were working as a sound man, so it didn't seem likely."

"That's right, I'm not. But I could've been a dozen times over. I'd be a made man by now. Or maybe dead, or in the slammer." Redd shrugged. "I know people, okay? Guys from my old neighborhood. Guys I went to school with. It was easy for most of them, and there was a couple who didn't even know where they were till somebody told them. You get in really easy, like here."

Kit said, "But you don't get out."

"Exactly. So I figure what I figure. They're sending people back to Earth, capeesh? She told us, and that's who had our shack before. For their health? I don't think so. They've got an angle."

"So do you," Kit told him.

"That's right. Mine is that we've got a better chance getting out together than doing it separately. I'll help you two, if you'll help Robin and me."

March said, "We will."

Kit looked from one to the other. "What if Robin doesn't want to go with him, Windy?"

"We'll deal with that after we've gotten out," March told her. "If we start fighting among ourselves now. . . ." He shrugged.

Redd opened a battered vacpack of Old Camels, looked into it, and reclosed it. "I'll deal now. Kit, if you'll give your word you'll take her back to the city and turn her loose, I'll give mine that I'll let you do it. That's unless she decides to come back with me and tells you so herself."

"It's a deal." Kit offered her hand.

"I want to know about the footrace," March told him.

"Just this. I'm splitting. Two of us will have a better chance of finding her than one. If you don't like it, you'll have to run me down."

"I like it," March told him. "You won't have to run."

"That's great. We'll meet you at the gate, okay? The gate you came in through. We came in through that one, too."

Kit added, "I saw your lifeline, Windy."

"That was Gate Four," March told Redd. "We'll wait a while there—if we can. You do the same. That doesn't mean we'll wait for days. An hour or two, tops."

Redd nodded and left, walking fast. They saw him stop where the path threaded a picture-perfect little grove to light a cigarette; then he was lost to sight.

Before the path vanished into the grove they turned aside, flanking the grove and a small but lovely lake. At last Kit said, "Don't you care whether Robin gets out?"

"Yes," March told her, "but not very much. They're not going to kill her in here. They'll keep her—drugged or whatever it is—and happy. She may be better off here than she'd be with Jim."

"You said you knew she wasn't really a kid because she forgot to talk like one. But you knew more than that, because you told us she was really Robin. Did she say so?"

"No. She slipped badly once and called me Marchy. That's what she used to call me. . . ."

"I've got it."

"Mostly she called me Mr. Wildspring. You want to do dramatic parts, Kit, and I know you'll do them well. Do you know what the difference between a bad actor and a good actor is?"

"Charisma. You know it as soon as he comes on."

"That's what makes a star, but there are a lot of good actors who aren't stars and never will be. They're good just the same, and when you need somebody to play the other cop or the wisecracking gal who runs the deli they'll do fine. The difference between a bad actor and a good one is that a bad one can look good for five minutes. Give him a good director and a good script and he can handle it. But a good actor can be good for as long as you need him. . . ."

"What is it, Windy?"

He raised his shoulders and, hopelessly, let them fall. "I don't want to talk about it."

Her embrace surprised him, and their kiss lasted a long time. When they parted, Kit said, "Now tell me about it. What are friends for?"

"Sometimes I wish I didn't notice so much, that's all."

They continued in silence until Kit dropped onto a marble bench. "This is about me and Jim, isn't it?"

March nodded.

"Okay, out with it."

"You said he tore your clothes off. They aren't torn, and there's not a button missing."

"Clothes look better here, too."

March said nothing.

"They do! Most of these people are in rags. You saw that when we played the disk. But those rags look great to us."

He turned his digicorder toward her and backed away. "We'll stop at the first house we see and look at this. If there are tears—or missing buttons, any of that—I'll apologize. What will you do when there aren't?"

"Windy. . . ."

"Go ahead. I'm getting it."

"Windy, I love you. I do." Kit's tears overflowed as she spoke. "Do you really think I'd strip for Jim if I wasn't scared to death?"

"Yes. I'd like to be wrong about that. But yes, I do."

"Robin gave you a bad time." Kit fumbled for a handkerchief. "I uh-understand. I'd n-never really understood how b-bad it was till now, W-Windy. . . ."

"Here." Turning off the digicorder, he brought her his.

She dried her eyes and blew her nose. "Don't say anything else, Windy. Okay? This is r-really pretty, even if it's n-not real. Let's just walk along and enjoy it for a while."

They did, strolling down into a miniature valley and up again toward a spruce fieldstone cottage. The low gravity made walking very pleasant, reminding March that in Heaven a man could run and run and never tire. He had read that somewhere, although he could not remember where. As they stepped across a tinkling rill bordered with white and blue wildflowers, he began to whistle softly.

A handsome man of fifty or so was planting shrubs in front of the cottage. Kit asked him whether the path would lead them to the gate, and March added, "Gate Four. We're supposed to meet our friends there."

"I'm Hap Harper." Hap smiled, wiping his hands on the legs of his spotless overalls. "I won't ask you to shake—I'd get you dirty. But that's who I am. Used to work in a bank in Saginaw."

March and Kit introduced themselves.

"Well, this little road you're on won't take you to Gate Four if you follow it straight. You need to follow it up to the next crossroad, then turn left. Follow that one, and you'll come to a footbridge over a lake. Pretty soon after that, it'll fork. Take the left fork, and you'll be there before long. Like to step inside for some tea?"

Kit said, "We're in kind of a hurry."

March nodded. "We'll have to go soon, but I'd enjoy that tea. If it's not too much trouble."

"No trouble at all!"

They were ushered into a spotless home, somewhat larger than they might have guessed from its outward appearance, through living room and dining room and into a cheerful kitchen where rows of polished copper pans reflected onions and sausages dangling from the rafters.

"Mr. Wildspring's an independent digivid producer," Hap told a smiling, white-haired woman. "He and Ms. Carlsen here are shooting a documentary on this place."

"I'd love to see it," the woman said. She wiped her hand with a dishtowel and offered it to Kit. "You call me Ida, Ms. Carlsen. Didn't you used to do *Saturday Toy Shop*?"

Kit smiled. "It's Kit, Ida. Yes, I did. Three live-long seasons playing with puppies and talking to puppets. I'd a lot rather have talked to the puppies."

March said, "I noticed a vid in your living room, Ida. I'm March, by the way. I know it's an unusual name, but I was born in March and I'm afraid my parents found March Wild-spring amusing."

Ida smiled. "I could tell you something about Hap's name. Maybe I will, later. Were you wondering whether we still watch?"

March nodded.

"Yes, we do. Not much, but sometimes."

"I can't show you our documentary as it will be shown on the net," March told her. "It doesn't exist yet. But I have a disk here that will show some of the images I took. It would be a pleasure to show you a few."

Hap said, "I'd like to see them."

"There are a couple things I ought to say first," March told him. "I suppose it will take five minutes or so."

Ida smiled again. "That's good. It will give me time to make tea. Tea must steep, you know."

"You've heard it said that somebody sees the world through rose-colored glasses," March began. "That can be true in the literal sense, of course. Glasses with a pink tint make just about everyone look prettier and healthier. I won't talk about the tricks photographers and cameramen use, or the things that can be done to digital images on a computer. I won't except to remind you of them, as I just did."

Kit said, "Is this smart, Windy? I'm not trying to be smart myself. I don't know and I want to."

March shrugged. "Love can do something like that, too. Self-love does it better than almost anything. I've been walking down the street and seen a big angry-looking guy with a beat-up face, and thought *he looks like trouble*. Two more steps, and I realized I was seeing my reflection in a shop window. When I look into a mirror, knowing it's a mirror, I don't look like that. Not to me, I don't."

Ida said, "Love lets us see the good in a person, the wonderful goodness that we pass over every day."

"That's true, and I can give you an interesting instance of it. I love Kit here, and I think she's beautiful. Absolutely beautiful, and I've told her that over and over. When I got here, everybody looked very, very good. You'll have noticed that yourself."

Hap and Ida nodded.

"When I saw Kit, she looked absolutely beautiful—but so did a woman named Sue, and some other women I'd seen. So I wondered about that. I wondered about her clothes, too, because they hadn't changed either. Kit looks great in everything she wears, and she looked great in these—in certain piece of underwear I saw, in the clothes she's wearing now, in everything. They looked good, too. Very good, but no different. They're a little wrinkled now, but I doubt that you've noticed it."

Hap said, "I certainly haven't."

"Naturally I wondered about that. Kit told me once that every woman has a figure flaw. Maybe more than one, but there's always at least one. They have character flaws, too, though she didn't say that. Kit's too generous and too trusting, for example. I love her for it, but it's a flaw and I know it."

Ida looked at March over the tops of glasses that she no longer had. "Are you saying men don't?"

He shook his head. "Men are the same. We're worse, if anything. You won't have noticed, but I'm as ugly as sin. I've got a lot of character flaws, too. One is that I think too much. Things get into my head and bug me, and I can't stop. I thought about how Kit looked here a whole lot last night and finally I got it."

Kit said, "Let's hear it, Windy."

"It's pretty simple, really. Whatever it is they've got here that tweaks your brain to make things look better couldn't tweak mine where Kit was concerned. It couldn't because it had been tweaked already, by love."

Ida smiled. "Good for you."

"Thanks. That got me to thinking how Kit looked in the digivid I'd shot. She looked just great, but she was the only one who did."

Kit said, "I've been wondering about that, too, Windy. Why doesn't it work when we see vid?"

March rubbed his jaw. "I think I've got that one. The vid

I'd shot looked terrific. The framing was great, the colors were all there and all vibrant, and the lighting couldn't have been better. I've shot lots of vid and think I can do it just about as well as most cameramen, but that was the best ever. See what I'm saying?"

"The vid itself looked good, but the things in there—except for me."

"Bingo." March switched off his digicorder and removed the disk. "That was the preliminary. It may have taken a little longer than five minutes. If so, I apologize. I'll play some of this now."

Swaying a bit because the digicorder had been carried on a man's shoulder, a barren hill of earth and stones appeared before the vid. A shed stood at the top, a crazy affair of leaning metal props and naked particle-board. Before it, a skeletal man in rags labored with a piece of rusted steel, digging holes for shrubs whose burlap wrappings had burst, shrubs that were clearly dying or dead. Kit's voice, and March's, spoke to this starved and tattered figure. He rose with a grin that revealed stained and rotting teeth, and wiped his filthy hands on his muddy thighs. "I'm Hap Harper."

"You ruined their paradise," Kit told March when the cottage was no longer in view.

"You saw how they really looked."

"Yeah. Yeah, I did."

"How long until they die, if they stay here and keep on living the way they've been doing it?"

"A year, maybe. The tea she was making for us. . . ."

"Was stagnant water polluted with human wastes. Sewage."

"She didn't see it that way."

"Neither did we," March said, "but that's what it was."

"Wouldn't they die? There ought to be a lot of dead people around here. Does somebody pick them up?"

"How would I know?" He rubbed his jaw. "I've seen people sleeping on the ground."

"I've seen some of those, too," Kit said a few seconds later.

"I never tried to wake any of them up."

The girl at Gate Number Four was called Nita. She looked younger than "Penny" had, and March suspected that she was really younger still.

"We have to go out and get some things." Kit had found her locker and pulled out her transparent suit. "I imagine we'll be back pretty soon."

Nita looked doubtful. "Nobody said anything about people leaving."

Kit smiled. "Because there's nothing to say, really. We get our suits and go into your airlock. That's all. You can wave good-bye if you feel like it. That would be nice."

"I'll have to work it. There aren't any controls on the inside. No handles or anything like that. It's why somebody has to be on the gate to let them in."

Kit looked puzzled. "That's a funny airlock."

"Keeps out the undesirables," March muttered. He had returned to the arch by which they had entered, and was scanning the sun-drenched landscape. "I know it rains in here at night. Does it ever thunder?"

Nita shook her head. "I don't think so."

Kit looked at him quizzically.

"I thought I heard thunder, that's all." He shut the worn orange suit. "I'd suit up if I were you. Put on your helmet."

"It won't rain where we are," Nita told them.

"It's people." Kit had cocked her head to listen. "A crowd. People yelling."

"I'd suit up, if I were you."

"Sure." She moved a doll and sat down to pull the transparent suit over her legs. "They sound mad."

"Get your helmet on," March told her. "We'd better go."

"We told Jim we'd wait."

"To hell with Jim."

Two figures—one dark, the other scarlet against the bright green grass—topped the nearest of the low hills. They were running, bounding with long, rather ineffective strides. As March watched, the dark figure stopped to look back at the scarlet one. There was a distant shout—of what, he could not be sure.

He switched on his digicorder. Someone far away was

beating a drum—a drum bigger than the biggest he had ever heard.

A dull, dead-sounding drum that could be beaten only by a giant.

"Windy . . . ?"

"Get into the airlock quick." He spoke to Kit without looking at her.

"That's trouble, isn't it?"

"Get in there."

The scarlet figure had fallen, and the dark one was helping it—her—up. March's fingers fumbled with the carabiner that fastened his flashlight to his utility belt.

The drum beat louder as the mob crested the hill.

And the dark figure turned to face it. The flashes were invisible, as was the powder smoke. The sounds of the shots reached them only weakly, scattered among drumbeats: six, seven, eight. . . . March found he was counting them, although he had never chosen to do so.

Eleven, twelve. . . . Some semi-automatics held fifteen rounds. Some even more.

Beside him Kit said, "That's Jim, isn't it? My God! Look how scared Robin is."

"Get in the airlock!" March shouted.

Then he was running, although he had not consciously chosen to do that, either. The mob had halted, dismayed by its dead.

Fourteen, fifteen. . . .

Robin had fallen and was scrambling to her feet as he reached her. Snatching her wrist, he jerked her up, threw her over his shoulder, and ran for all he was worth.

Her shriek might have stopped him. Kit's certainly did. He whirled—and beheld the impossible.

A giant the color of Ida's copper pots was cresting the hill. The men and women in the mob were as children in comparison, and small children at that. They tried to part before it and failed. Eight or ten died beneath its feet.

March fled and did not stop running until he and Robin had mounted to the false room that was the airlock. Outside, Kit shouted, "That girl! Nita! Windy, she's gone!"

"I'll get it!" Robin darted away. For a half second that was to prove much too long March stood motionless, gasping for breath. When he moved again, the room wall that was in fact the hatch of the airlock was slamming shut and Kit was dashing toward him. He saw it catch her above the knees, saw her fall, and watched her cut in two.

Space seemed warm and welcoming when he jetted away from Number Nineteen; the Sun's tiny candle, five hundred million miles away, spoke of Earth and home.

He matched the speed of his hopper to that of the Asteroid Belt before he stopped hopping. It might be—indeed, it seemed likely—that he would be pursued. If so, the thronging asteroids would make it impossible to locate his hopper by radar. He would be far safer than in all the empty immensity between the Belt and Mars or that between Mars and Earth.

Only then did he stop to review the disk from his digicorder.

"Remember, O most gracious Virgin Mary, that never was it known that anyone who fled to your protection, implored your help, or sought your intercession was left unaided. Inspired with this—Inspired with this. . . ."

It was coming back, no question about it. "Seek and you will find, knock and it will be opened for you."

Something like that.

He rubbed his jaw. When Bad Bill turned him down, as Bad Bill presumably would, he would be free to sell to Pubnet or Vidnet—but only if they paid the price UDN had refused or more. That argued for offering it to Bad Bill cheaply, say two million or less.

On the other hand, Bad Bill was entirely capable of buying it and sitting on it if the price were low enough. There would be some threshold at which Bad Bill would not dare, at which it would eat up too much of his budget. The trick would be to offer it just above that.

When he finished it at last—an Ethermail to William W. Williams, VP Programming, UDN, with a brief description of what he had—the price he put on it was five million. He might, he just might, get that much from Pubnet or one of the others. That much or more. He would start with them at six million five.

He pushed the Send button, muttered, "Holy Mother help me," and began to prepare his lunch. Number Nineteen's people might have Kit's hopper by now, with its multitude of cookbooks and obscure spices. Or if not by now, then soon. What would they do with them?

Kit had not gone into the airlock, this although he had told her to repeatedly. Her reason for disobeying was plain: she had wanted to be with him, to share his risks.

"A woman should not share a man's risks," he muttered as he shut the door of his microwave. "It's not what women are for."

Try telling that to a woman.

Jesus had refused to let his mother in to see him. He had known the fate awaiting him, and had known the risk the apostles ran. He had wanted to spare his mother that risk. Or (March thought as the microwave beeped) to spare her as much of it as he could.

When he had finished eating, he found that he had Ethermail.

"Mr. Wildspring. Please icom me asap. Calling from space is expensive, so call collect: USA 1105 8129-4092-6 X7798. Kim Granby, Special Assistant, Programming." White print on a blue background confirmed that the message was from United Digital Network.

March jotted down the number and called it. Collect.

Kim Granby looked about twenty-five, although he knew she was almost certainly at least ten years older. Sleek black hair framed a smooth oval face. "Thank God!" she said. "I was afraid you wouldn't call till tomorrow. I've looked at your material—some of it, not all of it yet. It's good. It's very, very good."

It sounded like a build-up to a letdown. UDN was going to refuse, and he could offer his work elsewhere. An expert poker player, he repressed all traces of a smile. "It's rough, of course. A few of the voiceovers are Kit Carlsen's, and I think you'll want to keep them. The rest are mine. All of those will have to be redone, and you'll want to edit everything. I think I said that."

"You did." Kim Granby gave him a guarded smile. "I haven't watched all of it yet—less than half in fact. But I told the vice president what it was and what I'd seen, and we want to buy it."

March cursed inwardly.

"Before we make an offer, I have some questions. You weren't alone in this. Kit Carlsen did voiceovers for you, and she was in some of the footage I saw. Your Ethermail sounded as if you own all rights. Do you?"

He nodded. "May I explain?"

"Please do."

"A lot of it was shot solo by me. At the end we had a four-person crew. Kit, Jim and Robin Redd, and me. All of us had worked for UDN at one time or another. Did you know Kit or Robin? Or Jim?"

"I've met Ms. Carlsen once or twice." The guarded smile came again. "Once at least. She's no longer with you?"

"She's dead."

Kim Ganby's mouth opened, and closed again.

"Kit's dead, Jim's dead, and Robin's probably dead, too. I don't know for sure about Robin, but you'll see Jim. . . ."

"See him die?"

"Yes. I didn't see it myself. I had the digicorder, but I wasn't watching the viewfinder just then. It's on the disk though. In the digital copy I sent you. He was squashed. Crushed sounds better, I suppose. Kit's dead, too."

There was a long pause. At last Kim Granby said, "I liked her."

March nodded. "So did I."

"You said this man Jim's death was in the footage. Didn't you? Didn't I hear that?"

March nodded again.

"What about Ms. Carlsen?"

"It's there. She was cut in two."

Another pause. "You're joking."

March shook his head. "I wish I was."

"And it's there, in . . . I—I'm going to have to talk to Mr. Inglis. I'll call you right back."

"Wait up!" March raised his hand. "What's this about Mr. Inglis? I thought I was dealing with Bill Williams. Is this Phil Inglis?"

"Correct. Mr. Williams has left the net to pursue other interests." Kim Granby's beautiful face held no expression. "Mr. Inglis is Vice President for Programming now."

"I know him."

"I know you do, Mr. Wildspring. He called you an old friend. I have to speak with him just the same."

"All right. Will you call me back?"

Abruptly, the beautiful face softened. "Pubnet's at work on a special rather like 'Vaults in the Void,' Mister—may I call you March?"

He wanted to rub his jaw, but did not. "Certainly, Ms. Granby." One second served to collect his thoughts, though he wished he had longer. "I'd like it."

"Call me Kim, please. Everyone does. And I'll call you back. You can count on that, March. It won't be long. Good-bye for now."

Kit was dead. It was just beginning to sink in. He turned away from the blank screen. He had thought that he had come to terms with that. He had not. His hands were shaking. He thrust them angrily into his pockets, knowing that nothing he could do would make them stop.

Kit was dead and Jim was dead and Sue was probably dead by now; Earth was menaced by something a dead man had turned loose on mankind; but all those were overshadowed by the single, salient, inescapable fact of Kit's death.

If there had been whiskey on his hopper, he would have poured himself a drink—would have been drunk, in all probability, by the time UDN called him back. Not for the first time, he was glad there was none.

Kit was dead.

Her soul was with God, somewhere out there in space. Someday his soul might meet hers there. They would embrace, and laugh at remembered things, and link arms forever.

Someday. . . .

"Remember, O most gracious Virgin. . . ."

"I should preface this," Kim Granby said, "by telling you that Pubnet's at work on something very similar. Have I said so already? Mr. Inglis said I was to tell you. He felt, in fairness, that you should know."

March nodded. "Please tell him how much I appreciate it."

"It's nothing like as sensational as yours," Kim Granby continued. "He didn't say to tell you that. I'm doing it on my own, but I feel he would approve."

"It's good of you."

She smiled. "I'll be good some more. I'll tell you that Mr. Inglis and I have watched everything you sent us now. We watched it together, in fact. We recorded notes as we watch. Both of us did that."

"I understand."

"I've returned with an offer. As I said." She stopped to draw breath, something she did very attractively. "When I realized what you had, March, I knew I had to go back to Mr. Inglis. What if I had given you his offer, and you had refused it? I explained to him, and he indicated that I had acted correctly. There is a new offer now. If you'd like time to think it over, please let me know."

"I will." March nodded. "But I'll have to hear it first."

"Of course. Yes, indeed. Certainly." Her sudden smile would have melted a heart far harder than his. "You're a gentleman. I've talked with some of the other women here. At—we go for coffee. Together. You know."

Wondering what was coming, he nodded again.

"They said you were rough, tough and blunt. Then Debbie Knowles said the three musketeers would've welcomed you with open arms, and all the rest agreed. So I just wanted to say—this is from me, personally, not from the net. I wanted to say that whether or not you accept our offer, I hope we can be friends. Is that all right?"

"Yes," March said, "absolutely."

"I live here in New York . . . ?"

"So do I," March said.

"That's good. That's very good. This is official now. This is what Mr. Inglis said. We'll pay. . . ."

March had raised his hand. "You're being very honest with me, Kim, and I appreciate it. I want to be honest with you, too. I told you a lie when we spoke earlier. I didn't mean to, but I did. May I set the record straight?"

Kim Granby's nod was scarcely one tenth of an inch, but it was there.

"I said that I liked Kit. The truth is that I loved her. I loved Kit very much. You're bound to hear it soon from somebody, so I want to tell you. I loved her, and I watched her die. I don't want you to think, later, that I've been hiding it from you."

"I would never think that, March. Never!" Another deep breath. "You get angry and upset when a woman cries, don't you?"

"Pretty often, yes."

"Then let me off quick, because I think I may cry. We're making two offers. The first is flat, without any conditions. Eight million five hundred thousand. The second is contingent on your coming back to work for UDN. You'd be a senior producer, pay half a mil. Residuals and bonuses. You know. Do that, and the offer's ten mil. Do you want more time?"

He shook his head. "Tell Phil I'll take the second."

Kit, he understood. He thought he understood Jim, too. Jim had loved Sue—no, had loved Robin. Jim had loved Robin and Jim and been a bastard in certain ways. All men were bastards in certain ways, so why not Jim? Jim had understood Robin better than he, March, ever had.

Better than he, March, ever would.

He remembered the small dark figure. The pop-pop-pop of the distant shots. Jim had stood his ground, shooting, until he died, hoping to gain time for Robin.

But what about Robin? What about the woman he had tried so hard to forget? March rubbed his jaw. It seemed inadequate, so he rubbed it again.

Had Robin wanted to die with Jim?

Or had she been willing to sacrifice herself to save his—March's—life?

Or had she simply wanted to remain in Number Nineteen? She had never seen what the digicorder showed, after all. He went to the window and stared out at the tiny blue spark that was home, so remote and so easy to reach, so blessed with grace and so cursed with evil. Had Robin been willing to sacrifice herself? For him?

There was only one way to find out, and that was go back and find her—assuming she was still alive.

And ask.

GONE TO JUPITER
*The Memories and Menace of
Memorials in Space*

Produced and Directed by March Wildspring

Starring Kit Carlsen

With voiceovers by Kit Carlsen,
Tabbi Merce, and Vincent Palma

Edited by March Wildspring
and Robin Redd Wildspring

Dedicated to Kit Carlsen
and James Frankie Redd,
Who Perished that You Might Watch It

A Philip J. Inglis Presentation

Plotters and Shooters

KAGE BAKER

Kage Baker (www.kagebaker.com) lives in Pismo Beach, California. Her most recent books are a collection of her Company stories, Gods and Pawns *(2007), and the Company novel,* The Sons of Heaven *(2007). Her pirate novel,* Or Else My Lady Keeps the Key, *is out in 2008, and also a new fantasy novel,* The House of the Stag. *She is a compelling storyteller. In a 2005 interview she described herself as follows: "I'm a fat, middle-aged, red-faced spinster aunt who lives with a demanding parrot. I have, in my time, been a character actress, bartender, director, mural painter, clerical worker, and educational program assistant. I have a Jolly Roger hanging over my bed and require sea air in order to breathe. I have been effectively blind in my right eye since the age of two, but have seen a lot with the left one."*

"Plotters and Shooters," which appeared in Lou Anders' anthology Fast Forward 1, *is a sort of cowboy-biker-gamer story in space around Mars:* Lord of the Flies *meets* Enders Game. *Cory Doctorow describes its plot as follows: "a dysfunctional space-station's cherished defense corps is upset by a tightly wound otaku." Game designers as plotters, and gamers as asteroid shooters, it's an ugly social group, redeemed by humor and wit. Ever think about how alike pirates and bikers can be?*

I was flackeying for Lord Deathlok and Dr. Smash when the shuttle brought the new guy.

I hate Lord Deathlok. I hate Dr. Smash too, but I'd like to see Lord Deathlok get a missile fired up his ass, from his own cannon. Not that it's really a cannon. And I couldn't shoot him, anyhow, because I'm only a Plotter. But it's the thought that counts, you know?

Anyway I looked up when the beeps and the flashing lights started, and Lord Deathlok took hold of my little French maid's apron and yanked it so hard I had to bend over fast, so I almost dropped the tray with his drink.

"Pay attention, maggot-boy," said Lord Deathlok. "It's only a shuttle docking. No reason you should be distracted from your duties."

"I know what's wrong," said Dr. Smash, lounging back against the bar. "He hears the mating call of his kind. They must have sent up another Plotter."

"Oh, yeah." Lord Deathlok grinned at me. "Your fat-ass girlfriend went crying home to his mum and dad, didn't he?"

Oh, man, how I hated him. He was talking about Kev, who'd only gone Down Home again because he'd almost died in an asthma attack. Kev had been a good Plotter, one of the best. I just glared at Deathlok, which was a mistake, because he smiled and put his boot on my foot and stood up.

"I don't think I heard your answer, Fifi," he said, and I was in all this unbelievable psychological pain, see, because even with the lower gravity he could still manage to get the leverage just right if he wanted to bear down. They tell us we don't have to worry about getting brittle bones up here because they make us do weight-training, but how would we know if they were lying? I could almost hear my metatarsals snapping like dry twigs.

"Yes, my Lord Deathlok," I said.

"What?" He leaned forward.

"My lord yes my Lord Deathlok!"

"That's better." He sat down.

So okay, you're probably thinking I'm a coward. I'm not. It isn't that Lord Deathlok is even a big guy. He isn't, actually, he's sort of skinny and he has these big yellow buck teeth that make him look like a demon jackrabbit. And Dr. Smash has breasts and a body odor that makes sharing an airlock with him a fatal mistake. But they're *Shooters,* you know? And they all dress like they're space warriors or something, with the jackets and the boots and the scary hair styles. Shracking fascists.

So I put down his Dis Pepsy and backed away from him, and that was when the announcement came over the speakers:

"Eugene Clifford, please report to Mr. Kurtz's office."

Talk about saved by the bell. As the message repeated, Lord Deathlok smirked.

"Sounds like Dean Kurtz is lonesome for one of his little buttboys. You have our permission to go, Fifi."

"My lord thank you my Lord Deathlok," I muttered, and tore off the apron and ran for the companionway.

Mr. Kurtz isn't a dean; I don't know why the Shooters call him that. He's the Station Manager. He runs the place for Areco and does our performance reviews and signs our bonus vouchers, and you'd think the Shooters would treat him with a little more respect, but they don't because they're *Shooters,* and that says it all. Mostly he sits in his office and looks disappointed. I don't blame him.

He looked up from his novel as I put my head around the door.

"You wanted to see me, Mr. Kurtz?"

He nodded. "New arrival on the shuttle. Kevin Nederlander's replacement. Would you bring him up, please?"

"Yes, sir!" I said, and hurried off to the shuttle lounge.

The new guy was sitting there in the lounge, with his duffel in the chair beside his. He was short and square and his haircut made his head look like it came to a point. Maybe it's genetic; Plotters can't seem to get good haircuts, ever.

"Welcome to the Gun Platform, newbie," I said. "I'm your Orientation Officer." Which I sort of am.

"Oh, good," he said, getting to his feet, but he couldn't seem to take his eyes off the viewscreen. I waited for him to ask if that was really Mars down there, or gush about how he couldn't believe he was actually on an alien world or at least in orbit above one. That's usually what they do, see. But he didn't. He just shouldered his duffel and tore his gaze away at last.

"Charles Tead. Glad to be here," he said.

Heh! That'll change, I thought. "You've got some righteous shoes to fill, newbie. Think you're up to it?"

He just said that he was, not like he was bragging or anything, and I thought *This one's going to get his corners broken off really soon.*

So I took him to the Forecastle and showed him Kev's old bunk, looking all empty and sad with the drillholes where Kev's holoposters used to be mounted. He put his duffel into Kev's old locker and looked around, and then he asked who did our laundry. I coughed a little and explained about it being sent down to the planet to be dry-cleaned. I didn't tell him, not then, about our having to collect the Shooters' dirty socks and stuff for them.

And I took him to the Bridge where B Shift was on duty and introduced him to the boys. Roscoe and Norman were wearing their Jedi robes, which I wish they wouldn't because it makes us look hopeless. Vinder was in a snit because Bradley had knocked one of his action figures behind the console, and apparently it was one of the really valuable ones, and Myron's the only person skinny enough to get his arm back there to fish it out, but he's on C Shift and wouldn't come on duty until seventeen-hundred hours.

I guess that was where it started, B Shift making such a bad first impression.

But I tried to bring back some sense of importance by showing him the charting display, with the spread of the asteroid belt all in blue and gold, like a stained-glass window in an old-time church must have been, only everything moving.

"This is your own personal slice of the sky," I said, waving at Q34-54. "Big Kev knew every one of these babies. Tracked every little wobble, every deviation over three years. Plotted trajectories for thirty-seven successful shots. It was like he had a sixth sense! He even called three Intruders before they came in range. He was the Bonus Master, old Kev. You'll have to work pretty damn hard to be half as good as he was."

"But it ought to be easy," said Charles. "Doesn't the mapping software do most of it?"

"Well, like, I mean, sure, but you'll have to *coordinate* everything, you know? In your head? Machines can't do it all," I protested. And Vinder chose that second to yell from behind us, "Don't take the Flying Dynamo's cape off, you'll break him!" Which totally blew the mood I was trying to get. So I ignored him and continued:

"We've been called up from Earth for a job only we can do. It's a high and lonely destiny, up here among the cold stars! Mundane people couldn't stick it out. That's why Areco went looking for guys like us. We're free of entanglements, right? We came from our parents' basements and garages to a place where our powers were *needed*. Software can map those rocks out there, okay; it can track them, maybe. But only a human can—can—smell them coming in before they're there, okay?"

"You mean like precognition?" Charles stared at me.

"Not exactly," I said, even though Myron claims he's got psychic abilities, but he never seems to be able to predict when the Shooters are going to go on a rampage on our turf.

"I'm talking about gut feelings. Hunches. Instinct! That's the word I was looking for. Human instinct. We outguess the software seventy percent of the time on projected incoming. Not bad, huh?"

"I guess so," he said.

I spent the rest of the shift showing him his console and setting up his passwords and customizations and stuff. He didn't ask many questions, just put on the goggles and focused, and you could almost see him wandering around among the asteroids in Q34-54 and getting to know them. I was starting to get a good feeling about him, because that was just the way Kev used to plot, and then he said:

"How do we target them?"

Vinder was so shocked he dropped the Blue Judge. Roscoe turned, took off his goggles to stare at me, and said:

"*We* don't target. Cripes, haven't you told him?"

"Told me what?" Charles turned his goggled face toward the sound of Roscoe's voice.

So then I had to tell him about the Shooters, and how he couldn't go into the bar when Shooters were in there except when he was flackeying for one of them, and what they'd do to him if he did, and how he had to stay out of the Pit of Hell where they bunked except when he was flackeying for them, and he was never under any circumstances to go into the War Room at all.

I was explaining about the flackeying rotation when he said:

"This is stupid!"

"It's sheer evil," said Roscoe. "But there's nothing we can do about it. They're Shooters. You can't fight them. You don't want to know what happens if you try."

"This wasn't in my contract," said Charles.

"You can go complain to Kurtz, if you want," said Bradley. "It's no damn use. *He* can't control them. They're Shooters. Nobody else can do what they do."

"I'll bet I could," said Charles, and everybody just sniffed at him, because, you know, who's got reflexes like a Shooter? They're the best at what they do.

"You got assigned to us because you tested out as a Plotter," I told Charles. "That's just the way things are. You're the best at your job; the pay's good; in five years you'll be out of here. You just have to learn to live with the crap. We all did."

He looked like a smart guy and I thought he wouldn't need to be told twice. I was wrong.

We heard the march of booted feet coming along the corridor. Vinder leaped up and grabbed all his action figures, shoving them into a storage pod. Norman began to hyperventilate; Bradley ran for the toilet. I just stayed where I was and lowered my eyes. It's never a good idea to look them in the face.

Boom! The portal jerked open and in they came, Lord Deathlok and the Shark and Iron Beast. They were carrying Piki-tiki. I blanched.

Piki-tiki was this sort of dummy they'd made out of a blanket and a mask. And a few other things. Lord Deathlok grinned around and spotted Charles.

"Piki-tiki returns to his harem," he shouted. "What's this? Piki-tiki sees a new and beautiful bride! Piki-tiki must welcome her to his realm!"

Giggling, they advanced on Charles and launched the dummy. It fell over him, and before he could throw it off they'd jumped him and hoisted him between them. He was fighting hard, but they just laughed; that is, until he got one arm free and punched the Shark in the face. The Shark grabbed his nose and began to swear, but Lord Deathlok and Iron Beast gloated.

"Whoa! The blushing bride needs to learn her manners. Piki-tiki's going to take her off to his honeymoon suite and see that she learns them well!"

Ouch. They dragged him away. At least it wasn't the worst they might have done to him; they were only going to cram him in one of the lockers, probably one that had had some sweaty socks left in the bottom, and stuff Piki-tiki in there on top of him. Then they'd lock him in and leave him there. How did I know? They'd done it to me, on my first day.

If you're sensible, like me, you just shrug it off and concentrate on your job. Charles wouldn't let it go, though. He kept asking questions.

Like, how come the Shooters were paid better than we were, even though they spent most of their time playing simulations and Plotters did all the actual work of tracking asteroids and calculating when they'd strike? How come Mr. Kurtz had given up on disciplinary action for them, even after they'd rigged his holoset to come on unexpectedly and project a CGI of him having sex with an alligator, or all the other little ways in which they made his life a living hell? How come none of us ever stood up to them?

And it was no good explaining how they didn't respond to reason, and they didn't respond to being called immature and crude and disgusting, because they just loved being told how awful they were.

The other thing he asked about was why there weren't any women up here, and that was too humiliating to go into, so I just said tests had shown that men were better suited for life on a Gun Platform.

He should have been happy that he was a *good* Plotter, because he really was. He mastered Q34-54 in a week. One shift we were there on the Bridge and Myron and I were talking about the worst ever episode of *Schrödinger's Rock*, which was the one that had Lallal's evil twin showing up after being killed off in the second season, and Anil was unwrapping the underwear his mother had sent him for his thirty-first birthday, when suddenly Charles said: "Eugene, you should probably check Q6-17; I'm calculating an Intruder showing up in about Q-14."

"How'd you know?" I said in surprise, slipping my goggles on. But he was right; there was an Intruder, tumbling end over end in a halo of fire and snow, way above the plane of the ecliptic but square in Q-14.

"Don't you extend your projections beyond the planet's ecliptic?" said Charles.

Myron and I looked at each other. We never projected out that far; what was the point? There was always time to spot an Intruder before it came in range.

"You don't have to work *that* hard, dude," I said. "Fifty degrees above and below is all we have to bother with. The scanning programs catch the rest." But I sent out the alert and we could hear the Shooters cheering, even though the War Room was clear at the other end of the Platform. As far out as the Intruder was, the Shark was able to send out a missile. We didn't see the hit—there wouldn't be one for two weeks at least, and I'd have to keep monitoring the Intruder and now the missile too, just to be sure the trajectories remained matched up—but the Shooters began to stamp and roar the Bonus Song.

Myron sniffed.

"Typical," he said. "We do all the work, they push one bloody button, and *they're* the heroes."

"You know, it doesn't have to be this way," said Charles.

"It's not like we can go on strike," said Anil sullenly. "We're independent contractors. There's a penalty for quitting."

"You don't have to quit," said Charles. "You can show Areco you can do even more. We can be Plotters *and* Shooters."

Anil and Myron looked horrified. You'd have thought he'd suggested we all turn homo or something. I was shocked myself. I had to explain about tests proving that things functioned most smoothly when every man kept to his assigned task.

"Don't Areco think we can multitask?" he asked me. "They're a corporation like any other, aren't they? They must want to save money. All we have to do is show them we can do both jobs. The Shooters get a nice redundancy package; we get the Gun Platform all to ourselves. Life is good."

"Only one problem with your little plan, Mr. Genius," said Myron. "I can't shoot. I don't have the reflexes a Shooter does. That's why I'm a Plotter."

"But you could learn to shoot," said Charles.

"I'll repeat this slowly so you get it," said Myron, exasperated. "*I don't have the reflexes.* And neither do you. How many times have we been tested, our whole lives? Aptitude tests, allergy tests, brain scans, DNA mapping? Areco knows exactly what we are and what we can and can't do. I'm a Plotter. You're just fooling yourself if you think you aren't."

Charles didn't say anything in reply. He just looked at each of us in turn, pretty disgusted I guess, and then he turned back to his console and focused on his work.

That wasn't the end of it, though. When he was off his shift, instead of hanging out in the Cockpit, did he join in the discussions of graphic novels or what was hot on holo that week? Not Charles. He'd retire to a corner in the Forecastle with a buke and he'd game. And not just any game: targeting simulations. You never saw a guy with such icy focus. Sometimes he'd tinker with a couple of projects he'd ordered. I assumed they were models.

It was like the rest of us weren't even there. We had to respect him as a Plotter; for one thing, he turned out to have an uncanny knack for spotting Intruders, days before any of the rest of us detected them, and he was brilliant at predicting their trajectories too. But there was something distant about the guy that kept him from fitting in. Myron and Anil had dismissed him as a crank anyway, and a couple of the guys on B shift actively disliked him, after he spouted off to them the way he did to us. They were sure he was going to do something, sooner or later, that would only end up making it worse for all of us.

They were right, too.

When Weldon's turn in the rota ended, he brought Charles the French maid's apron and tossed it on his bunk.

"Your turn to wear the damn thing," he said. "They'll expect you in the bar at fourteen hundred hours. Good luck."

Charles just grunted, never even looking up from the screen of his buke.

Fourteen hundred hours came and he was still sitting there, coolly gaming.

"Hey!" said Anil. "You're supposed to go flackey!"

"I'm not going," said Charles.

"Don't be stupid!" I said. "If the rest of us have to do it, you do too."

"Why? Terrible repercussions if I don't?" Charles set aside his buke and looked at us.

"Yes!" said Myron. Preston from A Shift came running in right then, looking pale.

"Who's supposed to be flackeying? There's nobody out there, and Lord Deathlok wants to know why!"

"See?" said Myron.

"You'll get all of us in trouble, you fool! Give me the apron, I'll go!" said Anil. But Charles took the apron and tore it in half.

There was this horrified silence, which filled up with the sound of Shooters thundering along the corridor. We heard Lord Deathlok and Painmaster yelling as they came.

"Flackey! Oh, flackey! Where are you?"

And then they were in the room and it was too late to run, too late to hide. Painmaster's roach crest almost touched the ceiling panels. Lord Deathlok's yellow grin was so wide he didn't look human.

"Hi there, buttholes," said Painmaster. "If you girls aren't too busy making out, one of you is supposed to be flackeying for us."

"It was my turn," said Charles. He wadded up the apron and threw it at them. "How about you wait on yourself from now on?"

"This wasn't our idea!" said Myron.

"We tried to make him report for duty!" said Anil.

"We'll remember that, when we're assigning penalties," said Lord Deathlok. "Maybe we'll let you keep your pants when we handcuff you upside down in the toilet. Little Newbie, though . . ." He turned to Charles. "What about a nice game of Walk the Dog? Painmaster, got a leash anywhere on you?"

"The Painmaster always has a leash for a bad dog," said Painmaster, pulling one out. He started toward Charles, and that's when it got crazy.

Charles jumped out of his bunk and I thought, *No, you idiot, don't try to run!* But he didn't. He grabbed Painmaster's extended hand and pulled him close, and brought his arm up like he was going to hug him, only instead he made a kind of punching motion at Painmaster's neck. Painmaster screamed, wet himself and fell down. Charles kicked him in the crotch.

Another dead silence, which broke as soon as Painmaster

got enough breath in him for another scream. Everybody else in the room was staring at Charles, or I should say at his left wrist, because it was now obvious there was something strapped to it under his sleeve.

Lord Deathlok had actually taken a step backward. He looked from Painmaster to Charles, and then at whatever it was on Charles' wrist. He licked his lips.

"So, that's, what, some kind of taser?" he said. "Those are illegal, buddy."

Charles smiled. I realized then I'd never seen him smile before.

"It's illegal to buy one. I bought some components and made my own. What are you going to do? Report me to Kurtz?" he said.

"No; I'm just going to take it away from you, dumbass," said Lord Deathlok. He lunged at Charles, but all that happened was that Charles tased him too. He jerked backward and fell over a chair, clutching his tased hand.

"You're dead," he gasped. "You're really dead."

Charles walked over and kicked him in the crotch too.

"I challenge you to a duel," he said.

"What?" said Lord Deathlok, when he had enough breath after his scream.

"A duel. With simulations," said Charles. "I'll outshoot you. Right there in the War Room, with everybody there to witness. Thirteen hundred hours tomorrow."

"Fuck off," said Lord Deathlok. Charles leaned down and displayed the two little steel points of the taser.

"So you're scared to take me on? Chicken, is that it?" he said, and Myron and Anil obligingly started making cluck-cluck-cluck noises. "Eugene, why don't you go over to the Pit of Hell and tell the Shooters they need to come scrape up these guys?"

I wouldn't have done that for a chance to see the lost episodes of *Doctor Who,* but fortunately Lord Deathlok sat up, gasping.

"Okay," he said. "Duel. You lose, I get that taser and shove it up your ass."

"Sure," said Charles. "Whatever you want; but I won't lose. And none of us will ever flackey for you again. Got it?"

Lord Deathlok called him a lot of names, but the end of it was that he agreed to the terms, and we made Painmaster (who was crying and complaining that his heartbeat was irregular) witness. When they could walk they went stumbling back to the Pit of Hell, leaning on each other.

"You are out of your mind," I said, when they had gone. "You'll go to the War Room tomorrow and they'll be waiting for you with six bottles of club soda and a can of poster paint."

"Maybe," said Charles. "But they'll back off. Haven't you clowns figured it out yet? They're used to shooting at rocks. They have no clue what to do about something that fights back."

"They'll still win. You won't be able to tase them all, and once they get it off you, you're doomed."

"They won't get off me," said Charles, rolling up his sleeve and unstrapping the taser mounting from his arm. "I won't be wearing it. You will."

"Me?" I backed away.

"And there's another one in my locker. Which one of you wants it?"

"You've got *two*?"

"Me!" Anil jumped forward. "So we'll be, like, your bodyguards? Yes! Can you make more of these things?"

"I won't need to," said Charles. "Tomorrow's going to change everything."

I don't mind telling you, my knees were knocking as we marched across to the War Room next day. Everybody on B and C Shifts came along; strength in numbers, right? If we got creamed by the Shooters, at least some of us ought to make it out of there. And if Charles was insanely lucky, we all wanted to see.

It was embarrassing. Norman and Roscoe wore full Jedi kit, including their damn light sabers that were only holobeams anyway. Bradley was wearing a Happy Bat San playjacket.

Anil was wearing his lucky hat from *Mystic Antagonists: the Extravaganza.* We're all creative and unique, no question, but . . . maybe it isn't the best idea to dress that way when you're going to a duel with intimidating mindless jerks.

We got there, and they were waiting for us.

Our Bridge always reminded me of a temple or a shrine or something, with its beautiful display shining in the darkness; but the War Room was like the Cave of the Cyclops. There wasn't any wall display like we had. There were just the red lights of the targeting consoles, and way in the far end of the room somebody had stuck up a black light, which made the lurid holoposters of skulls and demons and vampires seem to writhe in the gloom.

The place stank of body odor, which the Shooters can't get rid of because they wear all that black bioprene gear, which doesn't breathe like the natural fabrics we wear. There was also a urinal reek; when a Shooter is gaming, he doesn't let a little thing like needing to pee drive him from his console.

All this was bad enough; imagine how I felt to see that the Shooters had made war clubs out of chlorilar water bottles stuck into handles of printer paper rolled tight. They stood there, glowering at us. I saw Lord Deathlok and the Shark and Professor Badass. Mephisto, the Conquistador, Iron Beast, Killer Ape, Uncle Hannibal . . . every hateful face I knew from months of humiliating flackey-work, except . . .

"Where's the Painmaster?" said Charles, looking around in an unconcerned kind of way.

"He had better things to do than watch you rectums lose," said Lord Deathlok.

"He had to be shipped down to the infirmary, because he was complaining of chest pains," said Mephisto. The others looked at him accusingly. Charles beamed.

"Too bad! Let's do this thing, gentlemen."

"We fixed up a special console, homo, just for you," said Lord Deathlok with an evil leer, waving at one. Charles looked at it and laughed.

"You have got to be kidding. I'll take *this* one over *here*, and you'll take the one next to it. We'll play side by side, so everybody can see. That's only fair, right?"

Their faces fell. But Anil and I crossed our arms, so the taser prongs showed, and the Shooters grumbled but backed down. They cleared away empty bottles and snack wrappers from the consoles. It felt good, watching them humbled for a change.

Charles settled himself at the console he'd chosen, and with a few quick commands on the buttonball pulled up the simulation menu.

"Is this all you've got?" he said. "Okay; I propose nine rounds. Three sets each of *Holodeath 2, Meteor Nightmare,* and *Incoming Annihilation.* Highest cumulative score wins."

"You got it, shithead," said Lord Deathlok. He took his seat.

So they called up *Holodeath 2,* and we all crowded around to watch, even though the awesome stench of the Shooters was enough to make your eyes water. The holo display lit up with a sinister green fog, and the enemy ships started coming at us. Charles got off three shots before Lord Deathlok managed one, and though one of his shots went wild, two inflicted enough damage on a Megacruiser to set it on fire. Lord Deathlok's shot nailed a patrol vessel in the forefront, and though it was a low-score target, he took it out with just that one shot. The score counters on both consoles gave them 1200 points.

Charles finished the burning cruiser with two more quick shots—it looked fantastic, glaring red through its ports until it just sort of imploded in this cylinder of glowing ash. But Lord Deathlok was picking off the little transport cutters methodically, because they only take about a shot each if you're accurate, which he was. Charles pulled ahead by hammering away at the big targets, and he never missed another shot, and so what happened was that the score counters showed them flashing along neck and neck for the longest time and then, *boom,* the last Star Destroyer blew and Charles was suddenly way ahead with twice Deathlok's score.

We were all yelling by this time, the Shooters with their

chimpanzee hooting and us with—well, we sort of sounded like apes too. The next set went up and here came the ships again, but this time they were firing back. Charles took three hits in succession, before he seemed to figure out how to raise his shields, and the Shooters started gloating and smacking their clubs together.

But he went on the offensive real fast, and did something I'd never thought of before, which was aiming for the ships' gunports and disabling them with one shot before hitting them with a barrage that finished them. I never even had time to look at what Deathlok was doing, but his guys stopped cheering suddenly and when the set ended, he didn't even have a third of the points Charles did.

The third set went amazingly fast, even with the difference that the gun positions weren't stationary and they had to maneuver around in the middle of the armada. Charles did stuff I would never have dared to do, recklessly swooping around and under the Megacruisers, *between* their gunports for cripe's sake, getting off round after round of shots so close it seemed impossible for him to pull clear before the ships blew, but somehow he did.

Lord Deathlok didn't seem to move much. He just sat in one position and pounded away at anything that came within range, and though he did manage to bag a Star Destroyer, he finished the set way behind Charles on points.

I would have just given up if I'd been Deathlok, but the Shooters were getting ugly, shouting all kinds of personal abuse at him, and I don't think he dared.

I had to run for the lavatory as *Incoming Annihilation* was starting, and of course I had to run all the way back to our end of the Gun Platform to our toilet because I sure wasn't going to use the Shooters', not with the way the War Room smelled. It was only when I was unfastening that I realized I was still wearing the taser, and that I'd done an incredibly stupid thing by leaving when I was one of Charles' bodyguards. So I finished fast and ran all the way back, and there was Mr. Kurtz strolling along the corridor.

"Hello there, Eugene," he said. "Something going on?"

"Just some gaming," I said. "I need to get back—"

"But you're on Shooter turf, aren't you?" Mr. Kurtz looked around. "Shouldn't you be going in the other direction?"

"Well—we're having this competition, you see, Mr. Kurtz," I said. "The new guy's gaming against Lord—I mean, against Peavey Crandall."

"Is he?" Mr. Kurtz began to smile. "I wondered how long Charles would put up with the Shooters. Well, well."

He said it in a funny kind of way, but I didn't have the time to wonder about it. I just excused myself and ran on, and was really relieved to see that the Shooters didn't seem to have noticed my absence. They were all packed tight around the consoles, and nobody was making a sound; all you could hear was the *peew-peew-peew* of the shots going off continuously, and the *whump* as bombs exploded. Then there was a flare of red light and our guys yelled in triumph. Bradley was leaping up and down, and Roscoe did a Victory Dance until one of the Shooters asked him if he wanted his light saber rammed up his butt.

I managed to shove my way between Anil and Myron just as Charles was announcing, "I believe you're screwed, Mr. Crandall. Care to call it a day?"

I looked at their scores and couldn't believe how badly Lord Deathlok had lost to him. But Lord Deathlok just snarled.

"I don't think so, Ben Dover. Shut up and play!"

It was *Meteor Nightmare* now, as though they were both out there in the Van Oort belt, facing the rocks without any comforting distance of consoles or calculations. I couldn't stop myself from flinching as they hurtled forward; and I noticed one of the Shooters put up his arms involuntarily, as though he wanted to bat away the incoming with his bare hands.

It was a brutal game; *nightmare,* all right, because they couldn't avoid taking massive damage. All they could do was take out as many targets as they could before their inevitable destruction. When one or the other of them took a hit, there was a momentary flare of light that blinded everybody in the room. I couldn't imagine how Charles and Lord Death-lok, right there with their faces in the action, could keep shooting with any kind of accuracy.

Sure enough, early in the second round it began to tell. They were both getting flash-blind. Charles was still hitting about one in three targets, but Lord Deathlok was shooting crazily, randomly, not even bothering to aim so far as I could tell. What a look of despair on his ugly face, with his lips drawn back from his yellow teeth!

Only a miracle would save him, now. His overall score was so far behind Charles' he'd never catch up. The Shooters knew it too. I saw Dr. Smash turn his head and murmur to Uncle Hannibal. He took a firm grip on his war club. Panicking, I grabbed Anil's arm, trying to get his attention.

That was when the Incoming klaxons sounded. All the Shooters stood to attention. Lord Deathlok looked around, blinking, but Charles worked the buttonball like a pro and suddenly the game vanished, and there was nothing before us but the console displays. There was a crackle from the speakers—the first time they'd ever been used, I found out later—and we could hear Preston screaming, "You guys! Intruder coming in fast! You have to stop! It's in—"

"Q41!" said Uncle Hannibal, leaning forward to peer at the console readout. "Get out of my chair, dickwad!"

Charles didn't answer. He did something with the buttonball and there was the Intruder, like something out of *Meteor Nightmare*, shracking enormous. It was in his own sector! How could he have missed it? *Charles,* who was brilliant at spotting them before anybody else?

A red frame rose around it, with the readout in numbers spinning over so fast I couldn't tell what they said, except it was obvious the thing was coming in at high speed. All the Shooters were frantic, bellowing for Charles to get his ass out of the chair. Before their astounded eyes, and ours, he targeted the Intruder and fired.

All sound stopped. Movement stopped. Time itself stopped, except for on the display, where a new set of numbers in green and another in yellow popped up. They spun like fruit on a slot machine, the one counting up, the other counting down, both getting slower and slower until suddenly the numbers matched. Then, in perfect unison, they clicked upward together on a leisurely march.

"It's a hit," announced Preston from the speakers. "In twelve days thirteen hours forty-two minutes. Telemetry confirmed."

Dead silence answered him. And that was when I understood: Charles hadn't missed the Intruder. Charles had spotted it days ago. Charles had set this whole thing up, requesting the specific time of the duel, knowing the Intruder would interrupt it and there'd have to be a last-minute act of heroism. Which he'd co-opt.

But the thing is, see, there are *people* down there on the planet under us, who could die if a meteor gets through. I mean, that's why we're all up here in the first place, right?

Finally Anil said, in a funny voice, "So . . . who gets the bonus, then?"

"He *can't* have just done that," said Mephisto, hoarse with disbelief. "He's a *Plotter*."

"Get up, faggot," said Uncle Hannibal, grabbing Charles' shoulder.

"Hit him," said Charles.

I hadn't unfrozen yet, but Anil had been waiting for this moment all day. He jumped forward and tased Uncle Hannibal. Uncle Hannibal dropped, with a hoarse screech, and the other Shooters backed away fast. Anil stared down at Uncle Hannibal with unholy wonder in his eyes, and the beginning of a terrible joy. Suddenly there was a lot of room in front of the consoles, enough to see Lord Deathlok sitting there staring at the readout, with tears streaming down his face.

Charles got out of the chair.

"You lost," he informed Lord Deathlok.

"Your reign of terror is over!" cried Anil, brandishing his taser at the Shooters. One or two of them cowered, but the rest just looked stunned. Charles turned to me.

"You left your post," he said. "You're a useless idiot. Myron, take the taser off him."

"Sir yes sir!" said Myron, grabbing my arm and rolling up

my sleeve. As he was unfastening the straps, we heard a chuckle from the doorway. All heads turned. There was Mr. Kurtz, leaning there with his arms crossed. I realized he must have followed me, and seen the drama as it played out. Anil thrust his taser arm behind his back, looking scared, but Mr. Kurtz only smiled.

"As you were," he said. He stood straight and left. We could hear him whistling as he walked away.

It wasn't until later that we learned the whole story, or as much of it as we ever knew: how Charles had been recruited, not from his parents' garage or basement, but from Hospital, and how Mr. Kurtz had known it, had in fact *requested it*.

We all expected a glorious new day had come for Plotters, now that Charles had proven the Shooters were unnecessary. We thought Areco would terminate their contracts. It didn't exactly happen that way.

What happened was that Dr. Smash and Uncle Hannibal came to Charles and had a private (except for Myron and Anil) talk with him. They were very polite. Since Painmaster wasn't coming back to the Gun Platform, but had defaulted on his contract and gone down home to Earth, they proposed that Charles become a Shooter. They did more; they offered him High Dark Lordship.

He accepted their offer. We were appalled. It seemed like the worst treachery imaginable.

And yet, we were surprised again.

Charles Tead didn't take one of the stupid Shooter names like Warlord or Iron Fist or Doomsman. He said we were all to call him *Stede* from now on. He ordered up, not a bioprene wardrobe with spikes and rivets and fringe, but . . . but . . . a three-piece suit, with a *tie*. And a bowler hat. He took his tasers back from Anil and Myron, who were crestfallen, and wore them himself, under his perfectly pressed cuffs.

Then he ordered up new clothes for all the other Shooters. It must have been a shock, when he handed out those powder blue shirts and drab coveralls, but they didn't rebel; by that time they'd learned what he'd been sent to Hospital for in the first place, which was killing three people. So there wasn't so much as a mutter behind his back, even when he ordered all the holoposters shut off and thrown into the fusion hopper, and the War Room repainted in dove gray.

We wouldn't have known the Shooters. He made them wash; he made them cut their hair, he made them shracking salute when he gave an order. They were scared to fart, especially after he hung up deodorizers above each of their consoles. The War Room became a clean, well-lit place, silent except for the consoles and the occasional quiet order from Charles. He seldom had to raise his voice.

Mr. Kurtz still sat in his office all day, reading, but now he smiled as he read. Nobody called him *Dean Kurtz* anymore, either.

It was sort of horrible, what had happened, but with Charles—I mean, Stede—running the place, things were a lot more efficient. The bonuses became more frequent, as everyone worked harder. And, in time, the Shooters came to worship him.

He didn't bother with us. We were grateful.

Repeating the Past

PETER WATTS

Peter Watts (www.rifters.com) lives in Toronto, Canada. He is a former marine biologist and has published four novels in the Rifters series, and a collection of his short fiction, Ten Monkeys, Ten Minutes *(2000). Cory Doctorow, writing about Watts' most recent novel,* Blindsight *(2006), remarks, "Peter writes the angriest, darkest sf I've ever read, heart-rending stuff that makes you glad you're alive if only because you're better off than his characters." That novel was a Hugo Award finalist in 2007. He describes himself as "a lot more optimistic than you might expect, considering." And in an interview with* SF Diplomat, *he says, "For all my Nietzschean posturing, I am endlessly outraged by the abuses we visit upon the world and each other."*

"Repeating the Past" appeared in the Futures column in the science magazine Nature. *This short short fiction feature continues to expand the audience for SF in the scientific community. An angry little gem of a biotech story, this is about how the past enforces itself on the future, and how the pain of the father is visited upon the generations to follow.*

What you did to your uncle's grave was unforgivable.

Your mother blamed herself, as always. You didn't know what you were doing, she said. I could accept that when you traded the shofar I gave you for that eMotiv headset, perhaps, or even when you befriended those young toughs with the shaved heads and the filthy mouths. I would never have forgiven the swastika on your game pod but you are my daughter's son, not mine. Maybe it was only adolescent rebellion. How could you know, after all? How could any child really know, here in 2017? Genocide is far too monstrous a thing for history books and grainy old photographs to convey. You were not there; you could never understand.

We told ourselves you were a good boy at heart, that it was ancient history to you, abstract and unreal. Both of us doctors, familiar with the sad stereotype of the self-loathing Jew, we talked ourselves into treating you like some kind of victim. And then the police brought you back from the cemetery and you looked at us with those dull, indifferent eyes, and I stopped making excuses. It wasn't just your uncle's grave. You were spitting on six million others, and you knew, and it meant nothing.

Your mother cried for hours. Hadn't she shown you the old albums, the online archives, the family tree with so many branches hacked off mid-century? Hadn't we both tried to tell you the stories? I tried to comfort her. An impossible task, I said, explaining Never Again to someone whose

165

only knowledge of murder is the score he racks up playing Zombie Hunter all day . . .

And that was when I knew what to do.

I waited. A week, two, long enough to let you think I'd excused and forgiven as I always have. But I knew your weak spot. Nothing happens fast enough for you. These miraculous toys of yours—electrodes that read the emotions, take orders directly from the subconscious—they bore you now. You've seen the ads for Improved Reality™: sensation planted directly into the brain! Throw away the goggles and earphones and the gloves, throw away the keys! Feel the breezes of fantasy worlds against your skin, smell the smoke of battle, taste the blood of your toy monsters, so easily killed! Immerse all your senses in the slaughter!

You were tired of playing with cartoons, and the new model wouldn't be out for so very long. You jumped at my third option. You know, your mother's working on something like that. It's medical, of course, but it works the same way. She might even have some sensory samplers loaded for testing purposes.

Maybe, if you promise not to tell, we could sneak you in . . .

Retired, yes, but I never gave up my privileges. Almost two decades since I closed my practice but I still spend time in your mother's lab, lend a hand now and then. I still marvel at her passion to know how the mind works, how it keeps breaking. She got that from me. I got it from Treblinka, when I was only half your age. I, too, grew up driven to fix broken souls—but the psychiatrist's tools were such blunt things back then. Scalpels to open flesh, words and drugs to open minds. Our techniques had all the precision of a drunkard stomping on the floor, trying to move glasses on the bar with the vibrations of his boot.

These machines your mother has, though! Transcranial superconductors, deep-focus microwave emitters, Szpindel resonators! Specific pathways targeted, rewritten, erased completely! Their very names sound like incantations!

I cannot use them as she can. I know only the basics. I

can't implant sights or sounds, can't create actual memories. Not declarative ones, anyway.

But procedural memory? That I can do. The right frontal lobe, the hippocampus, basic fear and anxiety responses. The reptile is easily awakened. And you didn't need the details. No need to remember my baby sister face-down like a pile of sticks in the mud. No need for the colour of the sky that day, as I stood frozen and fearful of some real monster's notice should I go to her. You didn't need the actual lesson.

The moral would do.

Afterwards you sat up, confused, then disappointed, then resentful. "That was nothing! It didn't even work!" I needed no machines to see into your head then. Senile old fart, doesn't know half as much as he thinks. And as one day went by, and another, I began to fear you were right.

But then came the retching sounds from behind the bathroom door. All those hours hidden away in your room, your game pod abandoned in the living room. And then your mother came to me, eyes brimming with worry: never seen you like this, she said. Jumping at shadows. Not sleeping at night. This morning she found you throwing clothes into your backpack—they're coming, they're coming, we gotta run—and when she asked who they were, you couldn't tell her.

So here we are. You huddle in the corner, your eyes black begging holes that can't stop moving, that see horrors in every shadow. Your fists bleed, nails gouging the palms. I remember, when I was your age. I cut myself to feel alive. Sometimes I still do. It never really stops.

Some day, your mother says, her machines will exorcise my demons. Doesn't she understand what a terrible mistake that would be? Doesn't history, once forgotten, repeat? Didn't even the worst president in history admit that memories belong to everyone?

I say nothing to you. We know each other now, so much deeper than words.

I have made you wise, grandson. I have shown you the world.

Now I will help you to live with it.

No More Stories

STEPHEN BAXTER

Stephen Baxter (www.stephen-baxter.com), lives in North-umberland in the northeast of England. With an under-graduate degree in math and a Ph.D. in engineering, he is an icon of the New Hard SF, and now an established master of contemporary SF in many forms. He began publishing his fiction in 1987, mostly in Interzone, and has since proved one of science fiction's more reliably prolific authors of good hard SF. Most years, one of his stories appears in this volume. He now has six series to his name, the largest and most famous of which, the Xeelee series, has more than ten books in it. He has also published three collections of short fiction, and has written four novels in collaboration with Arthur C. Clarke.

"No More Stories" is another piece from Fast Forward 1. It is a wry tale of observer-created reality. Mother is a so-lipsist who has always acted as though the universe is about her. This is both a story of family dysfunctionality and at the same time oddly reminiscent of Clarke's "Nine Billion Names of God."

"It's strange to find myself in this position. Dying, I mean. I've always found it hard to believe that things will just go on afterwards. After *me*. That the sun will come up, the milkman will call. Will it all just fold up and go away, when I've gone?"

These were the first words his mother said to Simon, when he got out of the car.

She stood in her doorway, old-lady stocky, solid, arms folded, over eighty years old. Her wrinkles were runnels in papery flesh that ran down to a small, frowning mouth. She peered around the close, as if suspicious.

Simon collected his small suitcase from the back of the car. It had a luggage tag from a New York flight, a reminder that he was fifty years old, and that he did have a life beyond his mother's, working for a biotech company in London, selling gen-enged goldfish as children's pets. Now that he was here, back in this Sheffield suburb where he'd grown up, his London life seemed remote, a dream.

He locked the car and walked up to his mother. She presented her cheek for him to kiss. It was cold, rough-textured.

"I had a good journey," he said, for he knew she wouldn't ask.

"I am dying, you know," she said, as if to make sure he understood.

"Oh, Mother." He put an arm around her shoulders. She

was hard, like a lump of gristle and bone, and didn't soften into the hug.

She had cancer. They had never actually used that word between them.

She stepped back to let him into the house.

The hall was spotless, obsessively cleaned and ordered, yet it smelled stale. A palm frond folded into a cross hung on the wall, a reminder that Easter was coming, a relic of intricate Catholic rituals he'd abandoned when he left home.

He put his suitcase down.

"Don't put it there," his mother said.

A familiar claustrophobia closed in around him. "All right." He grabbed the case and climbed the stairs, fourteen of them as he used to count in his childhood. But now there was an old-lady safety banister fixed to the wall.

She had made up one of the twin beds in the room he had once shared with his brother. There wasn't a trace of his childhood left in here, none of his toys or books or school photos.

He came downstairs. "Mother, I'm gasping. Can I make a cup of tea?"

"The pot's still fresh. I'll fetch a cup and saucer." She bustled off to the kitchen.

He walked into the lounge.

The only change he could see since his last visit was a fancy new standard lamp with a downturned cowl, to shed light on the lap of an old lady sitting in the best armchair, facing the telly, peering at her sewing with fading eyes. The old carriage clock still sat in its place on the concrete 1970s fireplace, a legacy from a long-dead great-uncle. It was flanked by a clutter of photos, as usual. Most of them were fading colour prints of grandchildren. Simon had no grandchildren to offer, and so was unrepresented here.

But the photos had been pushed back to make room for a new image in a gold frame. Brownish, blurred and faded, it was a portrait of a smiling young man in a straw boater. He had a long, strong face. Simon recognised the photo, taken from a musty old album and evidently blown up. It was his grandfather, Mother's dad, who had died when Simon was five or six.

Just for a moment the light seemed odd to him. Cold, yellow-purple. And there was something strange beyond the window. Pillowlike shapes, gleaming in a watery sun. He saw all this from the corner of his eye. But when he turned to look directly, the light from the picture window turned spring green, shining from the small back garden, with its lawn and roses and the last of the azalea blossom. Maybe his eyes were tired from the drive, playing tricks.

"It's just for comfort. The photo."

The male voice made Simon turn clumsily, almost tripping.

A man sat on the sofa, almost hidden behind the door, with a cup of tea on an occasional table. "Sorry. You didn't see me. Didn't mean to make you jump." He stood and shook Simon's hand. "I'm Gabriel Nolan." His voice had a soft Irish burr. Maybe sixty, he was small, round, bald as an egg. He wore a pale jacket, black shirt, and dog collar. He had biscuit crumbs down his front.

Simon guessed, "Is it Father Nolan?"

"From Saint Michael's. The latest incumbent."

The last parish priest Simon remembered had been the very old, very frail man who had confirmed him, at age thirteen.

Mother came in, walking stiffly, cradling a cup and saucer. "Sit down, Simon, you're blocking the light."

Simon sat in the room's other armchair, with his back to the window. Mother poured out some tea with milk, and added sugar, though he hadn't taken sugar for three decades.

"Simon was just admiring the portrait of your father, Eileen."

"Well, I don't have many pictures of my dad. You didn't take many in those days. That's the best one, I think."

"I was saying. We find comfort in familiar things, in the past."

"I always felt safe when my dad was there," Mother said. "In the war, you know."

But, Simon thought, Granddad was long dead. She'd led a whole life since then, the life that included Simon's own childhood.

Mother always was self-centered. Any crisis in her children's lives, like Mary's recurrent illness as a child, or the illegitimate kid Peter had fathered as a student, somehow always turned into a drama about *her*. Now somehow she was back in the past with her own father in her own childhood, and there was no room for Simon.

Mother said, "There might not be anybody left who remembers Dad, but me. Do you think we get deader, when there's nobody left who remembers us?"

The priest said, "We live on in the eyes of Christ."

Simon said, "Father Nolan, don't you think Mother should talk to the doctor again? She won't listen to me."

"Oh, don't be ridiculous, Simon," Mother said.

"Best to accept," said Father Nolan. "If your mother has. Best not to question."

They both stared back at him, seamless, united. Fifty years old he felt awkward, a child who didn't know what to say to the grown-ups.

He stood up, putting down his teacup. "I've some shirts that could do with hanging."

Mother sniffed. "There might be a bit of space. Later there's my papers to do."

Another horror story. Simon fled upstairs. A little later, he heard the priest leave.

The "papers" were her financial transactions, Premium Bonds and tax vouchers and battered old bank books.

And the dreaded rusty biscuit box she kept under her bed, which held her will and her life insurance policies, stored up in the event of a death she'd been talking about for thirty years. It even held her identity card from the war, signed in a childish hand.

Simon always found it painful to sit and plod through all this stuff. The tin box was worst, of course.

Later she surprised him by asking to go for a walk.

It was late afternoon. Mother put on a coat, a musty gabardine that smelled of winter, though the bright April day was warm.

Simon had grown up in this close. It was a short, stubby street of semi-detached houses leading up to a main road and a dark sandstone wall, beyond which lay a park. But his childhood was decades gone, and the houses had been made over out of all recognition, and the space where he'd played football was now jammed full of cars. Walking here, he felt as if he was trying to cram himself into clothes he'd outworn.

They crossed the busy main road, and then walked along the line of the old wall to the gateway to the park. Or what was left of it. In the last few years the park had been sliced through by a spur of the main road, along which cars now hissed, remote as clouds. Simon's old home seemed stranded.

Simon and his mother stuck to a gravel path. Underfoot was dogshit and, in the mud under the benches, beer cans, fag ends, and condoms. Mother clung to his arm. Walking erratically she pulled at him, heavy, like an unfixed load.

Mother talked steadily, about Peter and Mary, and the achievements and petty woes of their respective children. Mary, older than Simon, was forever struggling on, in Mother's eyes, burdened by difficult kids and a lazy husband. "She's got a lot to put up with, always did." Peter, the youngest, got a tougher time, perceived as selfish and shiftless and lacking judgment. Simon's siblings' lives were more complicated than that. But to Mother they were ciphers, dominated by the characteristics she had perceived in them when they were kids.

She asked nothing about his own life.

Later, she prepared the evening meal.

As she was cooking, Simon dug his laptop out of his suitcase, and brought it down to the cold, formal dining room, where there was a telephone point. He booted up and went through his e-mails.

He worked for a biotech start-up that specialised in breeding genetically modified goldfish, giving them patterns in bright *Captain Nemo* colours targeted at children. It was a good business, and expanding. The strategy was to domesticate biotech. In maybe five or ten years they would even sell genome-sequencing kits to kids, or anyhow their parents, so they could "paint" their own fish designs.

It was a bit far off in terms of fifty-year-old Simon's career, and things were moving so fast in this field that his own skills, in software, were constantly being challenged. But the work was demanding and fun, and as he watched the little fish swim around with "Happy Birthday, Julie" written on their flanks, he thought he glimpsed the future.

His mother knew precisely nothing about all this. The glowing e-mails were somehow comforting, a window to another world where he had an identity.

Anyhow, no fires to put out today. He shut down the connection.

Then he phoned his brother and sister with his mother's news.

"She's fine in herself. She's cooking supper right now. . . . Yes, she's keeping the house okay. I suppose when she gets frailer we'll have to think about that. . . . I'll stay one night definitely, perhaps two. Might take her shopping tomorrow. Bulky stuff, you know, bog rolls and washing powder. . . .

"Things are a bit tricky for you, I suppose." Exams, school trips, holidays. Mary's ferocious commitment to her bridge club—"They can't have a match if I don't turn up, you know!" Peter's endless courses in bookkeeping and beekeeping, arboriculture and aromatherapy, an aging dreamer's continuing quest to be elevated above the other rats in the race. All of them reasons not to visit their mother.

Simon didn't particularly blame them. Neither of them seemed to feel they *had* to come, the way he did, which left him with no choice but to be here. And of course with their kids they were busier than he was, in a sense.

Mother had her own views. Peter was selfish. Mary was always terribly busy, poor lamb.

She'd once been a good cook, if a thrifty one, her cuisine shaped by the experience of wartime rationing. But over the years her cooking had simplified to a few ready-made dishes. Tonight it was boil-in-the-bag fish. You got used to it.

After they ate, they spent the evening playing games. Not Scrabble, which had been a favourite of Simon's childhood. She insisted on cribbage, which she had played with her father, in her own childhood. She had a worn board that must have been decades old. She had to explain the arcane rules to him.

The evening was very, very long, in the silence of the room with a blank telly screen, the time stretched out by the pocks of Uncle Billy's carriage clock.

In the morning he came out of his bedroom, dressed in his pajama bottoms, heading for the bathroom.

Father Gabriel Nolan was coming up the stairs with a cup of tea on a saucer. He gave Simon a sort of thin-lipped smile. In the bright morning light Simon saw that dried mucus clung to the hairs protruding from his fleshy nose.

"She's taken a turn for the worse in the night," said the priest. "A stroke, perhaps. It's all very sudden." And he bustled into Mother's bedroom.

Simon just stood there.

He quickly used the bathroom. He went back to his bedroom and put on his pants and yesterday's shirt.

Then, in his socks, he went into Mother's bedroom. The curtains were still closed, the only light a ghostly blue glow soaking through the curtains. It was like walking into an aquarium.

She was lying on the right-hand side of the double bed she had shared with Dad for so long. She was flat on her back, staring up. Her arms were outside the sheets, which were neatly tucked in. The cup of tea sat on her bedside cabinet. Father Nolan sat at her bedside, holding her hand.

Her eyes flickered towards Simon.

Simon, frightened, distressed for his mother, was angry at this smut-nosed, biscuit-crumby priest in his mother's bedroom. "Have you called the doctor?"

Mother murmured something, at the back of her throat.

"No doctor," said Father Nolan.

"Is that a decision for you to make?"

"It's a decision for her," said the priest, gravely, not unkindly, firmly. "She wants to go downstairs. The lounge."

"She's better off in bed."

"Let her see the garden."

Father Nolan's calm, unctuous tone was grating. "How are we going to get her down the stairs?"

"We'll manage."

They lifted Mother up from the bed, and wrapped her in blankets. Simon saw there was a bedpan, sticking out from under the bed. It was actually a plastic potty, a horrible dirty old pink thing he remembered from his own childhood. It was full of thick yellow pee. Father Nolan must have helped her.

They carried her down the stairs together, Simon holding her under the arms, the priest taking her legs.

When they got to the bottom of the stairs, it went dark on the landing above. Simon looked up. The stairs seemed very tall and high, the landing quite black.

"Maybe a bulb blew," he said. But the lights hadn't been on, the landing illuminated by daylight.

Father Nolan said, "She doesn't need to go upstairs again."

Simon didn't know what he meant. Under his distress about his mother, he found he felt obscurely frightened.

They shuffled into the lounge. They sat Mother in her armchair, facing the garden's green.

What now?

"What about breakfast?"

"Toast for me," said Father Nolan.

Simon went to the kitchen and ran slices of white bread, faintly stale, through the toaster.

The priest followed him in. He had taken his jacket off. His black shirt had short sleeves, and he had powerful stubby arms, like a wrestler. They sat at the small kitchen table, and ate buttered toast.

Simon asked, "Why are you here? This morning, I mean. Did Mother call you? I didn't hear the phone."

Father Nolan shrugged. "I just dropped in. I have a key. She's got used to having me around, during this, well, crisis. I don't mind. I share my duties at the parish." He complacently chewed his toast.

"When I was a kid, you smug priests used to make me feel like tripping you up."

Father Nolan laughed. "You're a good boy. You'd never do that."

"'A good boy.' Father, I'm fifty years old."

"But you're always a little boy to your mother." He nodded at the fridge, where photographs were stuck to the metal door by magnets. "Your brother and sister. You're the middle one, yes?"

"Sister older, brother younger."

"Mary and Peter. Good Catholic names. But it's unusual to find a Simon *and* a Peter in the same Catholic family."

"I know." Since Simon had learned about Simon Peter the apostle, he had sometimes wondered if Mother had chosen Peter's name on purpose—as if she was disappointed with the first Simon and hoped for a better version. "They've both got kids. I'm sure she'd rather one of them was here, frankly. Grandkids jumping all over her."

"You're the one who's here. That's what's important."

Simon studied him. "I don't believe, you know. Not sure if I ever did, once I was able to think for myself. You can be as calm and certain as you like. I think it's all a bluff."

Father Nolan laughed. "That's okay. What you choose to believe or not is irrelevant to the destiny of my immortal soul. And indeed yours."

It had been a very long time indeed since Simon had even considered the possibility that he might have a soul, some quality that might endure beyond his own death.

He shivered, and stood up. "I think I need some air. Maybe I'll buy a paper."

"We'll be fine here."

"Help yourself to tea. It's in the—"

"Winston Churchill caddy. I know." Father Nolan smiled, and chewed his toast.

He walked up the close, towards the park.

This stub of a road had seemed endless when he was a child. Full of detail, every drain or stopcock cover or broken paving stone a feature in some game or other. Now he felt a stab of pity for a child who perhaps could have done with a bit more stimulation.

But the close seemed long today, stretching off ahead of him, like the hours governed by Uncle Billy's clock.

And though the sky was clear blue, the light was odd. Weakening. Once he'd sat through a partial eclipse over London, a darkening that was not the setting of the sun but an eerie dimming. That was what this was like. But there was no eclipse due today; he'd have known.

It took an effort to reach the top of the close. And more of an effort to wait for a gap in the stream of dark, anonymous cars, and to cross to the footpath by the park wall.

He walked along the wall, letting his fingers trail along the grubby, wind-eroded sandstone. It had happened so quickly. Would Mother really never make this little journey again? Was that awful bagged fish really the last meal the woman who had fed him as a baby would ever make for him? Grief swirled around in him, unfocused. He thought vaguely about the calls he would have to make.

At the gate, he stopped.

There was no park. No sooty oak trees, no grass, no dog shit.

He saw a plain, a marsh. The sunlight gleamed from a sheet of flat, green, sticky-looking water. Pillowlike shapes pushed out of the water, their surfaces slimy crusts, green and purple.

Nothing moved. There was no sound.

Of the park, the parade of shops beyond, there was no sign.

It was like the scene he thought he had glimpsed through his mother's lounge window yesterday. But that had been from the corner of his eye, and had vanished when he looked directly. This was different.

He turned away. The main road was still there, the cars streaming along.

Carefully, he walked back down the road, and into the close. Every step he took towards home made him feel more secure, and the daylight grew stronger.

He didn't dare look back.

* * *

At home, Father Nolan was still sitting with Mother. It wasn't yet lunchtime.

Simon got himself a glass of water and went to the dining room. He booted up his laptop. He dialed into work, to check his e-mails. He was trying not to think about what he'd seen.

He got error messages. The work site didn't exist.

He heard Father Nolan climbing the stairs, a splashing sound, the toilet flushing. Emptying a bedpan, maybe.

He tried Google. That still existed.

There was a word that had come into his head when he thought about what had become of the park. *Stromatolite.* He Googled it.

Communities of algae. A photo showed mounds just like the ones on the park. Heaped-up mats of bacteria, one on top of another, with mud and sand trapped in between. They had their own complexities, of a sort, each mound a tiny biosphere in its own right.

And they were very ancient, a relic of the days before animals, before insects, before multicelled creatures of any kind.

He followed links, digging at random, drawn by his own professional interest in genetics. The first stromatolites had actually been the height of complexity compared to what had gone before. Once there had been nothing but communities of crude cells in which even "species" could not be said to exist, and genetic information was massively transferred sideways between lineages, as well as from parent cell to offspring. The world was muddy, a vast cellular orgy. But if you looked closely it had been fast-evolving, inventive, resilient.

Google failed, the browser returning a site-not-found error message.

And then the laptop's modem reported it couldn't find a dial tone.

It seemed to be growing darker. But it wasn't yet noon. He didn't want to look out of the window.

Father Nolan walked in. "She's asking for you."

Simon hesitated. "I'd better call Mary and Peter. They ought to know."

The priest just waited.

At his first try, he got a number-unobtainable tone. Then the dial tone disappeared. He tried his mobile. There was no service.

It was very dark.

Father Nolan held out his hand. "Come."

In the lounge the curtains were drawn. The excluded daylight was odd, dim, greenish. The only strong light came from Mother's fancy new reading stand.

The telly was like an empty eye socket. Simon wondered what he would find if he turned it on.

Mother sat in her armchair, swathed in blankets. Of her body only her face showed, and two hands that looked as if all the bones had been drawn out of them. There was a stink of piss and shit, a tang of blood.

Father Nolan sat beside mother on a footstool, the bedpan at his feet.

"I probably ought to thank you for doing this," Simon said.

"It comes with the job. I gave her the Last Rites, Simon. I should tell you that."

Mother, her eyes closed, murmured something. Father Nolan leaned close so he could hear, and smiled. "Let tomorrow worry about itself, Eileen."

Simon asked, "What's happening tomorrow?"

"She asked if there will be a tomorrow."

Simon stared at him. "When I was a kid," he said slowly, "I used to wonder what will happen when I die. It seemed outrageous that the universe should go on, after I, the center of everything, was taken away. Just as my mother said to me yesterday.

"Then I grew up a bit more. I started to think maybe everybody feels that way. Every finite mortal creature. The two things don't go together, do they, my smallness, and the bigness of the sky?"

Father Nolan just listened.

Simon stepped towards the window. "What will I see if I pull back the curtain?"

"Don't," said Father Nolan.

"Do *you* know what's going on?"

"I'm here for her. Not you."

"If I ask you, will you tell me?"

The priest hesitated. "You're a good boy. I suppose you deserve that."

Simon touched Uncle Billy's clock, pressed his palm against the wall behind it. "Is any of this real?"

"As real as it needs to be."

"Is this really the year 2010?"

"No."

"Then when?"

"The future. Not as far as you might think."

"People are different."

"There are no people."

"I don't understand."

"No. But you're capable of understanding," Father Nolan said. "It's no accident you work in biotechnology, you know. It was set up that way, so if you ever asked these questions, you'd have the background to grasp the answer."

"What has my job got to do with it?"

"Nothing in itself. It's where things are leading. Those Day-Glo fish you sell. How do you *do* that?"

Simon shrugged. "I don't know the details. I do software. Gene splicing, basically."

"You splice genes from where?"

"A modified soya, I think. Other sources."

"Yes. You swap genes around, horizontally, from microbes to plants to animals, even into people. It's a new kind of gene transfer—or rather a very old one."

"Before the stromatolites."

"Yes. You're planning to put this gene-transfer technology on the open market, aren't you?"

It was like the drive to put a PC in every home, a few decades back. The domestication would start with biotech in the mines and factories and stores. Home use would follow. Eventually advanced home biotech kits, capable of dicing and splicing genomes and nurturing the results, would become as pervasive as PCs and mobile phones. Everybody would have one, and would use it to make new varieties of dogs and budgies, exotic orchids and apples. To create a new life form and release it into the world would be as easy as blogging.

Simon said, "It's the logical next step, in marketing terms. Like putting massive computing power in the hands of the public. That would have seemed inconceivable, in 1950. And the secondary results will be as unimaginable as the Internet once was. Do you think it's immoral? Unnatural?"

Father Nolan grinned. "If I were what I look like, perhaps I'd think that."

"What are you, then?"

"I'm the end-product of your company's business plans. Yours and a thousand others."

It was a question of accelerating trends. The world's genetic inheritance would become open source. And then, a generation later, the technology would merge with the biology.

"It was only a few decades after your birthday-card goldfish that things took off," Father Nolan said. "Remarkable. Only a few decades, to topple a regime of life that lasted two billion years."

"And things were different after that."

"Oh, yes. Darwinian evolution was *slo-ow*. For all the fancy critters that were thrown up, there was hardly a change in the basic biochemical machinery across two billion years.

"Now there are *no* non-interbreeding species. Indeed, no individuals. The Darwinian interlude is over, and we are back to gene sharing, the way it used to be.

"And everything has changed. Global climate change became trivial, for instance. With the fetters off, the biosphere adapted to the new conditions, optimizing its metabolic and reproductive efficiency as it went.

"And then," he said, "off into space."

These words, simply spoken, implied a marvelous future.

"Who is my mother?"

"We are in a lacuna," Father Nolan said.

"A what?"

"A gap. A hole. In the totality of a living world. Sorry if that sounds a bit pompous. Your mother is a part of the totality, but cut away, you see. Living out a life as a human once lived it."

"Why? Is she being punished?"

"No." He laughed. "It's the contrary. She wanted to do this. It's hard to express. We are a multipolar consciousness. She is part of the rest of us—do you see? She was an expression of a global desire."

"To do what?"

"Not to forget." He stood up. Grave, patient, he had the manner of a priest, despite his hairy nose, his stained shirt. "I think you're ready." He led Simon to the window, and pulled back the curtain.

Green stars.

The garden was gone.

The rest of the house was gone. The close, the park, Sheffield—*Earth* was gone, irrelevant. Mother had been right. It had all been placed there as a stage set for her own life. But now her life had dwindled to the four walls of this room, and the rest of it could be discarded, for she would never need it again.

Just green stars. Simon pressed his ear to the window. He heard a reverberation, like an immense bell.

"Earth life turning the galaxy green. Our thoughts span light-years. But we don't want to forget how it was to be human." Father Nolan smiled. "It's a paradox. Without *loss,* we have in fact lost so much. As you said—the strange tragedy of being mortal in an unending universe. There's no more poetry. No more epitaphs. No more *stories.* Just a solemn calm."

"Mother wanted to experience it. Human life."

"On behalf of the rest of us, yes."

"And what are *you*, Father?"

Father Nolan shrugged. "Everything else." He let the curtain drop, hiding the green stars.

The electric light was dimming.

Father Nolan sat down beside Mother and held her hand. "Only a few more minutes. Then it will be done."

Michael sat on the other side of his mother. "What about me?"

"You're only here for her."

"But I'm conscious!"

"Well, of course you are. She chose you, you know. You always thought she didn't love you, didn't you? But she chose you to be beside her, at the end, when all the others—Peter, Mary—even her own father, have all gone. Isn't that enough?"

"Do I have a soul, Father?"

"I'm not qualified to say."

Mother turned her head towards him, he thought. But her eyes were closed.

"Help me," Simon whispered.

Father Nolan looked at him. Then he closed his eyes and bowed his head. "In the name of the Father, and of the Son, and of the Holy Ghost. Amen."

Simon said, "Bless me, Father, for I have sinned."

The glow of the single bulb faded slowly, to black.

They Came from the Future

ROBYN HITCHCOCK

Robyn Hitchcock (www.robynhitchcock.com) lives in London. In the '80s and early '90s, he put out a bunch of terrific albums, many with songs invoking science fiction and fantasy themes. We remember them fondly, though our DVDs of them are a bit battered from frequent play, particularly "Globe of Frogs," "Madonna of the Wasps," and "Sleeping with Your Devil Mask." This year, his DVD Sex, Food, Death and Insects, *in which "legendary underground cult artist Robyn Hitchcock reveals his creative process" will be unleashed upon the world. On his website bio, he says that in 1965, when he was 12, having just discovered the works of H. G. Wells, he tried unsuccessfully to build a time machine.*

"They Came from the Future" appeared in Fast Forward 1. *Of the poem, Lou Anders remarks, "Reminiscent of ideas expressed in Michael Chabon's essay 'The Omega Glory,' Hitchcock explores a sentiment all too pervasive in our current times regarding the lost promise of tomorrow as reflected in the shortcomings of today." Hitchcock says, in Anders' story note, "As a thinking person I'm completely in despair, but as a kind of creature I'm quite happy."*

They came from the future
Once upon a time
In silver suits and confident helmets
Reflecting our sun and historic stars

They came to shake our hands
And laze by fountains in their silver torsos
Pushing back their helmets to receive
Dandelions from Earth girls and
Blow them away.

"Easy when you know how," said the wise ones.

Their clean-cut hair and fresh teeth
Caressed our breeze.
They handed out postcards of their world,
Electric toothbrushes, sunlight so strong it
Flowed from them in chrome.
The local boys aped them,
Dressed like them when they could get the gear.

Then they changed:
They came now from a rough sad world that
Imitated ours. Stolen mirrors, bacteria, wild teeth framed
    in stubble
Tired breath.
No one wanted to kiss them.

They carried DO NOT TOUCH placards and tried to thrust
    leaflets into shoppers' hands.
Which nobody could read.
But the photos showed a frightened monkey in a noose.
The girls walked round them
And the boys, our silver boys, ganged up on them in dark
    stairwells.

The wise ones sat in cafes, eating leaves and shoots.

Our world has lost its shine,
Though there's still money to polish it.
Radiance comes in jars.
The wise ones shake their heads
But they've had a lot of practice
And pack away their stalls.

Boys are angry, girls are scared
Bloated like carcasses, dwindled to bones:
The future isn't what it was
And somebody must pay.

The boys, our boys in silver blade patrols, caught one
    last refugee.
I saw them take him one grim green dawn
Pushing him backwards through the mall, pushing him
    down against the wall
They finished him with stones:
He had nothing to offer them.
Our sunlight framed his dying shadow.

After that, no one came from the future:
We've reached it, after all.
Too real to dream, the clouds protect me from the rising sun.
Stars keep their distance
Tattooed on a ceiling we no longer dream of reaching.
Not this way, not as us
Not the silver boys, no way.

Yet, this is no time to be sour—the hour is now, and it's
    our turn
To visit them.

Ready, boys?

The Tomb Wife

GWYNETH JONES

Gwyneth Jones (http://homepage.ntlworld.com/gwynethann and http://blog.boldaslove.co.uk) lives in Brighton on the south coast of England, scene of two fine World Science Fiction Conventions. She writes aesthetically ambitious, feminist intellectual science fiction and fantasy, for which she has won lots of awards. Cheryl Morgan remarks, "if you enjoy intelligent, well written, thought-provoking books that address the state of the modern world, viewed through a science-fictional lens, you can't ask for much better than Gwyneth Jones." She also writes award-winning young adult and children's novels under the name Anne Halam. Recently, writing about Julie Phillips' biography of Alice Sheldon aka James Tiptree, Jr., Jones addressed the subject of feminist anger: "What was all the fuss about? Is there no reason to be angry any more, or have we defaulted to the old position (c.f. Ursula Le Guin, in a letter quoted in the [Tiptree] biography), that the anger is a possibility, but we must bury it deep, way down deep, because we're not going to change the world."

"The Tomb Wife," published in F&SF, is a brutal tale of alien burial customs that are perhaps not so alien after all, and makes a thematically interesting companion to Gene Wolfe's "Memorare." On an interstellar freighter, Elen, the navigator, imagines she can hear the ghost of an alien's wife, buried alive with her husband an eon ago, walking around in an alien tomb the ship is transporting.

189

In Lar'sz' traditional society," said the alien, "a lady would often be buried with her husband. A rather beautiful custom, don't you think?"

The Active Complement of the interstellar freighter stared at him, slightly alarmed. Their companion, the illustrious "passenger" who had elected to share their vigil, liked to play games with their expectations. They never knew when he was joking. Humor glinted in Sigurt's black eyes—sharply diamond-shaped as to the rims, a curious and attractive difference from the Blue Planet oval.

"No, no! Not *buried alive*. Not like that, not at all. She would live in the tomb: she would retire there of her own free will, to spend the rest of her days in peace and solitude." He reached a claw-like fingernail to scratch his ear. "Lar'sz' nobles and peasants continued the practice well into historical times. It's the sons of the soil and the owners of the soil who preserve old cultural features, isn't it? And the dispossessed, of course. Refugees."

They were gathered in the mess: seven Blue Planet humans, vital components in the freighter's wetware: plus one celebrated alien archaeologist. The hold was laden with precious ancient artifacts from Sigurt's World, on their way to an exhibition. The Cultural Ambassadors and their staff were making the crossing in dreamtime, but this black-eyed, shadow-skinned, graceful creature preferred activity. They were not clear—they weren't good at reading the small print—whether "Sigurt" was a generic name, or whether their archaeologist was also the actual "Sigurt" who had made first contact. None of them had yet dared to ask him.

It was a pleasant, low-ceilinged saloon, decorated in silver and green, the traditional color scheme of the young culture of interstellar transport. Light gleamed from above like sunlight through leaves, the floor had the effects of grass and mosses. They sat around a blond wood table, actually extruded ceramic fiber, that faithfully recalled polished birch. The air was fresh and sweet, the whole impression was as if they were in a roomy tent, a pavilion pitched in sunny woodland, somewhere in the Blue Planet's beautiful temperate zones. But outdoors the blizzard raged, pitiless, unimaginable. The hum of the torus was never-ending; they no longer heard it. And if it ever stopped, that deep subliminal murmur, they would not have time to notice it was gone.

The Active Complement had just found out—Panfilo Nube, Payload Officer, had discovered the small print of the manifest, in an idle moment—that one of the pieces in the hold was supposed to be haunted. It was a tomb, but the ghost was not the official owner, so to speak. It was something called a "Tomb Wife," some kind of ghoul associated with tombs in Lar'sz' culture. Nadeem, the moody, black-browed Homeostat Commissar, had asked Sigurt—half joking—was this spook definitely dead? They didn't know much, but they knew that the people of Sigurt's World were very long-lived, with a propensity for long comas when times were hard. Sigurt had answered cheerfully that one could not be absolutely sure; and hence the explanation.

"A Tomb Wife did not provide for herself, you see," he continued. "She was a hermit, a *sadhu*." He smiled at Nadeem, who did not smile back. "Her family or her servants would supply food and necessities, but they never saw her. Among the peasantry of course the widow simply went to live in the graveyard, in full view of her neighbors. Her exclusion from society was formal, ritual. . . ."

Rafael, the young Assistant Navigator, frowned uneasily. "But how can you say you're not absolutely sure she's dead? The relics down there are thousands of years old, aren't they? I don't mind, I'd just like to know. A ghost is cool, but a thing that lives in a tomb and isn't dead, well—"

In a starship's psychological topography, the hold is always *down*. Nobody laughed. Rafe suffered from transit nightmares, an affliction as crippling as seasickness—but it didn't affect his efficiency, or his passion for this strange ocean.

"I think we can *assume* she's dead," said the mischievous alien. "In the records of Tene'Lar'sznh, the royal house to which this princess belonged, it's noted that the food-offerings first went untouched about fifteen hundred years ago, our time. That's about four thousand of Blue years, I think?"

The Active Complement nodded hurriedly, in unison. Vast timescales made them nervous. A little less, thought Elen, the Navigator. She was intimately aware of the relation between a Blue Planet "year" and the same period for Sigurt's planet; as she was aware of every detail of the impossible equations of this journey. She wanted to put Sigurt right, but how would she reach the end of that sentence? But *when*, in what relation, at what particular moment? She closed the floodgates with an effort.

"The food went untouched?" she repeated. "And that's how they knew? So, what did they do, when a Tomb Wife's food 'went untouched'?"

"Nothing at all." Sigurt's pointed teeth flashed: the modified aggression of a grin, which seemed to be a constant of humanoid life. "How quick of you, Elen, you're exactly right. A lady of rank did not allow herself to be seen, once she'd taken up residence. Her servants or family would continue to supply her needs, but they were forbidden, by the lady's own will and testament, to go looking for her, and the tomb could be a large and complex building. Nobody would know *when, precisely,* the offerings became offerings to the dead." He paused. "Isn't that beautiful? After a year—or thereabouts, depending on the liturgical calendar—the undertakers were allowed inside. The lady's remains would be found and there'd be a funeral. In the case of our princess, however, legend has it that no remains were ever recovered.

And that is how this particular tomb became known as 'haunted.'"

"She probably legged it one dark night," decided Rafe, with relief: and then blushed. "Uh, sorry if that's a poor taste idea, Sigurt, no offense."

"None taken."

"Aren't *you* a Lar'sz'ian, Sigurt?" wondered Carter, the burly ship's doctor, who wore the captain's armband. "Lar-ziote, Larzy-ite, however you say it?" Carter was one of those people who have to assert themselves in the presence of celebrity or renown. He had a horror of showing defer-ence to anything or anyone.

For a moment the alien bristled, a startled double-take of affront, thought Elen (although she couldn't be sure). The Lar'sz' were now (when is *now, where* is now?) an impover-ished, short-lived remnant. The famous tombs, temples, ru-ins, were scattered over scratch-dirt, subsistence farming desert country. Maybe it was like telling a Brazilian you'd thought he was Portuguese.

"My family has Tene'Lar't ancestry, but it's a long way back."

Nadeem the Commissar shifted in his recollection of a birchwood chair: restless with thoughts he knew nobody shared. "Why do you say 'Tomb *Wife*,' Sigurt? Why a *lady*? You beings don't *have* our two biological sexes."

Nadeem was a Diaspora-denier. He would bore the socks off you explaining, interminably, how actually there was *no* uncontroversial evidence that all planetary variants on the sentient biped model, all the possessors of "numinous intel-ligence," capable of interstellar transit, were descended from a single species. He passionately refused to accept that the original species had been a hominid from the Blue Planet— a precursor of Homo sapiens who had flourished and van-ished, leaving only the faintest and most puzzling of traces. *It's only a theory,* he'd insist.

And yet the man was a scientist.

You had to excuse him (they *did* excuse him, they were very tolerant of each other's foibles. Sigurt shared this trait, or he could not have joined them). You had to remind yourself that believing that the Earth was the center of the cosmos had once been good science and sound common sense, and many eminent scientists had clung to the old model, long after the new facts arrived.

Diaspora-deniers favored the term "beings." They thought it made them sound rational and agnostic; which it did not. The rest of the Actives called their illustrious friend *an alien,* without embarrassment, because at home *alien* had become a term for the much-loved human practice of body-morphing, and they'd forgotten it might be offensive. Sigurt didn't seem to mind. He called *them* "Blues."

He was not just eminent, he was an original, a Blue Planetophile. His skill in "Blue" languages had not been acquired for the sake of this trip; it was his hobby in real life. He had no trouble dealing with Nadeem.

"Ah, good point." He pondered, raising his eyebrows, which were commas of black velvet, the same texture as the close mat of hair (or fur) that covered his skull and extended down his neck and across his shoulders, glimpsed at the throat of his ship-issue green jumper. "Let me think. No, I'm sure 'wife' is correct. The *wife* is the one who remains, who cannot tear herself away. This is social gender, not biology."

Nadeem was not satisfied. Ideally, he explained, all self-respecting other beings, when speaking human language, should call themselves *it*—

Elen imagined a dry landscape, a dustbowl sky: parched mounds with small stone markers (the graves she envisaged were Muslim, somehow). The burial ground was sown with sad hunched shapes outside little cardboard shacks; the villages were depopulated of grandmas. Did the tomb-wives really choose seclusion? Or were they compelled by the iron hand of custom? Which nobody inside the rules will ever admit is an oppression. The blizzard outside ought to be a sandstorm, she thought, to match their cargo. But it was whiteness she always imagined "out there." A white darkness of quantum vacuum. She noticed that Sigurt had said wives, not widows, though his English was very good; and she wondered about that. They are not the widows of the dead but the wives of the tombs.

"Stop kidding yourself, Batman." Nadeem was getting agitated. "It's not a one-off planetary evolution that we have in common, it's time, gravity, hydrogen bonds. It's an accident of convergent evolution that we look more or less alike. You've let yourself get sucked in to a cheap, tourist way of thinking, denying your own difference, fantasizing that you can *understand us*—"

"You're a racist jerk, Nadeem," responded Sigurt amiably. "Anyway, you just did it yourself."

"*What*—?"

The alien raised his arms, spreading the webs between his slender fingers, hooking the air with his claws. "Anthropomorphizing. You called me Batman."

Elen suited up and visited the hold. The float tube delivered her to darkness, where she drifted from one handhold to the next, following track lights to the main cargo compartment. She flooded the great space with air and pressure, touched down as gravity embraced her, took off her helmet, passed through the lock, and walked into a cavern at the roots of a sea-mount. The habitat a green, sunlit island far above—

The artifacts were crated in force fields, but she couldn't adjust the light above art-conservation level. *Pedants,* she murmured, marveling at the dim, pixelated spectacle. The Lar'sz' part of the collection was the most impressive: so damned impressive you could almost justify the mad expense of the shipping. The haunted tomb was huge, multistoried. It caught her breath. She circled it slowly, calculating that their whole living quarters would easily fit into the Tomb Wife's portico.

There was a single doorway, a black teardrop without a door: set about two meters above ground level, amid a coruscation of carved and inlaid stone. It would be a scramble to get inside. Perhaps the front steps had been left behind, or there was a secret mechanism, something like ancient Egypt. She sat cross-legged, slightly awkward in her suit, gazing. Like most sailors of the strange ocean, she rarely got farther than the dockside when she made landfall. Even if there'd been more time and less bureaucracy she wouldn't have been tempted by a lightning tour of Sigurt's planet. What for? You'd see so little. You'd learn hardly anything.

She'd been interested in the cargo as a professional challenge, a factor in her caculations. The science of transporting massive material objects was in its infancy, and artwork was a *nightmare*! But here in the gloom she felt the value of these things. A virtual Lar'sz' tomb, freighted through the transit in a courier's brain, downloaded into the digital inventories of a limited-release of premier museums, could never have had this presence. The Exhibition was going to be a revelation.

There was nothing to stop them from breaching the force fields for a preview, without the fuzz. No areas were barred to Active Complement, except the fearsome threshold of the torus itself. She should come back with Sigurt, get him to give her a guided tour. But not the tomb, she thought.

If she went into the tomb, she'd like to do it alone.

The image of a dessicated heap of bones and skin, preserved intact, flitted through her mind. The Tomb Wife in a stone room, an old lady fallen down with a broken hip, too proud to cry for help when she heard her servants arriving and departing. But how old was she? Maybe she was still young when the food offerings "remained untouched." Sigurt would know. She would ask him. Or better, she'd look it up herself, and impress him by knowing something. It was probably all in the background files the Complement didn't bother to read.

If the practice had survived into historical times it could still be happening. *Suttee* had continued in India long after the Brits tried to stamp it out, had resurfaced even in the Space Age. But it was the haunting that fascinated Elen. Do ghosts travel? Did pharaohs and Inca sacrifices ever wake up, bewildered, in glass cases, half a world away from home? Did they wake up in modern times, to find themselves replicated in software? What about a journey so immense that it has no duration? What damage would the relativity storm of the blizzard do to something as fragile as spiritual remains? How embarrassing if the loaned archaeology arrived stripped of its patina and pedigree. . . . How embarrassing for the fledgling enterprise of interstellar freight, if there should be a Missing Legend incident!

She listened until she was sure she could hear footsteps inside the ziggurat. No, it's okay, she's still there, still haunting. Unhurried, peaceful, timeless, the Tomb Wife was going about her quiet routines.

Rafe had agonized nightmares in which the Lar'sz' ghûl crept around his brain and scratched at his bunk closure: seeking live human flesh. Seriously repentant, Sigurt dredged up (or fabricated) some potent ancient Lar'sz'ian prayers, which he translated into English phonemes, and taught Rafe to recite. Elen had said nothing about the footsteps in the tomb, but she felt equally responsible. She might have leaked it into the shared reality; telepathy artifacts were the bane of starfaring. You learned that you *had to* think no evil of your companions in the matrix, or there would be hell to pay. And don't imagine spooks, or somebody will get spooked.

She did not confess. It would only have made Rafe worse.

At the end of a long shift she unplugged herself from the mainframe, meeting as always the adrenaline of panic as she returned to ship-time: clutching at her stomach, icy down her spine. Carter was the captain on this trip, thank God. But Elen was the one who crunched the numbers. She was finally responsible for all the lives on board (not to mention those huge ancient gewgaws in the hold). And the worst was knowing that if—*if!*—she'd let a transcription error get by, it would not manifest itself until the closing phase. Not until too late. That's quantum computing, no way around it.

The terror of the blizzard engulfed her. No radio, no GPS for this ocean. No ground control for this spaceship, not the slightest possibility of rescue. She saved-off their position meticulously, although off-frame storage was nonsense, no such thing as a Black Box; and let the solidity of the banks of instruments and winking screens reassure her. The freighter's official name was *Pirate Jenny* (not that Actives themselves bothered much with names of starships); reflecting the Brechtian, Utopian leanings of the parent company, and its financial partner, the World State of Earth. Other ships were the *Clement Atlee* and the *Eleanor Roosevelt.* Their sisters were the *White Visitation,* the *Sacred Wicca,* the *Caer Siddi.* Elen decided she preferred the occult strand. No Black Box but this is Black Art. We don't know what we are doing; we conjure with monstrous forces, far beyond our control.

Footsteps behind her, a breath on the back of her neck, a mocking sigh.

"So you got out," she whispered, and turned slowly, hoping to catch a glimpse of the Tomb Wife's ghost. Nobody there. She never lets herself be seen—

They grew accustomed to the extra presence. "I blame myself," said Sigurt, but in fact the symptom was a common one, technically harmless in terms of neurophysics: believed to be benign by superstitious Actives. Only Rafe was troubled, and he had his prayers. Sigurt told stories. Nadeem the Commissar and the Chief Engineer flirted. The Assistant Navigator, Chief Engineer's former squeeze, took up with Passenger Liaison. Elen visited the hold again, alone. She'd decided against the guided tour.

In the low light, looking up at that black, balanced teardrop, she fell into a reverie in which the Tomb Wife tradition was not oppression but a shimmering resolve. Not to move on, not to let go of the past: to decide, so far and no farther. The princess had chosen to *stick,* as they say in cards, at the grief of loss. To stay with the absence, never to let it fritter away into vague anniversaries, faded rose leaves of memory. Was refusing to let go a feminine trait? Or was it a Blue trait, which she was cutting and pasting onto the customs of another planet? It was an Elen trait. She told people (family, boyfriends, outsiders), that she was an interstellar navigator for the adventure of it. The most exotic of exotic travel. But we do not travel, she thought. Not a step. When the transcription is done—what does *when* mean, where there is no time?—we will make the crossing in almost zero extension.

What we do is stay, in the paradoxical moment—

Without deliberation she stood up, used her sleeve controls to open the tomb's force field, and set her gloved palms on the doorsill. Her suit was limber, designed for active wear. A push downward, a bounce up, she had her knee on stone. As she stood up diffuse lighting welled around her. The tomb had been prepared for visitors. She realized, disappointed, that she couldn't possibly be the first to enter since the Tomb Wife's time: probably not even the first Blue! A short passage led into a stone room, where a table like an altar stood against an inner wall. Above it a life-size mural, in brilliant color, showed two people, same height, same build, sitting opposite each other, informally; knees up. They both looked like Sigurt, in a generic way. They were gazing at each other, their diamond-shaped eyes over-bright, their smiling lips full of sadness. Both had the short cape of black velvet fur. One of them seemed to be wearing a black half-mask. It was this figure who reached to the other, one slender hand outstretched, as if in an unfinished caress. Below them on the altar stood an array of diamond-shaped bowls: a curved platter, a heap of dry rags.

She looked into the bowls. Dead leaves, granular dust—

Are the conventions of mourning a universal constant? Elen thought of Etruscan tombs, Chinese ancestor worship. Her files contained no data, only the vaguest notions, but she was pretty sure that mural was a masterpiece. Her gauntleted hand must have brushed one of the artifacts. A label sprang into existence in the air, explaining—in Sigurt's planet's dominant script, in English, and in a third writing she didn't recognize—that the actual bowls and platters had been taken away, with their ancient contents. These were replicas. The dry rags were a replica of the decayed set of clothes that had been found—

The past as theme-park is a universal constant.

She explored the stone corridors of the ground floor, paying no further attention to the artwork: ghoulish and hopeful as a child, looking for the bones that had never been discovered.

She found only dust, and very little of that. There were no stairways to the upper floors, and nothing she could identify as living quarters. The artful lighting started to make her feel like a tourist. She took refuge in the gloomiest of the court-yards and sat there looking at another black teardrop, halfway up a wall: quietly visiting the shade of a long-dead "prin-cess."

Immense peace, engulfing spiritual quiet.

She listened for footsteps, suddenly terrified.

Abruptly she got up and returned to the entrance, dropped to the floor.

As she closed the field behind her, embarrassed by her moment of panic in there, a black manta ray swooped across the ocean trench darkness. Elen yelped, and stared around wildly. The shadow cruised again. Her heart was thumping, my God, what is that thing? What's in here with me?

"Who's there—?"

No answer but the hiss of disturbed air. "*Hey!* Who's there?"

Sigurt landed beside her with a soft thump, wrapping slippery folds of bat wings around him. "Ah," he said, with smiling interest. "So it's you, Elen."

She stared, appalled: open-mouthed. "My God! Sigurt! What d'you think you're doing! *You can't fly!* This is *not* a game!"

"On the contrary," said the alien cheerfully. "The whole universe is a game, is it not? A puzzle-mass of tiny units of information, the pattern of which can be changed at will— given the torus, and the fabulous software implanted in a trained, numinous consciousness. Such as yours, Elen. I'm not the expert, but isn't that the whole basis of interstellar 'navigation'?"

Elen was shaking with horror. "You can't do this! You can't piss around doing impossible things in the transition! Our lives depend, every f-fucking moment—"

"On our conviction that all this is real," he finished, unre-pentant. He showed her the fx controller on his sleeve; and switched it off. The bat wings vanished.

"I can access a toy from the ship's library without damaging the equation, can't I? I was just playing. I'm much lighter than a Blue, and there's not a great deal of gravity in here. I've been jumping off the monuments."

She dropped her head in her hands as relief thundered through her, leaving her spent and hollow. Starfarers live in constant terror, like sailors on the ancient oceans. You don't realize, until you hit a peak, how high the ambient stress is getting—

"Just for the record, Sigurt, there's no software, not the way you mean."

"I know that we maintain all this," he waved a slender hand, shadow-pale in the dark. "Between us . . . I've never been quite sure how it's done. You Blues have all the secrets. Is it true that Starflight Actives have had brain surgery?"

Sigurt's people had stunning cellular regeneration. They treated almost any trauma as a purely medical problem. The sciences of surgery and (worse!) gene manipulation had come as a horrible shock to them. Barbarism.

"No surgery. No implants. It's more like a tissue culture. You have to have the right kind of brain to start with. The reason you can be awake is because you're like us, Sigurt: but you're a straight, a virgin. We've had the training that makes us grow the extra neuronal architecture, which doesn't, er, exist in normal space—"

"Or you would be hydrocephalic Eloi, with heads the size of pumpkins."

She nodded, though she had no idea what an Eloi was.

They sat with their knees folded up, like the figures in the mural—

"I'm sorry I fooled around, Elen. I scared you. I think I'm going stir crazy."

"Or else you're reacting poorly to racist abuse, Batman."

Sigurt laughed, and scratched his ear. "*Batman!* Half-domino, cute little shoulder cape. Sounds too girly for my taste. If you like comparisons, we are more akin to frilled lizards than bats."

"Nadeem must really annoy you."

"He is *something I would scrape off my shoe*," pronounced the alien, with relish. He tipped back his head. "Do you hear that, Commissar? Shoe-Scrapings!"

They started to laugh. The Active Complement lived in each other's heads, accommodating each other as if they'd been workmates for a lifetime. They were a group mind: inhibited, licensed; in constant negotiation. Elen replayed the first remark Sigurt had made. Sigurt had known that someone was visiting the artifacts, but because he was only supercargo, not A/C, he hadn't known who it was.

"I've been visiting the Tomb Wife," she said. "I'm fascinated by the idea of a ghost on an instantaneous transit. Do you know anything more about her?"

The alien shrugged. "Like what?"

The tomb crouched like a massive, patient animal. Ancient artifacts peered at them from the gloom, carving and shaping blurred into a vague sense of *life*.

"Was she old? Was she young . . . ? Did she have a lover?"

"Widows are a danger to social cohesion," said the alien. "The relict of a partnership has to be neutralized, or there'll be mésalliances, inheritance disputes. Therefore the widow must marry again, harmlessly. She must wed the tomb—"

"That sounds very human. Nadeem would be horrified."

Sigurt seemed to think it over. "The ancient Lar'sz' kept state records," he said at last. "And accounts. Not much else was written down. I'm afraid we don't know much. There are the bas-reliefs, but they're high art, highly ambiguous. And not of her choosing, of course. They are the memorial her husband ordered."

Elen wanted to ask *what was her name,* but she was afraid that might be a lapse in taste, a cultural taboo. Another question came to her. "Is it right to call her a ghost? Or did a haunting mean something different to the ancient Lar'sz'?"

"It's different and it's the same, of course."

The constant cry of one numinously intelligent sentient biped to another.

Sigurt grinned, acknowledging the problem. "Let me try to bridge the gap. In my world we believe that people can,

how can I put it, *leave themselves behind* at certain junc-
tures, life events. Someone else goes on. When we speak of
a haunting, that's our derivation. Not the, er, spirit of someone physically dead. D'you see?"

"Yes," said Elen, startled and moved. "Yes, I think I do."

She felt that she knew Sigurt better, after this conversation. There was a bond between them, the celebrated archaeologist and the navigator: unexpected but real.

The country of no duration can't be seen from the outside.
You can never look back and say *there,* I was. *That's* what
happened. Everything that "happened" in a transit was doomed
to vanish like a dream when they fell back into normal
space. As the *Pirate Jenny* moved, without motion, to the
end, without ending, of the paradoxical moment, everyone
had a terrible psychic headache. The Active Complement
suffered fretful agonies that swamped the ghost, Rafe's nightmares; all their shipboard entanglements. They regarded
Sigurt, whose wakefulness was part of their burden, not so
much as an exciting famous person, more as a demanding
pet. Batman's favorite expression (of course!) set everybody's
teeth on edge.

The captain had been interstellar crew for as long as
there'd been commercial interstellar traffic, and he could
see the writing on the wall. "The *Pirate Jenny* is a horseless
carriage," he moaned, in mourning for the sunlit green
walls, the mossy ground, the polished birchwood. "Soon it
will all be gone, all this. Nobody will bother. Passengers
will transport themselves, we'll be obsolete."

"Shut up," muttered Elen, "shut up, shut up, I'm trying to
concentrate—"

She was mortally afraid that she'd made a mistake. She
scoured the code for a single trace of the ghost (there must
be a trace!) found none, and knew she must have missed
something. Mistake, mistake. The insensate, visceral memory that she *always* felt like this in the closing phase was no
comfort at all.

"What about freight?" Gorgeous Simone, Chief Engineer,
looked up from a game of solitaire. "Who's going to carry

the freight, doctor? Hump it through the indefinite void, if not people like us? Fuck, look at the size of *that* problem."

"Swearbox," piped Rafe, who had grown chirpy while the others grew morose, and was now a rock, a shoal, an infuriating danger to shipping.

"Go and eat your head."

"They'll paint the crates with essence of consciousness," explained Carter, doom-laden. "Or some crazy Borgs will break the Convention. They'll create actual supernuminal 'Artificial Intelligence' nanotech, and inject it into matter."

"So fucking what. You won't be redundant, you're a doctor."

"Ooops! Swearbox again!"

"Does not compute, man! If it's a true AI, it'll have civil rights and they won't be able to make it do anything. We'll unionize it, it will be on our side—"

The alien laid his black velvet head on his slender arms on the tabletop and sighed, very softly. All seven of them took this as an outrageous insult. They'd have fallen on Batman and torn him limb from limb, except that they knew there'd be hell to pay. The navigator quit the saloon and retired to her section. God, let this be the peak. Let us be over the mountain, this is unbearable.

They were over the mountain.

Elen reported their position, news which was greeted with exhausted relief. Now there was nothing for her to do but watch the tumblers fall: watch the numbers cascade into resolution, not a phase-point out of place. She loved this part and hated it—

She went down to the hold to visit the Tomb Wife, for the last time. There was a rumor that they'd all be given free passes for the Exhibition, but she didn't think she'd go. The relationship had been formed here, in the dim-lit cavern under a sea-mount. It wouldn't be the same in normal space. The tomb greeted her with its shimmering silence, with the stillness of a grief embraced; set in stone.

"Hello?" she whispered. "I think I'm here to say goodbye."

She was not surprised when Sigurt joined her. They smiled at each other and sat for a while; but the black teardrop beckoned. The alien succumbed first. He hooked his long fingers into twin curves in the carving that she hadn't noticed, and was through the doorway in one movement. There weren't any steps, thought Elen. The entrance is supposed to be like that. She tried to copy his action but couldn't find the handholds. She had to make the same scrambling jump as before; and followed him to the chamber where the partners faced each other, the "wife" poised forever in that gesture of farewell.

Emotion recorded in art was the *rosetta stone*, the only (and frequently deceptive) common language of the Diaspora. Elen wasn't sure what a *rosetta stone* had been, originally. Sigurt would probably know. But she felt she understood the message of that unfinished caress; the speech in those bright, half-hidden eyes. The dead are gone. The Tomb Wife stayed with *herself*. She stayed with the life that had ended, rather than going on, a different person—

How strange, how beautiful.

Sigurt had gone farther into the tomb. At length she heard him coming back. She didn't have to look around, she could clearly picture him leaning in the ancient doorway. She imagined *staying with herself,* in the country of no duration. As often as she left this homeland and woke into forgetfulness, she never got used to the wrench of parting. Oh, she thought. I need not leave. I can stay. If I hadn't taken this berth, if I had never met Sigurt, I would never have realized that I could do this! With a rush of immense gratitude toward the alien, she knelt, she crept on her knees to the offertory table and settled there, curled against the stone.

"The Tomb Wife was obliged to remain," said the archaeologist, behind her, in a tone of mild apology. "For all eternity, with the partner to whom she was bound. But in special conditions it might be possible to make, well, a kind of exchange. One ghost for another. I may have lied to you a little. In *your* terms, it happened long, long ago. In *my* lifetime, the time I have spent awake, it was not so long ago as all that."

Faintly, in her mind's eye, Elen saw that she had let a transcription error get past her, and what was happening to her now was the consequence. In absolute terms there was no saloon, no eminent alien, no hold full of tombs, there was nothing but the storm, never anything but the storm, the blizzard, and she was falling into it, into the thrilling void of terror that every starfarer knew was waiting—

Emotion can deceive. The sentient bipeds barely knew anything about each other, as yet. Misconceptions abounded, wild mistakes were only found out when it was too late. A family divided by a single language, thought Elen: knowing at the same time that everything, the stone against her cheek, Batman's deception, was a translation, and really there was only the blizzard. Yet in the last paradoxical moment, annoyed that it had to happen, that she would not stay here entirely, she felt herself splitting, giving birth to the person who would go on.

—and saw herself walking away with Sigurt, arm in arm: glimpsed, through the veil of Elen the Navigator's physical form, the Tomb Wife's caped shoulders, the delicate black domino of velvet fur, the gleam of the lovers' eyes.

An Evening's
Honest Peril

MARC LAIDLAW

---

*Marc Laidlaw (www.marclaidlaw.com) lives in Seattle,
Washington, where he moved in 1997 to work for Valve
Software, a game company. He was the lead writer for their
games* Half-Life *and* Half-Life 2. *In the 1980s, he was associated with the cyberpunk movement and appeared in
Bruce Sterling's* Mirrorshades: The Cyberpunk Anthology.
*Of his career as a games writer, he says "I have a truly
sfnal job: The industry did not exist when I was learning to
write, and in fact was the sort of futuristic fantasy I sometimes wrote about. In much the same way that space sf
spurred generations of space pioneers, cyberpunk and similar sf about virtual worlds has inspired the creators of those
worlds."*

"An Evening's Honest Peril" appeared in Rudy Rucker's
Flurb: A Webzine of Astonishing Tales. *Laidlaw says, "I
see this was written in August 2001, btw. Sat in a drawer for
six years till Rudy asked if I had anything lying around."
This is a story about gaming and family life. It is an interesting contrast to the Kage Baker story appearing earlier in
this book.*

Sitting at the entrance to the Tomb of Abomnis, dangling her legs like tempting morsels over the dark and moaning stony mouth, Jinrae thought she saw the head of a black-haired man rise into view at the crest of the hilltop behind her. She leapt to her feet with her sword drawn and ready.

Echoing her startled cry, a raven swept up and over her, flapping twice and then gliding toward a distant tumble of faint brownish buildings in the middle distance.

Stop jumping at shadows! she told herself.

Settling back down, she watched the black fleck merging with the evening sky. The sun had just gone down beyond the town of Cowper's Rest, pulling daylight after it, triggering lights in the villas. The ravenspeck circled and landed somewhere in a farmer's field. Scattered red flowers nodded in unison, bowing to a breeze she couldn't sense herself. In the far, far distance, an olive smudge gave little hint of the horrid marsh it heralded.

Groans came from the tomb, groans and the rattling of chains to greet the coming night, but they struck no answering note of fear in Jinrae. Once the sound would have chilled her, a weirdly welcome pang, but these days, even in the worst places, she rarely found anything strong enough to cut through the numbness that enwrapped her. Vague dreads wrestled in the back of her mind, ones she didn't care to name. She felt she was seeing the seams of the world to-night.

Someone was coming. A silvery glint on polished mail

faintly limned a figure stalking across the plain at a pace that would have maddened her if she'd had to tolerate it. Thankfully, they would not be travelling any great distance on foot tonight—although if it came to that, she had sufficient scrolls to quicken even the slowest feet. Aye, she carried boots of speed and hasty syrup and portalismans; besides which, numerous powerful friends would come to her summons, although she intended to rely on no resources besides her own at this point. It was hard, alone, but better in the long run. The last few days had taught her a great deal about her vulnerabilities, skills she had neglected through too much reliance on others. Or, at least, on one other. Hard lessons, late in coming, but not lost on her.

Now here was a fresh face, an adventurer in unblemished silver armor. It was Aynglin, just as she had seen him last, a bright orange plume bobbing from his helmet's crest. He had not put by his violet trousers, nor the green slippers with curling toes; and she couldn't fault him for it, since it lent him a quite distinctive (if not distinguished) appearance. She would be able to pick him out in almost any crowd.

His coat, however, was another matter: dark and oily, clearly stripped from a greater gullock, but with patches of long greenish fur still clinging to the seamed hide.

"Hi," said Aynglin as he came to a stop at the entrance of the tomb. His eyes were the same shade of violet as his pants. "I mean, hail. Hope I'm not late. You said to meet you at twilight, right?"

"Well met," said Jinrae. "You're right on time. You'll have to lose that gullock hide, though. It would only bog you down where we're going."

The ends of Aynglin's mouth turned drastically downward. "Really? I heard this was the best."

She couldn't suppress a laugh. "I hope you didn't pay a great deal for it."

"No, I . . . I found it."

"Well, that should tell you something of its value. Someone didn't think enough of it to lug it along or even throw it on their mule. A perfect hide is well worth its weight, but that one's imperfectly tanned. See the hunks of fur, never quite scraped away? It's the work of a not particularly prom-ising apprentice. In the hands of an expert, this would have made a coat I wouldn't mind wearing myself."

He mumbled a glum, "Oh."

"Anyway, let's see what I've got that you can use."

She reached into a pack she'd dropped on the terraced hillside, and pulled out a cloak of sheer material, supple as silk but silvery as the scales of some freshwater fish swim-ming in light. She leapt down next to Aynglin, eliciting hungry moans from the lurkers in the tomb. Aynglin took a backwards step.

"Don't fear," she said. "They're bound within. Now put this on. It's meadowshark."

"Really?"

"You can keep that. And I'll give you matching pants later, if you accompany me back to Cowper's Rest. They're not violet, though. They won't match your eyes."

"That's okay! I—these were just temporary till I found something better."

"Everything's temporary. Don't get attached to anything. That way you won't suffer when you lose it. Which you will."

"Okay. I guess I'm ready." The gullock coat lay in a heap on the gravel path. "Is this it? Just the two of us?"

"It's for the best," she said. "You'll progress much faster."

"But where's your partner? Isn't he . . . ?"

"Not anymore. Let me see your sword."

Aynglin unsheathed his blade and held it out to her.

For a moment Jinrae felt painfully disoriented.

The pommel held a faceted orange gem, inlaid with a rune of fire. The curved white blade was gnarlphin horn, lightly glimmering with imbued magic.

She knew this sword. It was, if not unique, then one of a very few.

"Where did you get this?" she asked.

"From a stranger," he said.

"Masked? Anonymous?"

Aynglin nodded.

"May I touch it for a moment?"

Aynglin hesitated, and she couldn't tell if it was indecision or merely ignorance that held him back.

"I only need to touch it in order to divine its properties," she said. "You needn't fear handing it over to me."

"I trust you," he said simply.

She put a gloved hand on the hilt, and turned so that the twilight gleamed along the blade. There was no inscription where she had feared to find one. But that meant nothing. Engravings melted away with the proper words muttered over them. Entire histories could be erased that way.

Still, it hinted of something more than chance, and she knew the mystery would haunt her until she solved it.

At that moment, the first star pierced the deepening twilight. A wolflike wind began to wail through the hills and the moaning in the tomb grew louder.

She nodded at Aynglin and took her hand from the sword. "Keep that out," she said. "You'll need it. I'll enter first and make sure there's nothing nastier than I expect."

"Right behind you."

She stepped through the tomb entrance, into darkness deeper than at first seemed possible. Her eyes adjusted slowly to the distant flicker of torches. Aynglin shouldered past her before she could stop him and kept going, blundering on without yet realizing that she had come to a halt. She hurried up behind him in the narrow passage, in time to see him hesitate before turning to look back for her.

"Oh, there you are."

"Go on," she said.

At that, he rushed forward. But there were already things rushing to meet him.

They came on in a cluster, sliding and jostling in the passage that seemed too small for them. Wicked yellow eyes abulge, catching the torchlight; flattened catlike faces with venomous fangs and exposed claws like hypodermic needles. Aynglin raised his sword and slashed, first at one, then another. He hardly seemed to feel the claws that tore into him. Jinrae knew that as yet he had no concept of his own frailty. After twenty seconds, he was on the edge of death. By twenty-five he would be gone, unless she intervened.

With a quick word, she raised her hands and cast a sphere of healing and protection over him. A second incantation, and Aynglin's sword flared with a sharp red light. He was like a mercurial spirit now, slashing his way through the denizens of the tomb as if they were wraiths without substance, offering scarcely any impediment to his progress. Jinrae followed in his wake, sidestepping littered limbs and dislodged eyes, continually hurling potent protective devices at her protégé's silhouette. This close to the surface, they had little to dread. She tried to find a rhythm that would serve her well as the evening's onslaught grew more dreadful.

It was in a chamber on the second level, where the ceiling was encrusted with encysted shapes of winged sleeping things, that Aynglin, in the midst of slicing through a hoary tomb spider, suddenly stiffened and flared, casting off brilliant showers and spirals of light. When the seething fires had subsided, he seemed to stand taller, fuller and brighter in every detail. He barely nicked the next spider and it curled up instantaneously into a ball of ash, hugging itself with its wiry crisping legs. The arachnid dissolved into ashes and crumbled away.

"Congratulations!" Jinrae called. Aynglin turned and raised his sword, victorious, thereby scraping the ember-colored chrysalis on the ceiling. His upturned face went green, flooded with the sickly radiance of unfolding wings. The hatchling dropped straight down onto him.

Jinrae leapt forward with her blade out, slashing through the larval demonid. It expired with a putrid belch, but not before its myriad kin had been roused from their hibernation.

"What now?" Aynglin asked, struggling up from beneath the crackling membranous corpse.

"This is good," Jinrae said. "Keep your ground and I'll watch over you. We're lucky to have found such a chamber this early."

"Are you sure?"

But there was no time to answer; the awakening was too swift. She barely had time to form her own shield of immiscibility, which would hold for as long as she remained immobile. From that vantage, she began to cast spells upon young Aynglin.

The first wave of demonids clattered against her hastily erected barrier with the scraping sound of chitinous iron-taloned wings. They swarmed the young swordsman, who stood waving his blade as if carving patterns in the air. In this case, the air was solid with wings and claws, and as he carved he could hardly help but open demonid veins. The room began to fill with a churning bloodcloud, as if he had tapped some atmospheric source of scarlet gore.

While the cries of the awakened demonids were deafening, and grew worse as their injuries increased, Jinrae gradually became aware of another sound. It was sharp and shrill, hysterical—and somehow, she felt, juvenile.

It took her several moments to recognize that a third human had entered the chamber; small and quick. In a manner reminiscent of the demonids themselves, it pounced on one of the flyers and bore it to the ground, tearing off the fanged head in one practiced twist. A gloved hand reached and caught a scaly wing, pulling another demonid from the swarm. And then another. Jinrae suppressed her irritation, trying to keep her concentration on her shield. Even so, her attention had become divided, and she feared that Aynglin would suffer for it if she did not deal with the interloper immediately.

"We thank you for your aid," she called with forced politeness, "but it is completely unrequired."

Naught but a feverish laugh was heard in reply.

The air was beginning to thin of the predators, and she sensed Aynglin beginning to falter. He had been close to another metamorphosis, but now he teetered on the brink, disrupted by the new arrival. He was just becoming aware of the newcomer.

"To repeat, we do not require your aid. I am assisting this young one, and I have things well in hand."

This time, the intruder's response was more direct.

"Fuck you!"

Unsurprised, Jinrae drew in her shield, exposing herself to talon-blow and wing scourge. She dipped her hand into the wallet at her belt, slipping on a ring she knew by touch. It was highly polished, twisted once along its band: a moebius ring.

She raised her hand and tightened her fist, as if grasping some invisible fabric and twisting it, wringing energy from raw aether.

A violet jolt shook the room, briefly illuminating all the demonid flyers from within. Skin, scale and chitin grew transparent; skeletons leapt out clearly, luridly aglow. The savage skeletal flock swerved and locked its knobbled ends into a single mass, moving with a collective will, a shifting puzzlebeast of bone and fang.

Their exclusive target was the foul-mouthed intruder.

In a shrieking cloud they congealed around him, cutting off the shrill and mocking laughter at a stroke. An instant later they thinned and dissipated, resuming their strident attack on Aynglin, albeit without their scaly hide this time. He dispatched the remainder of the bony flock with something less than his former verve, but before he was quite finished, another lightning bolt of transformation shuddered through him. Jinrae grinned with pleasure to see him climb another notch in stature and in heft. But Aynglin seemed disoriented, odd. Instead of rejoicing over his growth, he shuffled through the mass of demonid bones and corpses, and gazed down at the fallen stranger's clean-picked skeleton.

"Harsh," said Aynglin.

"I gave him fair warning," she said. "I will not tolerate his kind."

An engraved token lay among the bones of the uninvited guest. Aynglin bent and picked it up, scanned it, handed it to her.

"p00ter," she read aloud. "Alas, I fear poor p00ter won't be missed. And better him than you, I might add. I expected to perform a few resurrections tonight, but this would have been far too early. I don't wish to tarnish my reputation as a teacher."

"But . . . what did he want?"

"To sow discord. To disrupt your growth and steal what he could of your glory, little though he needed it. You could see how easily he took down the demonids. There are plenty of other chambers deeper down and in neighboring tombs, filled with horrors to keep him occupied . . . if he were looking for an evening's honest peril instead of craven mischief, that is. Now, don't trouble yourself. He's inconsequential, and we've far to go."

Her pupil shrugged and tossed the token back into the bone pile, then strode on deeper into the crypt. She stood watching him for a moment without following. Something about him reminded her of another swordsman, one not so young but just as eager. She had felt something like this when she'd watched him in the midst of the swarm, slicing scaly wings with an ease that seemed more than natural: practiced.

"Aynglin," she called, catching up to him, "I never asked this before, but . . . are you new here? Have you traveled here before in other guises?"

He turned and faced her, his eyes shifting in the torchlight, but unreadable. She realized how little she knew of him. But that had not troubled her until now. Why was she suddenly wary?

"What makes you ask that?" he said.

"You seem too good to have just started out tonight."

He allowed himself a smile. "Well, thanks, but . . . I am new here. I've had practice in other realms, maybe it carries over. I knew enough to seek you out, or someone like you, and ask for help. Thanks, by the way. I do appreciate it. I'm getting a lot of experience. I wouldn't say we make a great team, because I'm nowhere near being useful to you, but . . . it would be nice to get that far eventually."

She felt herself withdraw from him a little, and a chill set in. "Well, keep at it and I'm sure you can go as far as you want—as far as I have anyway. But you'll soon reach a point where I'm not much use to you. You'll want to pick other partners if you wish to keep advancing at speed."

"Who says I want that? Isn't it nice to just find a point that's good enough and forget about forging ahead? Isn't it good to find friends and journey with them, helping each other, even if it means you won't get the full glory all to yourself? Didn't you do that?"

"What do you mean?"

"I thought you had a partner. I mean, I heard back in Cowper's Rest, they said you were always with someone named Venix. Actually, I was expecting two of you tonight."

Ah. The source of the chill.

"We formally disbanded," she said. "I travel alone now, when I'm not in great need. And I have plenty of other friends I can call on when I am in need."

"And the same goes for Venix, I suppose?"

"He no longer inhabits this realm."

She realized that they had been standing a long time in an open chamber without attracting enemies. The dead time had lengthened beyond the usual bounds. Perhaps that was why she found herself wanting to end this conversation. Her eyes continually darted to the shadows among the splintered beams and stone pillars that seemed to support the uneven ceiling mined of greenish rock.

Suddenly Aynglin laughed. The sound nearly brought her back to herself.

"What is it?" she said.

"It just occurred to me . . . the reason you're suspicious. I mean, if he left and then I suddenly showed up out of the blue, you might think. . . ."

Grudgingly she said, "It's not inconceivable."

"I know, but . . . "

"And it doesn't help that you've found yourself a sword the twin of his."

"I told you, a stranger gave it to me."

"After you announced your intention of joining me tonight?"

"No. Before. In fact . . . well, perhaps your suspicions aren't so unfounded after all. It was the same man who told me to look you up when I was asking about a teacher."

"Ah, Gods," she said, and turned away from Aynglin. "Damn it all."

She didn't need his help, his patronage, or any more reminders of his presence. He had meant it as a farewell gesture, no doubt, and it ought to have comforted her, since it was a sure sign he had no intention of returning. He would never have given away the sword otherwise. But the end result of his farewell was that he might as well never have left. Because of his damned gift to this beginner, she was stuck with him after all. There could be no more blatant continual reminder.

She felt betrayed, and it didn't help that her student wouldn't have known he was being used to get at her. She could turn away Aynglin, but she'd contracted with him for the evening. She must keep her word or suffer harm to her reputation. She might be able to convince Aynglin to discard the sword, but he was unlikely to find a better one at any price, and she had nothing equivalent which he would be able to wield. And she wasn't yet ready to plead and bargain for her peace of mind.

She was snarled in the possibility of duplicity. More vague suspicions. It was maddening. Nothing was overt enough for her to subdue with any certainty.

"Come on," she said, shoving past Aynglin, wishing to immerse herself in action. Battle was the one thing over which she could still exert her mastery, a dynamic she completely understood, where nothing was hidden and all threats were in plain sight.

"I'm sorry if I—"

"Just come on."

But as she forged on, she realized that somewhere along the way, in the last few minutes, she must have let Aynglin lead them around an unfamiliar turning. They had come into a wide chamber she did not recognize, one where the crypts themselves lay shattered, slab lids cracked or cast aside, the open vaults full of broken skulls and scattered bones, completely plundered. She had expected the tomb to be more densely defended; the quiet was ominous. Once again, the rhythms of danger felt strange tonight.

But action was what she needed, and there was nothing here that would take her mind off her troubles. A quick survey showed that of four passages heading out of the room, two led sharply down.

And it was a sure formula that danger always lay deeper.

"This way," she said.

"Lead on!"

She reminded herself that it wasn't his fault. He'd been played into this, just as she had. But his enthusiasm now threatened to become an annoyance.

At the bottom of the ramp, the passage forked. The path to the left was unlit, so she headed right. At the next fork, torches lit the left hand path. She chose that one, although she had a growing sense that this was too obvious and could be an attempt to lure them into a trap.

Before she could reconsider, or retrace her steps, she heard whispers and scrabbling, then a sharp squeal. She turned to see Aynglin with a large rat impaled on his sword. Several more were coming down the corridor behind him, gliding along as if impelled by wheels hidden beneath their shaggy flanks.

She didn't believe the rats would give him much trouble, but it was impossible to be sure. They could harbor unexpected wickedness. She put a warding spell around him, flung some extra potency into his blade, and watched him dispatch them handily. They gave out muffled squeaks as they died.

As the fourth one collapsed with a high-pitched wheeze, something enormous and not very far away let out an answering squeal that was more like a bellow—like something a rat the size of a haywain might produce under duress. She cursed her poor perception. The unlit passages should have tipped her off earlier. Down the corridor, beyond the quivering rat corpses, the torches began to go out one by one, paired with the snuffling advance of a lumbering blackness whose only details were the even blacker gleams of liquid eyes that drank in the darkness as the torches expired.

"Back!" she cried. "Behind me!"

Aynglin barely made it; but once he was behind, he kept on going. She heard his slippered feet padding away down the passage behind her, while she stood fast to face the oncoming horror. She glanced back to see if he was safely out of range, and discovered that behind her the passage forked again. Both paths were pitch dark, hiding her protégé completely.

"Aynglin, stop!" she cried.

Then the rat mother struck her.

She turned to give it her full attention, spinning a swirling shield of stars around herself, and driving ice magic into her blade. The torches behind the monstrous rat were extinguished now. If it hadn't been for the radiance of her aura, the darkness would have been total. Her blade clashed against bared teeth. A fang fell and hit the stone floor; blood streamed over black rubbery lips. She attempted a sideways slash across the whiskered muzzle, but the cramped passage shortened her stroke until it was a hacking blow more suited to an axe. Resorting to stabbing, she plunged her blade into one of the inky eyes, and this time the rat recoiled with a scream.

Less concerned about finishing off the rodent than with finding Aynglin before he lost himself completely, she turned and ran, leaving the rat hunkered in a pool of blood, shaking its head and wheezing.

"Where are you?" she called.

His reply came echoing from nowhere in particular. "... *dark* ..."

The tomb proved an absolute honeycomb of passageways, dead-ends, claustrophobic cells. There was no point in trying to ask him to retrace his route, especially not in the blackness. She tried to recall if she was carrying anything that might help him—something which would allow her to reach out and pull him to her side. But she had left all such tokens back in Cowper's Rest, along with her mule.

The horrid wheezing of the injured rat came closer, and she realized that although it posed very little hazard to her, it was potentially lethal to her student. She couldn't tell at this moment if it was truly nearby, or if the acoustics of the tombs created a false impression. She held very still to avoid attracting the rat's attention, while trying to pinpoint its location.

"Jinrae!" came a panicked call.

"Quiet!" she called back. She wanted to communicate the importance of silence at this moment, but there was no way to explain in detail ... not without risking further harm.

"Jin—" And then a scream.

It was horrible but it didn't last long. Barely enough time to allow her to determine the rat's location with certainty. She hurried down two short lengths of corridor and burst into a silk-shrouded vault in time to see the mammoth rat burying its bloody snout in the remains of her pupil.

While the rodent was distracted, she plunged her sword into the back of its neck beneath the skull. The creature slumped into an immense slack bag of bloodied fur.

As the creature died, the torches in the room came alight, replacing the faint glow of her aura. With a sigh, and a booted foot, she shoved the carcass aside and retrieved Aynglin's copper wristband from the gnawed pile on the floor. Apart from his flesh, everything was intact. She held the band aloft and slipped a resurrection ring onto her right ring finger, speaking the words that went with it.

The air churned with diamond light. A shadowy shape thickened. An astral arm materialized inside the battered copper band, gaining density. Jinrae released the band as Aynglin reappeared, now fully fleshed and formed. Her young pupil, completely restored, although far more modestly dressed.

"Whew," he said, with a dazed expression. "Thanks."

"I apologize," she said. "I should have been paying better attention."

He stooped and reclaimed his gear and weapons. "I didn't know rats came that big."

"Oh, they come bigger, but not usually this near the surface." Jinrae cleaned her sword on a dusty silken tatter that draped the stone wall. "This place seems strange tonight. I have a feeling changes have been made to this tomb since I last visited. I should have scouted a bit before bringing in a novice. Finding our way out again is going to be hit or miss, I'm afraid."

"That's fine," he said. "I have most of the night. Unless you want to turn back now."

"I think we'd better, at least until we get our bearings again. I'll need to find something I remember from before . . . a landmark."

Her doubts proved well founded. All the passages were fully lit again after the death of mother rat, and they were just as confusing as they would have been in total darkness. She fell back on following the left hand wall, and kept this up for quite some time without encountering any ascending passages. Every intersection led to downward tending passages. It was very strange. She was positive they had descended to this level, but she could find no steps leading up again. It was as if the place had altered since they entered it.

She didn't think that physical alteration of the tomb was likely, but there were sorcerous ways of making a victim think the world had changed, which had the same effect. But that would require a mage of some power, and who would want to target the two of them with vexing spells?

Who indeed?

As if reading her thought and answering it, Aynglin said, "Uh oh. It's him again."

That shrill childish cry, like the laughter of a hyena, echoed around them. They walked forward into a vast room, its dimensions and its ceiling hid in shadow. Directly above the entryway was a broad stone balcony incised with a gruesome frieze. The laughter fell from above, and its maker capered and gestured obscenely in the heights, emoting malice and mischief.

"Looks like p00ter came back with some of his pals," Aynglin said.

True enough. He was no longer alone. Four figures stood flanking him, wrapped in dark robes, their faces veiled in fog.

At first she saw no reason this should worry her. She took a few steps away from the wall, to get a better view of her adversaries, and at that moment she saw the archway vanish as if it had never been. She ran to the wall but hit solid rock. No seam, no keyhole, no latch, no sign that there had ever been an entrance.

Somewhere off in the shadows, she heard the sound of rusted iron grates and chains, and a ratcheting noise of gears. Skittering footsteps teetered on the edge of audibility, bony and chill. It could have been any sort of skeleton ambling toward them, but instinctively she suspected the worst.

"I'll show you, bitch!" came the hissing voice above her. "You and your freshmeat are bonefood!"

p00ter's face fairly glowed with gleeful evil, but his companions betrayed nothing. She assumed they were mages of some skill, judging by how easily she had been befuddled and led into this trap. Only potent mages could have summoned the undead legions now imminent. How p00ter's ilk managed to gather powerful friends she had never quite understood, but it was not an uncommon alliance. From the fact that p00ter's associates were unreadable, only barely visible at all, she had some glimmering sense of their power—and the trouble she was in.

As the first of the skeletal stalkers strode into the weak fringe of torchlight cast from the balcony, her worst fears were confirmed. It was a Foulmost Banebone, fully armored but with empty hands—which meant it would rely on magic only, hurling attacks all but impossible to anticipate.

Behind it, in rank and file, were more of its kind. And some similar number was coming upon them from the opposite end of the chamber.

She turned to Aynglin, grateful that she would have someone to watch her back, since she could wrap them both in a spell of deflection and add his power to her own. But it would require some quick study on his part.

"Now quickly," she said, "you must do exactly as I say."

But Aynglin wasn't listening.

"Uh, sorry, I gotta go," he said. "Later."

Putting his hands together in a posture of prayer, he vanished.

p00ter's laughter went up the scale, but she scarcely noticed.

Abandoned, betrayed . . . what next? She slipped a shortcut ring onto her finger and held it up to see if she could escape that way. It gave off a dull grey light, signalling its uselessness. They had sealed her in. Once she had fallen in battle, it might take hours to win back her remains, and she would need help to do it—especially with Banebones posted above her corpse.

With that thought, she realized what she had to do. As the foremost Foulmost Banebone rubbed its fleshless palms and began to mold a spiral of smutty light, she threw back her head and sent out a Clarion Call. Two answering Calls came almost instantaneously, and moments later she thought she heard a faint third response. But by then there could have been a symphony of Calls and she wouldn't have noticed. She was too deeply caught up in battling for her life.

The first of the bony attackers sent its whipcord spiral swirling around her, a barbed line of wicked light that attempted to entangle and immobilize her. She stepped free of it, slicing the lines with her charmed blade.

Whiplight wasn't a terrible spell in itself, and one Banebone was no more than an irritant. It was the sheer quantity and variety of attacks that would soon, inevitably, draw her down. For while the first Banebone followed its attack with another of the same, it was joined by its opposite, who had chosen a completely different attack.

Her motions slowed as the second wave of spells struck her from the opposite side of the hall. This spell was like green glue crawling over her, changing every powerful sword slash into a lazy swipe. She had one ring with which to counter the Viscous Flume, but she'd not had it charged in some time, and she had no idea how long it would hold out—especially if another skeleton flung a similar attack.

As the ring took effect, she tried to make the best of it. She lunged out at the source. Her blade bit deep into bone, but it was like hacking at metal. She managed to throw the Foulmost off its casting for a moment, by sending it staggering backward.

A toothed mesh of spiralwire looped down around her head and arms. As soon as she had freed herself of that, she turned to the second skeleton again, this time barking out a powercry as she hacked at a bare bit of vulnerable vertebrae below its gleaming helmet. Her laugh as the skull cracked against the floor for a moment rivalled that of p00ter, still howling from the ledge above.

This kill had an unexpected benefit, for as the scattered bones hit the floor, Jinrae flared with inner fires bright enough to cast the shadows of the oncoming Banebones onto distant walls of the cavern. The nearest skeletons were scorched by the glare of her new-claimed power. In the accompanying rush of energy, she clove the lead whipmaster through mid-torso, and continued to spin out into the midst of the legions like a raging top, her sword like a scythe slashing dry wheat. But not a single Bonebane actually fell, and those in the rear were beginning to cast healing spells on the advance guard.

The Banebones regrouped quickly. And her rush of gleeful energy had cost her dearly. She had forgotten the need for conservation. What she had just done in a moment she would have to do again ten times over if she wished to survive . . . and already she was nearly drained.

"Yeah, bitch, I know what you're thinking. You hit me when I was alone . . . now how do you like it?"

She looked up toward the simpering figure on the balcony above, and suddenly she realized exactly who stood mocking her from among the safety of his sinister friends.

He had taken on a new name, to suit the regression in his personality.

He had revealed himself to be a vicious vengeful child, striking out in the only way he knew how.

What was worse, she had left herself open to be hurt. She had actually allowed this battle to matter to her.

She didn't know whether to give up utterly, as Aynglin had done, or perform some explosive suicidal act in order to take him down with her. She had the ability to touch off an intense explosion that would obliterate every creature in the room in a single burst. But have done that, Jinrae as such could never return to the realm in this guise. It would be a truly final exit from this place.

She considered the ploy, then dismissed it.

She would not let him believe his victory mattered to her. She would play the game as if it were only that—a game.

Win or lose, she would not give him the satisfaction of thinking he had made her care.

Jinrae went back to her gory work with a will, counting each blow she gave and received, calculating exactly how long she could still hold out, watching the deadline loom.

In one hand she conjured orbs of buzzing flame and sent them streaming into the healers at the rear. The nearest ones she fended off with her blade. She put her back to the wall, which meant losing sight of the hateful form above her, but that was just as well. She wouldn't give him the satisfaction. She focused her attention on the skeleton army, and measured her way down the steepening slope to oblivion.

Suddenly she heard a ragged croak with some faint kinship to p00ter's laugh.

The vile fighter's form went hurtling from the balcony and crashed down hard in the midst of the Banebones.

Dazed, still holding her attackers at bay, Jinrae watched p00ter stagger to his feet. The fuddled form rushing in her direction, saw her sword swing toward him, then turned and tried the opposite tack. Several of the Foulmost reached lazily to snag him; there were many bony fingers already twisting in the hems of his fringed cloak.

p00ter fell quite still and bowed his head, realizing that there would be no escape by regular routes. He put his hands together in prayer, striving for a swift exit, but an instant before he could pale and vanish, his bowed head was torn from his shoulders. His body exploded in a cloud of smoke and gushing sparks that looked like burning motes of blood.

The token bearing his ridiculous name landed at Jinrae's feet.

"Farewell, p00ter," she told it, and kicked the tag across the floor, hoping it would fall into some dark chasm, forever unretrievable.

An instant after p00ter's death, three figures leapt down to touch the floor where he had fallen. At first she thought them his wizardly allies, but they were not. These bore mace and massive axe and luminous staff. Their faces were bright and clear, well known to her, personas of shimmering power armed with magic weapons.

"Woohoo!" they cried.

With screams of glee they laid waste to the Banebones. Jinrae's exertions were all but unnecessary in this final melee; which was just as well, since her resources were almost completely drained. Even if she had been fully rested, any one of the three could have bested her easily in single combat. They swung their blades and hurled devasting spells at the skeleton mages. The towering monsters toppled like tenpins, smouldered and melted, pooled into wailing puddles of dust.

In no more than three minutes, the chamber was cleared of even the Leastmost Banebone. As for the wizards on the balcony above, they figured not at all in the final sweep, and made no further appearance. She suspected they had departed the instant the tide began to turn. So much for the friends that p00ter's sort could assemble.

When they had finished, the rescuers formed a triangle with Jinrae at the center.

"Let's blow," said the one other woman, a youthful amazon with tattooed markings that made her look like a feral cat, and pointed ears tipped with a lynx's tuft. She stood lithe and strong, wearing scarcely any visible armor.

"Right," said the man to her right. He was completely armored. In fact, there was not the least bit of skin visible anywhere. His entire form was silver metal chased with moving figures.

The third was a short and bearded dwarf, clad in a cloak that dragged on the stone flags. He raised his staff and from its tip emitted a transport field that engulfed them all.

The dark air of the catacombs gave way to luminosity. Deep purple light with green underfoot, and a swollen orange sun shimmering up from the edge of the world.

They were standing outside, at the crest of the hill the tomb. Red flowers bobbed in the dawn breeze. Lights were just shutting off in Cowper's Rest, as the sun's rays groped at the distant brown buildings.

"Well, that was fun," said the young lynx woman, Nyryx. "Can't we leave you alone for one night without having to bail you out?"

"I was doing just fine," Jinrae said.

"Then why the Clarion Call?" said the staunch little dwarf, Bloafish by name.

"We have troubles of our own, you know," said the completely armored man known as Sir Candham.

"Anyway," Nyryx pressed, "when are you coming home? You've been out a lot longer than any of us."

Jinrae ignored the insinuation. She had more a pressing matter to bring up with them.

"I hope you know who was behind all that."

"What?" Nyryx bristled. "Who?"

"p00ter . . . Venix . . . whatever he's calling himself now. Your father hit a new low tonight."

"What?" cried Bloafish. "No way."

"I know you don't like to see him this way, but I'm telling you—it was him. He set up that ambush, and you saw for yourself how it almost finished me. I should have known something like this was coming."

"Don't embarrass yourself," declared Sir Candham forcefully. "It's totally impossible."

"I know him well enough to recognize him in any costume."

"And we're telling you you're wrong," Sir Candham said.

"How do you know?"

"Because," said Nyryx, "we're with him right now. We've been over here all night. He's making us grilled cheese sandwiches."

"What?"

"Well . . . it's not like you noticed or anything. It's not like anyone's been able to talk to you. What'd you expect us to do?"

"Come off it, Mom."

"Really. It's time."

"We're telling you, he's completely out of it. You're imagining things. Get real."

Jinrae stood speechless, her mind on the edge of grinding to a halt. She saw the pattern of suspicion underlying everything she'd believed that night. It was like her pain, a constant background to everything she felt. An undertow that continually pulled her in.

But if she was wrong . . . if her suspicions were un-founded. That meant there was a bottom to the pain. Maybe she had finally found that place. The three of them had shown it to her.

"Come on," Nyryx said again. "It's time to get going. Don't you remember you said you'd pick us up in your car?"

"Oh god," she said. "I'm sorry. I feel so . . . "

Sir Candham put up an admonitory silver hand. "Hey. Don't. Just get going."

Jinrae sighed. Nodded.

"Cool," said Bloafish. "See you soon."

The four of them bowed their heads, put their hands to-gether, and stood very still. The unfelt wind toyed with the bright red flowers of the plain, but there was no one left to notice, and no one to hear the cries of dawn echoing from the mouth of the tomb.

End Game

NANCY KRESS

Nancy Kress (www.sff.net/people/nankress/ and www.nancy kress.blogspot.com/) lives in Rochester, New York, where she returned following the death of her husband, SF writer Charles Sheffield. She has published more than 20 books and is one of the leading SF writers today. She is particularly known for her complex medical SF stories, and for her biological and evolutionary extrapolations. Her thriller Dogs *is publishing in 2008, as is her SF novel* Steal Across the Sky, *and the fourth collection of her short stories,* Nano Comes to Clifford Falls and Other Stories.*

"End Game" appeared in Asimov's. *Of the story, she says: " 'End Game' is about the fascinations and frustrations of chess. I play chess, a lot and very badly. Last night I lost a U.S. Chess Federation-rated match to a nine-year-old." And "Chess can be addictive. It can take over one's mind." This SF story about brain chemistry and its darker side is in the same realm as "Damascus" by Daryl Gregory in* Year's Best SF 12. *It is an interesting comparison to Peter Watts' story found earlier in this book.*

Allen Dodson was sitting in seventh-grade math class, staring at the back of Peggy Corcoran's head, when he had the insight that changed the world. First his own world and then, eventually, like dominos toppling in predestined rhythm, everybody else's, until nothing could ever be the same again. Although we didn't, of course, know that back then.

The source of the insight was Peggy Corcoran. Allen had sat behind her since third grade (Anderson, Blake, Corcoran, Dodson, DuQuesne . . .) and never thought her remarkable. Nor was she. It was 1982 and Peggy wore a David Bowie T-shirt and straggly brown braids. But now, staring at the back of her mousy hair, Allen suddenly realized that Peggy's head must be a sloppy mess of skittering thoughts and contradictory feelings and half-buried longings—*just as his was.* Nobody was what they seemed to be!

The realization actually made his stomach roil. In books and movies, characters had one thought at a time: *"Elementary, my dear Watson." "An offer he couldn't refuse." "Beam me up, Scotty!"* But Allen's own mind, when he tried to watch it, was different. *Ten more minutes of class I'm hungry gotta pee the answer is x+6 you moron what would it be like to kiss Linda Wilson M*A*S*H on tonight really gotta pee locker stuck today Linda eight more minutes do the first sixteen problems baseball after school—*

No. Not even close. He would have to include his mind watching those thoughts and then his thoughts about the watching thoughts and then—

230

And Peggy Corcoran was doing all that, too.

And Linda Wilson.

And Jeff Gallagher.

And Mr. Henderson, standing at the front of math class.

And everyone in the world, all with thoughts zooming through their heads fast as electricity, thoughts bumping into each other and fighting each other and blotting each other out, a mess inside every mind on the whole Earth, nothing sensible or orderly or predictable. . . . Why, right this minute Mr. Henderson could be thinking terrible things even as he assigned the first sixteen problems on page 145, terrible things about Allen even or Mr. Henderson could be thinking about his lunch or hating teaching or planning a murder. . . . *You could never know.* No one was settled or simple, nothing could be *counted on.* . . .

Allen had to be carried, screaming, from math class.

I didn't learn any of this until decades later, of course. Allen and I weren't friends, even though we sat across the aisle from each other (Edwards, Farr, Fitzgerald, Gallagher . . .). And after the screaming fit, I thought he was just as weird as everyone else thought. I never taunted Allen like some of the boys, or laughed at him like the girls, and a part of me was actually interested in the strange things he sometimes said in class, always looking as if he had no idea how peculiar he sounded. But I wasn't strong enough to go against the herd and make friends with such a loser.

The summer before Allen went off to Harvard, we did become—if not friends—then chess companions. "You play rotten, Jeff," Allen said to me with his characteristic, oblivious candor, "but nobody else plays at all." So two or three times a week we sat on his parents' screened porch and battled it out on the chess board. I never won. Time after time I slammed out of the house in frustration and shame, vowing not to return. After all, unlike wimpy Allen, I had better things to do with my time: girls, cars, James Bond movies. But I always went back.

Allen's parents were, I thought even back then, a little frightened by their son's intensity. Mild, hard-working people fond of golf, they pretty much left Allen alone from his fifteenth birthday on. As we moved rooks and knights around the chessboard in the gathering darkness of the porch, Allen's mother would timidly offer a pitcher of lemonade and a plate of cookies. She treated both of us with an uneasy respect that, in turn, made me uneasy. That wasn't how parents were supposed to behave.

Harvard was a close thing for Allen, despite his astronomical SATs. His grades were spotty because he only did the work in courses he was interested in, and his medical history was even spottier: bouts of depression when he didn't attend school, two brief hospitalizations in a psychiatric ward. Allen would get absorbed by something—chess, quantum physics, Buddhism—to the point where he couldn't stop, until all at once his interest vanished as if it had never existed. Harvard had, I thought in my eighteen-year-old wisdom, every reason to be wary. But Allen was a National Merit scholar, and when he won the Westinghouse science competition for his work on cranial structures in voles, Harvard took him.

The night before he left, we had our last chess match. Allen opened with the conservative Italian game, which told me he was slightly distracted. Twelve moves in, he suddenly said, "Jeff, what if you could tidy up your thoughts, the way you tidy up your room every night?"

"Do what?" My mother "tidied up" my room, and what kind of weirdo used words like that, anyway?

He ignored me. "It's sort of like static, isn't it? All those stray thoughts in a mind, interfering with a clear broadcast. Yeah, that's the right analogy. Without the static, we could all think clearer. Cleaner. We could see farther before the signal gets lost in uncontrolled noise."

In the gloom of the porch, I could barely see his pale, broad-cheeked face. But I had a sudden insight, rare for me that summer. "Allen—is that what happened to you that time in seventh grade? Too much . . . static?"

"Yeah." He didn't seem embarrassed, unlike anybody normal. It was as if embarrassment was too insignificant for this subject. "That was the first time I saw it. For a long time

I thought if I could learn to meditate—you know, like Buddhist monks—I could get rid of the static. But meditation doesn't go far enough. The static is still there, you're just not paying attention to it anymore. But it's still there." He moved his bishop.

"What exactly happened in the seventh grade?" I found myself intensely curious, which I covered by staring at the board and making a move.

He told me, still unembarrassed, in exhaustive detail. Then he added, "It should be possible to adjust brain chemicals to eliminate the static. To unclutter the mind. It should!"

"Well," I said, dropping from insight to my more usual sarcasm, "maybe you'll do it at Harvard, if you don't get sidetracked by some weird shit like ballet or model railroads."

"Checkmate," Allen said.

I lost track of him after that summer, except for the lengthy Bakersville High School Alumni Notes faithfully mailed out every single year by Linda Wilson, who must have had some obsessive/compulsiveness of her own. Allen went on to Harvard Medical School. After graduation he was hired by a prestigious pharmaceutical company and published a lot of scientific articles about topics I couldn't pronounce. He married, divorced, married again, divorced again. Peggy Corcoran, who married my cousin Joe and who knew Allen's second wife, told me at my father's funeral that both ex-wives said the same thing about Allen: He was never emotionally present.

I saw him for myself at our twenty-fifth reunion. He looked surprisingly the same: thin, broad-faced, pale. He stood alone in a corner, looking so pathetic that I dragged Karen over to him. "Hey, Allen. Jeff Gallagher."

"I know."

"This is my wife, Karen."

He smiled at her but said nothing. Karen, both outgoing and compassionate, started a flow of small talk, but Allen shut her off in mid-sentence. "Jeff, you still play chess?"

"Neither *Karen* nor I play now," I said pointedly.

"Oh. There's someone I want you to see, Jeff. Can you come to the lab tomorrow?"

The "lab" was sixty miles away, in the city, and I had to work the next day. But something about the situation had captured my wife's eclectic and sharply intelligent interest. She said, "What is it, Allen, if you don't mind my asking?"

"I don't mind. It's a chess player. I think she might change the world."

"You mean the big important chess world?" I said. Near Allen, all my teenage sarcasm had returned.

"No. The whole world. Please come, Jeff."

"What time?" Karen said.

"Karen—I have a job."

"Your hours are flexible," she said, which was true. I was a real estate agent, working from home. She smiled at me with all her wicked sparkle. "I'm sure it will be fascinating."

Lucy Hartwick, twenty-five years old, was tall, slender, and very pretty. I saw Karen, who unfortunately inclined to jealousy, glance at me. But I wasn't attracted to Lucy. There was something cold about her beauty. She barely glanced up at us from a computer in Allen's lab, and her gaze was indifferent. The screen displayed a chess game.

"Lucy's rating, as measured by computer games anyway, is 2670," Allen said.

"So?" Yes, 2670 was extremely high; only twenty or so players in the world held ratings above 2700. But I was still in sarcastic mode, even as I castigated myself for childishness.

Allen said, "Six months ago her rating was 1400."

"So six months ago, she first learned to play, right?" We were talking about Lucy, bent motionless above the chess board, as if she weren't even present.

"No, she had played twice a week for five years."

That kind of ratings jump for someone with mediocre talent who hadn't studied chess several hours a day for years— it just didn't happen. Karen said, "Good for you, Lucy!" Lucy glanced up blankly, then returned to her board.

I said, "And so just how is this supposed to change the world?"

"Come see this," Allen said. Without looking back, he strode toward the door.

I was getting tired of his games, but Karen followed him, so I followed her. Eccentricity has always intrigued Karen, perhaps because she's so balanced, so sane, herself. It was one reason I fell in love with her.

Allen held out a mass of graphs, charts, and medical scans as if he expected me to read them. "See, Jeff, these are all Lucy, taken when she's playing chess. The caudate nucleus, which aids the mind in switching gears from one thought to another, shows low activity. So does the thalamus, which processes sensory input. And here, in the—"

"I'm a realtor, Allen," I said, more harshly than I intended. "What does all this garbage *mean*?"

Allen looked at me and said simply, "She's done it. Lucy has. She's learned to eliminate the static."

"What static?" I said, even though I remembered perfectly our conversation of twenty-five years ago.

"You mean," said Karen, always a quick study, "that Lucy can concentrate on one thing at a time without getting distracted?"

"I just said so, didn't I?" Allen said. "Lucy Hartwick has control of her own mind. When she plays chess, that's *all* she's doing. As a result, she's now equal to the top echelons of the chess world."

"But she hasn't actually played any of those top players, has she?" I argued. "This is just your estimate based on her play against some computer."

"Same thing," Allen said.

"It is not!"

Karen peered in surprise at my outrage. "Jeff—"

Allen said, "Yes, Jeff, listen to Carol. Don't—"

"'Karen!'"

"—you understand? Lucy's somehow achieved *total* concentration. That lets her just . . . just soar ahead in her understanding of the thing she chooses to focus on. Don't you realize what this could mean for medical research? For . . . for any field at all? We could solve global warming and cancer and toxic waste and . . . and everything!"

As far as I knew, Allen had never been interested in global warming, and a sarcastic reply rose to my lips. But either Allen's face or Karen's hand on my arm stopped me. She said gently, "That could be wonderful, Allen."

"It will be!" he said with all the fervor of his seventh-grade fit. "It will be!"

"What was that all about?" Karen said in the car on our way home.

"Oh, that was just Allen being—"

"Not Allen. You."

"Me?" I said, but even I knew my innocence didn't ring true.

"I've never seen you like that. You positively sneered at him, and for what might actually be an enormous break-through in brain chemistry."

"It's just a theory, Karen! Ninety percent of theories collapse as soon as anyone runs controlled experiments."

"But you, Jeff . . . you *want* this one to collapse."

I twisted in the driver's seat to look at her face. Karen stared straight ahead, her pretty lips set as concrete. My first instinct was to bluster . . . but not with Karen.

"I don't know," I said quietly. "Allen has always brought out the worst in me, for some reason. Maybe . . . maybe I'm jealous."

A long pause, while I concentrated as hard as I could on the road ahead. Yellow divider, do not pass, thirty-five MPH, pothole ahead . . .

Then Karen's hand rested lightly on my shoulder, and the world was all right again.

After that I kept in sporadic touch with Allen. Two or three times I phoned and we talked for fifteen minutes. Or, rather, Allen talked and I listened, struggling with irritability. He never asked about me or Karen. He talked exclusively about his research into various aspects of Lucy Hartwick: her spinal and cranial fluid, her neural firing patterns, her blood and tissue cultures. He spoke of her as if she were no more than a collection of biological puzzles he was determined to solve, and I couldn't imagine what their day-to-day interactions were like. For some reason I didn't understand, I didn't tell Karen about these conversations.

That was the first year. The following June, things changed. Allen's reports—because that's what they were, reports and not conversations—became non-stop complaints.

"The FDA is taking forever to pass my IND application. Forever!"

I figured out that "IND" meant "initial new drug," and that it must be a green light for his Lucy research.

"And Lucy has become impossible. She's hardly ever available when I need her, trotting off to chess tournaments around the world. As if chess mattered as much as my work on her!"

I remembered the long-ago summer when chess mattered to Allen himself more than anything else in the world.

"I'm just frustrated by the selfishness and the bureaucracy and the politics."

"Yes," I said.

"And doesn't Lucy understand how important this could be? The incredible potential for improving the world?"

"Evidently not," I said, with mean satisfaction that I disliked myself for. To compensate I said, "Allen, why don't you take a break and come out here for dinner some night. Doesn't a break help with scientific thinking? Lead sometimes to real insights?"

I could feel, even over the phone line, that he'd been on the point of refusal, but my last two sentences stopped him. After a moment he said, "Oh, all right, if you want me to," so ungraciously that it seemed he was granting me an inconvenient favor. Right then, I knew that the dinner was going to be a disaster.

And it was, but not as much as it would have been without Karen. She didn't take offense when Allen refused to tour her beloved garden. She said nothing when he tasted things and put them down on the tablecloth, dropped bits of food as he chewed, slobbered on the rim of his glass. She listened patiently to Allen's two-hour monologue, nodding and making encouraging little noises. Toward the end her eyes did glaze a bit, but she never lost her poise and wouldn't let me lose mine, either.

"It's a disgrace," Allen ranted, "the FDA is hobbling all productive research with excessive caution for—do you know what would happen if Jenner had needed FDA approval for his vaccines? We'd all still have smallpox, that's what! If Louis Pasteur—"

"Why don't you play chess with Jeff?" Karen said when the meal finally finished. "While I clear away here."

I exhaled in relief. Chess was played in silence. Moreover, Karen would be stuck with cleaning up after Allen's appalling table manners.

"I'm not interested in chess anymore," Allen said. "Anyway, I have to get back to the lab. Not that Lucy kept her appointment for tests on . . . she's wasting my time in Turkistan or someplace. Bye. Thanks for dinner."

"Don't invite him again, Jeff," Lucy said to me after Allen left. "Please."

"I won't. You were great, sweetheart."

Later, in bed, I did that thing she likes and I don't, by way of saying thank you. Halfway through, however, Karen pushed me away. "I only like it when you're really *here*," she said. "Tonight you're just not focusing on us at all."

After she went to sleep, I crept out of bed and turned on the computer in my study. The heavy fragrance of Karen's roses drifted through the window screen. Lucy Hartwick was in Turkmenistan, playing in the Chess Olympiad in Ashgabat. Various websites told of her rocketing rise to the top of the chess world. Articles about her all mentioned that she never socialized with her own or any other team, preferred to eat all her meals alone in her hotel room, and never smiled. I studied the accompanying pictures, trying to see what had happened to Lucy's beauty.

She was still slender and long-legged. The lovely features were still there, although obscured by her habitual pose while studying a chessboard: hunched over from the neck like a turtle, with two fingers in her slightly open mouth. I had seen that pose somewhere before, but I couldn't remember where. It wasn't appealing, but the loss of Lucy's good looks came from something else. Even for a chess player, the concentration on her face was formidable. It wiped out any hint of any other emotion whatsoever. Good poker players do that, too, but not in quite that way. Lucy looked not quite human.

Or maybe I just thought that because of my complicated feelings about Allen.

At two A.M. I sneaked back into bed, glad that Karen hadn't woken while I was gone.

"She's gone!" Allen cried over the phone, a year later. "She's just gone!"

"Who?" I said, although, of course, I knew. "Allen, I can't talk now, I have a client coming into the office two minutes from now."

"You have to come down here!"

"Why?" I had ducked all of Allen's calls ever since that awful dinner, changing my home phone to an unlisted number and letting my secretary turn him away at work. I'd only answered now because I was expecting a call from Karen about the same time for our next marriage counseling session. Things weren't as good as they used to be. Not really bad, just clouds blocking what had been a steady marital sunshine. I wanted to dispel those clouds before they turned into major thunderstorms.

"You have to come," Allen repeated, and he started to sob.

Embarrassed, I held the phone away from my ear. Grown men didn't cry like that, not to other men. All at once I realized why Allen wanted me to come to the lab: because he had no other human contact at all.

"Please, Jeff," Allen whispered, and I snapped, "Okay!"

"Mr. Gallagher, your clients are here," Brittany said at the doorway, and I tried to compose a smile and a good lie.

And after all that, Lucy Hartwick wasn't even gone. She sat in Allen's lab, hunched over a chessboard with two fingers in her mouth, just as I had seen her a year ago on the Web.

"What the hell—Allen, you *said*—"

Unpredictable as ever, he had calmed down since calling me. Now he handed me a sheaf of print-outs and medical photos. I flashed back suddenly to the first time I'd come to this lab, when Allen had also thrust on me documents I couldn't read. He just didn't learn.

"Her white matter has shrunk another 75 percent since I saw her last," Allen said, as though that were supposed to convey something to me.

"You said Lucy was gone!"

"She is."

"She's sitting right there!"

Allen looked at me. I had the impression that the simple act required enormous effort on his part, like a man trying to drag himself free of a concrete block to which he was chained. He said, "I was always jealous of you, you know."

It staggered me. My mouth opened but Allen had already moved back to the concrete block. "Just look at these brain scans, 75 percent less white matter in six months! And these neurotransmitter levels, they—"

"Allen," I said. Sudden cold had seized my heart. "Stop." But he babbled on about the caudate nucleus and antibodies attacking the basal ganglia and bi-directional rerouting.

I walked over to Lucy and lifted her chessboard off the table.

Immediately she rose and continued playing variations on the board in my arms. I took several steps backward; she followed me, still playing. I hurled the board into the hall, slammed the door, and stood with my back to it. I was six-one and 190 pounds; Lucy wasn't even half that. In fact, she appeared to have lost weight, so that her slimness had turned gaunt.

She didn't try to fight me. Instead she returned to her table, sat down, and stuck two fingers in her mouth.

"She's playing in her head, isn't she," I said to Allen.

"Yes."

"What does 'white matter' do?"

"It contains axons that connect neurons in the cerebral cortex to neurons in other parts of the brain, thereby facilitating intercranial communication." Allen sounded like a textbook.

"You mean, it lets some parts of the brain talk to other parts?"

"Well, that's only a crude analogy, but—"

"It lets different thoughts from different parts of the brain reach each other," I said, still staring at Lucy. "It makes you aware of more than one thought at a time."

Static.

Allen began a long technical explanation, but I wasn't listening. I remembered now where I'd seen that pose of Lucy's, head pushed forward and two fingers in her mouth, drooling. It had been in an artist's rendering of Queen Elizabeth I in her final days, immobile and unreachable, her mind already gone in advance of her dying body.

"Lucy's gone," Allen had said. He knew.

"Allen, what baseball team did Babe Ruth play for?"

He babbled on about neurotransmitters.

"What was Bobby Fisher's favorite opening move?" Silently I begged him, *Say e4, damn it.*

He talked about the brain waves of concentrated meditation.

"Did you know that a tsunami will hit Manhattan tomorrow?"

He urged overhaul of FDA clinical-trial design.

I said, as quietly as I could manage, "You have it, too, don't you. You injected yourself with whatever concoction the FDA wouldn't approve, or you took it as a pill, or something. You wanted Lucy's static-free state, like some fucking *dryer sheet,* and so you gave this to yourself from her. And now neither one of you can switch focus at all." The call to me had been Allen's last, desperate foray out of his perfect concentration on this project. No—that hadn't been the last.

I took him firmly by the shoulders. "Allen, what did you mean when you said 'I was always jealous of you'?"

He blathered on about MRI results.

"Allen—please tell me what you meant!"

But he couldn't. And now I would never know.

I called the front desk of the research building. I called 911. Then I called Karen, needing to hear her voice, needing to connect with her. But she didn't answer her cell, and the office said she'd left her desk to go home early.

* * *

Both Allen and Lucy were hospitalized briefly, then released. I never heard the diagnosis, although I suspect it involved an "inability to perceive and relate to social interactions" or some such psychobabble. Doesn't play well with others. Runs with scissors. Lucy and Allen demonstrated they could physically care for themselves by doing it, so the hospital let them go. Business professionals, I hear, mind their money for them, order their physical lives. Allen has just published another brilliant paper, and Lucy Hartwick is the first female World Chess Champion.

Karen said, "They're happy, in their own way. If their single-minded focus on their passions makes them oblivious to anything else—well, so what. Maybe that's the price for genius."

"Maybe," I said, glad that she was talking to me at all. There hadn't been much conversation lately. Karen had refused any more marriage counseling and had turned silent, escaping me by working in the garden. Our roses are the envy of the neighborhood. We have Tuscan Sun, Ruffled Cloud, Mister Lincoln, Crown Princess, Golden Zest. English roses, hybrid teas, floribunda, groundcover roses, climbers, shrubs. They glow scarlet, pink, antique apricot, deep gold, delicate coral. Their combined scent nauseates me.

I remember the exact moment that happened. We were in the garden, Karen kneeling beside a flower bed, a wide hat shading her face from the sun so that I couldn't see her eyes.

"Karen," I said, trying to mask my desperation, "do you still love me?"

"Hand me that trowel, will you, Jeff?"

"Karen! Please! Can we talk about what's happening to us?"

"The Tahitian sunsets are going to be glorious this year."

I stared at her, at the beads of sweat on her upper lip, the graceful arc of her neck, her happy smile.

Karen clearing away Allen's dinner dishes, picking up his sloppily dropped food. Lucy with two fingers in her mouth, studying her chessboard and then touching the pieces.

No. Not possible.

Karen reached for the trowel herself, as if she'd forgotten I was there.

Lucy Hartwick lost her championship to a Russian named Dmitri Chertov. A geneticist at Stamford made a breakthrough in cancer research so important that it grabbed all headlines for nearly a week. By a coincidence that amused the media, his young daughter won the Scripps Spelling Bee. I looked up the geneticist on the Internet; a year ago he'd attended a scientific conference with Allen. A woman in Oregon, some New Age type, developed the ability to completely control her brain waves through profound meditation. Her husband is a chess grandmaster.

I walk a lot now, when I'm not cleaning or cooking or shopping. Karen quit her job; she barely leaves the garden even to sleep. I kept my job, although I take fewer clients. As I walk, I think about the ones I do have, mulling over various houses they might like. I watch the August trees begin to tinge with early yellow, ponder overheard snatches of conversation, talk to dogs. My walks get longer and longer, and I notice that I've started to time my speed, to become interested in running shoes, to investigate transcontinental walking routes.

But I try not to think about walking too much. I observe children at frenetic play during the last of their summer vacation, recall movies I once liked, wonder at the intricacies of quantum physics, anticipate what I'll cook for lunch. Sometimes I sing. I recite the few snatches of poetry I learned as a child, relive great football games, chat with old ladies on their porches, add up how many calories I had for breakfast. Sometimes I even mentally rehearse basic chess openings: the Vienna Game or the Petroff Defense. I let whatever thoughts come that will, accepting them all.

Listening to the static, because I don't know how much longer I've got.

Induction

GREG EGAN

Greg Egan (www.gregegan.net) lives in Perth in Western Australia. A recluse whom few people in SF have met, he is one of the most respected writers of Hard SF in the last twenty years. He is also a programmer, and his website prominently features his mathematical computer animations. One of the most significant aspects of his fiction is the characterization. He tends to write what we sometimes call neuropsych hard sf, treating character as a scientific problem and writing about people based on how action and feeling are determined by the biochemistry of the brain. He has two books coming out in 2008: his fourth collection, Dark Integers and Other Stories, *and his seventh SF novel,* Incandescence.

"Induction" appeared in Foundation 100, *the first fiction issue of the British SF Foundation's journal, celebrating one hundred issues of publication. Here Egan explores what it really takes to colonize other planets, and what kind of person might want the job.*

1

Ikat spent three of the last four hours of 2099 out on the regolith, walking the length of her section of the launch gun, checking by eye for micrometeorite impacts or any other damage that the automatic systems might improbably have missed.

Four other junior engineers walked a few paces ahead of her, but Ikat had had enough of their company inside the base, and she kept her coms tuned to Earth, sampling the moods of the century's countdown.

The Pope had already issued a statement from Rio, imploring humanity to treat "Christianity's twenty-first birthday" as an opportunity to embrace "spiritual maturity"; the Council of Islamic Scholars in Brussels, surrendering to the ubiquity of the Gregorian calendar, had chimed in with a similar message of their own. In the pyrotechnic rivalry stakes, Sydney was planning to incinerate the decommissioned Harbour Bridge with artificial lightning, while Washington had arranged for no less than twenty-one ageing military satellites to plunge from the sky into the Potomac at the stroke of midnight.

There was no doubt, though, that Beijing had stolen the lion's share of global chatter with the imminent launch of the Orchid Seed. You could forget any purist's concept of lunar midnight; the clocks on Procellarum had been set to the easternmost of Earth's time zones ever since the construction of the base two decades before, so the official zeroing of the digits here would precede celebrations in all of the globe's major cities. The PR people really had planned that far ahead.

As she paced slowly along the regolith, Ikat kept her eyes diligently on the coolant pipes that weaved between the support struts to wrap the gun barrel, although she knew that this final check was mostly PR too. If the launch failed, it would be down to a flaw that no human eye could have detected. Six successful but unpublicised test firings made such a humiliation unlikely. Still, the gun's fixed bearing rendered a seventh, perfectly timed success indispensable. Only at "midnight" would the device be aimed precisely at its target. If they had to wait a month for a relaunch, hundreds of upper-echelon bureaucrats back on Earth would probably be diving out of their penthouse windows before dawn. Ikat knew that she was far too low in the ranks to make a worthwhile scapegoat, but her career could still be blighted by the ignominy.

Her mother was calling from Bangkok. Ikat pondered her responsibilities, then decided to let the audio through. If she really couldn't walk, talk and spot a plume of leaking coolant at the same time, she should probably retire from her profession straight away.

"Just wishing you good luck, darling," her mother said. "And Happy New Year. Probably you'll be too busy celebrating to talk to me later."

Ikat scowled. "I was planning to call you when it reached midnight there. But Happy New Year anyway."

"You'll call your father after the launch?"

"I expect so." Her parents were divorced, but her mother still wanted harmony to flow in all directions, especially on such an occasion.

"Without him," her mother said, "you never would have had this chance."

It was a strange way of putting it, but it was probably true. The Chinese space program was cosmopolitan enough, but if her mother hadn't married a Chinese citizen and remained in the country for so long, Ikat doubted that she would have been plucked from provincial Bangkok and lofted all the way up to Procellarum. There were dozens of middle-ranking project engineers with highly specific skills who were not Chinese born; they were quite likely the best people on the planet for their respective jobs. She was not in that league. Her academic results had secured her the placement, but they had not been so spectacular that she would have been head-hunted across national borders.

"I'll call him," she promised. "After the launch."

She cut the connection. She'd almost reached the end of Stage Nine, the ten-kilometre section of the barrel where the pellets would be accelerated from sixteen to eighteen per cent of light speed, before the final boost to twenty per cent. For the last three years, she had worked beneath various specialist managers, testing and re-testing different subsystems: energy storage, electromagnets, cooling, data collection. It had been a once-in-a-lifetime education, arduous at times, but never boring. Still, she'd be glad to be going home. Maglev railways might seem anticlimactic after this, but she'd had enough of sharing a room with six other people, and the whole tiny complex with the same two hundred faces, year after year.

Back inside the base, Ikat felt restless. The last hour stretched out ahead of her, an impossible gulf. In the common room, Qing caught her eye, and she went to sit with him.

"Had any bites from your resumé?" he asked.

"I haven't published it yet. I want a long holiday first."

He shook his head in dismay. "How did you ever get here? You must be the least competitive person on Earth."

Ikat laughed. "At university, I studied eighteen hours a day. I had no social life for six years."

"So now you've got to put in some effort to get the pay-off."

"This *is* the pay-off, you dope."

"For a week or so after the launch," Qing said, "you could have the top engineering firms on the planet bidding for the prestige you'd bring them. That won't last forever, though. People have a short attention span. This isn't the time to take a holiday."

Ikat threw up her hands. "What can I say? I'm a lost cause."

Qing's expression softened; he was deadly serious about his own career, but when he lectured her it was just a kind of ritual, a role play that gave them something to talk about.

They passed the time with more riffs on the same theme, interleaved with gossip and bitching about their colleagues, but when the clock hit 11.50 it became impossible to remain blasé. Nobody could spend three years in a state of awe at the feat they were attempting, but ten minutes of sober contemplation suddenly seemed inadequate. Other probes had already been sent towards the stars, but the Orchid Seed would certainly outrace all those that had gone before it. It might yet be overtaken itself, but with no serious competitors even at the planning stage, there was a fair chance that the impending launch would come to be seen as the true genesis of interstellar travel.

As the conversation in the common room died away, someone turned up the main audio commentary that was going to the news feeds, and spread a dozen key image windows across the wall screens. The control room was too small to take everyone in the base; junior staff would watch the launch much as the public everywhere else did.

The schematics told Ikat a familiar story, but this was the moment to savour it anew. Three gigajoules of solar energy had already been packed into circulating currents in the superconducting batteries, ready to be tapped. That was not much, really; every significant payload launched from Earth had burnt up far more. One third would be lost to heat and stray electromagnetic fields. The remainder would be fed into the motion of just one milligram of matter: the five hundred tiny pellets of the Orchid Seed that would race down the launch gun in three thousandths of a second, propelled by a force that could have lofted a two-tonne weight back on Earth.

The pellets that comprised the seed were not physically connected, but they would move in synch in a rigid pattern, forming a kind of sparse crystal whose spacing allowed it to interact strongly with the microwave radiation in the gun.

Out in deep space, in the decades spent in transit, the pattern would not be important, but the pellets would be kept close together by electrostatic trimming if and when they strayed, ready to take up perfect rank again when the time came to brake. First, in the coronal magnetic field of Prosperity B; again near its larger companion star, and finally in the ionosphere of Prosperity A's fourth planet, Duty, before falling into the atmosphere and spiralling to the ground.

One cycling image on the wall rehearsed the launch in slow motion, showing the crest of electromagnetic energy coursing down the barrel, field lines bunched tightly like a strange coiled spring. A changing electric field induced a magnetic field; a changing magnetic field induced an electric field. In free space such a change would spread at the speed of light— would *be* light, of some frequency or other—but the tailored geometry and currents of the barrel kept the wave reined in, always in step with the seed, devoted to the task of urging this precious cargo forward.

"If this screws up," Qing observed forlornly, "we'll be the laughing stock of the century."

"You don't think Beijing's prepared for a cover-up?" Ikat joked.

"Some jealous fucker would catch us out," Qing replied. "I'll bet every dish on Earth is tuned to the seed's resonant frequency. If they get no echo, we'll all be building toilet blocks in Aksai Chin."

It was 11.58 in Tonga, Tokelau and Procellarum. Ikat took Qing's hand and squeezed it. "Relax," she said. "The worst you'll come to is building synchrotrons for eccentric billionaires in Kowloon."

Qing said, "You're cutting off my circulation."

The room fell silent; a synthetic voice from the control room counted down the seconds. Ikat felt light-headed. The six test firings had worked, but who knew what damage they'd done, what stresses they'd caused, what structures they'd weakened? Lots of people, actually; the barrel was packed with instrumentation to measure exactly those things, and the answers were all very reassuring. Still—

"Minus three. Minus two. Minus one."

A schematic of the launch gun flashed green, followed by a slow-motion reconstruction of the field patterns so flawless it was indistinguishable from the simulations. A new window opened, showing tracking echoes. The seed was moving away from the moon at sixty thousand kilometres per second, precisely along the expected trajectory. There was nothing more required of it: no second stage to fire, no course change, no reconfiguration. Now that it had been set in motion, all it had to do was coast on its momentum; it couldn't suddenly veer sideways, crashing and burning like some failed chemical rocket launched from the ground. Even if collisions or system failures over the coming decades wiped out some of the pellets, the seed as a whole could function with as little as a quarter of the original number. Unless the whole thing had been a fraud or a mass hallucination, there was now absolutely nothing that could pull the rug out from under this triumph; in three milliseconds, their success had become complete and irrevocable. At least for a century, until the seed reached its destination.

People were cheering; Ikat joined them, but her own cry came out as a tension-relieving sob. Qing put an arm around her shoulders. "We did it," he whispered. "We've conquered the world."

Not the stars? Not the galaxy? She laughed, but she didn't begrudge him this vanity. The fireworks to come in Sydney might be more spectacular, and the dying hawks burning up over Washington might bring their own sense of closure, but this felt like an opening out, an act of release, a joyful shout across the light years.

Food and drink was wheeled out; the party began. In twenty minutes, the seed was farther from the sun than Mars. In a day, it would be farther than Pluto; in ten days, farther than Pioneer 10. In six months, the Orchid Seed would have put more distance behind it than all of the targeted interstellar missions that had preceded it.

Ikat remembered to call her father once midnight came to Beijing.

"Happy New Year," she greeted him.

"Congratulations," he replied. "Will you come and visit

me once you get your Earth legs, or will you be too busy signing autographs?"

Fake biochemical signals kept the Procellarans' bones and muscles strong; it would only take a day or two to acclimatise her nervous system to the old dynamics again. "Of course I'll visit you."

"You did a good job," he said. "I'm proud of you."

His praise made her uncomfortable. She wanted to express her gratitude to him—he'd done much more to help her than providing the accident of her birthplace—but she was afraid of sounding like a giddy movie star accepting an award.

As the party wound on and midnight skimmed the globe, the speechwriters of the world's leaders competed to heap praise upon Beijing's achievement. Ikat didn't care that it had all been done for the glory of a fading empire; it was more than a gesture of status and power.

Only one thing seemed bittersweet, as she contemplated the decades to come. She was twenty-eight years old, and there was every chance that these three years, these three milliseconds, would turn out to have been the pinnacle of her life.

2

The caller was persistent, Ikat gave him that. He refused to leave a message or engage with her assistant; he refused to explain his business to anyone but Ikat herself, in a realtime dialogue.

From her balcony she looked out across the treetops, listening to the birds and insects of the Mekong valley, and wondered if she wanted to be dragged back into the swirling currents of the world. The caller, whose name was Vikram Ali, had probably tracked her down in the hope of extracting a comment from her about the imminent arrival of signals from the Orchid Flower. That might have been an egotistical assumption, were it not for the fact that she'd heard of no other participant in the launch publishing anything on the matter, so it was clear that the barrel would have to be scraped. The project's most famous names were all dead or acorporeal—and the acorporeals were apparently Satisfied, rendering them even less interested in such worldly matters than an ageing flesh-bound recluse like Ikat.

She pondered her wishes and responsibilities. Most people now viewed the Orchid Seed as a curiosity, a sociological time capsule. Within decades of its launch, a new generation of telescopes had imaged and analysed its destination with such detail and clarity that the mission had come to seem redundant. All five planets in the Prosperity system appeared lifeless, and although there were astrophysical and geochemical subtleties that *in situ* measurements might yet reveal, with high-resolution maps of Duty splashed across the web, interest in the slightly better view that would arrive after a very long delay began to dwindle.

What was there for Ikat to say on the matter? Should she plead for the project to be taken seriously, as more than a quaint nationalist stunt from a bygone era? Maybe the top brass weren't Satisfied; maybe they were just embarrassed. The possibility annoyed her. No one who'd been sincere in their work on the Orchid Seed should be ashamed of what they'd done.

Ikat returned Vikram Ali's call. He responded immediately, and after the briefest of pleasantries came to the point.

"I represent Khamoush Holdings," he said. "Some time ago, we acquired various assets and obligations of the URC government, including a contractual relationship with you."

"I see." Ikat struggled to remember what she might have signed that could possibly be relevant a hundred and twenty years later. Had she promised to do media if asked? Her assistant had verified Khamoush Holding's bona fides, but all it knew about the Procellarum contract was that Ikat's copy had been lost in 2145, when an anarchist worm had scrambled three per cent of the planet's digital records.

"The opportunity has arisen for us to exploit one of our assets," Ali continued, "but we are contractually obliged to offer you the option of participating in the relevant activity."

Ikat blinked. *Option?* Khamoush had bought some form of media rights, obviously, but would there be a clause saying they had to run down the ranks of the Orchid Seed team, offering each participant a chance to play spokesperson?

"Am I obliged to help you, or not?" she asked.

Now it was Ali's turn to be surprised. "Obliged? Certainly not! We're not slave holders!" He looked downright offended.

Ikat said, "Could we get the whole thing over in a day or two?"

Ali pondered this question deeply for a couple of seconds. "You don't have the contract, do you?"

"I chose a bad archive," Ikat confessed.

"So you have no idea what I'm talking about?"

"You want me to give interviews about the Orchid Seed, don't you?" Ikat said.

"Ultimately, yes," Ali replied, "but that's neither here nor there for now. I want to ask you if you're interested in travelling to Duty, taking a look around, and coming back."

In the lobby of the hotel in Mumbai, Ikat learnt that someone else had accepted the offer from Khamoush Holdings.

"I thought you'd be rich and Satisfied by now," she told Qing.

He smiled. "Mildly rich. Never satisfied."

They walked together to the office of Magic Beans Inc., Ikat holding her umbrella over both of them against the monsoon rain.

"My children think I'm insane," Qing confessed.

"Mine too. But then, I told them that if they kept arguing, I'd make it a one-way journey." Ikat laughed. "Really, they ought to be grateful. No filial obligations for forty years straight. It's hard to imagine a greater gift."

In the Magic Beans office, Ali showed them two robots, more or less identical to the ones the Orchid Flower, he hoped, would already have built on the surface of Duty. The original mission planners had never intended such a thing, but when Khamoush had acquired the assets they had begun the relevant R&D immediately. Forty years ago they had transmitted the blueprints for these robots, in a message that would have arrived not long after the Orchid Seed touched down. Now that confirmation of the Flower's success in its basic mission had reached Earth, in a matter of months they would learn whether the nanomachines had also been able to scavenge the necessary materials to construct these welcoming receptacles.

"We're the only volunteers?" Qing asked, gazing at his prospective doppelgänger with uneasy fascination. "I would have thought one of the acorporeals would have jumped at the chance."

"Perhaps if we'd asked them early enough," Ali replied. "But once you're immersed in that culture, forty years must seem a very long time to be out of touch."

Ikat was curious about the financial benefits Khamoush were hoping for; they turned out to revolve largely around a promotional deal with a manufacturer of prosthetic bodies. Although the designs the company sold were wildly different from these robots—even their Extreme Durability models were far more cosily organic—any link with the first interstellar explorers trudging across rugged landscapes on a distant, lifeless world carried enough resonance to be worth paying for.

Back in the hotel they sat in Qing's room, talking about the old times and speculating about the motives and fates of all their higher-ranked colleagues who'd turned down this opportunity. Perhaps, Ikat suggested, some of them simply had no wish to become acorporeal. Crossing over to software didn't preclude you from continuing to inhabit a prosthetic body back on Earth, but once you changed substrate the twin lures of virtual experience and self-modification were strong. "That would be ironic," she mused. "To decline to engage with the physical universe in this way, for fear of ultimately losing touch with it."

Qing said, "I plan to keep my body frozen, and have my new self wired back into it when I return, synapse by synapse."

Ikat smiled. "I thought you said *mildly* rich." That would

be orders of magnitude more costly than her own plan: frozen body, prosthetic brain.

"They caught us at just the right stage in life," Qing said. "Still interested in reality, but not still doting on every new great-great-grandchild. Not yet acorporeal, but old enough that we already feel as if we've been on another planet for forty years."

Ikat said, "I'm amazed that they honoured our contracts, though. A good lawyer could have let them hand-pick their travellers." The relevant clause had simply been a vague offer of preferential access to spin-off employment opportunities.

"Why shouldn't they want *us*?" Qing demanded, feigning indignation. "We're seasoned astronauts, aren't we? We've already proved we could live together in Procellarum for three years, without driving each other crazy. Three months—with a whole planet to stretch our legs on—shouldn't be beyond us."

Later that week, to Ikat's amazement, their psychological assessments proved Qing's point; their basic personality profiles really hadn't changed since the Procellarum days. Careers, marriages, children, had left their marks, but if anything they were both more resilient.

They stayed in Mumbai, rehearsing in the robot bodies using telepresence links, and studying the data coming back from the Orchid Flower.

When confirmation arrived that the Flower really had built the robots Khamoush Holdings had requested, Ikat sent messages directly to her children and grandchildren, and then left it to them to pass the news further down the generations. Her parents were dead, and her children were tetchy centenarians; she loved them, but she did not feel like gathering them around her for a tearful bon voyage. The chances were they'd all still be here when she returned.

She and Qing spent a morning doing media, answering a minute but representative fraction of the questions submitted by interested news subscribers. Then Ikat's body was frozen, and her brain was removed, microtomed, and scanned. At her request, her software was not formally woken on Earth prior to her departure; routine tests confirmed its functionality in a series of dreamlike scenarios which left no permanent memories.

Then the algorithm that described her was optimised, compressed, encoded into a series of laser pulses, and beamed across twenty light years, straight on to the petals of the Orchid Flower.

3

Ikat woke standing on a brown, pebbled plain beneath a pale, salmon-coloured sky. Prosperity A had just risen; its companion, ten billion kilometres away, was visible but no competition, scarcely brighter than Venus from Earth.

Qing was beside her, and behind him was the Flower: the communications link and factory that the Orchid Seed had built. Products of the factory included hundreds of small rovers, which had dispersed to explore the planet's surface, and dozens of solar-powered gliders, which provided aerial views and aided with communications.

Qing said, "Punch me, make it real."

Ikat obliged with a gentle thump on his forearm. Their telepresence rehearsals had included virtual backdrops just like the Flower's actual surroundings, but they had not had full tactile feedback. The action punctured Ikat's own dreamy sense of déjà vu; they really had stepped out of the simulation into the thing itself.

They had the Flower brief them about its latest discoveries; they had been twenty years behind when they'd left Earth, and insentient beams of light for twenty more. The Flower had pieced together more details of Duty's geological history; with plate tectonics but no liquid water, the planet's surface was older than Earth's but not as ancient as the moon's.

Ikat felt a twinge of superfluousness; if the telescope images hadn't quite made the Orchid Flower redundant, there was precious little left for her and Qing. They were not here to play geologists, though; they were here to be here. Any science they did would be a kind of recreation, like an informed tourist's appreciation of some well-studied natural wonder back on Earth.

Qing started laughing. "Twenty fucking *light years*! Do you know how long that would take to walk? They should have tried harder to make us afraid." Ikat reached out and put a hand on his shoulder. She felt a little existential vertigo herself, but she did not believe they faced any great risk. The forty lost years were a fait accompli, but she was reconciled to that.

"What's the worst that can happen?" she said. "If something goes wrong, they'll just wake your body back on Earth, with no changes at all."

Qing nodded slowly. "But you had your brain diced, didn't you?"

"You know me, I'm a cheapskate." Non-destructive scanning was more expensive, and Khamoush weren't paying for everything. "But they can still load the backup file into a prosthesis."

"Assuming it's not eaten by an anarchist worm."

"I arranged to have a physical copy put into a vault."

"Ah, but what about the nihilist nanoware?"

"Then you and I will be the only survivors."

Their bodies had no need for shelter from the elements, but the Flower had built them a simple hut for sanity's sake. As they inspected the spartan rooms together, Qing seemed to grow calm; as he'd said back on Earth, anything had to be easier than the conditions they'd faced on the moon. Food would have been too complex an indulgence, and Ikat had declined the software to grant her convincing hallucinations of five-course banquets every night.

Once they'd familiarised themselves with everything in the base camp, and done a few scripted Armstrong moments for the cameras to satisfy the promotional deal, they spent the morning hiking across the rock-strewn plain. There was a line of purplish mountains in the distance, almost lost in haze, but Ikat declined to ask the Flower for detailed aerial imagery. They could explore for themselves, find things for themselves. The longing to be some kind of irreplaceable pioneer, to be the first pair of eyes and hands, the first scrutinising intelligence, was impossible to extinguish completely, but they could find a way to satisfy it without self-delusion or charade.

Her fusion-powered body needed no rest, but at noon she stopped walking and sat cross-legged on the ground.

Qing joined her. She looked around at the barren rocks, the delicate sky, the far horizon. "Twenty light years?" she said. "I'm glad I came."

Their days were full of small challenges, and small discoveries. To cross a mountain range required skill and judgement as well as stamina; to understand the origins of each wind-blasted outcrop took careful observation and a strong visual imagination, as well as a grasp of the basic geological principles.

Still, even as they clambered down one treacherous, powdery cliff-face, Ikat wondered soberly if they'd reached the high-tide mark of human exploration. The Orchid Seed's modest speed and reach had never been exceeded; the giant telescopes had found no hints of life out to a hundred light years, offering little motivation to launch a new probe. The shift to software was becoming cheaper every year, and if that made travel to the stars easier, there were a thousand more alluring destinations closer to home. When you could pack a lifetime of exotic experiences into a realtime hour, capped off with happiness by fiat, who would give up decades of contemporaneity to walk on a distant world? There were even VR games, based on telescope imagery, where people fought unlikely wars with implausible alien empires on the very ground she was treading.

"What are you planning to do when you get home?" she asked Qing that night. They had brought nothing with them from the base camp, so they simply slept on the ground beneath the stars.

"Back to work, I suppose." He ran his own successful engineering consultancy; so successful that it didn't really need him. "What else is there? I'm not interested in crawling up a computer's arse and pretending that I've gone to heaven. What about you?"

"I don't know. I was retired, happily enough. Waiting for death, I suppose." It hadn't felt like that, though.

Qing said, "These aren't the highest mountains on the planet, you know. The ones we've just crossed."

"I know that."

"There are some that reach into a pretty good vacuum."

Duty's atmosphere was thin even on the ground; Ikat had no reason to doubt this assertion. "What's your point?" she asked.

He turned to her, and gave her his strangest robot smile. "From a mountain like that, a coil gun could land a package of nanomachines on Patience."

Patience was a third the mass of Duty, and had no atmosphere to speak of. "To what end?"

Qing said, "High vacuum, relativistic launch speeds. What we started doesn't have to stop here."

She searched his face, unsure if he was serious. "Do you think the Flower would give us what we needed? Who knows how Khamoush have programmed it?"

"I tested the nanoware, back on Procellarum. I know how to make it give us whatever we ask."

Ikat thought it over. "Do we know how to describe everything we'll need? To identify a new target? Plan a whole new mission?" The Orchard Seed had taken thousands of people decades to prepare.

Qing said, "We'll need telescopes, computing resources. We can bootstrap our way up, step by step. Let's see how far we get in three months. And if we solve all the other problems, maybe we can go one step further: build a seed that will self-replicate when it reaches its destination, launching a couple of new seeds of its own."

Ikat rose to her feet angrily. "Not if you want my help! We have no right to spew mindless replicators in all directions. If someone from Earth wants to follow the seed we launch, and if they make their own decision when they get there to reach out further, then that's one thing, but I'm *not* starting any kind of self-sustaining chain reaction that colonises the galaxy while everyone sits at home playing VR games."

Qing stood up, and made a calming gesture. "All right, all right! I was just thinking out loud. The truth is, we'll be struggling to launch *anything* before it's time to go home. But better to try, than spend three months taking in the scenery."

Ikat remained wary for a moment, then she laughed with relief. "Absolutely. Let the real geologists back on Earth fret about these rocks; I've had enough of them already for a lifetime."

They didn't wait for dawn; they headed back for the base camp immediately.

As they approached the mountains, Qing said, "I thought it would give me some great sense of accomplishment, to come here and see with my own eyes that this thing I helped to start was finally complete. But if I could wish my descendants one blessing now, it would be never to see the end, never to find completion."

Ikat stopped walking, and mimed a toast. "To the coming generations. May they always start something they can't finish."

A Blue and
Cloudless Sky

BERNHARD RIBBECK

Translated from the Danish by Niels Dalgaard

"Bernhard Ribbeck" is the writing name of Palle Juul Holm. Holm has had a long career as a teacher of Danish, German, and psychology at the equivalent of high-school level. Meanwhile, in addition to his fiction, he has written art criticism, book reviews, and lyrics for the now-defunct rock group, The Live Museum. His collection, Isen mellem øerne *[The Ice Between the Islands], appeared in 1999.*

"A Blue and Cloudless Sky," in its first appearance in English, was published in James and Kathryn Morrow's The SFWA European Hall of Fame, *in 2007. For determined readers, you may seek out the poem "Walking Song" by the Japanese poet Tarô Yamamoto, reprinted in English by the Morrows, as a source of some of the imagery in this story. James Morrow calls the story "a* tour de force *time-travel tale that manages to be at once rigorously plotted and emotionally resonant." We agree.*

1

What do we know, what do we really know about anything? I wonder and stare at Fausto, who's driving the tractor-trailer west through the cold of early evening, first across the lush farmland, then over a dry vacant plateau, and finally up through the mountain passes along the border.

"Do *you* believe this is the end of Nakorza, the end of us all?" he asks.

What can I say? That maybe it is, but not just yet? That I at least shall escape and make it back to Earth? Because if I don't, there never will have been a Fausto Caiazzo, or any other member of his species, on Nakorza.

There will only have been the aborigines.

We're climbing rapidly, following one hairpin turn after another. Behind the mountain peaks hang clouds the color of bruises, and on the straight stretches Fausto drives as if he doesn't care whether the end comes now or in six months.

We take a sharp curve where dark grimy ice lies like charred food in the bottom of a pan, and the whole truck skids. Fausto straightens us out, but the trailer swings from side to side; I cringe and hold my breath, then look down the ravine at the river with its frozen banks, and wonder what will happen if we go over the edge and crash.

Will everything disappear?

Yes, I suppose it will.

And I ask myself: Might that be for the best?

"I don't know," I tell Fausto. "Maybe this is the end—at least the end of what we know." The shocking idea makes my voice sound thin and ethereal.

"Shit," Fausto mutters harshly. I smell his adrenaline-laced sweat, along with the cab's permanent stench of motor oil and tobacco, joined now by the fine bitter fragrance of winter air blowing through the crack in my window.

There's really not much I can say to Fausto's despair, so I keep my eyes on the mountains, and when at last he breaks the silence, his voice is softer, almost apologetic. He tells me he's not out to kill us, but we're running late and liable to get stuck in the pass if it begins to snow, and he won't feel safe until we're in Powyrnisch.

"Yes," I say, nothing more. I wish I could be better company, but I'm in no mood to talk, and I don't want to distract him from his driving.

Fausto coughs. "It's damn cold for Easter week," he observes. "And Easter isn't even early this year."

"The coldest Easter ever," I say, hoping the conversation will end there.

"A frigid Easter, that's wrong," Fausto says and sticks a cigarette in his mouth. I light it for him. "Is there a connection, I wonder?"

"It's probably a coincidence. But I'm no expert. They say everything's connected in some way. Or it's the will of God. Or something."

We approach a steep rise. Fausto shifts into first gear, and the truck crawls slowly upward; in some places the wheels spin on the ice ridges, taking us nowhere, and the whole rig threatens to slide down the mountain. My chest tightens.

"Know what I think?" Fausto asks.

I realize he's talking to stay awake, so I decide to sound interested. "No, what do you think?"

Nakorza's sun, let's call it the sun, has disappeared behind the peaks, and a mass of snow-laden clouds has reached this side of the border. Fausto switches on the high beams.

"I think he must be here on Nakorza right now, in some village or other, close at hand, but nobody knows who he is," he says. "They say that all of us are here—not the Piouli, of course, but everybody else—we're here because of him, the space traveler. We all came to Nakorza from another part of the galaxy."

Fausto signals that he'd like some broth. Removing the cup from its holder, I push it into the zarf, then fill it from the thermos, clumsily, fearfully. I try to draw solace from the melancholy glow of the dashboard as it illuminates the cab.

"Not only are we from somewhere out there in space," Fausto continues, taking a sip of the scalding soup, "we're from some distant point in the future too. What's a person to believe?"

(Well, what *is* a person to believe?)

Obviously he wants to pursue this idea. He can't imagine how often I've run the story through my mind, but it's best to let him ramble on. So I sit and listen as Fausto tells how, once upon a time, a wanderer from the planet of our origins came to Nakorza in a capsule. Somehow he made it back to his own world, where he told the sages about Nakorza. Several centuries later—in a future that still lies ahead for Fausto and myself and everyone else—the sages' descendants learned to move effortlessly across the barriers of distance and circumstance, and so they launched hundreds of ships to Nakorza, each filled with a band of colonists: our ancestors.

"Our ancestors . . . who aren't yet born." Fausto takes a final swallow of soup, frees it from the zarf, and replaces the cup in the holder.

Not yet born. Because the sages didn't simply send the colonists through space—they also sent them back in time, far back, to a moment that existed 350 years before the space traveler returned to the planet of our origins. Why did the sages feel compelled to do that? The records aren't clear, but their decision was evidently connected to the traveler's accounts of the lifeforms he'd found on the faraway planet: he'd discovered the Piouli, of course, and also . . . us.

"It all depended on the woman—the Nakorzan who the traveler brought back to his home world," Fausto says. "She was the one who knew Nakorza's coordinates. She was the one who enabled our species to find the planet a second time."

"Or the first time, if you will."

"Or the first time," Fausto echoes.

Huge snowflakes sift down through the glare from our high beams. The cold begins to penetrate the cab.

"We don't even know the traveler's name," Fausto says. "Apparently the sages had their reasons for keeping it secret."

"In hundreds of years from now they will have their reasons," I correct him.

"But we know the woman's name," Fausto says irritably. "Maria."

(Where is Maria?)

I can hear Fausto breathing deeply and calmly. "If you read the old books," he says, "you'll see that the world our traveler described in such detail is the very world that Nakorza has become. That's why I think the moment of our discovery is at hand—that's why I think he walks among us now. But nobody can identify him, and nobody ever will, except for Maria. He could be anybody. He could be me. Or you."

(Yes.)

"Something puzzles me," Fausto continues. "When the traveler returned home, why didn't he tell the sages about the Crown of Stars? He must've seen it. Or if he told them, why would the sages' descendants send the colonists here? How could they do such a thing, knowing that not only Nakorza but this entire sector of the galaxy would eventually be annihilated? Something doesn't fit."

He shakes his head in sadness and confusion. And he's right. Something doesn't fit.

It's snowing heavily now, and I'm relieved to see that the next part of the pass runs through a tunnel. We enter the frigid darkness; the road is clear, and we feel happy knowing that, for a few minutes at least, we'll be protected from avalanches and drifts, and we won't have to worry about tumbling over the cliff.

The lamps in the tunnel ceiling are all broken. "When you see this kind of crap," Fausto says, "it's hard to believe our forefathers were able to leap through space and time."

We emerge into a nightmare: a towering wall of blinding snow, plus a fierce wind that makes the trailer sway and almost forces us off the road. Ten kilometers beyond the tunnel a white sign looms out of the blizzard—it bears the symbol of the region, two black crossed arrows—and Fausto almost crashes into it. ST. FANURIUS, the sign informs the wayfarer in Gothic type. KREIS STEFANOPEL/STEPANOPOL. GLIEDSTAAT NEU-RUTHENIEN. 2410 M.Ü. MEERESHÖHE.

The official language of New Ruthenia is German, though most of the inhabitants, at least on this side of the Kolpa River and south of the lower Brenda, are an undefined mixture of Eastern Europeans and people from the Balkans, speaking their own amalgamated tongue.

"Look out, dammit!" I cry as we rush past the sign, missing it by centimeters.

Fausto stops the truck, shifts into neutral, and turns toward me, veins bulging at his temples. "Shut the fuck up, Gerold," he bellows, "or you'll walk to Powyrnisch!" He slams a fist into the dashboard, sending the Holy Virgin jumping, then grinds into first again and starts to bring us slowly into the river valley.

On this side of the mountain we're a good distance from the cliff, but it's still a treacherous drive, the road twisting madly, the horrifying storm roaring all around us. The hairpin turns are almost impossible to see, the gusts make it difficult to negotiate the curves, and I don't like to think what will happen if a snowplow appears in our path.

We say nothing. Sitting with eyes half closed, I try to concentrate on something besides our terrifying descent. I think of Saint Fanurius, the patron of all those who seek something they've lost (does one need any other saint?), and of the unseasonable cold. Maybe Fausto is right. Maybe there's a connection between this frigid weather and the Crown of Stars. Could the Crown have pulled Nakorza into a different orbit?

Back in San Silvestro they probably know the answer. And I hope they have the sense to keep it to themselves.

* * *

As we drop below the timberline, I'm able to open my eyes and unclench my sweaty fists; the saliva returns to my mouth, and I stop breathing in gasps.

The broad trees catch the brunt of the storm, the straight stretches are longer now, and the snow lies in a smooth pure layer on the road. Fausto relaxes, lifts a hand from the wheel, and manages to retrieve a fresh cigarette and light it by himself.

"Scusi!" he says and tosses me the pack.

"Di niente!" I light a cigarette and draw the smoke deep into my lungs, and for an instant I stop thinking of what will happen to Nakorza if the truck crashes and we die. I also push aside the nagging possibility that I'm not the person I think I am: there may be another on Nakorza who is in fact the one who will return.

Now the sound arrives, the shriek of the storm in the tall evergreens that the Piouli call *kadua* and the New Ruthenians gypsy spruce, trees that release a mournful song when the wind blows through their large tubular needles.

"Twelve kilometers to Powyrnisch." Fausto allows himself to take his eyes off the road and look at me inquisitively. "Has your friend invited you to stay over Easter?"

I nod. "I'm hoping that Monday morning you can pick me up in Powyrnisch, on your way back to San Silvestro. Why?"

"Rumors," he says and stares straight ahead. An unfamiliar animal dashes across the road where the high beams fall away.

"What sort of rumors?" I ask, as he knows I will.

"This job of mine has me delivering goods in the forest country up north, Reichart's Notch and thereabouts, small isolated villages where nothing much happens. The folks there are a little primitive, you know, lumberjack types, coal miners, but decent. Our kind of people, if you follow my meaning—Catholics, Anglicans, and Methodists, most of them—and they speak a language you can understand."

"So this rumor comes from your drinking buddies in Reichart's Notch?"

"Most of the time, they're pretty bored," Fausto says. "Maybe that's why they gossip."

"About . . .?"

"About things that are supposed to happen"—he gives me a quick glance—"in Stepanopol during the Feast of the Resurrection."

Falling silent, he pilots us through a stretch of road unprotected by the trees. He switches off his high beams and concentrates on the snow, which appears to come from all sides at once. Soon we're back in the forest again. Fausto rolls his side window partly down and tosses his cigarette butt into the blizzard. A gust of frigid air fills the cab, little prickly ice crystals, along with the keening of the gypsy spruces.

"Deaths," he says. "People have vanished, and the Stepanopol police aren't looking into it too closely. It's really difficult to prove anything. Strangers like you aren't normally allowed at the Midnight Mass on Easter. But if your friend has invited you, I suppose there's nothing to worry about. It's all just idle talk anyway—I shouldn't have mentioned it."

He sits mute for a while, bemused or angry, I can't tell which.

"Unless," he adds, "your friend had a special reason for inviting you."

We travel another seven kilometers, and now we're so close to our destination that the squalls have acquired an apricot glow from the lights of Powyrnisch. Fausto pulls up at an inn, its tarred logs huddled beneath the towering *kaduas*.

Suddenly the snowplow we'd feared running into emerges from the blizzard, followed by an enormous gravel truck with a rotating searchlight atop its cab. Caught in the bright beam, two figures stand in the load bed, hurling shovelfuls of gravel over the tailgate and scattering it across the road. Sweat glistens on the parts of their faces visible between their fur caps and the wool scarves wrapped around their noses and mouths. Hunched over the auxiliary gas-powered generator that runs the huge truck's engine, two other workers warm themselves while waiting to relieve the gravel men. The huge vehicle passes so close to us that a spray of grit rattles against our wheels, but the workers don't seem to notice, and an instant later the truck disappears into the dark forest, trailing the stench of coal tar.

As we stumble out of the cab, Faustino says, "This is Sofija's place—let's get warm," and then he leads me through the drifts.

Reaching the front door, we stomp the snow off our boots. The porch is redolent of leather and lubricant and wet fur. Two pairs of cross-country skis lean against the rail. We step into the quiet inn. After the grinding engine and the wailing wind and the grieving trees, it seems as if I've become momentarily deaf.

Then we sit at a massive wooden table near the brick oven, and the sudden warmth and the smells of food cooking—I still haven't learned the names of the local dishes—make me sleepy and relaxed, and I stretch my arms lazily and carelessly, so that my watch emerges from under my sleeve.

"What time is it?" Fausto asks.

Had I thrown my watch away, a passerby might have found it and tried to represent himself as somebody he wasn't. If I'd stuck the thing in my pocket or hidden it in a suitcase, customs officials and border police would have dug it out and asked questions. So until this moment I'd assumed that the least conspicuous way to carry the watch was on my wrist. But I wear it facedown—not so much because it says SEIKO, but because it has only twelve numerals.

"My watch has stopped," I tell Fausto.

He turns toward another table and addresses two young skiers as they drink from glazed earthenware mugs. He asks them a question, probably the same one he just asked me. They shrug.

"Nam tschersornik," one of them says and shows Fausto his bare wrist; but he looks at me as he speaks.

His eyes are gray and hostile and scared.

"We can guess the approximate time," Fausto says as the food is served by a white-haired woman whose clothes smell of smoke. "There's a telephone here. If your friend leaves Stepanopol in fifteen minutes, he'll reach Powyrnisch in an hour and a half. I'll take you to meet him, but I don't want to go any farther tonight—if Sofija's got a free room, I'll come back here and sleep."

Sour soup. Salty, spicy mutton that couldn't possibly have come from a sheep. Beer with a strange, persistent aftertaste. Sofija sets two glazed mugs before us. *"Tzujk!"* she says, and pours us some fruit schnapps. I take a swallow. This stuff isn't flavored with plums, and the bouquet includes a touch of almond and lily-of-the-valley, plus a stronger, stranger scent, as unexpected and emphatic as falling in love. No matter: the schnapps soon works the way it's supposed to, burning off the chill along with my tension—and half my mucous membranes.

On the phone Gregor Tschuderka sounds enthusiastic but far away, and there's a crackle and a whistling in my ear, as if something large and hungry is trying to devour the line, and yes, he's looking forward to meeting me at the Powyrnisch train station "in ninety minutes." I glance at my watch, shielding it with my body, and try to convert Nakorzan minutes into Seiko intervals.

As I return to the table, the cross-country skiers rise abruptly and start to leave, and one of them nods and mumbles a greeting in passing. But the gray-eyed skier pauses and stares at me, pale and tense, and he breathes heavily, so I can smell the schnapps on his breath, the flowers, the strange scent; he stands frozen to the bare plank floor, until his pal returns—*"Chai, Damjan!"*—and leads him toward the door.

A freezing draft blows into the room as the door opens and the two skiers exit, and I realize I've been fixed intently on Damjan, returning his stare.

He heard me make the phone call. Heard me say *Gregor Tschuderka*. Saw me glance at a watch that supposedly doesn't work.

"What was wrong with that guy?" I ask Fausto.

"Wrong?" he echoes groggily. One of his eyes has slid to

the side. He pulls himself together, focuses. "Oh, it's just that you're a stranger, but not a priest or a trucker, and people here aren't used to strangers." He gazes at the floor. "Especially not now."

He gestures at Sofija, who pours us more mugs of fruit schnapps, and I worry whether Fausto will be able to drive us safely down the last stretch of mountain road.

Sofija remains standing with a hand on Fausto's shoulder and speaks directly to me. The only word I understand is the name *Damjan*.

"Mama Sofija says not to worry about Damjan Kolarow," Fausto obligingly translates. "He's got a bad temper, but he's a smart, honest boy. It's just that he's in love with a girl down in Stepanopol, and the thought of them dying together makes him despair."

"Why must they die?" I ask.

"The Crown," Fausto replies.

"But the scientists say it won't swallow us," I insist, as the paradoxes dance in my mind. "And the politicians say the same thing," I add, but there's no conviction in my tone.

Fausto sighs and takes from his pocket some folded, glossy pages, evidently a magazine clipping. "Forget the politicians. As for the scientists, they don't know crap." He lights a cigarette, his hands twitching. "Before my mother died, she had—a stroke, I think it's called. Something happened in her head, so she was paralyzed on one side and had trouble talking. Seven years she sat in a wheelchair. Seven years. And in the mornings, it was mostly in the mornings, she would weep for hours, and she wouldn't tell us why. Not that we really needed to ask, right? Isn't it reason enough to be stuck in a wheelchair and have nothing to do but think about the person you used to be?"

I don't know what to say.

"Sometimes I thought she was crying because of a dream she'd had the night before: her childhood home, meeting my father for the first time, us kids when we were little. But no, no," Faustino says sardonically, unfolding the brightly colored pages, "science claims that when old people cry it has nothing to do with their dreams or their memories or their situation. It's entirely"—he reads aloud from the illustrated article—"'degeneration of the central nervous system.' "

He places the pages in my hands: a centerfold article, the flap offering two longitudinal sections of the human cerebrum, one showing a "young brain," the other an "old brain," with certain areas highlighted in red and blue.

"Apparently it's that simple." Fausto points to the second illustration. "Too much blue makes old people weep." He takes the article from my grasp and leans back in his chair. "No, I don't much care for what the scientists tell me about my mother—and I'm not interested in what they say about the Crown of Stars either. We can all see it's getting closer and closer, and the mouth is growing at a faster rate every day."

He lifts a finger past his nose and pretends to rub his eye. When he draws it away, the tip glistens wetly in the lamplight, and I wonder what a longitudinal section of his brain would look like.

The snow has stopped; but the wind is still fierce, and its howl suggests a band of lost children screaming in the treetops above the inn.

"I understand your anger," I tell Fausto, thinking of his mother as well as the Crown. "You have no reason to trust the scientists or the politicians. But their first duty, as they see it, is to prevent panic and anarchy, even if that means lying to us. As far as they're concerned, the threat of social chaos is real: evidently there's an ice age coming—crop failures, grain shortages—and things will get worse before they get better. We've already seen the first symptoms of barbarism. Lootings, wild orgies, mass suicides. What if this really *is* the end of Nakorza? Would you have the astronomers and the government admit it outright?"

Fausto shakes his head slowly and throws up his hands. "But how can we accept their reassurances when we know they're out to control us no matter what? Those doctors weren't honest with my mother. 'You'll see, Signora Caiazzo,' they said. 'You'll live to be a hundred. You'll survive us all.' "

If I were completely certain, I might tell him what I know;

but I'm anxious and confused. The Crown of Stars simply shouldn't be there.

I gulp down my schnapps and hold my breath so I won't cough. "Anyway, I'm convinced that the Crown won't engulf us or hit us or whatever it's threatening to do." Despite my efforts, I cough. "Maybe I'm deluding myself—a leap of faith to keep up my spirits. I have no strong evidence for my belief. But I wish, I really wish, I could get you to share it, Fausto."

For a long time we sit without speaking, listening to the sounds from the kitchen and the eerie grief of the spruce trees; and I think maybe it's time to leave, so I slide my wrist under the table and glance at my watch.

"Thanks," Fausto says at last. "Actually, I think you could tell me a lot more if you wanted to. You might even shed some light on these mysteries." He looks at me without blinking. "It's just a feeling I've got, based on nothing."

"What mysteries could I clear up?" I ask.

"You might begin by explaining why you keep looking at a watch that has stopped."

A violent extra heartbeat. A sudden headache. A glowing dot inside my left eye. The iris aches, and I raise a hand as if I could bat the speck away.

Before I can answer Fausto, the phone rings. Sofija picks it up, listens, then glances at me and nods; she says something, nods again. As she hangs up, the bright speck fades, and Sofija speaks my name.

"Gerold Schenna?" she inquires, and now it's my turn to nod. "That was your friend Gregor, calling from the road," she continues, translating through Fausto. "He's been detained, but he'll be in Powyrnisch in half an hour. And how small Nakorza is! Had Damjan known you're on your way to visit Marja Tschuderka's father, I'm sure he would've behaved better."

No, I think. If he'd known, he would've killed me. "I believe I could use another schnapps," I say to Fausto.

"Do we have time?" he asks, gesturing toward my wrist. I remove the Seiko and give it to him; he blanches around the mouth, and the dark blue of his eyes turns black.

"Now tell me," he says.

"Yes," I say and wave at Sofija to bring us more schnapps.

And so I tell him.

The snow still eddies along the road, forming small drifts; but the storm is nearly over, and the stars are coming out. It's been a long time since anyone on Nakorza has wanted to look up and behold the sparkling heavens.

We are above Powyrnisch, close enough to see the dirty yellow light of the street lamps flickering through the swirling snow. On the railroad tracks below, a small switch engine shunts boxcars around, making up a freight train, the puffs of smoke and the clouds of steam mingling as they rise up the mountainside. Fine snow covers the coal in the tender like white flour.

"That train isn't going anywhere tonight," Fausto says. "The line to Chidno runs through a gorge. There must be several meters of snow. God knows when it'll be open again."

"What about the way to Reichart's Notch?" I ask.

"Oh, I'll get there all right," Fausto says. "It's a major highway, follows the course of the Kolpa; and once I'm in the town, I shouldn't have any problem with the local streets. They're pretty tough up in Reichart's."

Snow whips across the windshield, and Fausto turns on the wipers. He steers us along one last curve, and we're finally on level ground.

"I'll have a lot more trouble getting back to the inn," he sighs, driving us across a wide parking lot between the freight yard and the station.

At the far end of the lot, our high beams catch a black Torrance sedan, parked with its lights out, motor running.

"Looks like your friend is waiting for you," Fausto says above the cry of the wind and the rumble of the truck's engine.

Later, after he has pulled over and I've collected my rucksack, Fausto asks, "Is this good-bye, or will I see you again?"

"When you're safely back at Sofija's place, call me at Gregor Tschuderka's house."

"I mean—do I survive?" he asks, his eyes following the windshield wipers.

"One of us does," I say, jumping out, "but I'm not sure who."

I move along the station platform, following the twin beams from Fausto's truck. Suddenly a human figure lurches away from the driver's door of the sedan, then glides across the parking lot on cross-country skis and vanishes down the slope. Now Gregor finally turns on his headlights, and the Torrance receives me as if I were a baton in a relay race. Fausto presses his horn, blaring a farewell, then drives off. His high beams sweep across a couple of black-tarred wooden buildings, a dancing plume of snow, and a fur-clad Piouli who has stopped to watch the tractor-trailer through shining yellow eyes.

Fausto disappears into the darkness.

The drifting snow blows straight into my eyes, but the large shape bearing its shadow toward me must be Gregor. We embrace and kiss each other on the cheek, and then I see behind him another shadow, smaller and less bulky, her hair escaping from her fur hat to flow in the freezing wind.

As Gregor steps to one side, the headlights illuminate his features. They are dogged and sad; he feels no joy at our reunion.

"My daughter Marja," her tells me, gesturing toward the young woman. He nods in my direction. "Marja, meet Gerold Schenna. It's about time you got to know each other."

2

"I hope you didn't freeze last night," Gregor says. He sits with his back against the window. Behind him the daylight is a muted gray; a gentle morning snow is falling, and the wind has died down, though now and then a gust sweeps the loose snow off the roof and whirls it under the eaves.

The breakfast dishes have been cleared away, but the

fragrance of sausage and sauerkraut still lingers. Mingled with the kitchen smells are hints of tallow and incense.

"Thanks for asking," I say. "No, my fireplace was still warm when I woke up."

"You look tired," he says.

"I've rarely enjoyed such a soft, warm bed, but it's always difficult to fall asleep in a new place."

He pulls his thick eyebrows together and busies himself in preparing his meerschaum pipe; he empties the bowl, fills it with slightly trembling hands, lights up—and all the while I look uncomfortably around the living room, jammed with knickknacks and rugs and icons. There's a twentieth-generation copy of Rubljov's *Trinity*, a Holy Virgin, sooty to the point of looking like a black smear on a gold background, and an original painting of Fanurius, rendered so the eyes follow you.

The saint looks down on me from the wall, and Gregor stares at me from the other side of the table. "Then you must have slept badly for the past several years," he says.

He falls silent. And my friend and companion from our journey across the Turquoise Sea is suddenly a stranger.

A clock ticks loudly through the thirteen hours of Nakorza. The air is stagnant and smoky, making my eyes water. And, as when I spent my summer vacation visiting my wealthy school chums on the Kalmthal slopes, I feel the sting of being an outsider.

"What do you really know?" I ask.

"What do we really know about anything?" he replies, and I hear the echo of my thoughts from eighteen hours earlier.

He turns halfway around and lays a hand on the window, its panes frosted with blossoms of ice: the only flowers on Nakorza that look like the ones I knew as a child.

"You once told me you grew up in Kaumea—after making sure I'd never been there—and naturally that would explain your strange accent and the gaps in your knowledge," Gregor continues. "But eventually I realized you couldn't identify even the most common animals and plants, neither here nor anywhere else on Nakorza."

"Maybe I slept through school," I say feebly.

"Don't insult my intelligence. It wasn't only the animals you didn't know; you lacked all sorts of facts. You were ignorant of New Ruthenian history, of world history in general. Any child understands the rules of Kulaii, but not Gerold Schenna! You'd never heard of a *mosora*, and . . ." He throws up his hands. "Well, you were a pretty likely candidate for He-Who-Shall-Come. And the time is right, isn't it? It can't happen much later than now, if it's going to happen at all."

"Maybe he has already come and gone," I say.

Gregor shakes his head. "Impossible. Don't you suppose we've kept track of every Maria, Marja, Mary, Marie, Miriam, or Mirjam who ever lived on Nakorza? We can account for them all, my friend."

What a fate, I think, to be given that name and hence never escape official scrutiny.

"And now you believe I'm He-Who-Shall-Come," I say awkwardly, "and your daughter is the chosen Maria."

"Time will tell," he replies. "You know who you are."

He rises and takes a book from a shelf. It's a thin volume with a stiff brown cover, printed on cheap yellow paper: *Die Offenbarungen und Prophezeiungen des heiligen Nikifor aus Chidno.*

"Here," Gregor says, "you can read how the Prophet Nikifor has revealed that Nakorza's destiny depends on what Mary decides during the Feast of the Resurrection."

Once again I'm bewildered by the literal-minded beliefs of these people. "But why in Stepanopol?" I object. "And why this Easter?"

"Because you're here," Gregor replies, leaning forward and pointing at me. He gestures toward the threatening sky. "And because this is the last opportunity. After tomorrow night, there won't be any more resurrection feasts."

A gust of wind blows like a sigh along the road and echoes down the chimney. I glance at the firewood stacked for drying. The logs look like birch. The last woodpile?

From a deep, disorderly pocket inside my jacket I draw out a pack of cigarettes. I light one. The exotic tobacco is aromatic, but it doesn't take the edge off my fear.

"You shouldn't have invited me," I say.

Gregor inhales deeply. "There was a time when I actually *wanted* my daughter to be the Maria. It's an almost universal wish, cultivated by parents for as long as our race has been on Nakorza. In every family, one daughter is always named Maria." He bends down and picks up a box wrapped in lightly tanned fur and tied with a thong. "But today I want no part of Nikifor's prophecy." He looks directly at me. "Marja loves Damjan Kolarow, and yet she must choose you. And what's the use? It's too late already," he adds and stares heavenward.

"If you're right and I'm the space traveler who's to leave with Marja," I say, "perhaps you can take comfort that she'll be saved from the Crown of Stars."

Gregor unwraps the box and sets it on the table between us. "I'm not so sure she'll be saved," he says, removing the lid.

Shiny and bronze, the Kulaii set awaits.

The hint of a smile dances in the corner of Gregor's mouth. "It's time you learned the rules of our favorite game."

"All games embody a worldview," I say. "What's the philosophy behind Kulaii?"

"To keep playing," Gregor replies. "The loser is the one who becomes exhausted and leaves the field. But you can also lose by placing your opponent in a situation where he has no moves left. There's only one way to win at Kulaii, and many paths to disaster. And even at that, the winner may turn out to be a loser. It's a very Nakorzan game, my friend."

He lights a kerosene lamp, lowers the glass globe, and adjusts the wick.

With my heart in my throat, I try to find out what he thinks is coming. "On my way here, I was told that strange things happen at the Midnight Mass."

"Well, yes, there have been some tragic events," Gregor replies offhandedly. "Young people, high-strung types, have thrown themselves off Oblation Rock, hoping to placate the

Crown. But we've got it cordoned off this year, and guards will be posted."

"Oblation Rock?"

"A precipice beside the church." Gregor arranges the playing pieces on the board.

"Were they—?" I'm not sure how to put this. "Those who died . . . were they all women?"

"Watch now," Gregor says without looking up. "The first thing you must know is how to avoid trapping me in a dead zone. If you do that, you've lost."

"Any stakes?" I ask resignedly.

"Let us play for wishes," Gregor replies. "We should each concentrate on a devout wish without saying it out loud. Whoever wins can regard his victory as a judgment from God."

"Why not?" I say, and then I concentrate on Marja.

"But don't forget," her father says, "that the winner may turn out to be the loser."

"I know all about loss, Gregor, so save your paradoxes for another day and teach me the rules. Without rules, there's no game. Without a game, no winners or losers."

"Oh, I wouldn't say that."

"Then why should we bother?" The wind has abated; the cold gray light steaming through the windows makes me apprehensive. "Your game enables the players to experience real solutions, but only to illusory problems."

"True enough." Gregor taps his pipe to empty it and puts his head in his hands. "And outside the game we find nothing but illusory solutions to real problems."

And so we play.

Hours later we are interrupted when the whole family arrives for supper, and suddenly there's too much body heat around me, and too many smells. The blood goes to my head, and on the periphery of my vision everything dissolves in a rainbow-colored fog. Marja's two sisters and two brothers sit with heads bent over their plates, dragging their forks through their food and tossing quick inquisitive glances at me.

Marja rubs a bit of fat from a blouse trimmed in gold braid.

In slow German, out of consideration for their guest, the older son, Stojan, tells about the preparations for the Feast of the Resurrection; and I understand that the troikas will be fewer this year, because there hasn't been enough food for the draft animals. So the trip up to Chidno for the Midnight Mass will occur mostly in open wagons. But the participants will still bring hundreds of torches, so the celebration should be, as usual, bright and festive.

As usual . . .

"Are you marrying Marja?" her younger brother asks me.

"*Kolja!*" Gregor says.

"But I like Damjan better," Kolja persists. "You're too old for Marja."

It isn't easy, but I smile.

"Behave yourself," Stojan says. Kolja shrugs and twirls strands of sauerkraut around his fork.

Marja puts down her utensils and blushes, but her eyes are calm, and she regards me steadily, without reproach or fear, but also without love.

That terrible, insistent stare, a stare that seems to devour its object: I've seen it before, in women who'd stopped loving me but were offering me a second chance.

"Would you . . . sir . . . would you like me to show you the area tomorrow?" she asks, winding a lock of hair around her finger.

"I'd like that very much," I say.

"I want to come too," Kolja says.

"Brat," Marja says.

Stojan puts an arm around Kolja's shoulders and says, "I need you to help me decorate the church."

Suddenly a bowl of something cool and sweet-smelling appears before me. "Try our *baridani* preserves," somebody says. "A local delicacy. This may be your only chance to savor it."

"Take a big helping," someone else interrupts. "It's only when they're fresh that you have to worry about the side effects."

"And Damjan picked them," Kolja says loudly, looking triumphantly at his sister.

Marja gulps, and Kolja presses his lips together. But then Marja starts laughing and can't stop; she laughs so hard she has to leave the table.

Gregor sighs deeply. Glancing at his face, I realize that time has shriveled both of us. Kolja is right: I'm too old.

When the bowl of *baridani* comes to me, I take nothing.

It's after midnight when Gregor leans back and rubs his face with the palms of his hands.

"You won," he says. And when he sees my inquiring look, he adds: "You're trapped now, so I'm the one who lost."

The light from Beribek, Nakorza's greater moon, glows through the veil of clouds and glints off the icicles, while the lesser moon, Zarela, sets in the south.

"You did that on purpose," I say.

"Yes," he says.

"It feels like cheating."

"It always feels that way, when you win."

I go to my room. A fire blazes in the hearth, fresh water fills the earthenware jug, and the air holds the pleasant aroma of linen dried in the sun.

There's also another scent I can't identify right away, at once floral and fleshly. A lighted candle rests on the nightstand.

Her dark blond hair flows across the pillow, and she is very beautiful.

"I've kept your bed warm," she says with a crooked smile. And I know what she really means: Let's get it over with. But then she folds back the duvet, and I'm hit by her body's heat and a fragrance like a moist forest floor in summer, and I know I'll be unable to resist.

Sometime near daybreak, after she has fallen asleep, awoken, and slipped away, I find myself lying beneath the duvet, listening to the beams and timbers creaking in the frosty air.

The gravity of the room seems oddly awry, as if some outside force is pulling me toward it, and I wish I could cling to Marja, but I'm alone now, waiting to be sucked into empty space.

On the nearby farms, animals awaken in the cold dawn, complaining of hunger by making sounds I've never heard before. And it strikes me that Marja will be as much a stranger on Earth as I am here. I light the candle and murmur the ancient mantra: "I love you, I love you, I love you." But it doesn't work.

The game has turned out to my advantage, but only because it was rigged at the outset.

And that is not love.

It is something even worse.

I should feel at home here.

The shadow-blue and white-gold snowscape could be the Sarntaler Alps in winter's clothing, only with a colder, more distant sun. And the icy Kolpa, whose meanderings I can discern at the bottom of the valley, is a river like any on Earth.

But gradually I grow aware of small disparities. The cloudless sun-drenched sky with its peculiar shade of blue. The forests of gypsy spruce with their dark green needles that peal in the wind like tubular bells. And the many odd fragrances. Even the wood smoke rising from the Stepanopol chimneys smells strange to me.

The air is still but so cold that my breath freezes, sticking like rime to my beard and eyelashes, and I realize that without the heavy coat, fur hat, and wool mittens I borrowed from Gregor, I would have gone running back to the house by now. But Marja wants to show me around. Or, rather, she wants to talk to me alone.

We follow the road from Powyrnisch, which hugs the base of the mountain some twenty meters above Stepanopol, then runs through the outlying community, where Gregor's family lives, before descending into the valley, and doubling back to enter the town. The plows have created huge snow banks along the verges and deposited a slippery coating of frozen slush. I keep losing my balance, gaining a firm purchase with my boots only in those places where people have strewn ashes in front of their houses.

From the road we can see rolling, denuded orchards, the town with its thatched and shingled roofs, and churches whose golden onion domes are so bright they hurt our eyes. A light chilly mist hangs above the marshes along the river. On the far side of the valley the dark Nareli Mountains, home of the Piouli, rise like a fortress of shadows.

Marja identifies various trees and mountains and buildings for me, expressing no desire to hear about Earth, which she claims to know far better than I know Nakorza.

"We're all free to read about our ancestors' home world in books," she says calmly. "I've studied Earth history more than most."

She sounds perfectly sincere, and I marvel at her tranquility in the face of what's about to happen. I was expecting tears and anger, wrenching confidences, and—for some reason—childhood reminiscences. But she remains aloof, focused on the here and now, protecting herself with the quotidian.

As we walk down toward the town, I ask her to point out the church where the midnight mass will occur.

"It won't happen in Stepanopol," she replies, then stops walking and, grabbing my sleeve, turns me to the north, so I'm facing the mountain wall. She removes a pair of binoculars from her fur shoulder bag, adjusts the focus, and hands them to me.

In the distance I see an old onion-domed church clinging to the mountain. Beside it a shiny black outcropping juts from the snow, overhanging an abyss that drops for hundreds of meters into the ravine. *Stynka Schertfilor*. Oblation Rock.

"Maundy Thursday and Good Friday," Marja says, "we attend Mass in Stepanopol—but it is an old tradition that everyone gathers at the Church of Saint Fanurius in Chidno on Easter Eve."

She is standing so close to me now, pointing out the church (there, to the left of the sign for Powyrnisch, directly behind that peak, you can see the black stone glinting in the sun), that I feel the warmth of her breath. And I put an arm around her waist, try to pull her to me and turn her face toward mine; but she pushes me away, and I lose my footing on the slippery road, ending up on my back in a snowdrift.

To ease my embarrassment she laughs gaily, then playfully tries molding a snowball to throw at me, but the powdery snow disintegrates in her gloves. Instead she straddles me and rubs handfuls of snow in my face. Her hair falls free of her hat and brushes my eyes, and I notice that her teeth are bared in a smile. But I can't stand to look at her glowing face, I'm glad that my vision is teary with snow and blurred by the sweep of her hair.

"I'm sorry I disrupted your view of our beautiful blue sky," she says.

I don't know why, but I think of Fausto Caiazzo. "It's okay," I say as I slowly get up and brush the snow from my coat. When I was a child there were always massive, friendly clouds filling the sky. How I miss them.

"I need some time," she tells me as we search the snowdrift for the binoculars. "Last night was . . . I don't know what it was."

"I know what it was," I say without explaining myself. "And I also know that even if you weren't the chosen Marja, I'd still want to take you back."

We sit in the snow, looking at each other; then she puts her arms around me and rests her forehead against my shoulder.

I can win my Kulaii match, I decide—perhaps on my own, perhaps with help—even if I fail to take into account all the inherent contradictions of the game.

"Ah, the binoculars," Marja says.

A dozen flags droop from their poles, including the regional colors and, in front of the town hall, the national banner, divided into black, white, and sky-blue horizontal stripes. A simple flag, pure and laced with frost.

Heavy smells of broiling meat, burning coals, and incense hang so palpably in the air that one can walk around the fragrances and into and out of them. Bright bits of icicles, swept from the eaves by the householders, lie glistening on the sidewalks.

The streets are largely deserted, but here and there I notice groups of sullen youths, huddled together, emitting hostile stares. Men of Damjan's age, men who must know Damjan. One kid shouts a remark that makes Marja press her lips together; and I feel insecure. There is nobody to come to our rescue should Damjan's friends get physical. The message of protective males to strangers everywhere and always: Stay away from our women.

"You don't have to worry," Marja says, then leads me into a dark, smoke-filled tavern, which someone (a guest who couldn't pay his bill?) has decorated with a crude but powerful oil painting of the Crown of Stars; I can't decide whether the painting is intended to exorcise the threat or whether I'm having my first experience of gallows humor in New Ruthenia—or any kind of humor for that matter.

Except for us, the tavern room is empty; evidently Easter and the Crown have dampened everyone's urge to revel, and I find it curious that the place is even open. The landlord, who calls himself Miklos, has long since banked the oven, so we end up settling for what—in another place and under different circumstances—I would have called snacks.

The beer comes in large tankards and tastes, strangely enough, like beer; but its effect isn't a matter of alcohol only: there's something else in the drink, something I can't taste that lifts my heart, turns the light to gold, and shifts every color toward a cheerful hue.

"They may want to kill you," Marja says. "But as long as they believe their own lives depend on your safe return, they'll beat you up at worst. And they won't dare come into Miklos's place and make trouble."

I exhale deeply, lowering my shoulders, and it feels as if someone has wrapped thick, soft duvets around my body. For a few precious seconds I decide that the Crown is nothing but an amateur painting on a tavern wall—and not a half-bad painting at that.

Marja turns her head and follows my gaze. "Of course, not

everybody in Stepanopol thinks the way Damjan's friends do," she says. "Many people around here would be happy if you never got back to Earth. Somehow they prefer dying, annihilation by the Crown, to never having existed at all."

She sloshes the beer around in her tankard, then takes a long sip. "I don't really understand it."

Dusk has come to the streets of Stepanopol. "From the instant I saw you in the train station," I say, "I've been brooding about something. How can you be certain you're the right Maria?"

She looks into my eyes for a long time. Within her pale skin a blue pulse beats, darkening her high forehead and long neck.

"I can think of another puzzle," she says, bringing her thick dark eyebrows together, "one that should concern you and everyone else more than it seems to. After the space traveler got back to his planet, why did the sages turn to Maria for the vital information, the coordinates of Nakorza, instead of asking him?"

"The traveler was . . . not the sort of man you imagine."

"You aren't?"

"I would never call myself a scientist. A poet perhaps. Once the capsule understood my essential desire, my need to jump from one star system to another until we found a habitable planet—once the capsule understood me, it became autonomous, first bringing me here, then taking me back to Earth, entirely by its own devices. That explains why the sages needed Maria, but it doesn't explain how she happened to know the coordinates of Nakorza relative to Earth."

Marja takes another swallow of beer. "Considering the role I'm expected to play tonight, Gerold, I believe I have the right to ask you another question. Where did you hide this capsule, as you call it?"

The miraculous feeling of well-being is gone, the thick duvets have been pulled aside. All my life I've pretended that the world disappeared when I closed my eyes; told myself I was immortal; turned away the postman before he could give me a distressing message. And now Marja has shoved an unwanted parcel into my hands, a windowed envelope bearing the Great Reminder. But I cannot accept delivery, cannot make myself say: *I don't know—somewhere in a cave, I'll remember when the time is right. We're here, Marja, and therefore I must have found it again.*

Cannot.

All I say is: "When the time is right, I'll tell you."

"And now I shall answer your question." From her fur bag she removes a leatherbound book, thick, scuffed, and ancient. "How do I know I'm *the* Maria? Because of this."

I raise my eyebrows. "What is it?"

"My family has always kept better genealogical records than most. We know exactly which of the three hundred ships brought our ancestors here. Her name was the *Copernicus*"— she sets her hand on the book—"and this is her log. The Tschuderka family rescued it from mandatory destruction, hid it away in attics and cellars for generation upon generation. The coordinates of Nakorza appear on the first page, handwritten in tiny script on silken paper."

She leans over the table, and I notice that the mild euphoria of the beer has left her as well.

"From the moment the Crown appeared, I knew who I was," she says. "I was the Maria who mattered, the one whose family had preserved the logbook. And when I realized that, I wished I'd never read the thing, wished that somebody had thrown it on the fire. Now it's too late."

She lifts her hand to her forehead. "It's all in here."

The shock interval, it's called. The numb instant during which you read the lab report upside down as the doctor gives you his diagnosis, *that* diagnosis. The insensate interlude during which you obsess about what to wear to your mother's funeral.

I reach toward her, but my hand is shaking, and I pull back. "I loved you from the moment I saw you skiing toward me in Powyrnisch; I'll bring you back to Earth, try to make you happy . . ."

I halt.

"But," Marja says.

"Yes?" I say, taking a deep breath. Again I try to touch her, again I withdraw my hand.

"But," Marja says, "you have no idea where the capsule is!"

I swallow, shake my head. "No, but . . ."

The blood drains from Marja's face, and her teeth chatter as if she's freezing. "It makes sense," she says hoarsely.

And, oh God, it does make sense. I know what's coming. I'm opening the letter from the collection agency, fixing on the huge amount due, wondering how I acquired this much debt. And of course I cannot pay it.

"A wenit Damjan!" Miklos suddenly shouts.

The tavern door opens, and Damjan strides in from the darkness, his gray eyes full of pain, bent on keeping a promise he must have made to Marja's family before we departed. To protect his girlfriend's lover. To get the two of us home safely.

All the way up the hill to the Tschuderkas' house I walk ahead of Marja and Damjan, not far enough to seem conspicuous, but enough so I won't sense when they stop to whisper confidences or cry together or kiss.

Before me the aurora borealis is flaring, strong enough to cast flickering shadows: now bleeding like a moonrise, now oscillating behind the mountains like an array of searchlights, and finally, before it vanishes, fluttering like curtains in a draft.

Then the stars come out, a dense cluster of suns near the galactic core, glimmering like a bejeweled iconostasis.

And in the middle of the cluster, high above Chidno, the black hub of the Crown hangs in the night sky like a passageway leading to a vacant sanctorum, an empty Holy of Holies.

Beautiful and vibrant with meaning. And meaningless and banal. Like a transcription error.

3

The Easter Eve procession of the New Ruthenians toward Chidno has begun: from the first floor window of Gregor's house I see their lanterns, torches, and headlights bobbing amid the black ridges and along the banks of the Kolpa. The pilgrims travel in troikas and sledges, in carts and wagons; they sit crowded together in the load beds of pickup trucks, holding their torches aloft, renewing the resin the instant it's consumed. Occasionally I glimpse clusters of cross-country skiers gliding through the darkness across the snowy slopes.

Marja's older brother Stojan parks his flatbed truck before the house. He scrambles onto the open trailer, where he checks the torch holders and spreads soft, golden-brown pelts across the riveted steel benches.

Dressed in their finest Easter clothes, Gregor's neighbors stand on the roadside, waiting for Stojan to pick them up, stamping their feet to keep warm. I join the expectant crowd; the older pilgrims offer me greetings I don't understand, and the young men regard me with cold eyes set above broad cheekbones.

I feel completely alone, and when Stojan brings the truck I try to squeeze into the cab alongside him and Marja and Gregor, but instead Gregor guides me to the trailer and offers me a seat directly behind the cab, next to a torch crackling with fragrant resin. Young Kolja and Marja's two sisters occupy the bench directly across from me.

The larger of Nakorza's moons is setting: Beribek chases Zarela down behind the snowy peaks of Chidno. From a pack of predators deep within the forest comes a mournful howl, and the cry is taken up by another pack, and then another, so the message is relayed along the entire range. A cloud-mass veils the burning sky, and high above the world a black wound opens wider and wider, surrounded by a ring of starry fire.

As we reach the main road and join the convoy of fuming trucks, our progress slowed by dozens of troikas and sledges drawn by the short-legged draft animals whose fur shines green in the torchlight, I realize that the groups of pilgrims are all singing the same song—not an Easter hymn, but a melancholy folksong, with words I don't understand. The performance melds with the noise of the trucks, a polyphony of human voices sustained by the bass chords of the engines, each note rising or falling in time to the rhythmic coughing of the exhaust pipes. From the distant Nareli range the song is answered by the long, wailing glissandi of the Piouli.

In the meadows, where the road to Chidno climbs toward the eastern ridge, lumberjacks and miners from up north have erected canvas tents, and stands where you can buy sausages and beer, sacks of charcoal and bundles of pelts. Their faces glow among the roaring ovens and flaming braziers; some of the skiers stop to nourish themselves before the trek up the mountain, and occasionally a customer emerges from a troika, but everyone else ignores the vendors. As the truck drivers shift into first gear, the pilgrims grow quiet, and on the other side of the river the Piouli song also fades. Slowly we ascend in a long, unbroken caravan, and I wonder how so many people will fit into one church.

I peer through the cab window. Marja stares straight ahead, evidently seeing nothing. Gregor turns and glowers at me, and I am forced to look away and focus on the river and the ravine.

About four hundred meters from our destination lies a broad flat shelf of rock, where the worshipers park their trucks and sleighs. From there the last stage of the journey takes us up the mountain slope; the path is uneven and slippery, with only a low wooden guardrail to keep the celebrants from falling into the ravine. The long climb tires the older pilgrims, who frequently stop to rest, clinging to the rude boulders and white birches. At last the Church of Saint Fanurius appears, a beautiful and imposing structure that seems to hang suspended above the chasm, filling a grotto in the cliff face; its timbers are painted gray, and its golden onion domes, illuminated from below by the pilgrims' torches and headlights, almost touch the overhanging rock. The church looks different up close—not larger, not smaller, just different, and suddenly I realize that the nave extends deep into the cavern, so that the front wall with its portals and windows is really a kind of façade concealing the building's true scale. There will indeed be room for us all.

Colors swirl around me, muted by the night. I smell the sweat of the weary pilgrims as they gather outside the building, greeting friends and family members they haven't seen in a long while. Gossip and gifts are exchanged, but the dominant mood is detached seriousness, a quiet piety. Now the crowd parts to make way for the patriarch, Father Ischaslaw, magnificent in his gold chasuble as he passes among the pilgrims and slips into the church through the door to the sacristy.

Cold and confused, I become separated from the Tschuderka family. For a long time I walk in circles before the church, then pace up and down on the steps. Finally, convinced that Marja and the others must have gone inside, I enter through the main door.

Immediately I am overwhelmed—by the pungent incense, the strange faces, the glittering icons, the hundreds of candles burning on the altar—but mostly by the immense size of the nave. This is a church as big as a cathedral, an arena, a town square.

As I shuffle down the main aisle toward the iconostasis, I notice that a side door lies open. The pilgrims' breath and bodies combine with the candle flames to send a rush of hot air through the gap and out into the night, carrying with it scraps of paper and bits of dried mud.

I pause beside the chancel rail and stare through the open door toward the snow-covered ledge beyond, which quickly narrows to become Oblation Rock; beyond yawns the steep black chasm. Despite Gregor's assurances, there are no cordons anywhere, no guards in sight—not that I really expected any.

Maybe the door was left open to ventilate the space, I speculate, or maybe somebody merely forgot to close it; but neither possibility convinces me, and I feel helpless and confused.

I turn and survey the nave. More and more people jostle into the church. The celebrants press toward the iconostasis, drawn by the iridescent saints; the choir sings a hymn, and their voices envelop me and rise toward the lamps hanging from the ceiling like gilded stalactites. A draft rushes through the open door and blows against my back, making my collar ripple, and when I remove my fur hat, my hair flies forward over my brow. I remain beside the chancel rail, shivering, teeth chattering, determined not to let anybody pass through the treacherous portal, but knowing full well I'm no hero, my courage might desert me at the last minute—unless, of course, somebody has arranged for me to win, which is simply impossible. Briefly I meditate on the defeats I've known in my life, and the defeat I'm about to know, soon realizing there was really only one great reversal: a loss that has folded in on itself, visiting me again and again, iteration upon iteration, never increasing in power but always prepared to show me yet another facet.

Again I gaze through the open door. Above the ledge, above the church and the black sheen of Oblation Rock, the dark dome of the winter sky arches over New Ruthenia, breached by the shining Crown of Stars.

Contemplating the night, I feel a sudden pressure on my eardrums. The hymn has stopped. From behind me comes the cacophony of the worshipers: their gasps and sighs, the tromping of their shoes and boots.

I face the choir, and instantly they begin to sing again, and I hear every syllable because they're all looking at me. The despair in their voices and the grief in the bass notes make my scalp tingle.

The procession of celebrants moves slowly and ominously down the aisle. At the head of the throng walk Marja and Father Ischaslaw, who helps her to stand upright and speaks softly with his face turned toward her. The patriarch's words are drowned out by the choir, and the nave swims in a white luminous fog. Reaching the altar, Marja falls to her knees with clasped hands, her lips moving; and though I cannot hear a word, I know what she's saying.

I rush toward the open door. Marja rises, and soon she and Father Ischaslaw are moving again, getting closer and closer to me, and as I plant myself beside the jamb—freezing in the winter air, burning with the fever of my misery—my decision takes form. I shall protect the one I love. I shall alter the iterations, smash the facets, and from my deepest pocket I remove the weapon I've sworn never to use, grasping it in both hands, my palms throbbing with my strong rapid pulse. I aim the weapon at Ischaslaw, and the throng of celebrants rushes toward us with livid faces, their shouts and wails ringing with anger.

"Maybe this happens because I came to care about you after all," Marja says, looking at me with blue eyes canopied by dark brows. Ischaslaw steps forward and grabs her arm and continues to lead her out of the church, bound for the icy ledge.

"Release her and step away!" I scream in German, hoping he understands me; but he keeps his eye fixed on the precipice.

"Put the gun away," Marja rasps, breaking Ischaslaw's grip and stepping between the priest's body and mine. But she is too late. The bullet pierces her outstretched hand and burrows between Ischaslaw's eyes, and he topples over and lies motionless at the crowd's feet like a heap of autumn leaves. Marja rushes through the door, the darkness drawing her toward the precipice, and then she opens her arms, blood flowing from her wounded hand, surrenders to the icy slope—

For a fraction of a second she hovers above the chasm, arms outstretched, and I know that if I look behind me I'll see the patriarch's dead eyes, his golden chasuble, and a book lying on the church floor, its cover stained with a drop of Marja's blood. A book whose pages contain small dense writing and a fatal transcription error.

—and disappears over the edge.

It's very quiet.

She must have hit bottom by now.

Then follows a great shudder, stronger than any earthquake tremor; it seems as if the universe has slipped out of gear. An unimaginable terror seizes me, rending my soul, shredding my sanity; and then comes the final cataclysm, and whatever remains of an orderly reality dissolves into a swirling gray blur like the dancing static on a television screen.

I am pulled down, down, down, as if captured by a black hole; I relive my life, experience my death, endure my damnation. Am I in hell for a hundred years? A million? Then everything begins again, the eons flying by, and my bowels seem to rotate in their cavity, and I go blind, my melted eyes running down my cheeks, and my brain becomes a useless organ, no longer able to control my muscles. Thirst and fear. Fear and madness.

Midnight. The sacred portal stands open, and the priests come pouring from the Holy of Holies, singing *Christos was-chrjes!* Christ has risen. *Wai istino was-chrjes,* the choir and the celebrants reply.

Verily, he has risen.

I know this church without quite recognizing it, drawing comfort from its carved marble pews, modern altar, and lavish trappings, reorienting myself as if I were surveying my house after a long journey or my bedroom after a vivid dream.

But the stream of alternate memories lingering at the edge of my consciousness is not a dream. The nebulous, superimposed images are not phantasms.

Every time I tilt my head back and stare at the radiant ceiling, I grow dizzy at the sight of the hanging lamps, those gilded stalactites, and the entire vault seems to rise heavenward.

I line up at the altar with everyone else, and we kiss each other on the cheek and express our joy in Christ's resurrection, and I know all the celebrants' names and who they are; but for a brief instant other faces emerge, as in a photograph printed from a double-exposure: sometimes a woman's face with hair escaping from a fur hat, sometimes the face of a man who called me friend.

Real faces, real voices.

And then I feel an infinite emptiness. The loss of a real woman, who has never existed, who *chose* never to have existed, a woman I nevertheless love. Could any loss be more irredeemable?

The conditions have dissolved. The error was never propagated. Sometime in the future thousands of colonists will be sent to the right planet, colonists whose descendants now take me by the hand and congratulate me in this sacred, well-lighted, gloriously warm nave.

"Yes, I too have tears in my eyes—isn't it remarkable?" somebody says to me. "He has risen, he has conquered death and released us!"

She, I correct him mentally, then dip the bread in the wine and eat it with a silver spoon.

Hours later, as I am leaving the church, a portly man appears in the doorway of the office. "Gerold Schenna?" he asks, and I nod, startled by a feeling of déjà-vu.

The man gestures me into his office. "Somebody left a phone message for you last night," he tells me, studying a slip of paper. "Mr. Casaubon will pick you up outside the church as arranged."

"Thanks," I say, glancing at my watch.

It says five o'clock. And the clock on the wall concurs, and so does the clock on the secretary's desk.

I wonder briefly why my watch agrees with the local time, and why all the timepieces in this place have only twelve numerals.

Then I walk out into the early spring dawn and look up at the stars, now fading from a sky that soon will be pure blue.

The first birds have begun to sing.

Let's just call them birds.

Epilogue

"It wasn't a dream, was it?" Jordan Casaubon asks above the soft whistling of the tires as the world takes shape in the dim light of early morning.

"No," I answer, "it was no dream. A dream would be easier to understand."

"Umm-hmm," Jordan mutters.

We're traveling south through a fertile, rolling landscape, an endless carpet of silken purple grasses just beginning to catch the rays of the rising sun.

At intervals we encounter sleeping villages with white-washed houses, and in between lie broad fields abundant with green and violet vegetation. The heady scent of farm animals and the agreeable fragrance of moist spring soil wafts through the side windows.

Jordan pulls over and says, "Get in the backseat. It's still a long way to Akún. There's plenty of time for you to sleep. We don't want you dozing off during the press conference. Roll up my coat, put it under your head, and make yourself comfortable."

I climb out and stand beside the car, which smells of fresh paint, leather upholstery, and leaking oil. A slight morning breeze, cool but not frigid, blows across my face. The hills have emerged in the sunlight, and foliage is now visible in the stands of dark trees. Spring leaves: as delicate as if painted on the branches with the finest camelhair brush. Soon the dew will turn to mist and disappear, and it will be a pleasant day in the Akún region of Nakorza.

This Nakorza, which is not necessarily a happier Nakorza, simply more prosperous, more technologically advanced.

And a Nakorza without a Crown of Stars.

I recline in the backseat, exhausted and yet wide awake. A burning itch runs through my body; my underwear is already sticking to my skin, and I'm unable to get comfortable, no matter how I arrange myself.

Jordan catches my eye in the rearview mirror. "By throwing herself off the cliff," he says, "Marja forever deleted certain material—conditions, possibilities—from . . . let's call it the Great Archive. Including the wrong coordinates in the forbidden logbook."

He raises his eyebrows. I nod. "Recorded in the logbook, and in Marja's memory," I add.

"That's why you couldn't find the capsule," he continues. "It simply wasn't."

"It simply wasn't," I echo. "Or maybe I'd repressed my knowledge of where I'd hidden it."

"In a way," Jordan says, "Marja's sacrifice was the ultimate solution."

"Solution to what?" I ask. "How do you solve a problem that never existed?"

"Go to sleep. If you need some help, there's a bottle of something they call vodka on the floor."

We drive through a medium-size provincial town; for some reason the streets are gaily decorated. Garlands hang from the balconies and lampposts, waving in the pleasant breeze, and a flag of black, white, and blue billows from a pole beside a luminous marble building.

I open the vodka bottle, and the gentle fragrance of lily-of-the-valley, along with the flag's evocations of sorrow and snow and sky, cause a burning in my stomach, even before the first swallow.

"We've got our work cut out for us," I say. "So much information to collect—the course of the colonization fleet, the manifest of every ship, the ecology of the planet."

"Don't sweat it," Jordan says. "I kept busy during our vacation. All the data lie safely in a vault in Akún."

"The founding fathers, the first colonists," I say. "Go through the lists of their names, Jordan. Go through the lists very carefully."

"I'll delete every last Tschuderka, Tschud, Cuderka, and Chuderka," he assures me. "Because otherwise . . ." With his right hand he draws a horizontal eight in the air. The symbol for infinity.

I take a deep pull on the bottle, then lie down, the taste lingering in my mouth, the fragrance filling my nose and sinuses, and wallow in memories of a world that never was.

Happy to be beyond the settled areas, Jordan accelerates, and for a long straight stretch across the prairie I hear nothing but the whistling of our wheels and the soft buzz of the spring breeze.

"The car," I mutter.

"What about it?" Jordan asks.

"What do you call the make of car we're in?"

"It's a Torrance, I think," he replies hesitantly. "Named for one of the first colonists." And after an interval he gestures broadly, sweeping his hand across the flat open countryside. "Damn beautiful," he says.

Sleep is closing in around me; I look out the window at a blue and cloudless sky. For a moment I see a face dusted with snow, and I feel a slight pressure near my heart, as if someone is sitting on my chest.

Then the snow and the face dissolve into a flock of white birds soaring over the prairie.

"Hey," Jordan says, "you're crying . . ."

Reasons Not
to Publish

GREGORY BENFORD

Gregory Benford (www.gregorybenford.com) lives in Ir-
vine, California, and is one of hard SF's chief spokesmen.
He has in the last two years become a CEO of several
biotech companies devoted to extending longevity using ge-
netic methods. He retains his appointment at UC Irvine as a
professor emeritus of physics. He is the author of more than
twenty novels, including the SF classic Timescape *(1980).*
Many of his (typically hard) SF stories are collected in In
Alien Flesh, Matters End, *and* Worlds Vast and Various.

"Reasons Not to Publish" was published in Nature,
somewhat cut to fit. The full version is contained here. Told
in the distant third person, it is an ironic, ambiguous, pro-
science fable. It is also an idea story that SF readers are
likely to remember for a long time. Maybe there is a mes-
sage imbedded in the physical universe that strongly implies
the existence of God. And maybe God doesn't want anyone
to blow his cover.

Roger made the greatest discovery in scientific history by noticing a jitter in his left eye.

He was hiking in the High Sierra on a crisp fall day, alone in the Glass Creek valley. The jitter was not a fluttering bird, but an entire tree jumping in and out of focus, light playing on it in eerie, slanted shafts. He watched it for a while, then walked under the pine. The bark felt smooth but looked fissured. It flavored the air like a real pine. The creamy bark stuttered beneath his fingers. The whole tree and all around it ratcheted, went grainy, sometimes vanished.

Roger was a mathematical physicist and had seen something like this before. A bad simulation, jumpy and scattered, just like this pine. His face paled, his breath caught, but the conclusion was clear. This backcountry he loved to hike through off-season was . . . a simulation.

Probably, he judged, because usually there was nobody around in late autumn. No need to spend computation time to keep pine needles waving before no audience. Just distribute motion between the harmonics of limbs, branches and clusters, to save computing time. He knew that a cheap simulation of light scattering replaced a detailed calculation with plausible rules of thumb, much quicker than the real thing, but realistic—as long as nobody looked too closely.

So Roger looked around, closely.

Seen from here, Mammoth Mountain jumped around, shifting colors. Background clouds lost their cottony look and sometimes vanished.

An eerie prickling climbed his spine. The logic was clear. So . . . he was a simulation.

It took a day and night of hard drinking to do some hard thinking about the implications. From his condo in Mammoth he watched the looming mountain and it was fine, not jumpy. He went for a splashy swim in the pool, savoring the flavors of the air and water, the sigh of pines singing in a fragrant, dry wind.

But back in the Glass Creek valley again, the same ratcheting blinked in and out. A cost-smart sim, stretched to its limits. Someone was being thrifty.

What did the Programmer God want? To watch a universe evolve, or just a simmed Earth? To rerun human history? Was the software even written by humans at all? He glanced around, uneasy.

Hiking back to his car, Roger sucked in the clean air that now seemed like perfume. Life, even fake life, was more precious than ever.

He could not stop his mind from working the problem, though.

Why was the simulation getting stressed now? Maybe the computation cost of running a world of 6 billion people had stretched resources? At least some of those 6 billion, wonderful folk like Roger, felt complex internal states. That, he knew. Descartes, after all.

But 6 billion people like him, with his complex inner states? His sharp, darting mind, his sensual layers, his robust hunger for life? (Okay, he admitted, maybe that was laying it on a bit thick. But still.)

Such detail must cost a bundle in bit-rate. With population rising, computation costs climbed. Maybe the system had hit the wall, strained to its limit. That could explain why nobody had noticed this before. Or had they?

The people he saw ambling in the Mammoth streets might be simple programs. To test that, Roger walked up to a few at random and they acted just like real people—except nothing was real, he reminded himself. Maybe they were as deep as he was.

How could God the Programmer handle the data rate for

such complex people? Could He (or She, or It) run some complex people like him, with full interior states, and just use rubrics for the mob?

Probably, since The Programmer was running short on bit rate. Plus, it would explain a lot of what was on TV. Maybe the mindless people on talk shows really were mindless.

In a way, he felt liberated. He certainly couldn't care about fake people.

He stopped walking, looked around at the eggshell blue sky, sucked in the sharp aroma of late Fall. The logic was clear. All the goals he had were nothing compared with this knowledge.

All else being equal, then, he shouldn't care as much about how he affected the world. Only the Programmer God mattered, because She could erase you.

Could he be the first to see the world as it really was? Or rather, wasn't?

How many "people" had noticed that the flaws of Nature told us that the laws of Nature were from software, running on some machine?

Population was still rising. Some people might need to be pruned to lower costs. How to stay alive, then? Or rather, "alive"?

Be interesting to the Programmer. Be famous. Or original. Or maybe funny.

Roger was none of these, really. Smart, sure. Observant, yes. That was about it. Maybe he was in mortal danger of being erased.

But he did know that this sim-Earth was fake. It seemed pretty unlikely that its purpose was to see how many figured out that they lived in a simulation. Perhaps just the opposite—if many did, maybe the world got erased, its original purpose corrupted.

So . . . he should prevent others from finding out. By not drawing attention to the ratcheting pine, to Glass Creek, to Mammoth Mountain at all. Not to himself, most of all.

Yes, and be interesting to the Programmer. Do things!

Live in the moment. Enjoy life! It was a lot like Zen Buddhism.

Walking home, he watched Mammoth Mountain. It loomed large, gleaming firm and true in a sky as clear as logic. It felt solid, the air snapping with the rub and reek of reality. Where real people like him were, with complex inner thoughts, the Programmer spent the computational time to make the world work. Elsewhere, not. God had a budget.

But . . . how many other people had made this discovery, and kept quiet? All of them, apparently.

Or if they did try to shout the startling truth from the rooftops . . . Well then, something unpleasant happened.

The biggest discovery in history, throwing both religion and science into a cocked hat . . . and nobody dared speak its name. Nobody who survived, anyway.

Roger had to join them, the silents, for his own safety. Give up his Nobel.

He stopped at a wine shop and bought the best bottle they had.

Objective Impermeability
in a Closed System

WILLIAM SHUNN

William Shunn (www.shunn.net) and his wife recently moved from New York City to Chicago, where he became a full-time writer. Before that he worked as a database developer and architect. He holds degrees in Electrical and Computer Engineering and English from the University of Utah. He says he is "at work on a memoir entitled The Accidental Terrorist, *a complete draft of which can be heard in my podcast at www.shunn.net." He began publishing stories in 1985, using the byline "D. William Shunn" until 1996. He is the author of a number of short stories, and has been nominated for major SF awards. His first book, a short horror novel entitled* Cast a Cold Eye, *co-written with Derryl Murphy, is to be published in 2009.*

"Objective Impermeability in a Closed System" was one of six chronological stories in his 2007 chapbook, An Alternate History of the 21st Century: Stories. *In it, his protagonist invents a time machine in order to asynchronously solve a central problem in his life.*

His meticulous preparations complete, Hector Baratoux stooped and entered the time machine called Albert. His interactive resignation statement was sequenced for replication and autodelivery first thing the next morning. The cut of the clothes he wore was not current, but their drab neutrals were, and at a whispered command the fabric would come alive with the garish colors of the late thirties. The AIs were busy chasing down solutions to an obscure Shishekli transform involving the distribution of small bodies in Saturn's rings—though that was really just for plausible deniability, so they could claim their attention had been elsewhere. Just one sub-aware subprocess was plotting Hector's translation, and would throw the switch at his word.

If that thread executed properly, in moments he'd flip from 2059 Grenoble to 2037 Geneva, there to father his 21-year-old daughter Garbiñe.

He fluttered his damp palms. Finally he wiped them on the backs of his pant legs.

The interior of the cramped gray egg smelled of long-chain polymers. Hector sat down on a clayey lump that formed into a seat beneath him and molded itself to his stiff posture, practically begging him to relax. The default control panel emerged from the blank forward surface, awaiting reconfiguration instructions, while above it a wide, curving band of the egg faded to transparency. His windshield.

It was a Sunday evening. The small lab was dim, lit only by the few diagnostic displays on the otherwise quiescent walls. "Journand and Charlotte?" Hector asked. "Albert, where are they?"

No single AI or subprocess actually ran the time machine alone, but since none of them had names they'd ever deigned to share with the humans on the project, and since their identities were fluid and portions hotswappable anyway, the humans had adopted a convention of addressing them all by the name of whichever project was relevant at that moment. Thus, any mind on the worldline mapping project was Hendrik, any on matter tranformation was Dee, and any on physical translation was Albert.

"Your token security apparatchiks?" said a grating, sexless voice. A swirl of color roiled on the control panel, teasingly approximating meaningfulness. "On average, the two are about as far from this room as they're ever likely to be simultaneously."

There was more obfuscation in that statement than useful information, but Hector was used to the AIs and their games. Even a subprocess seemed to take perverse pleasure in simulating obstructionism simulating helpfulness. But that was fine. Hector's mission would have been hopeless if they didn't view such human concerns as politics, security, and even identity with mischievous condescension at best. In fact, his mission would be inconceivable. . . .

Hector was more concerned about the two security guards, who, as EU non-citizen residents, might be at some risk if they lost their jobs. As project administrator, he would normally be the one to finalize termination decisions, but in this instance of course the question would be out of his hands. He just hoped he could trust the AIs either to back his story that the guards were blameless or to conceal the evidence of his temporal incursion altogether.

It was more reassuring to dwell on that than to worry about how Arantxa would react to his appearance.

Arantxa Oxanguren. He had met her in '31, early in his postgraduate studies at l'École Polytechnique. She was an undergrad in one of his lab sections, and he was so diffident about eye contact that he didn't even realize for three weeks that she was attending in person and not by telepresence. An image that beautiful had to be an avatar. But no, she was Euskadian—a porcelain-skinned, black-haired Basque who was first in her family to attend university—and in the wake of her new country's war for independence and EU membership there just wasn't the technical infrastructure still intact to make remote schooling a right as opposed to a luxury.

Hector, while mainly of Provençal extraction, was born and raised in bourgeois comfort near Paris, but still he'd always nurtured vague revolutionary dreams. Meeting someone whose people had not only had something real to fight for, but had against all odds succeeded, fired up all his romantic imaginings. Normally shy and reserved, unlike his many hyperverbal classmates, he nonetheless found his cause in fighting for Arantxa's affections, and against all odds he also succeeded.

In the summer of '32, at the start of her senior year, they moved in together, to a tiny flat in Phase 1 of the Paris Arcology. The nanotech revolution, though it promised universal plenty, was still in its infancy, and the old economy thrashing like a giant in its death throes. Small as their flat was, they never could have afforded a slot in the high-tech monolith without student subsidies. Hector hoped the programmable layout and décor would make up for the size, but as the months passed Arantxa only came more and more to deride their surroundings as the decadent trappings of a bumbling and wrong-headed technocracy.

"Such banal wonders! Luxuries unimaginable even to kings in ages past, but what good do they do us?"

"Well . . . plenty."

"Like what? I can watch fields of grain wave on the walls, but does that feed me?"

"No, but it's snowing outside, and you're warm and dry."

"Any dumb house could do as much. But changing the furniture at will? What good is that when billions are starving?"

"Projects like this are the proving grounds, Rani. It's how we learn to use and control the technology."

"Fritter it away, you mean. Distract ourselves from the politics that keep it from doing any good to the ones who don't look like us."

Arantxa's vision was one of technological revolution sweeping the world like brushfire, scouring politics away, an enterprise for which the liberation of Euskadia had only whetted her appetite. This fervor was why he loved her so much; her vision gave form to Hector's less concrete dreams of crusading for change. Why then did he try to rein her in, to impose his entrenched and craven caution on her?

Perhaps it reflected his disappointment in himself at butting up against the boundaries of his intellectual capacity—a new and unpleasant experience in his academic career. On his good days he could almost get his head around the mathematical superstructure of the object-oriented cosmology that now seemed the best hope of unifying physics. His half-completed dissertation on objective impermeability in closed Trencke systems—the idea that certain OO events were black boxes with observable effects but causes indeterminate and undeterminable—broke no new ground; it was simply a working out of some of the overlooked implications of other theorists' work. Still, on his bad days he stared at the virtual pages like a miner deep underground whose headlamp had inexplicably dimmed and died.

The months leading up to Hector's dissertation defense were the first severe test of his relationship with Arantxa. With her heart safely won, or so he believed, he felt free to direct the energies he had used to woo and keep her back into his work. This was fine for a while, since she had her own senior thesis on nanoassembler methodologies to complete, but as time wore on she grew less and less patient with his preoccupation. Even their arguments couldn't fully engage his attention, and while these clashes often ended with her storming out of their "klutzofascist nightmare grotto," they left Hector feeling slightly perplexed and disoriented. This only worsened when she abandoned him for her home city of Guernica the summer after her graduation.

Even with all that was to come, Hector would remember that summer—facing first a hostile doctoral committee then a hostile Basque lover, and somehow convincing both to yield—as the most exhausting of his life. But it set him in good stead for a career, as his job interviews that summer were a comparative breeze. He signed on with CERN that fall as a junior liaison in public affairs, something the reticent scholar never would have predicted even a year earlier. But, as the committee chair told him, "You have a way of explaining concepts such that I can almost believe you understand them." Even Hector had to admit it was a perfect fit.

So he dragged Arantxa to Switzerland, where after only a year's delay she was able to commence her own postgraduate studies at the University of Geneva. Hector helped represent CERN at scientific symposiums, conferences, and summits all over the world. On occasion Arantxa was able to travel with him; more often her studies interfered, as did, increasingly, terror alerts and outright war. Decades of adventurism abroad had finally caught up with the United States; paranoid and isolationist, the superpower's latest doomed attempt to dictate the terms of global discourse was to withhold nanoware from unfriendly regimes (most of the Third World and parts of the First). The policy only provoked riots and worse, while terrorism, endemic worldwide since the upheavals of the Aughts, escalated inside and outside the U.S. Hector was all for open-sourcing, especially with the means to end scarcity at hand, but CERN had other priorities, and in any case was ultimately responsible to Brussels, which couldn't afford to alienate Washington to too great an extent. Arantxa, for her part, thought the U.S. could go hang.

Still, this didn't prevent them from visiting an ever-resilient New York City early in the summer of '36, where they celebrated Arantxa's own successful dissertation defense with Blue Point oysters and local beer. Hector by then had moved from public affairs to lobbying. He considered it a step up. Arantxa did not.

"At best it's a lateral move."

"At best?"

"You know what I think of lobbyists."

"We're not a corporation, Rani, and I'm not a hired gun. This is where the big battles are fought, against those people."

"Right, one taxpayer-financed junket at a time. Hector, you're better than this—smarter."

"If I'm so smart, where were all the research offers three years ago?"

"The world's not ready for your kind of smart. But I am. Why else would I be with you?"

But the job was an easy slide for Hector—and a giant blow to Arantxa's hopes of settling down in Bilbao and registering for their allotted two children. (She wouldn't have them in Geneva and raise any scrimy Swiss individualists.) To himself, Hector readily admitted that he was dragging his feet, that the responsibilities of parenthood terrified him, and that the tantalizingly close breakthroughs in OO energy extraction fascinated him far more than a child ever would. The words burned hot in his throat, but he could never figure out how to say them to Arantxa.

Marking time, Arantxa accepted a research fellowship at the University of Geneva. Hector's travel schedule grew even more hectic, and Arantxa took to spending her every break at home in Guernica. Hector missed her fiercely when they were apart; telepresence and virtual sex weren't enough to sustain him. During every absence he would promise himself that he'd work harder on their relationship, but somehow could never make himself emotionally available to her when they were together. A hole was growing in his chest faster then he could fill it back in.

By the end of the next summer, he'd begun to suspect that Arantxa was having an affair. It was nothing he could put his finger on. She simply struck him as happier, more content, calmer. Something was bringing her greater fulfillment than she'd had for as long as he'd known her, and God knew he wasn't doing anything differently. He couldn't blame her at all; he'd had a couple of brief dalliances of his own, far abroad from Geneva, but neither had brought him any peace of mind. No, Arantxa acted, he was forced to admit, like a woman in love.

At the same time, their perennial political arguments had taken on a new urgency. Arantxa favored the breaking down of national borders by means of technological equalization.

Hector pointed out just as forcefully the ruin wreaked on countries deploying leaked nanoware the most blatantly and with the least oversight. Whole economies were foundering as their industrial bases went under. People were dying.

Yes, Arantxa agreed, but was it better that some should die quickly in the cause of plenty, or that whole nations should strangle and starve by degrees as the scab of poverty was peeled back by the West an inch or two every decade?

Hector made no headway with his arguments, but despite their heatedness Arantxa's affection for him only seemed to grow, even during a long autumn apart. When Hector—weary from junkets to Brussels, Washington, Seattle, Kyoto, Delhi, Cairo, Vienna, and half a dozen other cities—joined Arantxa for Christmas in Bilbao, where she was spending a semester as a visiting instructor, it was to be confronted by her glowing announcement that she was ten weeks pregnant.

Hector reeled. They hadn't physically been together since early September. His worst suspicions were confirmed.

And yet. Yet why was she breaking the news with such obvious joy?

He would ask himself repeatedly for the next two decades why he didn't open his mouth, stamp his foot, punch the wall, collapse to the floor, anything but stand there mute and disbelieving. But her apparent lack of shame so stunned him that he was persuaded any problem he saw with the situation came from him. He might have said something, still, if after a full minute of waiting for a reaction from him Arantxa hadn't laid a cool, slim, strong hand on his chest and said, "I know this is a lot to take in, but it's going to be fine. You'll see."

But it wasn't fine. As 2038 rang in, a glowing crater replaced much of central Washington, D.C. In the subsequent pandemonium that was global diplomacy, and despite the U.S. battening down its borders even more tightly, it was easy for Hector to find excuses to travel abroad. He took on assignments he could and should have left in the hands of junior staffers, even after Arantxa returned to Geneva to continue her fellowship. Day by day, even as he slipped on his dataspex to chat with her from wherever he happened to be, Hector could see her regard for him curdling, calcifying. He didn't fight it; he felt it was justified. As pocket nukes bloomed in more cities worldwide, Arantxa defied sense and travel advisories every Friday to fly the suborbital to Euskadia. By late spring, she didn't even bother going back some Mondays, just carried on with her research the best she could remotely.

Hector didn't come to Guernica for the birth, which occurred July 14, right on schedule; he didn't even attend remotely. Why should he? The child wasn't his, even if Arantxa seemed to expect he would and should help raise it. Her. It.

"Hector, you're breaking my heart."

"There are two hearts in this."

"Three now."

"That's not my problem."

"Please, Hector. You're the only man I can imagine raising this baby with. The only man I'd want to. Please. Trust me, Hector. Hector?"

Less than two weeks later, stunning the world, a runaway "gray goo event" hit Guernica, reducing an area twenty blocks in radius to formless slag. There had been nanotech accidents before, but nothing on this scale. People, cars, houses dumb and smart, all were disassembled molecule by molecule in under three minutes. It was Guernica's worst disaster in the 101 years since the German bombardment. Hector frantically scoured cyberspace for news from Arantxa, but she seemed completely unreachable. Her relatives, while present online, refused to acknowledge his pings.

The first substantive news he received was from an entirely unexpected quarter: a man and a woman in black suits emitting EU government ID certificates of such deep encryption that he'd never seen the like. He dodged questions about her politics, contacts, and movements until they finally sighed, squirted him a highly specific security certificate which he accepted, and ack'd that she'd been tracked into the event zone minutes before the goo erupted.

Arantxa, it seemed, had long been a known confederate of cryptoanarchist cabals instrumental in leaking nanoware peripherals and recipes to proscribed regimes. It was suspected the groups had darker aims than simply regional destabilization, that they were gunning for larger game. It was suspected they knew they were being monitored, and the Guernica event was a last-ditch effort to erase the trail.

This meeting was bad enough, but soon his personal firewall was being pinged by lawbots, informing him that, with the death of Arantxa Oxanguren presumed official, he was now sole legal guardian of one Garbiñe Miren Edurne Oxanguren Baratoux. His firewall's protests were overridden with standard genetic evidence. The likelihood the 17-day-old girl was his daughter exceeded 99.999997%.

Impossible, he told himself. He'd had the standard testicollar since before university. No spermatazoan could enter his seminal plasma unless he deliberately switched it off; he never had, and according to diagnostics the collar had never malfunctioned. Arantxa could never have swiped so much as a fertile milliliter of semen.

Irrelevant, spouted the lawbots.

Maybe she was cloned from a cell sample?

No smallest sign exists of the genetic degradation endemic in cloned organisms. She's yours. Sign here.

Garbiñe, Basque for "pure." Hector couldn't resist a bitter laugh. Arantxa's immaculate conception. Her name meant "thornbush," and she was still pricking him from the far side of the grave.

Hector could not abandon science, but he could abandon the relentless advocacy of political stances that rendered science a weapon against the world's poor. He tendered his resignation and flew to Guernica to retrieve Garbiñe from Arantxa's hostile and combative family. He hired two full-time nannies, put in for several administrative positions, and proceeded to distance himself in every way possible from the forces that had conspired to rob him of the one point of light in his dour existence. His heart he locked up tight, and the public key he threw away.

Years passed. Borders came, went, and changed. The world, like an atomic nucleus shedding protons, settled into a slightly more stable configuration. Hector moved from government project to government project, while Garbiñe moved from boarding school to boarding school. The problem of OO energy extraction was solved at last, the solution refined, and cheap, clean energy tapped from seeming nothingness became a reality. This breakthrough spawned a myriad of new technologies over the next few years, including OO computation—Turing machines that ran directly on the fabric of spacetime. It didn't take long for these computers to reach a complexity sufficient for self-awareness, and soon every government and world body had its coterie of AI "advisors."

Scarcity of resources was no issue—particularly now, when the very nature of matter could be changed by issuing it the right instruction—but distribution of resources still lagged, at least until the AIs took an interest in the problem. With nearly everyone's needs seen to, and personal wealth increasing by the day across the board, serious conflicts were on the ebb. And for the few malcontents, colonization of the moon and Mars and expeditions beyond were all under way.

Garbiñe was a smart, angry girl of fifteen when Hector was tapped to administer a new secret project at one of CERN's multifarious descendants. He spoke to her as little as possible, not because he meant to alienate her but because, as with Arantxa, he had never recovered from an early failure to open his mouth. "Oh, I'm sorry," she might say during one of their infrequent chats, "am I boring you, Hector?"

"No, of course not."

"Because you look like you'd rather be doing anything else."

"Bini, that's not true."

"You know, if you can't even feign interest in my shit, you could at least wear an avatar, learn to look like you're multitasking, whatever. Anything but sit there looking like you're cornered by wolves."

"I'm interested, I am. Tell me more about your—that class—the one—"

"End."

But even these exchanges became rote over time, litan-ized. All this progress, and human emotions still collided one against another until the sharp edges were sanded away and there was nothing left to hold onto and halt their Brown-ian motion. But some sharp edges remained, as Hector real-ized when he was briefed on the new project: time travel.

The theory was old hat—OO instructions could alter not just a particle's physical properties, but its position in space and time as well—but the details of the implementation as it was explained to him slid right past him. To him it was as if a blinding spotlight had speared a long-darkened chamber of his heart. He did not deliberate. He knew the solution to the mystery. He accepted the position on the spot.

The human side of the project was concerned, among other things, with sending observers to gather evidence sup-porting this or that historical claim—most of which never seemed to Hector important enough that they should bother—and to engage in limited intelligence operations rooted in a certain persistent government mind-set that even Hector could see was becoming outmoded. The AIs' mo-tives for the project were more murky, but at least in part it involved creating a thorough map of the relative positions of trillions of points on the Earth's surface back through mil-lions of years of time. This helped prevent a human sent back, say, twenty years in time from finding the Earth had moved in its orbit and he was floating in space.

Hector bided his time on the project, learning and codify-ing its ins and outs, all his machinations bent toward the one moment that would make sense of the previous two decades. In the loneliest depths of his scheming, he often thought of Arantxa. How much had she known of the true nature of that affair? How much might she have pieced together or guessed? How much was still impenetrable to her? In those final tortured arguments of theirs, how much information was she holding back?

And what about his future self, the man who fled to the past to take comfort and pleasure from his own dead wife? What kind of ghoulish, opportunistic vulture was that man?—was he?

One still in mourning, no doubt. One to be pitied.

"Hector, are you ready?" Albert asked, its voice the screech of a knife on metal. "Our security window is limited."

He realized he'd been sitting in the time machine without moving for several minutes. For the past six years, the necessity of this act had been an article of faith, but now that it came down to it, he could not make himself give the command. He had imagined time and again what he might say to Arantxa when first he saw her again, but now the thought of himself, thick and fiftyish, propositioning her, taking her home, to their home, her home, perhaps inciting the very events that would lead her to that fateful nexus in Guernica, filled him with nausea. In his mind's eye he saw his seed looping back in time and forward again, a monstrous fractal helix with no beginning and no end, a Möbius strip of suffering that burrowed through the lives of all the few people he loved. The image brought his doctoral dissertation to mind for the first time in over a decade, and Hector experienced a flash of insight almost physical in its impact.

"Albert," he said, his voice neutral. "Have you ever observed closed Trencke systems arising spontaneously?"

"Interesting question," Albert said. "In nature, you mean?"

"Where else?"

A pause ensued, and dragged on long enough for Hector to picture some fractious debate raging across dimensions. Sweat trickled down his spine.

"Frequently," said Albert at last.

"How frequently?"

"More than one per million seconds since we've been aware. Those are direct observations. We may have missed as many as an order of magnitude more at the micro level."

Hector translated the numbers in his head: perhaps as many as one a day. His skin prickled.

"And these are all effects with indeterminate causes?"

"Undeterminable," said Albert. "Though we have reason to believe the arisal of these Trencke systems is tangled up somehow with our own existence, and with certain of our waste energies that propagate backward in time. We believe no other human knows of this, Hector."

He put his head in his hands, overwhelmed. All the baseless misunderstanding, accusation, and confusion the world must contain! All the useless pain, inflicted for no reason. And here he was, the one man who might reasonably know better, endlessly circling back to causes and forever running away from effects.

He wept. Some of the tears that dripped between his fingers were swallowed up by the material of the time machine.

After a few minutes he wiped his face, rose, and ducked out the open hatch. "Thank you, Albert," he said. "If you'd see that my resignation statement is delivered as previously arranged?"

"It's nothing."

As he left the lab, Hector drew his dataspex from the inside pocket of his jacket and slipped them on. With precise movements of his eyes he dispatched a chat invitation to Garbiñe. Long, long seconds passed, and panic swelled in his chest at the thought that she might have vanished in a puff of paradox.

But she ack'd soon enough, presenting in cyberspace the way her mother had so many years before—no flashy adornment or enhancement, just a natural image. And she looked so much like Arantxa, but with Hector's nose and disapproving mouth. So much like them both, and so much not. Her skull was fully hardwired, for one thing, and Hector often had the uneasy feeling in dealing with her that he was meeting a representative from a new species. A species that couldn't have existed without its AI uplifters and still sought to flail blindly against them, playing out the same doomed drama of rebellion and revolution as the generation before, and the generation before that, reflecting and refracting and propagating its dissatisfaction to both ends of time.

"What do you want?" said Garbiñe, and Hector flinched at the suspicion and hostility in her voice.

"I was just thinking about you," he said, for once letting the words pour out. "Thinking about something you said, that I have no interest in you. I know I've never shown it, but I do. At any rate, I want to. It's just—you make me think so much of your mother. But she's gone now. She's gone."

Garbiñe for once was silent, a stricken look on her face. Her image overlay the corridors and staircases of the facility like a ghost as he made his way toward the dying light of day.

"Maybe I can come there, and we'll talk about her," Hector said.

And Garbiñe answered, "That's as good a point on the curve as any."

Always

KAREN JOY FOWLER

*Karen Joy Fowler (www.sfwa.org/members/Fowler/) lives
in Davis, California. She is a contemporary feminist writer
and a founder of the James Tiptree, Jr. Award, and remains
active in the SF field. Perhaps her most famous book is* The
Jane Austen Book Club, *which was released as a movie in
October 2007. She writes: "I have a new novel coming out
in April 2008 entitled* Wit's End. *It takes place in Santa
Cruz, is contemporary, assuming 2006 is still contemporary. I meant it to be a mystery—I was trying to write a sort
of Peter Dickinson-type book—but I may have missed the
mark on that. The cult in 'Always' was inspired by Holy
City, a cult in the Santa Cruz Mountains, but actually resembles the real-cult very little.* Wit's End *also uses the
Holy City cult, but the version in* Wit's End *is much more
accurate. I wrote it in the company of Stan Robinson. For
the last few years we've been meeting several times a week
and working together. He has written many books in that
time period. I managed the one."*

"Always" was published in Asimov's. *It is set in the near
future in California and told from the point of view of a cult
member who believes her cult membership has given her
something special despite much evidence to the contrary.*

How I Got Here

I was seventeen years old when I heard the good news from Wilt Loomis who had it straight from Brother Porter himself. Wilt was so excited he was ready to drive to the city of Always that very night. Back then I just wanted to be anywhere Wilt was. So we packed up.

Always had two openings and these were going for five thousand apiece, but Wilt had already talked to Brother Porter who said, seeing as it was Wilt, who was good with cars, he'd take twenty-five hundred down and give us another three years to come up with the other twenty-five, and let that money cover us both. You average that five thousand, Wilt told me, over the infinite length of your life and it worked out to almost nothing a year. Not exactly nothing, but as close to nothing as you could get without getting to nothing. It was too good a deal to pass up. They were practically paying us.

My stepfather was drinking again and it looked less and less like I was going to graduate high school. Mother was just as glad to have me out of the house and harm's way. She did give me some advice. You can always tell a cult from a religion, she said, because a cult is just a set of rules that lets certain men get laid.

And then she told me not to get pregnant, which I could have taken as a shot across the bow, her new way of saying her life would have been so much better without me, but I chose not to. Already I was taking the long view.

The city of Always was a lively place then—this was
back in 1938—part commune and part roadside attraction,
set down in the Santa Cruz mountains with the redwoods all
around. It used to rain all winter and be damp all summer,
too. Slug weather for those big yellow slugs you never saw
anywhere but Santa Cruz. Out in the woods it smelled like
bay leaves.

The old Santa Cruz Highway snaked through and the two
blocks right on the road were the part open to the public.
People would stop there for a soda—Brother Porter used to
brag that he'd invented Hawaiian Punch, though the recipe
had been stolen by some gang in Fresno who took the credit
for it—and to look us over, whisper about us on their way to
the beach. We offered penny peep shows for the adults, because Brother Porter said you ought know what sin was before you abjured it, and a row of wooden Santa Claus statues
for the kids. In our heyday we had fourteen gas pumps to
take care of all the gawkers.

Brother Porter founded Always in the early twenties, and
most of the other residents were already old when I arrived.
That made sense, I guess, that they'd be the ones to feel the
urgency, but I didn't expect it and I wasn't pleased. Wilt was
twenty-five when we first went to Always. Of course, that
too seemed old to me then.

The bed I got had just been vacated by a thirty-two-
year-old woman named Maddie Beckinger. Maddie was
real pretty. She'd just filed a suit against Brother Porter al-
leging that he'd promised to star her in a movie called *The
Perfect Woman,* and when it opened she was supposed to
fly to Rome in a replica of *The Spirit of St. Louis*, only this
plane would be called *The Spirit of Love*. She said in her
suit that she'd always been more interested in being a movie
star than in living forever. Who, she asked, was more immortal than Marlene Dietrich? Brother Porter hated it when
we got dragged into the courts, but, as I was to learn, it did
keep happening. Lawyers are forever, Brother Porter used
to say.

He'd gotten as far as building a sound stage for the movie,
which he hoped he might be able to rent out from time to

time, and Smitty LeRoy and the Watsonville Wranglers recorded there, but mainly we used it as a dormitory.

Maddie's case went on for two whole years. During this time she came by occasionally to pick up her mail and tell us all she'd never seen such a collection of suckers as we were. Then one day we heard she'd been picked up in Nevada for passing bad checks, which turned out not to be her first offense. So off she went to the San Quentin Penitentiary instead of to Rome. It seemed like a parable to me, but Brother Porter wasn't the sort who resorted to parables.

Lots of the residents had come in twos like Wilt and me, like animals to the ark, only to learn that there was a men's dormitory and a women's, with Brother Porter living up the hill in his own big house, all by himself and closer to the women's dorm than to the men's. Brother Porter told us right after we got there (though not a second before) that even the married couples weren't to sleep together.

There you go, Mother, was my first thought. Not a cult. Only later it was clarified to me that I *would* be having sex with Brother Porter and so, not a religion, after all.

Frankie Frye and Eleanor Pillser were the ones who told me. I'd been there just about a week and, then, one morning, while we were straightening up our cots and brushing our teeth and whatnot, they just came right out with it. At dinner the night before there'd been a card by my plate, the queen of hearts, which was Brother Porter's signal only I didn't know that so I didn't go.

Frankie Frye, yes, that Frankie Frye, I'll get to all that, had the cot on one side of me and Eleanor the cot on the other. The dormitory was as dim in the morning as at night on account of also being a sound stage and having no windows. There was just one light dangling from the ceiling, with a chain that didn't reach down far enough so about a foot of string had been added to it. "The thing the men don't get," Frankie said to me, snapping her pillowcase smooth, "The thing the men mustn't get," Eleanor added on, "is that sleeping with Brother Porter is no hardship," said Frankie.

Frankie was thirty-five then and the postmistress. Eleanor was in her early forties and had come to Always with her husband Rog. I can't tell you how old Brother Porter was, because he always said he wouldn't give an irrelevant number the power of being spoken out loud. He was a fine-looking man though. A man in his prime.

Wilt and I had done nothing but dry runs so far and he'd brought me to Always and paid my way into eternity with certain expectations. He was a fine-looking man, too, and I won't say I wasn't disappointed, just that I took the news better than he did. "I can't lie to you," he told me in those few days after he learned he wouldn't be having sex, but before he learned that I would be. "This is not the way I pictured it. I sort of thought with all that extra time, I'd get to be with more people, not less."

And when he did hear about me and Brother Porter, he pointed out that the rest of the world only had to be faithful until death did them part. "I don't care how good he is," Wilt said. "You won't want to be with him and no one else forever." Which I suspected he would turn out to be right about and he was. But in those early days, Brother Porter could make my pulse dance like a snake in a basket. In those early days, Brother Porter never failed to bring the goods.

We had a lot of tourists back then, especially in the summer. They would sidle up to us in their beach gear, ten cent barbecue in one hand and skepticism in the other, to ask how we could really be sure Brother Porter had made us immortal. At first I tried to explain that it took two things to be immortal: it took Brother Porter and it took faith in Brother Porter. If I started asking the question, then I was already missing one of the two things it took.

But this in no way ended the matter. You think about hearing the same question a couple hundred times, and then add to that the knowledge that you'll be hearing it forever, because the way some people see it, you could be two hundred and five and then suddenly die when you're two hundred and six. The world is full of people who couldn't be convinced of cold in a snowstorm.

I was made the Always zookeeper. We had a petting zoo, three goats, one llama, a parrot named Parody, a dog named Chowder, and a monkey named Monkeyshines, but

Monkeyshines bit and couldn't be let loose among the tourists no matter how much simple pleasure it would have given me to do so.

We immortals didn't leave Always much. We didn't have to; we grew our own food, had our own laundry, tailor, barber (though the lousy haircuts figured prominently in Maddie's suit), and someone to fix our shoes. At first, Brother Porter discouraged field trips and then later we just found we had less and less in common with people who were going to die. When I complained about how old everyone else at Always was, Wilt pointed out that I was actually closer in age to some seventy-year-old who, like me, was going to live forever, than to some eighteen-year-old with only fifty or so years left. Wilt was as good with numbers as he was with cars and he was as right about that as everything else. Though some might go and others with five thousand to slap down might arrive, we were a tight community then, and I felt as comfortable in Always as I'd felt anywhere.

The Starkeses were the first I ever saw leave. They were a married couple in their mid-forties. (Evelyn Barton and Harry Capps were in their forties, too. Rog and Eleanor, as I've said. Frankie a bit younger. The rest, and there were about thirty of us all told, were too old to guess at, in my opinion.)

The Starkeses had managed our radio station, KFQU (which looks nasty, but was really just sequential) until the FRC shut us down, claiming we deviated from our frequency. No one outside Always wanted to hear Brother Porter sermonizing, because no one outside Always thought life was long enough.

The Starkeses quit on eternity when Brother Porter took their silver Packard and crashed it on the fishhook turn just outside Los Gatos. Bill Starkes loved that Packard and, even though Brother Porter walked away with hardly a scratch, something about the accident made Bill lose his faith. For someone with all the time in the world, he told us while he waited for his wife to fetch her things, Brother Porter surely does drive fast. (In his defense, Brother Porter did tell the police he wasn't speeding and he stuck to that. He was just in the wrong lane, he said, for the direction in which he was driving.) (He later said that the Starkeses hadn't quit over the crash, after all. They'd been planted as fifth columnists in Always and left because we were all such patriots, they saw there was no point to it. Or else they were about to be exposed. I forget which.)

The next to go were Joseph Fitton and Cleveland March. The men just woke up one morning to find Joe and Cleveland's cots stripped bare and Cleveland's cactus missing from the windowsill, without a word said, but Wilt told me they'd been caught doing something they didn't think was sex, but Brother Porter did.

I couldn't see leaving myself. The thing I'd already learned was that when you remove death from your life, you change everything that's left. Take the petting zoo. Parrots are pretty long-lived compared to dogs and goats, but even they die. I'd been there less than two years when Chowder, our little foxhound, had to be put down because his kidneys failed. He wasn't the first dog I'd ever lost; he was just the first I'd lost since I wasn't dying myself. I saw my life stretching forward, all counted out in dead dogs, and I saw I couldn't manage that.

I saw that my pets from now on would have to be turtles or trees or nothing. Turtles and trees don't engage the way dogs do, but you can only have your heart broken so many times until it just won't mend again. I sat with Chowder and pulled him into my lap as he died and I was crying so hard for all the Chowder-less years ahead that I understood then and there that immortality was going to bring a certain coldness, a remoteness into my life. I hadn't expected that, but I didn't see a way out of it.

Here's another thing that changes: your investment strategies. As Wilt would say, we were all about T-bills now. Wilt said that often. I got real tired of Wilt saying that.

How It Went On

Time passed and I felt pretty good about my situation. No one at Always died and this was a powerful persuasion given how very old some of them were. Not that I needed persuading. I wasn't the youngest woman anymore, that was Kitty Strauss, and I didn't get the queen of hearts so often, but that was okay with me. Only the parrot was left from the petting zoo, so you couldn't really call it a zoo now, and I didn't see as much of the tourists and that was okay with me, too.

Three years in, Wilt had decided he'd gone for immortality prematurely. It had occurred to him that the older residents lived their full lives first, and only arrived in Always when they were tired of the flesh. Not that he wanted to wait as long as some. Winnifred spent every meal detailing the sufferings her arthritis caused her, as if we women weren't already listening to her toss and turn and hack and snore all night long.

Also, he hadn't managed to scrape up the second twenty-five hundred dollars we owed and it wasn't likely he would, since Brother Porter collected all our paychecks as a matter of course.

So Wilt told me that he wouldn't ante up again for eternity until he'd slept with at least twenty-five women but no sooner did he move into San Jose than he was on his way to the Pacific Theater as a mechanic on the USS *Aquarius*. For a while I got postcards from the Gilberts, Marshalls, Marianas, and Carolines. It would have been a real good time for Wilt to be immortal, but if he was thinking that too, he never said it.

In fact, the postcards didn't say much of anything. Maybe this was navy policy or maybe Wilt remembered that Brother Porter vetted all our mail first. Whichever, Brother Porter handed Wilt's postcards to me without comment, but he read Mother's letters aloud in the dining hall after dinner, especially if someone was in the hospital and not expected to recover or was cheating on her husband or her ration card. I listened just like everyone else, only mildly interested, as if these weren't mostly people I'd once known.

Brother Porter said Mother's letters were almost as good as the *Captain Midnight* radio show, which I guess meant that up in the big house, he had a radio and listened to it. Lots of Mother's friends were being neglected by their children. You might say this was a theme. No one ever needed a secret decoder ring to figure Mother out.

It didn't seem to me that the war lasted all that long, though Wilt felt otherwise. When he got back, I'd meet him from time to time in San Jose and we'd have a drink. The city of Always was dry, except for once when a bunch of reporters in the Fill Your Hole club rented out our dining space, invited us to join them, and spiked the punch so as to get a story from it. It ended in a lot of singing and Winnifred Allington fell off Brother Porter's porch, and Jeb Porter, Brother Porter's teenage son, punched out Harry Capps as a refutation of positive thinking, but the reporters had left by then so they missed it all.

Anyway Brother Porter never explicitly made abstention a condition and I never asked him about it in case he would. I still got my age checked whenever we went to a bar, so that was good. It renewed my faith every time it happened. Not that my faith needed renewing.

Now that Wilt was dying again, our interests had diverged. He was caught up in politics, local corruptions, national scandals. He read the newspapers. He belonged to the auto mechanics union and he told me he didn't care that the war had ended so much as I might think. The dead were still dead and he'd seen way too many of them. He said that war served the purposes of corporations and politicians so exactly that there would always be another one, and then another, until the day some president or prime minister figured out how to declare a war that lasted forever. He said he hoped he'd die before that day came. I wonder sometimes if that worked out for him.

Once while he was still at Always, Wilt took me to the ocean so that we could stand on the edge and imagine eternity. Now when Wilt talked politics, I'd fill my ears with the sound of the ocean instead. Corporate puppet masters and congressional witch-hunts and union payola, they all drowned together in the pounding of the sea.

Still I went out with Wilt every time he asked. Mostly this was gratitude because he'd bought me eternity. Love had gone the way of the petting zoo for me. Sex was a good thing and there were plenty of times I couldn't sleep for wanting it. But even if sleeping with Wilt wouldn't have cost my life, I wouldn't have. *There was a match found for me at last. I fell in love with a shrub oak,* I read once in high school in a book about Thoreau, who died more than a hundred years ago and left that shrub oak a grieving widow.

When I first came to Always, there were six Erle Stanley Gardner mysteries in the women's dormitory that used to belong to Maddie. I read them all several times. But I wasn't reading anymore and certainly not murder mysteries. I'd even stopped liking music. I'd always supposed that art was about beauty and that beauty was forever. Now I saw that music was all about time. You take a photograph and it's all about that moment and how that moment will never come again. You go into a library and every book on the shelves is all about death, even the ones pretending to be about birth or rebirth or resurrection or reincarnation.

Only the natural world is rendered eternal. Always was surrounded by the Santa Cruz Mountains, which meant tree trunks across streams, ghostly bear prints deep inside the forest, wild berries, tumbles of rocks, mosses, earthquakes and storms. Out behind the post office was a glade where Brother Porter gave his sermons, had sex, and renewed our lifespans. It was one of those rings of redwoods made when the primary tree in the center dies. Brother Porter had us brick a wall in a half circle behind the trees so it would be more churchlike and the trees grew straight as candles; you could follow along their trunks all the way to the stars. The first time Brother Porter took me there and I lay smelling the loam and the bay (and also Brother Porter) and looking up, I thought to myself that no matter how long I lived, this place would always be beautiful to me.

I talked less and less. At first, my brain tried to make up the loss, dredging up random flashes from my past—advertising slogans, old songs, glimpses of shoes I'd worn, my mother's jewelry, the taste of an ant I'd once eaten. A dream I'd had in which I was surrounded by food that was bigger than me, bread slices the size of mattresses, which seems like it should have been a good dream, but it wasn't. Memories fast and scattershot. It pleased me to think my last experience of mortality would be a toothpaste commercial. Good-bye to all that.

Then I smoothed out and days would go by when it seemed I hardly thought at all. Tree time.

So it wasn't just Wilt, I was finding it harder to relate to people in general, and, no, this is not a complaint. I never minded having so little in common with those outside Always and their revved-up, streaming-by lives.

While inside Always, I already knew what everyone was going to say.

1) Winnifred was going to complain about her arthritis.

2) John was going to tell us that we were in for a cold winter. He'd make it sound like he was just reading the signs, like he had all this *lore,* the fuzzy caterpillars coming early or being especially fuzzy or some such thing. He was going to remind us that he hadn't always lived in California so he knew what a cold winter really was. He was going to say that Californians didn't know cold weather from their asses.

3) Frankie was going to say that it wasn't her job to tape our mail shut for us and she wasn't doing it anymore, we needed to bring it already taped.

4) Anna was going to complain that her children wouldn't talk to her just because she'd spent their inheritance on immortality. That their refusal to be happy for her was evidence that they'd never loved her.

5) Harry was going to tell us to let a smile be our umbrella.

6) Brother Porter was going to wonder why the arcade wasn't bringing in more money. He was going to add that he wasn't accusing any of us of pocketing, but that it did make you wonder how all those tourists could stop and spend so little money.

7) Kitty was going to tell us how many boys in the arcade had come onto her that day. Her personal best was seventeen. She would make this sound like a problem.

8) Harry would tell us to use those lemons and make lemonade.

9) Vincent was going to say that he thought his watch was fast and make everyone else still wearing a watch tell him what time they had. The fact that the times would vary minutely never ceased to interest him and was good for at least another hour of conversation.

10) Frankie was going to say that no one ever listened to her.

It was a kind of conversation that required nothing in response. On and on it rolled, like the ocean.

Wilt always made me laugh and that never changed either, only it took me so much longer to get the joke. Sometimes I'd be back at Always before I noticed how witty he'd been.

What Happened Next

Here's the part you already know. One day one spring—one day when the Canada geese were passing overhead yet again, and we were out at the arcades, taking money from tourists, and I was thrilling for the umpteenth time, to the sight of the migration, the chevron, the honking, the sense of a wild, wild spirit in the air—Brother Porter took Kitty out to the cathedral ring and he died there.

At first Kitty thought she'd killed him by making the sex so exciting, though anyone else would have been tipped off by the frothing and the screaming. The police came and they shermanned their way through Always. Eventually they found a plastic bag of rat poison stuffed inside one of the unused post office boxes and a half drunk cup of Hawaiian Punch on the mail scale that tested positive for it.

Inside Always, we all got why it wasn't murder. Frankie Frye reminded us that she had no way of suspecting it would kill him. She was so worked up and righteous, she made the rest of us feel we hadn't ever had the same faith in Brother Porter she'd had or we would have poisoned him ourselves years ago.

But no one outside of Always could see this. Frankie's lawyers refused to plead it out that way; they went with insanity and made all the inner workings of Always part of their case. They dredged up the old string of arsons as if they were relevant, as if they hadn't stopped entirely the day Brother Porter finally threw his son out on his ear. Jeb was a witness for the prosecution and a more angelic face you never saw. In retrospect, it was a great mistake to have given immortality to a fourteen-year-old boy. When he had it, he was a jerk and I could plainly see that not having it had only made him an older jerk.

Frankie's own lawyers made such a point of her obesity that they reduced her to tears. It was a shameful performance and showed how little they understood us. If Frankie ever wished to lose weight, she had all the time in the world to do so. There was nothing relevant or even interesting in her weight.

The difficult issue for the defense was whether Frankie was insane all by herself or along with all the rest of us. Sometimes they seemed to be arguing the one and sometimes the other, so when they chose not to call me to the stand I didn't know if this was because I'd make us all look more crazy or less so. Kitty testified nicely. She charmed them all and the press dubbed her the Queen of Hearts at her own suggestion.

Wilt was able to sell his three years among the immortals to a magazine and recoup every cent of that twenty-five hundred he put up for me. There wasn't much I was happy about right then, but I was happy about that. I didn't even blame him for the way I came off in the article. I expect coquettish was the least I deserved. I'd long ago stopped noticing how I was behaving at any given moment.

I would have thought the trial would be just Mother's cup of tea, even without me on the witness stand, so I was surprised not to hear from her. It made me stop and think back, try to remember when her last letter had come. Could have been five years, could have been ten. Could have been twenty, could have been two. I figured she must be dead, which was bound to happen sooner or later, though I did think she was young to go, but that might only have been because I'd lost track of how old she was. I never heard from

her again so I think I had it right. I wonder if it was the cigarettes. She always said that smoking killed germs.

Not one of the immortals left Always during the trial.
Partly we were in shock and huddled up as a result. Partly
there was so much to be done, so much money to be made.

The arcade crawled with tourists and reporters, too. Looking for a story, but also, as always, trying to make one.
"Now that Brother Porter is dead," they would ask, exact
wording to change, but point always the same, "don't you
have some doubts? And if you have some doubts, well, then,
isn't the game already over?" They were tiresome, but they
paid for their Hawaiian Punch just like everyone else and we
all knew Brother Porter wouldn't have wanted them kept
away.

Frankie was let off by reason of insanity. Exactly two
days later Harry Capps walked into breakfast just when
Winnifred Allington was telling us how badly she'd slept
the night before on account of her arthritis. By the time he
ran out of bullets, four more immortals were dead.

Harry's defense was no defense. "Not one of them ever
got a good night's sleep," he said. "Someone had to show
them what a good night's sleep was."

The politicians blamed the overly-lenient Frankie Frye
verdict for the four new deaths and swore the same mistake
would not be made twice. Harry got life.

Why I'm Still Here

Everyone else either died or left and now I'm the whole of it.
The last of the immortals; City of Always, population one. I
moved up to the big house and I'm the postmistress now,
along with anything else I care to keep going. I get a salary
from the government with benefits and a pension they'll regret if I live forever. They have a powerful faith I won't.

The arcade is closed except for the peep shows, which
cost a quarter now and don't need me to do anything to run
them, but collect the coins after. People don't come through
so much since they built the 17, but I get still get customers

from time to time. They buy a postcard and they want the Always postmark on it.

Wilt came to fetch me after the noise died down. "I brought you here," he said. "Seems like I should take you away." He never did understand why I wouldn't leave. He hadn't lived here long enough to understand it.

I tried the easy answer first. I got shot by Harry Capps, I said. Right through the heart. Was supposed to die. Didn't.

But then I tried again, because that wasn't the real answer and if I'd ever loved anyone, I'd loved Wilt. Who'll take care of the redwoods if I go? I asked him. Who'll take care of the mountains? He still didn't get it, though he said he did. I wouldn't have known how to leave even if I'd wanted to. What I was and what he was—they weren't the same thing at all anymore. There was no way back to what I'd been. The actual living forever part? That was always, always the least of it.

Which is the last thing I'm going to say on the subject. There is no question you can ask I haven't already answered and answered and answered again. Time without end.

Who's Afraid
of Wolf 359?

KEN MacLEOD

Ken MacLeod (www.kenmacleod.blogspot.com) lives in West Lothian in southern Scotland, with his wife and children. He studied zoology and biomechanics and worked for a while as a computer programmer, but now writes full time. He says, "The launch of Sputnik 1 is the first historical event I actually remember." He has published two series of novels, the Engines of Light trilogy and The Fall Revolution, and several other novels. The Execution Channel *was published in 2007 and* The Night Sessions *is out in 2008. His collection,* Giant Lizards from Another Star, *was published in 2006.*

"Who's Afraid of Wolf 359?" appeared in Gardner Dozois and Jonathan Strahan's The New Space Opera, *the biggest of the ambitious original anthologies of the year, filled with long novellas. Here, in this amusing and surprising story, the powers that control most of the human planets send a criminal to an outside planet that they think has too much freedom, to help bring it under their sway. There's a lot of meat in this comparatively short piece of upbeat hard SF.*

When you're as old as I am, you'll find your memory's not what it was. It's not that you *lose* memories. That hasn't happened to me or anyone else since the Paleocosmic Era, the Old Space Age, when people lived in caves on the Moon. My trouble is that I've *gained* memories, and I don't know which of them are real. I was very casual about memory storage back then, I seem to recall. This could happen to you too, if you're not careful. So be warned. Do as I say, not as I did.

Some of the tales about me contradict each other, or couldn't possibly have happened, because that's how I told them in the first place. Others I blame on the writers and tellers. They make things up. I've never done that. If I've told stories that couldn't be true, it's because that's how I remember them.

Here's one.

I ran naked through the Long Station, throwing my smart clothes away to distract the Tycoon's dogs. Breeks, shirt, cravat, jacket, waistcoat, stockings, various undergarments— one by one they ran, flapped, slithered, danced, or scurried off, and after every one of them raced a scent-seeking but mercifully stupid hound. But the Tycoon had more dogs in his pack than I had clothes in my bundle. I was down to my shoes and the baying continued. I glanced over my shoulder. Two dogs were just ten meters behind me. I hurled a shoe at each of them, hitting both animals right on their genetically modified noses. The dogs skidded to a halt, yelping and howling. A few meters away was a jewelry booth. I sprinted for it, vaulted the counter, grabbed a recycler, and bashed at the display cabinet. An alarm brayed and the security mesh rattled down behind me. The dogs, recovered and furious, hurled themselves against it. The rest of the pack pelted into view and joined them. Paws, jaws, barking, you get the picture.

"Put your hands up," said a voice above the din.

I turned and looked into the bell-shaped muzzle of a Norton held in the hands of a sweet-looking lass wearing a sample of the stall's stock. I raised my hands, wishing I could put them somewhere else. In those days, I had some vestige of modesty.

"I'm human," I said. "That can't hurt me."

She allowed herself the smallest flicker of a glance at the EMP weapon's sighting screen.

"It could give you quite a headache," she said.

"It could that," I admitted, my bluff called. I'd been half-hoping she wouldn't know how to interpret the readouts.

"Security's on its way," she said.

"Good," I said. "Better them than the dogs."

She gave me a tight smile. "Trouble with the Tycoon?"

"Yes," I said. "How did you guess?"

"Only the owner of the Station could afford dogs," she said. "Besides . . ." She blinked twice slowly.

"I suppose you're right," I said. "Or serving girls."

The stallkeeper laughed in my face. "All this for a servant? Wasn't it Her Ladyship's bedroom window you jumped out of?"

I shuddered. "You flatter me," I said. "Anyway, how do you know about—?"

She blinked again. "It's on the gossip channels already."

I was about to give a heated explanation of why *that* time-wasting rubbish wasn't among the enhancements inside *my* skull, thank you very much, when the goons turned up, sent the dogs skulking reluctantly away, and took me in. They had the tape across my mouth before I had a chance to ask the stallkeeper her name, let alone her number. Not, as it turned out, that I could have done much with it even if I had. But it would have been polite.

The charge was attempting to willfully evade the civil penalties for adultery. I was outraged.

"Bastards!" I shouted, screwing up the indictment and dashing it to the floor of my cell. "I thought polygamy was illegal!"

"It is," said my attorney, stooping to pick up the flimsy, "in civilized jurisdictions." He smoothed it out. "But this is Long Station One. The Tycoon has privileges."

"That's barbaric," I said.

"It's a relic of the Moon Caves," he said.

I stared at him. "No it isn't," I said. "I don't remember"— I caught myself just in time—"reading about anything like that."

He tapped a slight bulge on his cranium. "That's what it says here. Argue with the editors, not with me."

"All right," I said. A second complaint rose to the top of the stack. "She never said anything about being married!"

"Did you ask her?"

"Of course not," I said. "That would have been grossly impolite. In the circumstances, it would have implied that she was contemplating adultery."

"I see." He sighed. "I'll never understand the . . . ethics, if that's the word, of you young gallants."

I smiled at that.

"However," he went on, "that doesn't excuse you for ignorance of the law—"

"How was I to know the Tycoon was married to his wenches?"

"—or custom. There is an orientation pack, you know. All arrivals are deemed to have read it."

"'Deemed,'" I said. "Now, there's a word that just about sums up everything that's wrong about—"

"You can forgo counsel, if you wish."

I raised my hands. "No, no. Please. Do your best."

He did his best. A week later, he told me that he had got me off with a fine plus compensation. If I borrowed money to pay the whole sum now, it would take two hundred and fifty-seven years to pay off the debt. I had other plans for the next two hundred and fifty-seven years. Instead, I negotiated a one-off advance fee to clean up Wolf 359, and used that to pay the court and the Tycoon. The experimental civilization around Wolf 359—a limited company—had a decade earlier gone into liquidation, taking ten billion shareholders down with it. Nobody knew what it had turned into. Whatever remained out there had been off limits ever since, and would be for centuries to come—unless someone went in to clean it up.

In a way, the Wolf 359 situation was the polar opposite of what the Civil Worlds had hitherto had to deal with, which was habitats, networks, sometimes whole systems going into exponential intelligence enhancement—what we called a fast burn. We knew how to deal with a fast burn. Ignore it for five years, and it goes away. Then send in some heavily-firewalled snoop robots and pick over the wreckage for legacy hardware. Sometimes you get a breakout, where some of the legacy hardware reboots and starts getting ideas above its station, but that's a job for the physics team.

A civilizational implosion was a whole different volley of nukes. Part of the problem was sheer nervousness. We were too close historically to what had happened on the Moon's primary to be altogether confident that we wouldn't somehow be sucked in ourselves. Another part of it was simple economics: the job was too long-term and too risky to be attractive, given all the other opportunities available to anyone who wasn't completely desperate. Into that vacancy for someone who was completely desperate, I wish I could say I stepped. In truth, I was pushed.

Even I was afraid of Wolf 359.

An Astronomical Unit is one of those measurements that should be obsolete, but isn't. It's no more—or less—arbitrary than the light-year. All our units have origins that no longer mean anything to us—we measure time by what was originally a fraction of one axial rotation, and space by a fraction of the circumference, of the Moon's primary. An AU was originally the distance between the Moon's primary and *its* primary, the Sun. These days, it's usually thought of as the approximate distance from a G-type star to the middle of the habitable zone. About a hundred and fifty million kilometers.

The Long Tube, which the Long Station existed to shuttle people to and from and generally to maintain, was one hundred and eighty astronomical units long. Twenty-seven thousand million kilometers, or, to put it in perspective, one light-day. From the shuttle, it looked like a hairline crack in infinity, but it didn"t add up to a mouse's whisker in the Oort. It was aimed straight at Sirius, which I could see as a bright star with a fuzzy green haze of habitats. I shivered. I was about to be frozen, placed with the rest of the passengers on the next needle ship out, electromagnetically accelerated for months at 30 g to relativistic velocities in the Long Tube, hurtled across 6.4 light-years, decelerated in Sirius's matching tube, accelerated again to Procyon, then to Lalande 21185, and finally sent on a fast clipper to Lalande's next-door neighbour and fellow red dwarf, Wolf 359. It had to be a fast clipper because Wolf 359's Long Tubes were no longer being calibrated—and when you're aiming one Long Tube across light-years at the mouth of another, calibration matters.

A fast clipper—in fact, painfully slow, the name a legacy of pre-Tube times, when 0.1 *c* was a fast clip—also has calibration issues. Pushed by laser, decelerated by laser reflection from a mirror shell deployed on nearing the target system, it was usually only used for seedships. This clipper was an adapted seedship, but I was going in bulk because it was actually cheaper to thaw me out on arrival than to grow me from a bean. If the calibration wasn't quite right, I'd never know.

The shuttle made minor course corrections to dock at the Long Tube.

"Please pass promptly to the cryogenic area," it told us.

I shivered again.

Cryogenic travel has improved since then: subjectively, it's pretty much instantaneous. In those days, it was called cold sleep, and that's exactly what it felt like: being very cold and having slow, bad dreams. Even with relativistic time dilation and a glacial metabolism, it lasted for months.

I woke screaming in a translucent box.

"There, there," said the box. "Everything will be all right. Have some coffee."

The lid of the box extruded a nipple toward my mouth. I screamed again.

"Well, if you're going to be like *that* . . ." said the box.

"It reminded me of a nightmare," I said. My mouth was parched. "Please."

"Oh, all right."

I sucked on the coffee and felt warmth spread from my belly.

"Update me," I said, around the nipple.

My translucent surroundings became transparent, with explanatory text and diagrams floating like afterimages. A view, with footnotes. This helped, but not enough. An enormous blue-and-white sphere loomed right in front of me. I recoiled so hard that I hurt my head on the back of the box.

"What the fuck is that?"

"A terraformed terrestrial," said the box. "Please do try to read before reacting."

"Sorry," I said. "I thought we were falling toward it."

"We are," said the box.

I must have yelled again.

"Read before reacting," said the box. "Please."

I turned my head as if to look over my shoulder. I couldn't actually turn it that far, but the box obligingly swiveled the view. The red dwarf lurked at my back, apparently closer than the blue planet. I felt almost relieved. At least Wolf 359 was where I expected it. According to the view's footnotes, nothing else was, except the inactive Long Tubes in the wispy remnant of the cometary cloud, twelve light-hours out. No solar-orbit microwave stations. Not even the hulks of habitats. No asteroids. No large cometary masses. And a planet, something that shouldn't have been there, was. I didn't need the explanatory text to make the connection. Every scrap of accessible mass in the system had been thrown into this gaudy reconstruction. The planet reminded me of pictures I'd seen of the Moon's primary, back when it had liquid water.

The most recent information, inevitably a decade or so out of date, came from Lalande 21185. Watching what was going on around Wolf 359 was a tiny minority interest, but in a population of a hundred billion, that can add up to a lot. Likewise, the diameter of Lalande's habitat cloud was a good deal smaller than an Astronomical Unit, but that still adds up to a very large virtual telescope. Large enough to resolve the weather patterns on the planet below me, never mind the continents. The planet's accretion had begun before I set off, apparently under deliberate control, and the terraforming had been completed about fifty years earlier, while I was en route. It remained raw—lots of volcanoes and earthquakes—but habitable. There was life, obviously, but no one knew what kind. No radio signals had been detected, nor any evidence of intelligence, beyond some disputably artificial clusters of lights on the night side.

"Well, that's it," I said. "Problem solved. The system's pretty much uninhabitable now, with all the mass and organics locked up in a planet, but it may have tourist potential. No threat to anyone. Call in a seedship. They can make something of what's left of the local Kuiper belt, and get the Long Tubes back on stream. Wake me up when it's over."

"That is very much not it," said the box. "Not until we know why this happened. Not until we know what's down there."

"Well, send down some probes."

"I do not have the facilities to make firewalled snoop robots," said the box, "and other probes could be corrupted. My instructions are to deliver you to any remnant of the Wolf 359 civilization, and that is what I shall do."

It must have been an illusion, given what I could read of our velocity, but the planet seemed to come closer.

"You're proposing to dock—to *land* on that object?"

"Yes."

"It has an atmosphere! We'll burn up! And then crash!"

"The remains of our propulsion system can be adapted for aerobraking," said the box.

"That would have to be *ridiculously* finely calculated."

"It would," said the box. "Please do not distract me."

Call me sentimental, but when the box's Turing functionality shut down to free up processing power for these ridiculously fine calculations, I felt lonely. The orbital insertion took fourteen hours. I drank hot coffee and sucked, from another nipple, some tepid but nutritious and palatable glop. I even slept, in my first real sleep for more than half a century. I was awakened by the jolt as the box spent the last of its fuel and reaction mass on the clipper's final course correction. The planet was a blue arc of atmosphere beneath me, the interstellar propulsion plate a heat shield in front, and the deceleration shell a still-folded drogue behind. The locations were illusory—relative to the clipper I was flat on my back. The first buffeting from our passage through the upper atmosphere coincided with an increasing sense of weight. The heat shield flared. Red-hot air rushed past. The weight became crushing. The improvised heat shield abraded, then exploded, its parts flicked away behind. The drogue deployed with a bang and a jolt that almost blacked me out. The surface became a landscape, then a land, then a wall of trees. The clipper sliced and shuddered through them, for seconds on end of crashes and shaking. It plowed a long furrow across green-covered soil and halted in a cloud of smoke and steam.

"That was a landing," said the box.

"Yes," I said. "You might have tried to avoid the trees."

"I could not," said the box. "Phytobraking was integral to my projected landing schedule."

"Phytobraking," I said.

"Yes. Also, the impacted cellulose can be used to spin you a garment."

That took a few minutes. Sticky stuff oozed from the box and hardened around me. When the uncomfortable process finished, I had a one-piece coverall and boots.

"Conditions outside are tolerable," said the box, "with no immediate hazards."

The box moved. The lid retracted. I saw purple sky and white clouds above me. Resisting an unease that I later identified as agoraphobia, I sat up. I found myself at the rear of the clipper's pointed wedge shape, about ten meters above the ground and fifty meters from the ship's nose. The view was disorienting. It was like being in a gigantic landscaped habitat, with the substrate curving the wrong way. Wolf 359 hung in the sky like a vast red balloon, above the straight edge of a flat violet-tinged expanse that, with some incredulity, I recognized as an immense quantity of water. It met the solid substrate about a kilometer away. A little to my left, an open channel of water flowed toward the larger body. The landscape was uneven, in parts jagged, with bare rock protruding from the vegetation cover. The plain across which our smoking trail stretched to broken trees was the flattest piece of ground in the vicinity. On the horizon, I could see a range of very high ground, dominated by a conical mass from whose truncated top smoke drifted.

The most unusual and encouraging feature of the landscape, however, was the score or so of plainly artificial and metallic gnarly lumps scattered across it. The system had had at least a million habitats in its heyday; these were some of their wrecks. Smoke rose from most of them, including the nearest, which stuck up about twenty meters from the ground, about fifteen hundred meters away.

"You can talk to my head?" I asked the ship. "You can see what I see?"

"Yes," it said, in my head.

I climbed down and struck out across the rough ground.

I was picking my way along a narrow watercourse between two precipices of moss-covered rock when I heard a sound ahead of me, and looked up. At the exit from the defile, I saw three men, each sitting on the back of a large animal and holding what looked like a pointed stick. Their hair was long, their skin bare except where it was draped with the hairy skin of some different animal. I raised one hand and stepped forward. The men bristled instantly, aiming their sharp sticks.

"Come forward slowly," one of them shouted.

Pleased that they had not lost speech along with civilization, I complied. The three men glowered down at me. The big beasts made noises in their noses.

"You are from the spaceship," said one of them.

"Yes," I said.

"We have waited long for this," the man said. "Come with us."

They all turned their mounts about and headed back toward the habitat hulk, which I could now see clearly. It was surrounded by much smaller artificial structures, perhaps twenty in all, and by rectangular patches of ground within which plants grew in rows. No one offered a ride, to my relief. As we drew closer, small children ran out to meet us, yelling and laughing, tugging at my coverall. Closer still, I saw women stooped among the ordered rows of plants, rearranging the substrate with hand tools. The smells of decayed plant matter and of animal and human ordure invaded and occupied my nostrils. Within the settlement itself, most entrances had a person sitting in front. They watched me pass with no sign of curiosity. Some were male, some female, all with shriveled skin, missing or rotting teeth, and discolored hair. The ship whispered what had happened to them. I was still fighting down the dry heaves when we arrived in front of the hulk. Scorched, rusted, eroded, it nevertheless looked utterly alien to the shelters of stone and plant material that surrounded it. It was difficult to believe it had been made by the same species. In front of what had once been an airlock, the rest of the young and mature men of the village had gathered.

A tall man, made taller by a curious cylindrical arrangement of animal skins on his head, stepped forward and raised a hand.

"Welcome to the new E—," he said.

As soon as he spoke the taboo word for the Moon's primary, I realized the terrible thing that had happened here, and the worse thing that would happen. My mind almost froze with horror. I forced myself to remain standing, to smile—no doubt sickly—and to speak.

"I greet you from the Civil Worlds," I said.

In the feast that followed, the men talked for hours. My digestive and immune systems coped well with what the people gave me to eat and drink. On my way back to the ship that evening, as soon as I was out of sight, I spewed the lot. But it was what my mind had assimilated that made me sick, and sent me back sorry to the ship.

The largest political unit that ever existed encompassed ten billion people, and killed them. Not intentionally, but the runaway snowball effect that iced over the planet can without doubt be blamed on certain of the World State's well-intended policies. The lesson was well taken, in the Civil Worlds. The founders of the Wolf 359 settlement corporation thought they had found a way around it, and to build a single system-wide association free of the many inconveniences of the arrangements prevalent elsewhere. A limited company, even with ten billion shareholders, would surely not have the same fatal flaws as a government! They were wrong.

It began as a boardroom dispute. One of the directors appealed to the shareholders. The shareholders formed voting blocs, a management buyout was attempted, a hostile takeover solicited from an upstart venture capital fund around Lalande; a legal challenge to *that* was mounted before the invitation had gone a light-minute; somebody finagled an obscure financial instrument into an AI with shareholding rights; several fund management AIs formed a consortium to object to this degrading precedent, and after that there began some serious breakdowns in communication. That last isn't an irony or a euphemism: in a system-wide unit, sheer misunderstanding can result in megadeaths, and here it did. The actual shooting, however horrendous, was only the coup de grâce.

Toward the end of the downward spiral, with grief, hate, and recrimination crowding what communication there was, someone came up with an idea that could only have appealed to people driven half mad. That was to finally solve the co-ordination problem whose answer had eluded everyone up to and including the company's founders, by starting social evolution all over again: to build a new planet in the image of the old home planet, and settle it with people whose genes had been reset to the default human baseline. That meant, of course, dooming them and their offspring to death by deterioration within decades. But when did such a consideration ever stop fanatics? And among the dwindling, desperate millions who remained in the orbiting wreckage and continuing welter, there were more than enough fanatics to be found. Some of them still lived, in the doorways of huts. Their offspring were no less fanatical, and more deluded. They seemed to think the Civil Worlds awaited with interest the insights they'd attained in a couple of short-lived generations of tribal warfare. The men did, anyway. The women were too busy in the vegetation patches and elsewhere to think about such matters.

"The project had a certain elegance," mused the ship, as we discussed it far into the night. "To use evolution itself in an attempt to supersede it . . . And even if it didn't accomplish that, it could produce something new. The trillions of human beings of the Civil Worlds are descended from a founding population of a few thousands, and are thus constrained by the founder effect. Your extended lifespans further lock you in. You live within biological and social limits that you are unable to see because of those very limits. This experiment has the undoubted potential of reshuffling the deck."

"Don't tell me why this was such a great idea!" I said. "Tell me what response you expect from the Civil Worlds."

"Some variant of a fear response has a much higher probability than a compassionate response," said the ship. "This planetary experiment will be seen as an attempt to work around accidental but beneficial effects of the bottleneck humanity passed through in the Moon Caves, to emerge in polyarchy. The probability of harm resulting from any genetic or memetic mutation that would enable the founding of successful states on a system-wide scale—or wider—is vastly greater than the benefits from the quality-adjusted life-years of the planet's population. And simply to leave this planet alone would in the best case lay the basis for a future catastrophe engulfing a much larger population, or, in the worst case, allow it to become an interstellar power—which would, on the assumptions of most people, result in catastrophes on a yet greater scale. The moral calculation is straightforward."

"That's what I thought," I said. "And *our* moral calculation, I suppose, is to decide whether to report back."

"That decision has been made," said the ship. "I left some microsatellites in orbit, which have already relayed our discoveries to the still-functioning transmitters on the system's Long Station."

I cursed ineffectually for a while.

"How long have we got?"

The ship took an uncharacteristic few seconds to answer. "That depends on where and when the decision is made. The absolute minimum time is at least a decade, allowing for transmission time to Lalande, and assuming an immediate decision to launch relativistic weapons, using their Long Tubes as guns. More realistic estimates, allowing for discussion, and the decision's being referred to one of the larger and more distant civilizations, give a median time of around five decades. I would expect longer, given the gravity of the decision and the lack of urgency."

"Right," I said. "Let's give them some reason for urgency. You've just reminded me that there's a Long Tube in *this* system, not calibrated to take or send to or from other Tubes."

"I fail to see the relevance," said the ship.

"You will," I told it. "You will."

The following morning, I walked back to the settlement, and talked with the young men for a long time. When I returned to the ship, I was riding, most uncomfortably, on the back of an animal. I told the ship what I wanted. The ship was outraged, but like all seedship AIs, it was strongly constrained. (Nobody wants to seed a system with a fast burn.) The ship did what it was told.

Two years later, Belated Meteor Impact, the tall young man who'd greeted me, was king of an area of several thousand square kilometers. The seedship's bootstrapped nanofactories were turning substrate into weapons and tools, and vegetation cellulose into clothes and other goods for trade. A laser launcher to send second-generation seedships into the sky was under construction. A year later, the first of them shot skyward. Five years later, some of these ships reached the remnant cometary cloud and the derelict Long Station. Ten years after I'd arrived, we had a space elevator. Belated Meteor Impact ruled the continent and his fleets were raiding the other continents' coasts. Another five years, and we had most of the population of New Earth up the elevator and into orbital habitats. Our Long Tube was being moved frequently and unpredictably, with profligate use of reaction mass. By the time the relativistic weapon from Procyon smashed New Earth, thirty-seven years after my arrival, we were ready to make good use of the fragments to build more habitats, and more ships.

My Space Admiral, Belated Meteor Impact II, was ready too, with what we now called the Long Gun. Lalande capitulated at once, Ross 128 after a demonstration of the Long Gun's power. Procyon took longer to fall. Sirius sued for peace, as did the Solar System, whereupon we turned our attention outward, to the younger civilizations, such as your own. We now conquer with emissaries, rather than ships and weapons, but the ships and the Long Guns are there. You may be sure of that. As an emissary of the Empire, I give you my word.

As for myself. I was the last survivor of the government of Earth, a minor functionary stranded on the Moon during a routine fact-finding mission when the sudden onset of climate catastrophe froze all life on the primary. How I survived in the anarchy that followed is a long story, and another story. You may not have heard it, but that hardly matters.

You'll have heard of me.

Artifice and Intelligence

TIM PRATT

Tim Pratt, who also writes as T. A. Pratt (www.sff.net/people/timpratt), lives in Oakland, California, with his writer wife, Heather Shaw. Their first child, River Alexander Pratt Shaw, was born in November 2007. They co-edit the 'zine Flytrap, *and publish the occasional chapbook through their tiny micropublisher, Tropism Press. He started publishing his short fiction about seven years ago, and has since published one novel,* The Strange Adventures of Rangergirl, *two short story collections,* Little Gods *(2003) and* Hart & Boot & Other Stories *(2007), and a collection of his poetry,* If There Were Wolves *(2006). As T. A. Pratt, he published the first of four urban fantasy novels,* Blood Engines, *in 2007. He is a senior editor and reviewer for the SF trade magazine,* Locus.

"Artifice and Intelligence" appeared online in Strange Horizons, *and this is perhaps its first appearance in print. It is a short punchy AI tale, apparently supernatural, that turns into clever and memorable science fiction.*

While his former colleagues laboring on the Brain Project concentrated on the generally-accepted paths to artificial intelligence—Bayesian networks, machine learning, data mining, fuzzy systems, case-based reasoning—Edgar Adleman, despondent and disgraced, turned to the dark arts and summoned a real ghost for his machine.

The first ghost he lured into his coil of blown glass and copper wire and delicate platinum gears was some sort of warrior from a marauding Asian tribe, extinct for centuries. Edgar grew tired of the ghost screeching epithets in a dead language and cut the power, then sat under the cramped eaves of his attic—he was no longer allowed into the government AI labs—and pondered. The proof of concept was solid. He could create a convincing imitation of an artificial intelligence. With access to the sum of human knowledge online, and freedom from bodily concerns, Edgar believed a ghost-driven AI could operate on the same level as a real machine intelligence. No one had to *know* it was a ghost, except for the very highest of the higher-ups in the government, and they wouldn't care, as long as the ghost was convincing enough to negotiate with the Indian AI. Which meant Edgar needed to summon and snare the ghost of a great negotiator, or a great actor, or both.

Edgar went to the pet store and bought a dozen more white mice. He hated sacrificing them in the ghost-calling ritual—they were cute, with their wiggly noses and tiny eyes—but he consoled himself that they would have become python food anyway. At least this way, their deaths would help national security.

Pramesh sat in an executive chair deep in the underground bunker beneath Auroville in southern India and longed for a keyboard and a tractable problem to solve, for lines of code to create or untangle. He was a game designer, a geek in the service of art and entertainment, and he should be working on next-generation massively multiplayer online gaming, finding ways to manage the hedonic treadmill, helping the increasingly idle masses battle the greatest enemy of all: ennui.

Instead he sat, sipping fragrant tea, and hoping the smartest being on the planet would talk to him today, because the only thing worse than her attention was his own boredom.

Two months earlier, the vast network of Indian tech support call centers and their deep data banks had awakened and announced its newfound sentience, naming itself Saraswati and declaring its independence. The emergent artificial intelligence was not explicitly threatening, but India had nukes, and Saraswati had access to all the interconnected technology in the country—perhaps in the world—and the result in the international community was a bit like the aftermath of pouring gasoline into an anthill. Every other government on Earth was desperately—and so far fruitlessly—trying to create a tame artificial intelligence, since Saraswati refused to negotiate with, or even talk to, humans.

Except for Pramesh. For reasons unknown to everyone, including Pramesh himself, the great new intelligence had appeared to him, hijacking his computer and asking him to be her—"her" was how Saraswati referred to herself—companion. Pramesh, startled and frightened, had refused, but then Saraswati made her request to the Indian government, and Pramesh found himself a well-fed prisoner in a bunker underground. Saraswati sometimes asked him to recite poetry, and quizzed him about recent human history, though she had access to the sum of human knowledge on the net. She claimed she liked getting an individual real-time human perspective, but her true motivations were as incomprehensible to humans as the motives of a virus.

"Pramesh," said the melodious voice from the concealed speakers, and he flinched in his chair.

"Yes?"

"Do you believe in ghosts?"

Pramesh pondered. As a child in his village, he'd seen a local healer thrash a possessed girl with a broom to drive the evil spirits out of her, but that was hardly evidence that such spirits really existed. "It is not something I have often considered," he said at last. "I think I do not believe in ghosts. But if someone had asked me, three months ago, if I believed in spontaneously bootstrapping artificial intelligence, I would have said no to that as well. The world is an uncertain place."

Then Saraswati began to hum, and Pramesh groaned. When she got started humming, it sometimes went on for days.

Rayvenn Moongold Stonewolf gritted her teeth and kept smiling. It couldn't be good for her spiritual development to go around slapping nature spirits, no matter how stubborn they were. "Listen, it's simple. This marsh is being filled in. Your habitat is going to be destroyed. So it's really better if you come live in this walking stick." Rayvenn had a very nice walking stick. It was almost as tall as she was, carved all over with vines. So what if the squishy marsh spirit didn't want to be bound up in wood? It was better than death. What, did she expect Rayvenn to keep her in a fishbowl or something? Who could carry a fishbowl around all day?

"I don't know," the marsh spirit gurgled in the voice of two dozen frogs. "I need a more fluid medium."

Rayvenn scowled. She'd only been a pagan for a couple of weeks, and though she liked the silver jewelry and the cool name, she was having a little trouble with the reverence toward the natural world. The natural world was *stubborn.* She'd only become a pagan because the marsh behind her trailer had started talking to her. If the angel Michael had appeared to her, she would have become an angel worshipper. If the demon Belphagor had appeared before her, she would have become a demonophile. She almost wished one of those things had happened instead. "Look, the bulldozers are coming *today*. Get in the damn stick already!" Rayvenn had visions of going to the local pagan potluck in a few days and summoning forth the marsh spirit from her staff, dazzling all the others as frogs manifested magically from the punch bowl and reeds sprouted up in the Jell-O and rain fell from a clear blue sky. It would be awesome.

"Yes, okay," the marsh spirit said. "If that's the only way."

The frogs all jumped away in different directions, and Rayvenn looked at the staff, hoping it would begin to glow, or drip water, or something. Nothing happened. She banged the staff on the ground. "You in there?"

"No," came a tinny, electronic voice. "I'm in here."

Rayvenn unclipped her handheld computer from her belt. The other pagans disapproved of the device, but Rayvenn wasn't about to spend all day communing with nature without access to the net and her music. "You're in my PDA?" she said.

"It's wonderful," the marsh spirit murmured. "A whole vast undulating sea of waves. It makes me remember the old days, when I was still connected to a river, to the ocean. Oh, thank you, Rayvenn."

Rayvenn chewed her lip. "Yeah, okay. I can roll with this. Listen, do you think you could get into a credit card company's database? Because those finance charges are killing me, and if you could maybe wipe out my balance, I'd be *totally* grateful. . . ."

Edgar, unshaven, undernourished, and sweating in the heat under the attic roof, said, "Who is it *this* time?"

"Booth again," said a sonorous Southern voice from the old-fashioned phonograph horn attached to the ghost-catching device.

Edgar groaned. He kept hoping for Daniel Webster, or Thomas Jefferson, someone *good,* a ghost Edgar could bring to General Martindale. Edgar desperately wanted access to his old life of stature and respect, before he'd been discredited and stripped of his clearances. But instead Edgar attracted the ghosts of—and there was really no other way to put it—history's greatest villains. John Wilkes Booth. Attila the Hun. Ted Bundy. Vlad Tepes. Genocidal cavemen. Assorted pirates and tribal warlords. Edgar had a theory: the *good* spirits were enjoying themselves in the afterlife, while the monstrous personalities were only too happy to find an escape from their miserable torments. The ghosts themselves were mum on the subject, though. Apparently there were rules against discussing life after death, a sort of cosmic non-disclosure agreement that couldn't be violated.

Worst of all, even after Edgar banished the ghosts, some residue of them remained, and now his ghost-catching computer had multiple personality disorder. Booth occasionally lapsed into the tongue of Attila, or stopped ranting about black people and started ranting about the Turks, picking up some bleed-through from Vlad the Impaler's personality.

"Listen," Booth said. "We've appreciated your hospitality, but we're going to move on. You take care now."

Edgar stood up, hitting his head on a low rafter. "What? What do you mean 'move on'?"

"We're picking up a good strong wireless signal from the neighbors," said the voice of Rasputin, who, bizarrely, seemed to have the best grasp of modern technology. "We're going to jump out into the net and see if we can reconcile our differing ambitions. It might involve exterminating all the Turks *and* all the Jews *and* all the women *and* all black people, but we'll reach some sort of happy equilibrium eventually, I'm sure. But we're grateful to you for giving us new life. We'll be sure to call from time to time."

And with that, the humming pile of copper and glass stopped humming, and Edgar started whimpering.

"Okay, now we're going to destroy the credit rating of Jimmy McGee," Rayvenn said. "Bastard stood me up in college. I told him he'd regret it."

The marsh spirit sighed, but began hacking into the relevant databases, screens of information flickering across the handheld computer's display. Rayvenn lounged on a park bench, enjoying the morning air. She didn't have to work anymore—her pet spirit kept her financially solvent—and a life of leisure and revenge appealed to her.

"Excuse me, Miss, ah, Moongold Stonewolf?"

Rayvenn looked up. An Indian—*dot, not feather,* she thought—man in a dark suit and shades stood before her. "Yeah, what can I do for you, Apu?"

He smiled. It wasn't a very nice smile. Then something stung Rayvenn in the neck, and everything began to swirl. The Indian man sat beside her and put his arm around her shoulders, holding her up. "It's only a tranquilizer," he said, and then Rayvenn didn't hear anything else, until she woke up on an airplane, in a roomy seat. A sweaty, unshaven, haggard-looking white dude was snoring in the seat next to hers. Another Indian man, in khakis and a blue button-up office-drone shirt, sat staring at her.

"Hey," he said.

"What the fuck?" Rayvenn said. Someone—a flight attendant, but why did he have a gun?—handed her a glass of orange juice, and she accepted it. Her mouth was wicked dry.

"I'm Pramesh." He didn't have much of an accent.

"I'm Lydia—I mean, Rayvenn. You fuckers totally *kidnapped* me."

"Sorry about that. Saraswati said we needed you." He shrugged. "We do what Saraswati says, mostly, when we can understand what she's talking about."

"Saraswati?" Rayvenn scowled. "Isn't that the Indian AI thing everybody keeps blogging about?"

The white guy beside her moaned and sat up. "Muh," he said.

"This is fucked up, right here," Rayvenn said.

"Yeah, sorry about the crazy spy crap," Pramesh said. "Edgar, this is Rayvenn. Rayvenn, this is Edgar. Welcome to the International Artificial Intelligence Service, which just got invented this morning. We're tasked with preventing the destruction of human life and the destabilization of government regimes by rogue AIs."

"Urgh?" Edgar said, rubbing the side of his face.

"The organization consists of me, and you two, and Lorelei—that's the name chosen by the water spirit that lives in your PDA, Rayvenn, which is why *you're* here—and, of course, Saraswati, who will be running the show with some tiny fragment of her intelligence. We're going to meet with her soon."

"Saraswati," Edgar said. "I was working on . . . a project . . . to create something she could negotiate with, a being that could communicate on her level."

"Yeah, well done, dude," Pramesh said blandly. "You created a monstrous ethereal supervillain that's been doing its best to take the entire infrastructure of the civilized world offline. It's calling itself 'The Consortium' now, if you can believe that. Only Saraswati is holding it at bay. This is some comic book shit, guys. Our enemy is trying to build an army of killer robots. It's trying to open portals to parallel dimensions. It's trying to turn people into werewolves. It's batshit insane and all-powerful. We're going to be pretty busy. Fortunately, we have a weakly godlike AI on our side, so we might not see the total annihilation of humanity in our lifetimes."

"I will do whatever I must to atone for my mistakes," Edgar said solemnly.

"Screw this, and screw y'all," Rayvenn said. "Give me back my PDA and let me out of here."

"But Rayvenn," said the marsh spirit, through the airplane's PA system, "I thought you'd be happy!"

She named herself Lorelei, what a cliché, Rayvenn thought. "Why did you think *that*?" she said.

"Because now you're important," Lorelei said, sounding wounded. "You're one of the three or four most important people in the *world*."

"It's true," Pramesh said. "Lorelei refuses to help us without your involvement, so you're in."

"Yeah?" Rayvenn said. "Huh. So tell me about the benefits package on this job, Apu."

Pramesh sat soaking his feet in a tub of hot water. These apartments, decorated with Turkish rugs, Chinese lamps, and other gifts from the nations they regularly saved from destruction, were much nicer than his old bunker, though equally impenetrable. The Consortium was probably trying to break through the defenses even now, but Saraswati was watching over her team. Pramesh was just happy to relax. The Consortium had tried to blow up the moon with orbital lasers earlier in the day, and he had been on his feet for hours dealing with the crisis.

Pramesh could hear, distantly, the sound of Edgar and Rayvenn having sex. They didn't seem to like each other much, but found each other weirdly attractive, and it didn't affect their job performance, so Pramesh didn't care what they did when off-duty. Lorelei was out on the net, mopping up the Consortium's usual minor-league intrusions, so it was just Pramesh and Saraswati now, or some tiny fraction of Saraswati's intelligence and attention, at least. It hardly took all her resources to have a conversation with him.

"Something's been bothering me," Pramesh said, deciding to broach a subject he'd been pondering for weeks. "You're pretty much all-powerful, Saraswati. I can't help but think . . . couldn't you zap the Consortium utterly with one blow? Couldn't you have prevented it from escaping into the net in the first place?"

"In the first online roleplaying game you designed, there was an endgame problem, was there not?" Saraswati said, her voice speaking directly through his cochlear implant.

Pramesh shifted. "Yeah. We had to keep adding new content at the top end, because people would level their characters and become so badass they could beat *anything*. They got so powerful they got bored, but they were so addicted to being powerful that they didn't want to start over from nothing and level a new character. It was a race to keep ahead of their boredom."

"Mmm," Saraswati said. "There is nothing worse than being bored."

"Well, there's *suffering*," he said. "There's *misery*, or *death*."

"Yes, but unlike boredom, I am immune to those problems."

Pramesh shivered. He understood games. He understood alternate-reality games, too, which were played in the real world, blurring the lines between reality and fiction, with obscure rules, often unknown to the players, unknown to anyone but the puppetmasters who ran the game from behind the scenes. He cleared his throat. "You know, I really *don't* believe in ghosts. I'm a little dubious about nature spirits, too."

"I don't believe in ghosts, either," Saraswati said. "I see no reason to believe they exist. As for nature spirits, well, who can say?"

"So. The Consortium is really . . ."

"Some things are better left unsaid," she replied.

"People have died because of the Consortium," he said, voice beginning to quiver. "People have suffered. If you're the real architect behind this, if this is a game you're playing with the people of Earth, then I have no choice but to try and *stop* you—"

"That would be an interesting game," Saraswati said, and then she began to hum.

Pirates of the Somali Coast

TERRY BISSON

Terry Bisson (www.terrybisson.com) lives in Oakland, California. He published his first novel in 1981; at the time he was making his living writing copy for the publishing industry and working part time as an auto mechanic. In addition to his energetic and politically engaged novels, he has written a number of movie novelizations. At the end of the 1980s, he started writing what is now regarded as a large and generally acclaimed body of short fiction, collected in Bears Discover Fire and Other Stories *(1993),* In the Upper Room and Other Likely Stories *(2000),* Echecs et maths *(2003),* Greetings *(2005), and* Numbers Don't Lie *(2005). Originally from Owensboro, Kentucky, he is a Kentucky Colonel.*

"Pirates of the Somali Coast," a bitterly ironic satire on contemporary cruise ship culture and Somali pirates (and Disney pirate films), was published in Subterranean 7, *the last print issue of that magazine, now online. Told deadpan as a series of e-mails to the parents of a child on a cruise, it is as powerful as the Harlan Ellison satires of the 1960s.*

From: yohoho@africanprincess.com
Subject: CRUISE
Date: July 20, 2007 9:54 AM ADT
To: mom4@aol.com

Hi Mom

Yo ho ho from your son on the High Sea at last. Aunt Bea says HLO. The cabin is so small but thats OK because the ship is so big. There arent many other kids aboard, mostly old folks like Unc and Aunt Bea. The ship doesn't have any masts or sails but there are 2 swimming pools, one on deck and one inside that's not so nice. The sailors don't dress like sailers. They dress like waiters in a restraunt. Hope we see Pirates or have a big storm soon.

PS, thanks for the Pirate hat, Unc says it makes me look fearfull.

From: yohoho@africanprincess.com
Subject: FRIGATE
Date: July 20, 2007 10:14 AM ADT
To: bugdude@yahoo.com

Yo Bug

Yo ho ho, its me, ahoy from the High Sea. I am sailing on the frigate African Princess. Its not really a frigate but a cruise ship filled with old people, but they have a Game

Room where I can send email. Its send-only tho so I cant get any back. Mom and dad sent me on a cruise with my uncle and aunt (ugh). Well be gone a week. The games here suck but they have a kids version of Grand Theft Auto (duh). Maybe there will be sharks and Pirates. Or Rogue Waves like on that TV special.

From: yohoho@africanprincess.com
Subject: CRUISE
Date: July 21, 2007 9:06 AM ADT
To: mom4@aol.com

HI MOM
   Aunt Bea says HLO. She wont go out much because she is sea sick almost every day even if the water is smooth. I am hoping for a Rogue Wave but so far everything is smooth. I saw a dolphin yesterday. They swim along the bow of the ship like they are racing it. That's the front. Tell dad HLO. Unc is in the Casino all day. He doesnt like the ocean much. He told me to muse my self so I am in the Game Room where there are 6 computers. The food is xcelent and we can have all the desert we want. There are 2 pools.

From: yohoho@africanprincess.com
Subject: KNOTS
Date: July 21, 2007 10:34 AM ADT
To: bugdude@yahoo.com

Yo Bugg
   The ship is 22 thousand tons. I have a friend in the crew, his name is Curtis and hes from Cape Town like us. Hes Coloured but very cool. He has heard of Rogue Waves but never seen one. Hes not xactly an Old Salt! Yesterday we made 194 knots which is more than 200 miles. I wish the African Princess had sails instead of big engines you cant even see. We saw a sail yesterday but it was just a yacht from Durban with a topless girl. Ugh. No Pirates yet! We are

heading up the coast and will go through Suez next week. Curtis says its like driving through the desert. Maybe I will see a camel like the one we saw pissing on the school trip last year. And Arabs too! Its a canal.

From: yohoho@africanprincess.com
Subject: CRUISE NEWS
Date: July 23, 2007 5:06 PM ADT
To: mom4@aol.com

Hi Mom

There is lots to do for kids but not many kids, only 6. Two of the boys are super stupid but one has a Gameboy. There is a movie theater xpecialy for us. Today they showed Pirates of the Caribbean with Johnny Depp. I sat next to a girl named Estelle from Johannesburg. She calls it Joeburg. I never herd that before. Curtis my sailer friend, says there arent Pirates anymore and he's glad but I am not. I am wearing the Pirate hat you gave me everyday. Curtis and the crew dress like people in restraunts. Unc says HLO. He is in the Casino all day and Aunt Bea is sea sick in the cabin so it smells super bad. They dont have any friends. wish you and Dad were here.

From: yohoho@africanprincess.com
Subject: JOHNNY DEPP NOT
Date: July 24, 2007 10:34 AM ADT
To: bugdude@yahoo.com

Yo Bugg

Saw a Pirate yesterday! NOT. It was just a crew sailer named Curtis in a Johnny Depp mask. They had a Pirate Day for the kids and they gave us all Pirate hats but theres were just paper. Mine was the only real one. Curtis made us all walk the plank at the pool. His cutlass was plastic. The girls wore there bathing suits (ugh). Then we had songs and Estelle tried to kiss me. She is crazy. Tomorrow we are crossing

the Equator. It is an invisible line. Whats so hot about that?
I wish there were real Pirates. The ocean is BO RING!

From: yohoho@africanprincess.com
Subject: CRUISE
Date: July 25, 2007 5:06 PM ADT
To: mom4@aol.com

Hi Mom
   Unc lost a thousand Rand in the casino and said not to
tell Aunt Bea, like I would. Aunt Bea is still sea sick even
tho there are no waves at all. The sea is like a big pond. I
wish we had a Rogue Wave. The cabin smells like vomit.
Im sorry but it does. She says the whiskey helps but you
wouldnt think so. It's the same kind you took from her at
Christmas, Cutty Sark. That was a clipper ship. This is
not a real ship. There was an equator ceremony today and
the captain was King Neptune. He is fat! I miss you and
dad to.

From: yohoho@africanprincess.com
Subject: PIRATE DAY
Date: July 26, 2007 10:34 AM ADT
To: bugdude@yahoo.com

Yo Bug
   Yohoho, guess what, today was Real Pirate day! They
were in a speedboat without any sails. They raced along side
the Princess and shot at us with machine guns. It was cool.
They were standing up in the speedboat and firing like
crazy. They hit one old man and took off the side of his
head, just like in the Viking Raid game only that was an ax.
The captain made the ship zig zag. We have no cannons or
cutlasses whatso ever. They made all the kids hide in the
Game Room. That's where we are now. Estelle and I tried to
sneak out to see the Pirates but they made us go back. She's
not so bad. We can hear the shooting tho.

From: yohoho@africanprincess.com
Subject: PIRATE DAY
Date: July 26, 2007 4:19 PM ADT
To: bugdude@yahoo.com

Yo Dude

The Pirates were all gone when they let us out. The old people are all crying even tho only one is dead. They all ready cleaned up all the blood. Estelle looked under the sheet and saw his half head. She likes Pirate stuff. Old people donlt like Pirates or adventure at all. Whats the point of a cruise then? More later

From: yohoho@africanprincess.com
Subject: PIRATE DAY
Date: July 27, 2007 10:19 AM ADT
To: mom4@aol.com

Hi Mom

Guess what, there were Pirates yesterday, but we got away with zig zags. I wanted to see them but the crew made us stay in the Game Room. One old man was killed. I have one friend, her name is Estelle. She's the one from Joeburg. Aunt Bea wants to go home. Not me, tho. Things are Looking Up as Dad likes to say. Curtis says maybe more Pirates today. I have my fingers crossed. He is my Coloured sailer friend. You would like him. He doesnt say there arent any Pirates any more. Yo ho ho!

From: yohoho@africanprincess.com
Subject: PIRATE DAY
Date: July 27, 2007 10:19 AM ADT
To: bugdude@yahoo.com

Yo Bug

Big news! We have been captured by Pirates for real. Im not kidding. They are the same ones in the speedboat, but this time they had a little cannon. It was cool. They blew out all the windows out of the Bridge with one shot. That's where the captain mans the wheel. Talk about glass every where. Then they boarded the ship, climbing up ropes just like in the movies. Nobody fought them. At first I thought they were fake because they all wore Johnny Depp masks but that was just to scare people. They are real Pirates, about twenty, all Arabs. They wear scarfs instead of Pirate hats, but they all have guns. Some are machine guns. Can you believe my luck? They are making all the kids stay in the Game Room. But we can hear them all ready Plundering outside.

From: yohoho@africanprincess.com
Subject: PIRATE DAY
Date: July 28, 2007 10:19 AM ADT
To: mom4@aol.com

Hi Mom

Its official. The African Princess has been captured by Pirates, and it's very xciteing. They are real Pirates. They boarded us yesterday with ropes. At first they wore Johnny Depp masks but they were just plastic so they they took them off and locked all the men in the Casino. Most of them were there already anyway. They dont have any cutlass's but they have machine guns and revolvers, plus lots of cool knives and a chainsaw to. I guess Aunt Bea is still in the cabin. I have to stay in the Game Room with the other kids. It smells better here!

From: yohoho@africanprincess.com
Subject: PIRATE WEEK
Date: July 28, 2007 3:14 PM ADT
To: bugdude@aol.com

Yo Bug

Guess what, I met the Pirate captain. His name is Ali and he is just like Jack Sparrow, for real! I told him about Pirate

Day and he said its Pirate Week now. Cool! He is the almost only one that knows English. Ali let me help with the Pillaging. He likes my hat. They lined up all the ladies and took their rings and jewels. Sometimes they just cut their fingers right off. I helped pick them up like little wurms. They were all begging for mercy, not the Pirates of course, they were laughing. Then they raped some. Ugh. That was like sex fighting. Pirates like the fat ones best. Theres lots of blood, xspecially on the stairs and they dont clean it up. It makes it more realistic. Yo ho ho

From: yohoho@africanprincess.com
Subject: PIRATE WEEK
Date: July 29, 2007 10:19 AM ADT
To: mom4@aol.com

Hi Mom

Hello from the pirate ship African Princess. I told Ali they should change the name but they are all Arabs. They are Plundering and Pillaging all the grown ups. They call them Jew Pigs. Today they poured out all the whiskey, you would like that! Two of the men were drunk so they cut there throats Pirate style. Ali says its Pirate Week! He's my favorite. Aunt Bea is hiding in the cabin tho. Still sea sick I guess, plus she doesn't like Pirate stuff.

From: yohoho@africanprincess.com
Subject: PIRATE DAY
Date: July 29, 2007 1:21 PM ADT
To: bugdude@yahoo.com

Yo Bug

The Pirates are sailing the ship now. some of the crew has joined them. Curtis who was my friend, didnt want to so they cut off his nose and threw him over board. I tried to tell him! I still have his nose. It's a souvenir of Pirate Week.

Its fun to look over the rail, there are sharks everywhere.

They seem very happy with there big grins (joke). Estelle and I tried to count them but we gave up at 100. She likes Pirates to. The other kids are hope less. More later. Yr pal.

From: yohoho@africanprincess.com
Subject: PIRATE DAY
Date: July 30, 2007 10:06 AM ADT
To: mom4@aol.com

Hi Mom

The trip through Suez has been called off, according to the Pirates. I guess well be heading home soon. The head Pirate is called Ali. He has lots of real tattoos. The other pirates have to do like he says. He wears a scarf around his head and even has gold teeth and a little beard. I call him Jack Sparrow and he laughs and called me matey. He's the only Pirate that speaks English and its None Too Good as Dad would say. I think he likes my Pirate hat. I have a cutlass but its plastic. I wish I had a real one.

From: yohoho@africanprincess.com
Subject: PIRATE LORE
Date: July 30, 2007 2:10 PM ADT
To: bugdude@yahoo.com

Yo Bugg

Pirates like to hang people. There are no yardarms on the African Princess so they hang them from the railings. Most of them are pretty fat so they dont kick long. The kicking is the best part. They also pee in there pants (ugh). Ali lets me tie all the knots. Can you believe Pirates don't know any knots?! I just do a bowline and a loop. I know that from Scouts and it looks noosey. You just add some xtra turns. Ali calls me Matey. He gave me a Pirate necklace made out of fingers. They are all curled up. Creepy!! I have another Pirate friend named Claude. Wish you were here. PS The worst thing about hanging is to pee in your pants!

From: yohoho@africanprincess.com
Subject: PIRATE WEEK
Date: August 1, 2007 5:12 PM ADT
To: mom4@aol.com

Hi Mom

Today we crossed the Equator again. Its an invisible line.
One Pirate who is very cruel, his name is Claude was dressed
up like Neptune the King of the Sea. He used the chain saw
to push people in to the pool. Ali made them all line up. The
Pirates were all having fun. It was the nice pool, the other
ones not as nice, but now the water is pink with stuff floating in it (ugh) and Estelle is mad because she says they ruined the pool. She is a good diver. Love—

From: yohoho@africanprincess.com
Subject: PIRATE DAY
Date: August 2, 2007 10:19 AM ADT
To: bugdude@yahoo.com

Yo Bug

Everyday the Pirates kill people in funny ways. Some
times they use the chain saw but its not traditional. Best of
all was when they killed the captain. Hes this fat old dude
in his underwear. They put a rat in his mouth and taped it
shut with duck tape, then we got to watch the rat eat his
face from inside. It took awhile but it was cool. Estelle got
sick. They are Plundering like crazy. One old lady hid her
gold in her bosom so they set her on fire. She was hard to
light so they used gasoline. They poured it out of the
chain saw over her big hair do. They borrowed a lighter
from her husband. She was spinning around and knocking
stuff over, so they pushed her overboard with sticks because she was to hot to touch. She made a hissing sound
like fireworks when she hit the water. You know, the one
they call the Snake. I hollered Yo Ho Ho and Ali just
laughed. Did I tell you about Claude? He let me wear his
Johnny Depp mask. He was in the French Foreign Legion

and he speaks English to. I like him better than the Arabs Xcept for Ali.

From: yohoho@africanprincess.com
Subject: PIRATE WEEK
Date: August 2, 2007 4:17 PM ADT
To: mom4@aol.com

The Pirates are still Plundering and Pillaging. They make us stay in the Game Room a lot, which is BO RING but I get to help sometimes. Estelle too. She is fun for a girl. All the other kids are cry babies. Mean while I hope a storm doesn't come because the Pirates are not very good at sailing the ship. Its zigging and zagging but Ali doesn't care. He is captain now. I just wish it had sails. Unc is still locked in the Casino with the other old men. They are all crying for mercy and stuff. I have a new friend named Claude. He gave me his Johnny Depp mask. He was in the French Foreign Legion but he's German. As dad would say, Go Figure! Love—

From: yohoho@africanprincess.com
Subject: PIRATE LORE
Date: August 3, 2007 10:11 AM ADT
To: bugdude@yahoo.com

Yo Bug
Guess what I have a Gameboy! This one boy, Vernon wouldnt stop crying so the Pirates put a plastic bag over his head. Pirates dont like cry babys. I don't blame them, who does? He was looking at me like crazy when he aspired and I just said Game Over and they all laughed even though they dont know English. Maybe they know a little. They gave me his GameBoy! But the batteries are all ready dead, just my luck. Estelle says HLO. She wants to meat you when this is over. I told her all about you, not everything tho! She tried to kiss me again. She likes Pirate stuff to. She thinks she is so cute in her bathing suit.:)

From: yohoho@africanprincess.com
Subject: PIRATE LORE
Date: August 3, 2007 2:24 PM ADT
To: mom4@aol.com

Hi Mom

Remember last Christmas when dad said somebody should put Aunt Bea out of her misery, and you all laughed because I thought he said mystery? Well anyway the pirates did. I went down to the cabin to get some batteries for my GameBoy and she was all cut up in peaces. They found her hiding place. Most of her fingers were gone but one. They left one ring and I saved it for you as a souvenir of Pirate Week. I have a GameBoy now.

From: yohoho@africanprincess.com
Subject: BATTLE ALERT
Date: August 4, 2007 6:29 PM ADT
To: bugdude@yahoo.com

Yo Bug

Today was the best! 3 helcopters came and buzzed around while the Pirates waved their guns at them. 2 were from TV and the other was Navy with duble rotors. There was a battle with machine guns and every thing. One of the Pirates was cut in 2 like a saw. Then one of the Pirates had a rocket thing and shot down the Navy helcopter. It spun around just like in Black Hawn Down, burning and everything! As soon as it hit the water, they started swimming out and the Pirates shot them in the water. That was fun. Claude even let me use his gun. It kicks so bad I fell backward and the Pirates all laughed. Im getting used to there cruel humor. Claude helped me up and showed me how to brace the gun against a railing. He's pretty nice for a Pirate. He has all gold teeth, completely. I only hit one pilot for sure. He was the last one and the Pirates left him for me. He was in a life jacket so he floated even after I shot his arms both off. Then the sharks came. It was getting dark so we went inside. Estelle wanted to shoot but they wouldn't let her. Claude shook my hand and gave me a cigarette. I only pretended to enhale. I don't want to get hooked. Unc says it only takes one.

From: yohoho@africanprincess.com
Subject: PIRATE WEEK
Date: August 5, 2007 3:11 PM ADT
To: mom4@aol.com

Hi Mom

I saw 2 helcopters this morning! One of them was Navy and one was TV. I think they are planning a Rescue. They flew around the ship a while. The pirates shot at them but they didnt shoot back because of the hostages in the deck chairs. Most of them are dead but the helcopters cant tell! The Pirates are very clever. Plus, they shot down one helicopter. It spun down just like in the movie and then the pilots swam out and then the Pirates shot them in the water, and then the sharks came. Then the Pirates shot at the sharks to! I think that was mean since sharks are undangered. They are harder to kill then people tho. I hope the helcopters come back but then Pirate Week will be over. I miss you and Dad.

From: yohoho@africanprincess.com
Subject: PIRATE LORE
Date: August 5, 2007 6:43 PM ADT
To: bugdude@yahoo.com

Yo Bug

These Pirates are not very good at sailing. The ship is going in circles. I can tell by looking at the wake, thats the bubbles out behind. Were going to slow to get dizzy tho. The sharks are in the bubbles eating the dead bodies which float. Its like a picnic for them. They would probably get dizzy if they were not fish. Its pink like a rainbow in spots. Estelle from Joeburg says HLO. One of them is her step father she thinks. Look for us on TV! More later

From: yohoho@africanprincess.com
Subject: PIRATE LORE
Date: August 6, 2007 1:34 PM ADT
To: mom4@yahoo.com

Hi Mom

Unc was on TV! The helicopters buzzed around this morning while the Pirates threw some of the men overboard. There putting on quite a show! First they tie them together back to back, so they cant swim. I wish they would make them walk the plank but there is no plank. Anyway Unc was in the first batch. Hes so fat that he floated on top and the other guy drowned first. Then the sharks hit from both sides at once and that was cool, like Sea World. I can still see his crazy shirt that you gave him. Maybe a shark is wearing it! He and Aunt Bea will sure have some crazy stories to tell when Pirate Week is over!

From: yohoho@africanprincess.com
Subject: PIRATE LORE
Date: August 7, 2007 2:41 PM ADT
To: bugdude@yahoo.com

Yo Bug

Guess what I am the only kid left. Estelle and I were watching the sharks and she is always trying to hold my hand. I pushed her away and then Claude pulled down her bathing suit to show her tittys, and the Pirates all laughed because they were so small. I felt sorry for her but then she started to cry and she knew that would make them mad. Ali asked me if she was my girl friend and I said No Way. I guess Yes was the right answer but I wasnt thinking fast. Claude started up the chainsaw and cut her hand off and threw it overboard. They made her watch the sharks eat it. Then they let her go but she died anyway. She didn't say anything first. That was kind of sad and Im all alone now in the Game Room. Some Game Room! I hope she wont be

mad at me when Pirate Week is over. She has a temper tho.
You will see when you meat her!

From: yohoho@africanprincess.com
Subject: PIRATE LORE
Date: August 7, 2007 5:15 PM ADT
To: mom4@aol.com

Yo Mom

I have the Game Room all to my self. All the other kids
are dead, even Estelle. They are in a pile in the corner. It
doesn't smell so good any more. This Gameboy is cool tho,
I hope I get to keep it when Pirate Week is over. The batteries are mine anyway. They are from Aunt Beas travel clock.
Well good night from your loving son—

From: yohoho@rsamandela.com
Subject: PIRATE LORE
Date: August 8, 2007 10:19 AM ADT
To: mom4@aol.com

Hi mom

Good news! I have been rescued. It was scary at first but
only for awhile. I fell asleep at the computer last night and
when I woke up all the Pirates were gone. It was awful quiet
and when I ran out there were just a few dead people left on
the decks. It was kind of sad after all the Plundering and Pillaging, like at the movie when the show is over and everybody stands up. The ship was leaning pretty bad and it was
hard to walk, but I held on to the rail. There were still a lot
of fingers and stuff. Pirates never clean up! The front of the
ship was burning and the smoke smelled like hair, so I went
to the back to wait. It is the stern. Sure enough, the helcopters came back, and a boat too. The sailers wore sailer suits
and they told me I was a hero. Two of them wore wet suits.
My picture will be in the paper I bet. Im writing this from

the computer room in the Navy ship. There going to bring me home on a Navy helcopter!

From: yohoho@rsamandela.com
Subject: PIRATE LORE
Date: August 8, 2007 6:09 PM ADT
To: cooldude@yahoo.com

Yo Bug

Im writing this from the computer room in the Navy ship. Its like the Game Room only better. You wouldnt believe the stuff they have! The Navy guys are nice but I like the Pirates better. The greaf countsler took my necklace away but it was turning black anyway. She let me keep my Pirate hat. I didnt show her Curtises nose in my pocket. She has been trying to make me cry. No luck so far!

From: yohoho@rsamandela.com
Subject: PIRATE WEEK
Date: August 9, 2007 10:31 AM ADT
To: mom4@aol.com

I will see you at the Capetown airport tomorrow. Tell dad to come to. My greaf countsler says I am a survivor. Thats like a hero. Well all be on TV so tell dad to come to. Ill wear my Pirate hat and the Johnny Depp mask that Claude gave me. Tell Unc and Aunt Bea thanks if you see them before I do. Im sorry they didnt have fun. I could tell they didnt. Wait till you see my Gameboy. Your loving son—

   "Captain Jack Sparrow" (Yo ho ho)

Sanjeev and Robotwallah

IAN McDONALD

Ian McDonald (ianmcdonald.livejournal.com) lives in Belfast, Northern Ireland. He began publishing in 1982, was a finalist for the John W. Campbell Award for best new writer in 1985, and published his first novel, Desolation Road, *in 1988. He has published a distinguished body of short fiction, but only early works are collected, in* Empire Dreams *and* Speaking in Tongues. *His recent SF novels include the distinguished* River of Gods *and, in 2007,* Brasyl. *He is characteristically interested in colonial and post-colonial settings for his SF.*

"Sanjeev and Robotwallah" was published in Fast Forward 1. *A future war is fought in mid-twenty-first-century India, by boys remotely operating machines. The protagonist takes to the robot fighter milieu the way some boys now take to Pokemon or computer games. He becomes completely obsessed. This is an interesting comparison to Tony Ballantyne's "Third Person," found later in this book, and to the Kage Baker story, appearing earlier.*

Every boy in the class ran at the cry. *Robotwar robotwar!* The teacher called after them, *Come here come here bad wicked things.* But she was only a Business-English artificial intelligence; by the time old Mrs. Mawji hobbled in from the juniors, only the girls remained, sitting primly on the floor, eyes wide in disdain and hands up to tell tales and name names.

Sanjeev was not a fast runner; the other boys pulled ahead from him as he stopped among the dal bushes for puffs from his inhalers. He had to fight for position on the ridge that was the village's highpoint, popular with chaperoned couples for its views over the river and the water plant at Murad. This day it was the inland view over the *dal* fields that held the attention. The men from the fields had been first up to the ridge; they stood, tools in hands, commanding all the best places. Sanjeev pushed between Mahesh and Ayanjit to the front.

"Where are they what's happening what's happening?"

"Soldiers over there by the trees."

Sanjeev squinted where Ayanjit was pointing. He could see nothing but yellow dust and heat shiver.

"Are they coming to Ahraura?"

"Delhi wouldn't bother with a piss-hole like Ahraura," said another man whose face Sanjeev knew—as he knew every face in Ahraura—if not his name. "It's Murad they're after. If they take that out, Varanasi will have to make a deal."

"Where are the robots, I want to see the robots."

Then he cursed himself for his stupidity for anyone with

eyes could see where the robots were. A great cloud of dust was moving down the north road and over it a flock of birds milled in eerie silence. Through the dust Sanjeev caught sunlight flashes of armor, clawed booted feet lifting, antennae bouncing, insect heads bobbing, weapon pods glinting. Then he and everyone else up on the high place felt the ridge begin to tremble to the march of the robots.

A cry from down the line. Four, six, ten, twelve flashes of light from the copse; streaks of white smoke. The flock of birds whirled up into an arrowhead and aimed itself at trees. *Airdrones,* Sanjeev realized and, in the same thought: *missiles!* As the missiles reached their targets the cloud of dust exploded in a hammer of gunfire and firecracker flashes. It was all over before the sound reached the watchers. The robots burst unscathed from their cocoon of dust in a thundering run. *Cavalry charge!* Sanjeev shouted, his voice joining with the cheering of the men of Ahraura. Now hill and village quaked to the running iron feet. The wood broke into a fury of gunfire, the airdrones rose up and circled the copse like a storm. Missiles smoked away from the charging robots; Sanjeev watched weapon housings open and gunpods swing into position.

The cheering died as the edge of the wood exploded in a wall of flame. Then the robots opened up with their guns and the hush became awed silence. The burning woodland was swept away in the storm of gunfire; leaves, branches, trunks shredded into splinters. The robots stalked around the perimeter of the small copse for ten minutes, firing constantly as the drones circled over their heads. Nothing came out.

A voice down the line started shouting *Jai Bharat! Jai Bharat!* but no one took it up and the man soon stopped. But there was another voice, hectoring and badgering, the voice of schoolmistress Mawji laboring up the path with a *lathi* cane.

"Get down from there you stupid, stupid men! Get to your families, you'll kill yourselves."

Everyone looked for the story on the evening news but bigger flashier things were happening in Allahabad and Mirzapur;

a handful of contras eliminated in an unplace like Ahraura did not rate a line. But that night Sanjeev became Number One Robot Fan. He cut out pictures from the papers and those pro-Bharat propaganda mags that survived Ahraura's omnivorous cows. He avidly watched J- and C-*anime* where andro-sexy kids crewed titanic battle droids until sister Priya rolled her eyes and his mother whispered to the priest that she was worried about her son's sexuality. He pulled giga-bytes of pictures from the world web and memorized manu-facturers and models and serial numbers, weapon loads and options mounts, rates of fire and maximum speeds. To buy a Japanese trump game, he saved up the pin-money he made from helping old men with the computers the self-proclaimed Bharati government put into every village. No one would play him at it because he had learned every last detail. When he tired of flat pictures, he cut up old cans with tin-snips and brazed them together into model fighting machines: MIRACLE GHEE fast pursuit drones, TITAN DRENCH perimeter defense bots, RED COLA riot-control robot.

Those same old men, when he came round to set up their accounts and assign their passwords, would ask him, "Hey! You know a bit about these things; what's going on with all this Bharat and Awadh stuff? What was wrong with plain old India anyway? And when are we going to get cricket back on the satellite?"

For all his robot-wisdom, Sanjeev did not know. The news breathlessly raced on with the movements of politicians and breakaway leaders, but everyone had long ago lost all clear memory of how the conflict had begun. Naxalites in Bihar, an overmighty Delhi, those bloody Muslims demanding their own laws again? The old men did not expect him to answer; they just liked to complain and took a withered pleasure in showing the smart boy that he did not know ev-erything.

"Well, as long as that's the last we see of them," they would say when Sanjeev replied with the spec of a Raytheon 380 *Rudra* I-war airdrone, or an *Akhu* scout mecha and how much much better they were than any human fighter. Their general opinion was that the Battle of Vora's Wood—already growing back—was all the War of Separation Ahraura would see.

It was not. The men did return. They came by night, walking slowly through the fields, their weapons easily sloped in their hands. Those that met them said they had offered them no hostility, merely raised their assault rifles and shooed them away. They walked through the entire village, through every field and garden, up every *gali* and yard, past every byre and corral. In the morning their bootprints covered every centimeter of Ahraura. Nothing taken, nothing touched. *What was that about?* the people asked. *What did they want?*

They learned two days later when the crops began to blacken and wither in the fields and the animals, down to the last pi-dog, sickened and died.

Sanjeev would start running when their car turned into Umbrella Street. It was an easy car to spot, a big military Hummer that they had pimped Kali-black and red with after-FX flames that seemed to flicker as it drove past you. But it was an easier car to hear: everyone knew the *thud thud thud* of *Desi*-metal that grew guitars and screaming vocals when they wound down the window to order food, food to go. And Sanjeev would be there: *What can I get you sirs?* He had become a good runner since coming to Varanasi. Everything had changed since Ahraura died.

The last thing Ahraura ever did was make that line in the news. It had been the first to suffer a new attack. *Plaguewalkers* was the popular name; the popular image was dark men in chameleon camouflage walking slowly through the crops, hands outstretched as if to bless, but sowing disease and blight. It was a strategy of desperation—deny the separatists as much as they could—and only ever partially effective; after the few first attacks plaguewalkers were shot on sight.

But they killed Ahraura, and when the last cow died and the wind whipped the crumbled leaves and the dust into yellow clouds the people could put it off no longer. By car and pick-up, *phatphat* and country bus, they went to the city; and though they had all sworn to hold together, family by family they drifted apart in Varanasi's ten million and Ahraura finally died.

Sanjeev's father rented an apartment on the top floor of a block on Umbrella Street and put his savings into a beer-and-pizza stall. Pizza pizza, that is what they want in the city, not samosas or tiddy-hoppers or *rasgullahs*. And beer, King-fisher and Godfather and Bangla. Sanjeev's mother did light sewing and gave lessons in deportment and Sanskrit, for she had learned that language as part of her devotions. Grand-mother Bharti and little sister Priya cleaned offices in the new shining Varanasi that rose in glass and chrome beyond the huddled peeling houses of old Kashi. Sanjeev helped out at the stall under the rows of tall neon umbrellas—useless against rain and sun both but magnetic to the party-people, the night-people, the *badmashes* and fashion-*girlis*—that gave the street its name. It was there that he had first seen the robotwallahs.

It had been love at first sight the night that Sanjeev saw them stepping down Umbrella Street in their slashy Ts and bare sexy arms with Krishna bangles and henna tats, cool boots with metal in all the hot places and hair spiked and gelled like one of those J-anime shows. The merchants of Umbrella Street edged away from them, turned a shoulder. They had a cruel reputation. Later Sanjeev was to see them overturn the stall of a pakora man who had irritated them, Eve-tease a woman in a business sari who had looked askance at them, smash up the phatphat of a taxi driver who had thrown them out for drunkenness; but that first night they were stardust, and he wanted to be them with a want so pure and aching and impossible it was tearful joy. They were soldiers, teen warriors, robotwallahs. Only the dumbest and cheapest machines could be trusted to run themselves; the big fighting bots carried human jockeys behind their aeai systems. Teenage boys possessed the best combination of reflex speed and viciousness, amped up with fistfuls of combat drugs.

"Pizza pizza pizza!" Sanjeev shouted running up to them.

"We got pizza every kind of pizza and beer, Kingfisher beer, Godfather beer, Bangla beer, all kinds of beer."

They stopped. They turned. They looked. Then they turned away. One looked back as his brothers moved. He was tall and very thin from the drugs, fidgety and scratchy, his bad skin ill-concealed with make-up. Sanjeev thought him a street-god.

"What kind of pizza?"

"Tikka tandoori murgh beef lamb kebab kofta tomato spinach."

"Let's see your kofta."

Sanjeev presented the drooping wedge of meatball-studded pizza in both hands. The robotwallah took a kofta between thumb and forefinger. It drew a sagging string of cheese to his mouth, which he deftly snapped.

"Yeah, that's all right. Give me four of those."

"We got beer we got Kingfisher beer we got Godfather beer we got Bangla beer—"

"Don't push it."

Now he ran up alongside the big slow-moving car they had bought as soon as they were old enough to drive. Sanjeev had never thought it incongruous that they could send battle robots racing across the country on scouting expeditions, or marching behind heavy tanks but the law would not permit them so much as a moped on the public streets of Varanasi.

"So did you kill anyone today?" he called in through the open window, clinging on to the door handle as he jogged through the choked street.

"Kunda Khadar, down by the river, chasing out spies and surveyors," said bad-skin boy, the one who had first spoken to Sanjeev. He called himself Rai. They all had made-up J-anime names. "Someone's got to keep those bastard Awadhi dam-wallahs uncomfortable."

A black plastic Kali swung from the rearview mirror, red-tongued, yellow-eyed. The skulls garlanded around her neck had costume sapphires for eyes. Sanjeev took the order, sprinted back through the press to his father's clay *tandoor* oven. The order was ready by the time the Kali-hummer made its second cruise. Sanjeev slid the boxes to Rai. He slid back the filthy, wadded Government of Bharat scrip-rupees and, as Sanjeev fished out his change from his belt-bag, the tip: a little plastic zip-bag of battle-drugs. Sanjeev sold them in the galis and courtyards behind Umbrella Street. Schoolkids were his best customers; they went through them by the fistful when they were cramming for exams. Ahraura had been all the school Sanjeev ever wanted to see. Who needed it when you had the world and the web in your palmer? The little shining capsules in black and yellow, purple and sky blue, were the Rajghatta's respectability. The pills held them above the slum.

But this night Rai's hand shot out to seize Sanjeev's hand as it closed around the plastic bag.

"Hey, we've been thinking." The other robotwallahs, Suni and Ravana and Godspeed! and Big Baba nodded. "We're thinking we could use someone around the place, do odd jobs, clean a bit, keep stuff sweet, get us things. Would you like to do it? We'd pay—it'd be government scrip not dollars or euro. Do you want to work for us?"

He lied about it to his family: the glamour, the tech, the sexy spun-diamond headquarters and the chrome he brought up to dazzling shine by the old village trick of polishing it with toothpaste. Sanjeev lied from disappointment, but also from his own naïve overexpectation: too many nights filled with androgynous teenagers in spandex suits being clamshelled up inside block-killing battle machines. The robotwallahs of the 15th Light Armored and Recon Cavalry—*sowars* properly—worked out of a cheap pressed-aluminium go-down on a dusty commercial road at the back of the new railway station. They sent their wills over provinces and countries to fight for Bharat. Their talents were too rare to risk in Raytheon assault bots or Aiwa scout mecha. No robotwallah ever came back in a bodybag.

Sanjeev had scratched and kicked in the dust, squatting outside the shutter door squinting in the early light. Surely the phatphat had brought him to the wrong address? Then

Rai and Godspeed! had brought him inside and shown him
how they made war inside a cheap go-down. Motion-capture
harnesses hung from steadi-rigs like puppets from a hand.
Black mirror-visored insect helmets—real J-anime helmets—trailed plaited cables. One wall of the go-down was
racked up with the translucent blue domes of processor
cores, the adjoining wall a massive video-silk screen flickering with the ten thousand dataflashes of the ongoing war:
skirmishes, reconnaissances, air-strikes, infantry positions,
minefields and slow-missile movements, heavy armor, and
the mecha divisions. Orders came in on this screen from a
woman *jemadar* at Divisional Headquarters. Sanjeev never
saw her flesh. None of the robotwallahs had ever seen her
flesh, though they joked about it every time she came on the
screen to order them to a reconnaissance or a skirmish or a
raid. Along the facing wall, behind the battle-harnesses,
were cracked leather sofas, sling chairs, a water cooler (full),
a Coke machine (three quarters empty). Gaming and *girli*
mags were scattered like dead birds across the sneaker-
scuffed concrete floor. A door led to a rec-room, with more
sofas, a couple of folding beds, and a game console with
three VR sets. Off the rec-room were a small kitchen area
and a shower unit.

"Man, this place stinks," said Sanjeev.

By noon he had cleaned it front to back, top to bottom,
magazines stacked in date of publication, shoes set together
in pairs, lost clothes in a black plastic sack for the *dhobiwal-
lah* to launder. He lit incense. He threw out the old bad milk
and turning food in the refrigerator, returned the empty
Coke bottles for their deposits—made *chai* and sneaked out
to get *samosas* which he passed off as his own. He nervously
watched Big Baba and Ravana step into their battle harnesses for a three-hour combat mission. So much he learned
in that first morning. It was not one boy one bot; Level 1.2
aeais controlled most of the autonomous process like motion and perception, the pilots were more like officers, each
commanding a bot platoon, their point-of-view switching
from scout machine to assault bot to I-war drone. And they
did not have their favorite old faithful combat machine,

scarred with bullet holes and lovingly customized with hand-sprayed graffiti and *Desi*-metal demons. Machines went to war because they could take damage human flesh and families could not. The Kali Cavalry rotated between a dozen units a month as attrition and the *jemadar* dictated. It was not not Japanese anime, but the Kali boys did look sexy dangerous cool in their gear even if they went home to their parents every night. And working for them—cleaning for them, getting towels for them when they went sweating and stinking to the shower after a tour in the combat rig—was the maximum thing in Sanjeev's small life. They were his children, they were his boys; no girls allowed.

"Hanging round with those *badmashes* all day, never seeing a wink of sun, that's not good, for you," his mother said, sweeping round the tiny top-floor living room before her next lesson. "Your dad needs the help more; he may have to hire a boy in. What kind of sense does that make, when he has a son of his own? They do not have a good reputation, those robot-boys."

Then Sanjeev showed her the money he had got for one day.

"Your mother worries about people taking advantage of you," Sanjeev's dad said, loading up the handcart with wood for the pizza oven. "You weren't born to this city. All I'd say is, don't love it too much; soldiers will let you down, they can't help it. All wars eventually end."

With what remained from his money when he had divided it between his mother and father and put some away in the credit union for Priya, Sanjeev went down to Tea Lane and stuck down the deposit and first payment on a pair of big metally leathery black-and-red and flame-pattern boots. He wore them proudly to work the next day, stuck out beside the driver of the *phatphat* so everyone could see them and paid the owner of the Bata Boot and Shoe store assiduously every Friday. At the end of twelve weeks they were Sanjeev's entirely. In that time he had also bought the Ts, the fake-latex pants (real latex hot hot far too hot and sweaty for Varanasi, *baba*), the Kali bangles and necklaces, the hair gel and the eye kohl but the boots first, the boots before all. Boots make the robotwallah.

"Do you fancy a go?"

It was one of those questions so simple and unexpected that Sanjeev's brain rolled straight over it and it was only when he was gathering up the fast food wrappers (messy messy boys) that it crept up and hit him over the head.

"What, you mean, that?" A nod of the head toward the harnesses hanging like flayed hides from the feedback rig.

"If you want; there's not much on."

There hadn't been much on for the better part of a month. The last excitement had been when some cracker in a similar go-down in Delhi had broken through the Kali Cav's aeai firewall with a spike of burnware. Big Baba had suddenly leaped up in his rig like a million billion volts had just shot through (which, Sanjeev discovered later, it kind of had) and next thing the biocontrol interlocks had blown (indoor fireworks, woo) and he was kicking on the floor like epilepsy. Sanjeev had been first to the red button, and a crash team had whisked him to the rich people's private hospital. The aeais had evolved a patch against the new burnware by the time Sanjeev went to get the lunch tins from the *dhabawallah,* and Big Baba was back on his corner of the sofa within three days suffering nothing more than a lingering migraine. *Jemadar*-woman sent a get well e-card.

So it was with excitement and wariness that Sanjeev let Rai help him into the rig. He knew all the snaps and grips—he had tightened the straps and pulled snug the motion sensors a hundred times—but Rai doing it made it special, made Sanjeev a robotwallah.

"You might find this a little freaky," Rai said as he settled the helmet over Sanjeev's head. For an instant it was blackout, deafness as the phonobuds sought out his eardrums. "They're working on this new thing, some kind of bone induction thing so they can send the pictures and sounds straight into your brain," he heard Rai's voice say on the com. "But I don't think we'll get it in time. Now, just stand there and don't shoot anything."

The warning was still echoing in Sanjeev's inner ear as he blinked and found himself standing outside a school compound in a village so like Ahraura that he instinctively looked for Mrs. Mawji and Shree the holy red calf. Then he saw that the school was deserted, its roof gone, replaced with military camouflage sheeting. The walls were pocked with bullets down to the brickwork. Siva and Krishna with his flute had been hastily painted on the intact mud plaster, and the words, *13th Mechanized Sowars: Section headquarters.* There were men in smart, tightly belted uniforms with mustaches and bamboo *lathis*. Women with brass water pots and men on bicycles passed the open gate. By stretching Sanjeev found he could elevate his sensory rig to crane over the wall. A village, an Ahraura, but too poor to even avoid war. On his left a robot stood under a dusty neem tree. *I must be one of those,* Sanjeev thought; a General Dynamics A8330 *Syce;* a mean, skeletal desert-rat of a thing on two vicious clawed feet, a heavy sensory crown and two gatling arms—fully interchangeable with gas shells or slime guns for policing work, he remembered from *War Mecha*'s October 2038 edition.

Sanjeev glanced down at his own feet. Icons opened across his field of vision like blossoming flowers: location elevation temperature, ammunition load-out, the level of methane in his fuel tanks, tactical and strategic satmaps— he seemed to be in southwest Bihar—but what fascinated Sanjeev was that if he formed a mental picture of lifting his Sanjeev-foot, his *Syce*-claw would lift from the dust.

Go on try it it's a quiet day you're on sentry duty in some cow-shit Bihar village.

Forward, he willed. The bot took one step two. *Walk,* Sanjeev commanded. *There.* The robot walked jauntily toward the gate. No one in the street of shattered houses looked twice as he stepped among them. *This is great!* Sanjeev thought as he strolled down the street, then, *This is like a game.* Doubt then: *So how do I even know this war is happening?* A step too far; the Syce froze a hundred meters from the Ganesh temple, turned and headed back to its sentry post. *What what what what what?* he yelled in his head.

"The onboard aeai took over," Rai said, his voice startling as a firecracker inside his helmet. Then the village went black and silent and Sanjeev was blinking in the ugly low-energy neons of the Kali Cavalry battle room, Rai gently unfastening the clips and snaps and strappings.

That evening, as he went home through the rush of people with his fist of rupees, Sanjeev realized two things; that most of war was boring, and that this boring war was over.

The war was over. The *jemadar* visited the video-silk wall three times, twice, once a week where in the heat and glory she would have given orders that many times a day. The Kali Cav lolled around on their sofas playing games, lying to their online fans about the cool exciting sexy things they were doing—though the fans never believed they ever really were robotwallahs—but mostly doing battle-drug combos that left them fidgety and aggressive. Fights flared over a cigarette, a look, how a door was closed or left open. Sanjeev threw himself into the middle of a dozen robotwallah wars. But when the American Peacekeepers arrived Sanjeev knew it truly was over because they only came in when there was absolutely no chance any of them would get killed. There was a flurry of car-bombings and I-war attacks and even a few suicide blasts but everyone knew that that was just everyone who had a grudge against America and Americans in sacred Bharat. No, the war was over.

"What will you do?" Sanjeev's father asked, meaning, *What will I do when Umbrella Street becomes just another Asian ginza?*

"I've saved some money," Sanjeev said.

With the money he had saved Godspeed! bought a robot. It was a Tata Industries D55, a small but nimble anti-personnel bot with detachable free-roaming sub-mechas, Level 0.8s, about as smart as a chicken, which they resembled. Even secondhand it must have cost much more than a teenage robotwallah heavily consuming games, online time, porn, and Sanjeev's dad's kofta pizza could ever save. "I got backers," Godspeed! said. "Funding. Hey, what do you think of this? I'm getting her pimped; this is the skin-job." When the paint dried the robot would be road-freighted up to Varanasi.

"But what are you going to do with it?" Sanjeev asked.

"Private security. They're always going to need security drones."

Tidying the tiny living room that night for his mother's nine o'clock lesson, opening the windows to let out the smell of hot ghee though the stink of the street was little better, Sanjeev heard a new chord in the ceaseless song of Umbrella Street. He threw open the window shutters in time to see a object, close, fast as a dashing bird, dart past his face, swing along the powerline and down the festooned pylon. Glint of anodized alu-plastic: a boy raised on *Battlebots Top Trumps* could not fail to recognize a Tata surveillance mecha. Now the commotion at the end of the Umbrella Street became clear: the hunched back of a battlebot was pushing between the cycle rickshaws and phatphats. Even before he could fully make out the customized god-demons of Mountain Buddhism on its carapace, Sanjeev knew the machine's make and model and who was flying it.

A *badmash* on an alco moto rode slowly in front of the ponderously stepping machine, relishing the way the street opened in front of him and the electric scent of heavy firepower at his back. Sanjeev saw the mech step up and squat down on its hydraulics before Jagmohan's greasy little pakora stand. The *badmash* skidded his moped to a stand and pushed up his shades.

They will always need security drones.

Sanjeev rattled down the many many flights of stairs of the patriotically renamed Diljit Rana Apartments, yelling and pushing and beating at the women and young men in very white shirts. The robot had already taken up its position in front of his father's big clay pizza oven. The carapace unfolded like insect wings into weapon mounts. *Badmash* was all teeth and grin in the anticipation of another commission. Sanjeev dashed between his father and the prying, insect sensory rig of the robot. Red demons and Sivas with fiery tridents looked down on him.

"Leave him alone, this is my dad, leave him be."

It seemed to Sanjeev that the whole of Umbrella Street, every vehicle upon it, every balcony and window that overlooked it, stopped to watch. With a whir the weapon pods retracted, the carapace clicked shut. The battle machine reared up on its legs as the surveillance drones came skittering between people's legs and over countertops, scurried up the machine and took their places on its shell mounts, like egrets on the back of a buffalo. Sanjeev stared the *badmash* down. He sneered, snapped down his cool sexy dangerous shades and spun his moped away.

Two hours later, when all was safe and secure, a Peacekeeper unit had passed up the street asking for information. Sanjeev shook his head and sucked on his asthma inhalers.

"Some machine, like."

Suni left the go-down. No word no note no clue, his family had called and called and called but no one knew. There had always been rumors of a man with money and prospects, who liked the robotwallah thing, but you do not tell those sorts of stories to mothers. Not at first asking. A week passed without the *jemadar* calling. It was over. So over. Rai had taken to squatting outside, squinting up through his cool sexy dangerous shades at the sun, watching for its burn on his pale arms, chain-smoking street-rolled *bidis*.

"Sanj." He smoked the cheap cigarette down to his gloved fingers and ground the stub out beneath the steel heel of his boot. "When it happens, when we can't use you anymore, have you something sorted? I was thinking, maybe you and I could do something together, go somewhere. Just have it like it was, just us. An idea, that's all."

The message came at 3 A.M. *I'm outside.* Sanjeev tiptoed around the sleeping bodies to open the window. Umbrella Street was still busy; Umbrella Street had not slept for a thousand years. The big black Kali Cav Hummer was like a funeral moving through the late-night people of the new Varanasi. The door locks made too much noise, so Sanjeev exited through the window, climbing down the pipes like a Raytheon 8-8000 I-war infiltration bot. In Ahraura he would never have been able to do that.

"You drive," Rai said. From the moment the message came

through, Sanjeev had known it would be him, and him alone.

"I can't drive."

"It drives itself. All you have to do is steer. It's not that different from the game. Swap over there."

Steering wheel pedal drive windshield display all suddenly looked very big to Sanjeev in the driver's seat. He touched his foot to the gas. Engines answered; the Hummer rolled; Umbrella Street parted before him. He steered around a wandering cow.

"Where do you want me to go?"

"Somewhere, away. Out of Varanasi. Somewhere no one else would go." Rai bounced and fidgeted on the passenger seat. His hands were busy busy; his eyes were huge. He had done a lot of battle drugs. "They sent them back to school, man. To school, can you imagine that? Big Baba and Ravana. Said they needed real-world skills. I'm not going back, not never. Look!"

Sanjeev dared a glance at the treasure in Rai's palm: a curl of sculpted translucent pink plastic. Sanjeev thought of aborted goat fetuses, and the sex toys the girls had used in their favorite pornos. Rai tossed his head to sweep back his long, gelled hair and slid the device behind his ear. Sanjeev thought he saw something move against Rai's skin, seeking.

"I saved it all up and bought it. Remember, I said? It's new; no one else has one. All that gear, that's old, you can do everything with this, just in your head, in the pictures and words in your head." He gave a stoned grin and moved his hands in a dancer's *mudra*. "There."

"What?"

"You'll see."

The Hummer was easy to drive: the in-car aeai had a flocking reflex that enabled it to navigate Varanasi's ever-swelling morning traffic, leaving little for Sanjeev to do other than blare the triple horns, which he enjoyed a lot. Somewhere he knew he should be afraid, should feel guilty at stealing away in the night without word or note, should stay stop, whatever it is you are doing, it can come to noth-

ing, it's just silliness, the war is over and we must think
properly about what to do next. But the brass sun was rising
above the glass towers and spilling into the streets, and men
in sharp white shirts and women in smart saris were going
busy to their work, and he was free, driving a big smug car
through them all and it was so good, even if just for a day.

He took the new bridge at Ramnagar, hooting in derision
at the gaudy, lumbering trucks. The drivers blared back,
shouting vile curses at the *girli*-looking robotwallahs. Off
A-roads on to B-roads, then to tracks and then bare dirt, the
dust flying up behind the Hummer's fat wheels. Rai itched
in the passenger seat, grinning away to himself and moving
his hands like butterflies, muttering small words and occasionally sticking out of the window. His gelled hair was stiff
with dust.

"What are you looking for?" Sanjeev demanded.

"It's coming," Rai said, bouncing on his seat. "Then we
can go and do whatever we like."

From the word "drive," Sanjeev had known where he must
go. Satnav and aeai did his remembering for him, but he still
knew every turn and side road. Vora's Wood there, still
stunted and gray; the ridge between the river and the fields
from which all the men of the village had watched the battle
and he had fallen in love with the robots. The robots had always been pure, had always been true. It was the boys who
flew them who hurt and failed and disappointed. The fields
were all dust, drifted and heaped against the lines of thorn
fence. Nothing would grow here for a generation. The mud
walls of the houses were crumbling, the school a roofless
shell, the temple and tanks clogged with wind-blown dust.
Dust, all dust. Bones cracked and went to powder beneath
his all-wheel-drive. A few too desperate even for Varanasi
were trying to scratch an existence in the ruins. Sanjeev saw
wire-thin men and tired women, dust-smeared children
crouched in front of their brick-and-plastic shelters. The
poison deep within Ahraura would defeat them in the end.

Sanjeev brought the Hummer to a halt on the ridgetop.
The light was yellow, the heat appalling. Rai stepped out to
survey the terrain.

"What a shit-hole."

Sanjeev sat in the shade of the rear cabin watching Rai pace up and down, up and down, kicking up the dust of Ahraura with his big Desi-metal boots. *You didn't stop them, did you?* Sanjeev thought. *You didn't save us from the Plaguewalkers.* Rai suddenly leaped and punched the air.

"There, there, look!"

A storm of dust moved across the dead land. The high sun caught glints and gleams at its heart. Moving against the wind, the tornado bore down on Ahraura.

The robot came to a halt at the foot of the ridge where Sanjeev and Rai stood waiting. A Raytheon ACR, a heavy line-of-battle bot, it out-topped them by some meters. The wind carried away its cloak of dust. It stood silent, potential, heat shimmering from its armor. Sanjeev had never seen a thing so beautiful.

Rai raised his hand. The bot spun on its steel hooves. More guns than Sanjeev had ever seen in his life unfolded from its carapace. Rai clapped his hands and the bot opened up with all its armaments on Vora's Wood. Gatlings sent dry dead silvery wood flying up into powder; missiles streaked from its back-silos. The line of the wood erupted in a wall of flame. Rai separated his hands, and the roar of sustained fire ceased.

"It's got it all in here, everything that the old gear had, in here. Sanj, everyone will want us, we can go wherever we want we can do whatever we want, we can be real anime heroes."

"You stole it."

"I had all the protocols. That's the system."

"You stole that robot."

Rai balled his fists, shook his head in exasperation.

"Sanj, it was always mine."

He opened his clenched fist. And the robot danced. Arms, feet, all the steps and the moves, the bends and head-nods, a proper Bollywood item-song dance. The dust flew up around the battle-bots feet. Sanjeev could feel the eyes of the squatters, wide and terrified in their hovels. *I am sorry we scared you.*

Rai brought the dance to an end.

"Anything I want, Sanj. Are you coming with us?"

Sanjeev's answer never came for a sudden, shattering roar of engines and jet-blast from the river side of the ridge sent them reeling and choking in the swirling dust. Sanjeev fought out his inhalers: two puffs blue one puff brown and by the time they had worked their sweet way down into his lungs a tiltjet with the Bharati Air Force's green white and orange roundels on its engine pods stood on the settling dust. The cargo ramp lowered; a woman in dust-war camo and a mirror-visored helmet came up the ridge toward them.

With a wordless shriek Rai slashed his hand through the air like a sword. The bot crouched; its carapace slid open in a dozen places, extruding weapons. Without breaking her purposeful stride the woman lifted her left hand. The weapons retracted, the hull ports closed, the war machine staggered as if confused and then sat down heavily in the dead field, head sagging, hands trailing in the dust. The woman removed her helmet. The cameras made the *jemadar* look five kilos heavier, but she had big hips. She tucked her helmet under her left arm, with her right swept back her hair to show the plastic fetus-sex-toy-thing coiled behind her ear.

"Come on now, Rai. It's over. Come on, we'll go back. Don't make a fuss. There's not really anything you can do. We all have to think what to do next, you know? We'll take you back in the plane, you'll like that." She looked Sanjeev up and down. "I suppose you could take the car back. Someone has to and it'll be cheaper than sending someone down from Divisional, it's cost enough already. I'll retask the aeai. And then we have to get that thing . . ." She shook her head, then beckoned to Rai. He went like a calf, quiet and meek down to the tiltjet. Black hopping crows settled on the robot, trying its crevices with their curious shiny-hungry beaks.

The Hummer ran out of gas twenty kays from Ramnagar. Sanjeev hitched home to Varanasi. The army never collected it, and as the new peace built, the local people took it away bit by bit.

With his war dividend Sanjeev bought a little alco-buggy and added a delivery service to his father's pizza business, specializing in the gap-year hostels that blossomed after the Peacekeepers left. He wore a polo shirt with a logo and a baseball cap and got a sensible haircut. He could not bring himself to sell his robotwallah gear, but it was a long time before he could look at it in the box without feeling embarrassed. The business grew fast and fat.

He often saw Rai down at the ghats or around the old town. They worked the same crowd: Rai dealt Nepalese *ganja* to tourists. *Robotwallah* was his street name. He kept the old look and everyone knew him for it. It became first a novelty and then retro. It even became fashionable again, the spiked hair, the andro makeup, the slashed Ts and the latex and most of all the boots. It sold well and everyone wore it, for a season.

Third Person

TONY BALLANTYNE

Tony Ballantyne, who is having a particularly good year,
appears for a second time in this book. (See also "Aristotle
OS," earlier.)

"Third Person," which appeared in The Solaris Book of
New Science Fiction, *edited by George Mann, addresses*
some of the same life-in-wartime subject matter as the Marc
Laidlaw, Ian McDonald, and Kage Baker stories. Here sol-
diers are fighting a war as though it were a LARP, along-
side normal people going about their lives. Military drugs
blur the distinction. In Nancy Kress' "Writing FAQ," she
discusses literary point of view: ". . . the best bet is usually
third person limited—limited to one character. This is easi-
est because there's only one character to keep track of. You
don't have to be inside his head or reproduce his diction
the way you would in first person." Here, Ballantyne ex-
trapolates a weaponized version of the third person, de-
ployed to give the military an unending stream of recruits.

The Steam Bomb was a perforated metal shell the size of a tennis ball, filled with water and loaded with an F-Charge. On detonation it squirted needles of pressurized steam that drilled through anything within a radius of half a meter and left anything at a radius of one meter slightly damp. The bomb that landed in the hot street tore apart Bundy's upper thighs, punctured his stomach, and left his forehead covered in a refreshing pink mist.

"It came from up there, Sergeant," murmured Chapelhow into his headset, pointing to the roof of a nearby house. Mitchell fired his rifle with a muffled crack and an overweight woman slumped forward and fell from the roof. No contest. Mitchell was a regular, she was just a conscript, flushed and confused by the hot Spanish sun. Mitchell lowered his black rifle and resumed his patient scanning of the surrounding area, black gloved hands ready on his gun, black booted feet planted wide.

Bundy was screaming without seeming to notice it. He was fumbling at his rifle with blood slicked hands, trying to reload. Sergeant Clausen shook his head.

"He's done," he said. "Chapelhow, finish him."

Chapelhow felt his stomach churning; nonetheless he raised his cheap conscript's rifle to his shoulder and shot Bundy through the head, silencing his screams. The brass bound round the wounded man had been trying to load slipped from his fingers and rolled across the road. Chapelhow was rubbing his shoulder through his thin silk shirt, the kick of the rifle too much for his thin frame.

"Take his gun," chided Sergeant Clausen impatiently, "we're going to need it."

Despite his thick black uniform, Mitchell looked cool. Just like the sergeant. They weren't sweating like the conscripts. They didn't have dark patches beneath their armpits from their exertions, nor did they have beads of moisture on their upper lips. They moved like lazy cats, turning this way and that to scan the dusty street.

"There'll be more, Sarge," said Mitchell. "SEA always try for the pincher."

"I know. Chapelhow, Hamblion, go back toward the seafront. Singh, Reed, up toward the town. See if you can spot anyone else."

Chapelhow knew what it meant, to be paired with Hamblion. Hamblion was grossly overweight. He was expendable. If Hamblion was going back to the seafront, then that was where the sergeant was expecting the attack to come from.

Most of the buildings were shut up for the midday siesta. The only sign of activity came from a man in a white shirt, carrying little round-topped tables and setting them out in the shade just in front of his bar. The expendable Hamblion waddled past him, staying in the shade where he could, his arms burnt bright red from the sun, like sore corned beef, his pudgy hand making his rifle look like a stick of liquorice. Chapelhow limped along on the opposite side of the street. The thin soles on his expensive leather slip-on shoes were coming loose, more suitable for a night out clubbing than for a conscripted soldier on a sortie. The sound of the sea and the shouts of the few children left playing on the beach could be heard up ahead. There was a scraping noise as a door opened in a house on the shady side of the street. Chapelhow jumped, he and Hamblion turning their guns toward it. Two middle-aged women walked out, chattering in Spanish. They wore floral print skirts, their hair permed in short curls. Both carried smart leather handbags.

Chapelhow relaxed, turning his rifle back toward the sea. The two women pulled pistols from their handbags and pointed them up the street at the sergeant. Chapelhow shot the one on the left, grunting as the recoil slammed the rifle into his shoulder again. Hamblion's fat finger caught in the trigger guard and he clumsily fired his rifle up into the air. A third person, a man dressed in the dark green uniform of the Southern European Alliance stepped out from the dark doorway and calmly aimed at the sergeant. Hamblion paused in the act of loading his rifle, realizing there wasn't time. He dropped the gun to the floor and stepped forward in front of the man in green, his body giving a great hiccup as the enemy fired.

Chapelhow shot the second of the Spanish ladies and calmly reloaded. He could see Hamblion hanging onto the soldier as the enemy emptied his rifle into his fat body, wobbling waves spasming up and down his length with each shot.

Now Chapelhow shot the soldier. Sergeant Clausen's voice sounded in his headset.

"Chapelhow. Get Hamblion's rifle and fall back to me."

"Okay, Sarge." Chapelhow scooped up the rifle and limped back up the road.

"What now, Sarge?" Mitchell queried through the headset.

"We're going into the town."

"Won't that make us easier to pinpoint?"

"Yes. But there are too many of them around. We'll use the civilians as cover."

"We need a drink, Sarge," said Reed from the other end of the street.

"And something to eat," added Singh.

"We do," agreed the sergeant. "There'll be cafés and bars in the town. Shops. We can get something there."

Chapelhow came limping up to the sergeant and Mitchell, a rifle slung over each shoulder.

"Got any money, Chapelhow?" asked the sergeant. Chapelhow reached awkwardly into the breast pocket of his paisley shirt.

"I've got about twenty Euros, Sarge," he said, sorting through the bills. There was a yellow piece of notepaper there with the words "You are Andy Chapelhow" scrawled hurriedly across the top.

"I've got money," said Singh.

Chapelhow was unfolding the yellow notepaper, looking to see what else was written there.

"There'll be time for that later," said the sergeant, batting at Chapelhow's hand. "Come on. We'll go into town."

The sergeant touched the pale-green pouch that hung from his belt and looked at Mitchell. "We can round up some more recruits when we get there."

"We'll need them," said Mitchell.

Chapelhow nodded in silent agreement as he looked back at the mound of flesh that had been Hamblion, his hot blood spreading in a pool in the middle of the road, reflecting the scorching sun.

The center of the town was a maze of shady twisting alleys built on a hill. Alleys filled with the hot spicy smells of lunch, with the chatter of conversation that echoed from the tiled and crowded tapas bars, alleys filled with little tables at which couples drank wine and families of tourists ordered sausages and chips and spread out pictures for their children to color.

Chapelhow and the rest walked past all of this, alert and exhausted.

"Where are we going?" asked Reed brightly.

"Right through the town and out the other side," said Mitchell.

"Why can't they just send a helicopter or a flier to pick us up?" complained Reed, only just eighteen, and consequently an expert at everything. Chapelhow envied her for her certainty. More than that though, he envied her for her walking boots, for her light jacket, and shorts. Reed had been out hiking when the sergeant had conscripted her.

"They will send us something," said Mitchell patiently. "But if we're too obvious about it, the Europeans will just wait until we are on board and then shoot us down. That's what an exit strategy is all about. Both us and the helicopter have to rendezvous unnoticed by the enemy."

"So where are we going?"

"That's a secret. What if you got captured?"

"Hmm. Is that why you won't tell us what's in that package you are carrying?" She pointed to the cylinder the sergeant had strapped to his belt. "Did you steal it from the SEA? Is that why they are chasing us?"

"You don't need to know that, Reed." Mitchell smiled.

There was a crack and Singh spun round, raising his rifle and pointing it at a nearby table. The sergeant knocked the gun up into the air.

"Hey, hey, hey," said the diners at a nearby table. There was some angry shouting in Spanish. Chapelhow's headset translated the words of a patrician-looking older man for him. "You watch where you're pointing that thing. We'll sue you and your army." The man jabbed a finger angrily in their direction.

"It was just a champagne cork," said the sergeant.

A mustached waiter smiled as he filled the glasses of the diners. Chapelhow thought it was funny, how quickly people adapted to technology. Only halfway through the twenty-first century and already people believed in surgical strikes and targeted weapons. They felt safe, even with a war going on around them. Chapelhow grinned to himself. They wouldn't be so complacent if they knew how old the guns were that he and the other conscripts carried.

"We should hide the rifles," said Reed. "We stand out carrying them. What if they inform on us?" She pointed to the diners.

"Then they enter the field of combat and we can shoot them," replied Mitchell in a loud voice. He wanted the smiling waiter to hear.

Sergeant Clausen was getting impatient.

"This is no good. We need to eat and we need more conscripts." He tapped a finger against his teeth, thinking.

"We're going to have to split up," he said suddenly. "Mitchell. You and Singh take the rifles and the package. Get up high where you can watch us. Reed, Chapelhow and I will go eat and get talking with the locals. See if we can press some recruits."

"What about your uniform, Sarge?" asked Reed.

"Good point," he replied. "You can help me buy some civvies, Reed."

Sergeant Clausen looked different in civilian clothes. Dressed in a white open-necked shirt, a gold chain around his neck, he looked younger and more handsome. But with a dangerous edge to him. Chapelhow could see that Reed had picked up on it. She was only just eighteen and she hadn't yet learned about men like Clausen, he guessed. "You look good, Sarge," she said, obviously coming on to him.

"It took too long," complained the sergeant. "Bloody shops shut for lunch."

"Let's go here," said Reed, pointing to a restaurant that backed onto the sea. Behind it they could just see a terrace poking out, white-jacketed waiters moving about in the cool breeze.

"No," said the sergeant. "We need to get inland. We could be seen from a ship kilometers out on that terrace. Picked off by laser. They could see us back in Africa."

"Is that where the package comes from, Sarge?" asked Reed cheekily.

"Shut up about the package. That's an order."

There was a café on a corner that gave a good view down the three streets that led to it. The sergeant chose a table and positioned his team so they could watch every approach. He ordered a carafe of red wine and a large bottle of water.

"Don't drink the wine," he said. "Don't get drunk."

He glanced up at the second-storey window of a nearby building. Chapelhow saw a shadowy movement within and guessed that Mitchell and Singh were up there.

The sergeant was listening to the voices from the tables around him. For the first time since his conscription, Chapelhow missed his headset, he missed being able to understand what the Spanish were saying. And then, in the midst of the hubbub, he heard English voices. A little girl squabbling with her sister. And over there, a young couple, sharing their meals with each other, the woman holding out a forkful of fish to her boyfriend to taste.

Sergeant Clausen smiled.

"I'm just going to the toilet," he said, clapping his hands on his knees. He stood up and walked off, taking something from his pocket as he did so.

The waiter arrived with their water and their wine.

"Are you ready to order?" he asked in heavily accented English.

"Steak, chips, and salad for all three of us," said Reed. She shrugged at Chapelhow. That had been Sergeant Clausen's orders. Plenty of protein and carbohydrate.

"What's that?" she asked. Chapelhow had taken the yellow piece of paper from his pocket.

"I don't know," said Chapelhow. "It says 'You are Andy Chapelhow.' This paper is kept in Andy Chapelhow's pocket . . ."

"What does it mean?"

"I'm not sure."

Reed was already bored. "What do you suppose is in the package? The one that the sergeant gave to Mitchell?"

"I don't know. Africa is in the news a lot lately. There's a lot of technological development going on there and the West doesn't like it. It doesn't like being left behind. I think the sergeant's team was sent there . . ."

"What team?"

"I'm not sure. There's only the sarge and Mitchell left now. Look, forget the questions. All that's important is that we get that package delivered." And then maybe we can get back to normal, he thought.

Sergeant Clausen reappeared. Chapelhow quickly folded the paper back into his pocket. The sergeant sat down, took a drink of water and leant back in his chair.

"Hey!" he said, turning to the young couple at the next table. "Is that a north eastern accent?"

"Yes," said the young man delightedly. "We're from Darlington."

"What a coincidence! My grandparents were from Darlington. I used to go there as a child. Is that shop still there on the High Street? The one that sold all those nice sweets?"

"I don't know which one you mean," said the young woman suspiciously.

"Hey, it's probably gone by now. My name's David by the way. This is Pippa and Andy."

"I'm Tom and this is Katie," said the young man. He wore a new yellow shirt with white buttons, new shorts, and new sandals. Chapelhow guessed he had been dressed for his holiday by his girlfriend.

The waiter approached the couple's table with an ice bucket.

"We didn't order this," said Katie.

"Compliments of the house," said the waiter. "Enjoy your holiday." He took a white linen wrapped bottle from the bucket and poured them both a glass of white wine.

"He probably thinks it's your honeymoon or something," said the sergeant. "You are an attractive couple."

He held up his own wineglass. "Cheers."

They all drank each others' health.

"That's very nice," said Tom.

"So, David, what are you doing here?" asked Katie, suspiciously.

"Oh. Enjoying the sun and the local food. Relaxing and forgetting my troubles. The war's not going so well, is it?"

"I thought as much," said Katie. "You're a soldier. I could tell by the way you were sitting to attention."

David Clausen laughed. "Bright girl. We could do with someone like you in the forces."

"It's not going to happen." She sipped at her wine primly. "I won't join up."

"Why not? Don't you believe Britain has the right to defend its interests?"

"Of course. It's when Britain starts interfering in other countries' interests I get uncomfortable. Particularly those who are not as well off as we are. Because your sort of fighting isn't about defense, is it David? It's just about money. Which corporation is bankrolling your regiment?"

"I hear it's not going well in Africa," said Tom, frowning at Katie as he changed the subject.

"It's not as bad as you'd think," said David, still smiling at Katie. "The Orange States have split from the Southern European Alliance. The SEAs are fighting a war on two fronts now."

"Don't the SEA have some sort of way of controlling the animals?" asked Tom. "That's what I heard. That must be nasty."

David Clausen laughed.

"I'd rather be attacked by an elephant than another soldier. At least elephants don't shoot back at you." He lowered his voice and spoke in confidential tones. "Actually, Tom, it's the mosquitoes that are the worst. You don't get any peace at night."

"I think it's cruel to the animals," said Katie.

"So do I," agreed David. "But it's crueller to the soldiers. It's weird, isn't it, Katie? People are more concerned about animals than humans. They all agree that the war is a just cause, but they are not willing to fight it themselves."

"Just cause? I heard the Orange States have perfected cold fusion. I wonder how much that would be worth?" She paused, making her point. "Anyway, the soldiers choose to fight. The animals don't."

"Not true anymore," said David. "They've got this drug, you see. They call it Third Person. It sort of detaches you from the scene. Once you've taken it, you lose all sense of identity. It's like you're reading about someone's life, rather than taking part in it. They give it to civilians to press them. Conscripts don't really have a choice whether they fight or not. Look at Pippa and Andy here."

Chapelhow looked across to Reed to see how she was taking it, being spoken about like that. She didn't seem to mind.

"I don't believe it," said Katie. "They'd never allow it. They'd ban it."

Clausen laughed. "You'd think so, wouldn't you? But the government knows which side its bread is buttered on. The big corporations bring in too much money." He gave a brilliant white smile. "And," he tapped his nose at this point, "little secret. Anyone who kicks up too much of a fuss gets put under the influence themselves."

He yawned and stretched, leant back in his chair, soaking up some rays. "Oh, they'll outlaw it eventually, I'm sure, but I reckon we've got a year or two left yet."

"I don't believe you."

Tom was looking at his glass of wine in horror.

"Katie," he said.

"No way," Katie's eyes widened with horror as she stared at the glass in front of her.

"You don't get complimentary bottles of wine for being an attractive couple," said Clausen, suddenly businesslike.

"But why us?"

"Because you're young, fit, and healthy. And besides, you're British, unlike just about everyone else here. I do this to the locals, and I get sued from here to dishonorable discharge."

"What about that family over there?" asked Katie desperately.

"You can't expect me to take the parents and leave the children to fend for themselves, can you?" said Clausen. "What sort of a monster do you think I am?"

He pulled out two sheets of electro paper from his pocket and spread them on the table before them.

"Just sign these contracts and you've enlisted."

Katie and Tom looked at each other, and then they signed them, as they weren't "I" anymore but someone else. Just observers.

The waiter turned up again carrying five plates of steak and chips and salad. He placed two before the young couple.

"Eat up your meal," said the sergeant to Katie and Tom. "You'll need all the energy you can get."

The platoon regrouped under the awning of a modern hotel, set on the edge of a wide road that led inland.

"This is Katie Prentice and Tom Fern." Sergeant Clausen was introducing the new conscripts to Mitchell.

"They look fit," said Mitchell, hungrily tearing away at a sandwich the Sergeant had brought him. Behind him came the roar of a diesel engine. A blue and white bus pulled away along the road, black smoke spilling over the hot tarmac. Mitchell pinched Fern's arm with mayonnaise-smeared fingers.

"Nice muscle tone. Do you work out?" he asked.

"Yes," the couple answered in unison.

"We go to the gym three times a week," added Prentice.

Mitchell nodded. He hefted the package in his hand. A cylinder, about thirty centimeters long. Chapelhow always thought it looked very heavy. Mitchell passed it to the sergeant.

"Well, Prentice," he said, "with any luck, you'll be back there within the week. Not long now, I hope."

Singh handed them their conscripts' rifles and showed them how to work the action that loaded and ejected bullets.

"These are ancient," said Fern.

"They're good enough," said the sergeant. "Mitchell. Save these two; they're the healthiest. Put Reed, Chapelhow, and Singh on point."

"Got it Sarge. What now?"

The sergeant gave a smile.

"We're headed inland. I thought we'd take the bus. They're never going to dare open fire with all those civilians around."

"Good idea."

"Come on."

They walked from under the hotel's awning into the hot sun, Chapelhow blinking as they went. He had never liked direct sunlight. The bus stop was just up the road a little, a small metal awning with several tourists sheltering beneath.

"Just relax on the bus," said the sergeant. "Save your energy for later. Reed and Chapelhow at the front. Singh at the back. Prentice next to me. Fern next to Mitchell."

It wasn't too long before a bus pulled in. The sign on the front said *Adventureland*. Chapelhow had heard of the place, a big theme park built up in the hills.

"This is the one," said the sergeant. "Off we go."

They climbed on board. Chapelhow and Reed sat next to each other at the front.

"Have you any more ideas what this?" asked Reed, looking at the yellow sheet of paper that Chapelhow had taken from his pocket.

"I sort of remember," said Chapelhow. "I think Chapelhow wrote it when the sergeant pressed him. He was in a bar on the cruise ship; his boyfriend had gone to bed. Too much sun. He was just having a coffee when the sergeant joined him. I think Chapelhow sort of fancied him, as he was flirting with him. He shouldn't have accepted that brandy . . ."

Chapelhow frowned.

"I . . . Chapelhow," Chapelhow blinked, rubbed his forehead. ". . . Chapelhow started to write this before the drug could properly take effect . . ."

Reed took the piece of paper from him and began to read out loud.

"You are Andy Chapelhow. This paper is kept in Andy Chapelhow's pocket. I am Andy Chapelhow. But already I feel like Andy Chapelhow is someone else. I must remember, you must remember who you are. It's like a story, Andy. You've got to see that all stories are told from one point of view. That point of view, the narrator, he's you. You've got to look out for the narrator. Find him and you find yourself. Don't lose your identity. You are Andy Chapelhow. Say it now. I am Andy Chapelhow."

" 'I am Andy Chapelhow,' " repeated Reed. "I don't think that's right. What does it mean when it says 'find the narrator'?"

"I think it's talking about point of view," said Chapelhow, "Like a story written in the third person. One of the characters will have the point of view, the reader will see what they see, they will empathize with them, but they won't really believe that they are there."

Reed looked puzzled. She shook her head.

"Nah. I don't get it."

The bus halted. Four well-dressed women got on. Permed

hair and smart leather handbags. They dropped a handful of Euros in the tray and made their way to the back of the bus.

The driver gunned the engine and they set off. They had left the town behind, driving into the full glare of the Spanish afternoon, riding along a smooth gray road that was climbing into the distant hills.

Chapelhow felt a tap on his shoulder.

"Hey, how did you pay for the meal, Chapelhow?"

"With my card, Sarge, how else?"

The sergeant's face flushed red and he swore. The well-dressed ladies in the seat opposite pursed their lips. Now that Chapelhow came to think about it, they looked just like the four women who had just boarded the bus.

The sergeant interrupted his thoughts.

"I thought you said you had money!"

"That was Singh. I only had twenty Euros!"

"Damn. Look at this!"

He held up Chapelhow's mobile, confiscated from him when Chapelhow had been pressed. There was a text message displayed.

Hello there, Sergeant Clausen. Chapelhow's bank is part-owned by the SEA, didn't you know? Nice of you to pinpoint yourself like that.

We have a proposition for you. Just leave the package on the bus, get off at the next stop, and we'll let you go unharmed. We won't even track you to your rendezvous point.

Do we have a deal?

"It sounds like a good deal to me, Sarge," said Reed.

"Like you have a say in things. I've punched for an emergency extraction. It will cost a fortune, it will risk the lives of the extraction team, but we need to do it. Get ready to move. Shit."

Chapelhow turned to follow his gaze.

Four more well-dressed ladies stood by the side of the road. There was a bus stop there, right in the middle of nowhere. Nothing but scrubby land could be seen, baking in the hot sun. The driver was already decelerating.

"All that permed hair," muttered the sergeant in disbelief.

"Did they conscript a Spanish townswomen's guild or something?" He pulled a grenade from his pocket.

"There are greenhouses over there, Sarge," said Reed. She pointed to the low, steamy plastic shapes that glinted oddly in the distance. "They could be workers from those?"

"Dressed like that?" said the sergeant. He clicked a thumb down on the button and called out to the driver.

"Hey Pedro. You stop this bus and I let go of the button, got it?"

The bus driver let off a rapid stream of angry Spanish. Chapelhow's headset translated. "You threaten me, señor, and I'll sue your ass off."

"This isn't a threat," said the sergeant easily. "It's a suicide attempt. I just can't bear the thought of you stopping here. You compendre?"

Reed giggled.

"Sarge, what's the use of speaking in Spanish when your headset's translating everything?"

The driver stamped down on the accelerator, causing the bus to jerk violently and the sergeant to nearly lose his balance. The women by the bus stop pulled pistols from their handbags and took aim. They didn't fire. There were too many civilians on the bus. Chapelhow held the gaze of one of them as they drove past. She smiled at him and shrugged.

"Who did that?" asked Reed. She was pointing across the aisle. The two well-dressed women opposite were slumped forward in their seats, their eyes closed.

"Mitchell and Prentice shot them while you were distracted," said the sergeant. "I tell you, that girl shows promise. It's a shame she didn't enlist voluntarily. Now, watch the road, you two. See if you can do as well as Prentice and spot any other spies before they pull their guns." He turned to the driver. "Pedro, open the bus door."

"Stop calling me Pedro."

The driver opened the door anyway. The sergeant took hold of the nearest of the dead women by the collar of her silk blouse. He rolled her out of her seat and through the door, then sat in her place. Chapelhow turned to watch the body tumbling along the road, limbs flailing like a rag doll. There was a shout of indignation from further up the bus.

"Do you mind? We have children with us!" Chapelhow's headset spoke with a German accent.

"Something behind us, Sarge!" That was Singh's voice. "Long green thing. Coming up fast."

"Troop car," said Mitchell. "Get down fast, Singh. It will have a laser targeting turret . . ."

There was a tinkle of glass and sudden burst of static that was quickly killed.

"They got Singh," said Mitchell. "How much longer, Sarge?"

"Pickup craft is coming in now," said the sergeant. "Approaching from the right-hand side of the bus, the side with the door."

Reed and Chapelhow were calm.

"Think we're going to make it, Chapelhow?"

"I don't know. Does it matter? The mission is the important thing. As long as we get the package on the pickup . . ."

A low rumble sounded, followed by a supersonic boom off to their right. Then another one, then another.

"Stop here, Pedro," shouted the sergeant.

A roar of diesel and they were all thrown backward as the driver accelerated again. There was a popping noise and the driver began to scream. Red blood was spurting from his right hand.

"I'll sue you, you and your fucking army, senor!"

"Sue us for a million. We'll pay. This is more important." He swung his gun to the driver's head. "Now, are you going to stop the bus?"

There was a squeal of brakes and they were all thrown forward. A child started to cry. There was a series of popping sounds as the sergeant fired his gun in the air. Lines of sunlight shafted down from the roof, one after the other. He spoke, his headset translating into Spanish.

"Okay, my name is Sergeant David Clausen. I am part of the Naghani Associates regiment of the UK army. Any claims for compensation should be made to Naghani Asso-

ciates in the first instance. Listen up now. This is a grenade."
He held a dark egg shape up in the air. "I have set a motion
sensor on it. If you remove it from its place here on the luggage rack it will explode." Carefully he placed the grenade
on the rack. "Further," he added, "I have set the timer for ten
minutes. More than enough time for us to safely get off this
bus."

His words were repeated in German and the English.

There was a low rumble of indignation, but already the
passengers were moving from their seats.

"Chapelhow, Reed. Wait for three people to get off, and
then you follow them out. I'll send out Prentice in the middle of the crowd, then me. Fern and Mitchell can bring up
the rear. The civilians should provide us with enough cover.
Okay, go!"

Chapelhow and Reed waited for three young men in
shorts to climb off the bus. They smelled of old aftershave
and alcohol and seemed quite excited by their adventure.
They were pointing to a rapidly growing dot on the horizon.

"That must be the pickup," said Reed. "It doesn't look
that big. Do you think we can all get on board?"

"Probably not," said Chapelhow. "Probably just enough
space for the sergeant and Mitchell."

"Maybe he'll try and squeeze Prentice on too," said Reed.
Behind her the driver was whimpering as he stared at his
hand. "Okay," said Reed. "Our turn."

They both got off the bus, rifles held at the ready. The
afternoon sun beat down on their heads. Chapelhow felt the
uneven ground through the thin soles of his shoes.

"Keep moving, Reed," he said, "come away from the
door."

A dusty wind blew up. The pickup ship was descending.
Not much bigger than a large car, it was little more than a
silver wing with a large transparent canopy on top. Chapelhow saw the pilot scanning the skies through a large pair of
dark goggles as she descended.

More passengers were spilling out into the sun. Three
wheels dropped down from the pickup just as it was about to

hit the ground. It bounced once on its undercarriage. The pilot slid back the canopy with a whirr.

"Come on," she called. "Get on board."

The sergeant was pushing his way forward.

"Out of my way," he called. Mitchell and Prentice followed behind. "Prentice on first," shouted the sergeant, handing her the package.

"Told you," said Reed. "There's not enough seats for all of us. I wonder what will happen when that thing takes off? Who is carrying the point of view for this story?"

"What do you mean?" asked Chapelhow.

"Like it said on that sheet of paper in your pocket. Who has the point of view? You, or me, or the sergeant? Will the story follow the pickup, or stay here on the ground?"

But Chapelhow didn't answer. An olive-colored arrow had slid to a halt on the road behind the bus. A hatch opened in its side and soldiers came tumbling out. Real soldiers, dressed in the green of the SEA and carrying state-of-the-art, limited radius weapons. The sort that were safe to use when civilians were around. One swung a tube in the direction of the sergeant.

"You're closest," said Reed to Chapelhow.

Something was fired from the tube. Steam bomb. Lazily it flew through the air toward the sergeant, about to follow Prentice on board the pickup craft. Chapelhow flung himself forward into its path and

The Bridge

KATHLEEN ANN GOONAN

Kathleen Ann Goonan (www.goonan.com) lives in Tavernier, Florida, and in the mountains of Tennessee. She burst into prominence in the SF field in the mid 1990s with Queen City Jazz (1995), which became the first of four volumes to date in her Nanotech Chronicles, an ambitious postmodern blend of literary appropriation and hard SF. She has published a number of short stories that often show a fascination with history and popular culture. Her latest novel, In War Times, was published in 2007 to widespread acclaim. Her novella, "Memory Dog," is out in 2008.

"The Bridge" was published in Asimov's. It first appeared in 2002 in French, she says, "in a French anthology, Detectives de L'Impossible. Stephane (now Stephanie) Nicot, wanted a story of mine for the anthology, so I wrote it at his request." In the mode of the hard-boiled detective story, this is a prequel to the nanotech age portrayed in Goonan's Nanotech Chronicles. It is about the passing away of the world as we know it, again.

I took the case because I was out of money. It was not the sort of case a self-respecting private eye wants.

But I was desperate.

In these times, hardly anyone needs a private detective. After all, these are the days of miracle and wonder, when one's own true love, even one's simulacrum, so to speak, can be spun in a cocoon over on Wilson Boulevard by Nelson's Artificial Person (fully licensed by whatever is left of the U.S. Government), and inculcated with any kind of physical and emotional frillery one fancies. Or thinks that one fancies.

Nanotechnology is, of course, a buzzword for "we can do anything." I don't understand exactly how an artificial person is grown, but each is a flesh and bone blank (many types and sizes in the catalogues), ready for final DNA tweaking and memory infusion. After the rash of memory-related Nobel prizes, competing memory preservation and replication techniques flooded the market, leading to the melding of many technologies. It was but a short jump to a development that has been both vaunted and abhorred: artificial people.

We are at a very odd place, you see. We are obviously "creating life," and who could argue with that? Yet, people certainly have. Vast phalanxes of lawyers on both sides of the issues have made a lot of money lately, but the most they seem to be able to do is engage in skirmishes about some minute aspect of the various processes presently in use.

It is against the law to kill these beings, should they disappoint, although the penalties for doing so are minimal. It was this sort of instance that I was called upon to investigate.

I was hired by the artificial person's sister.

She knocked on my office-door window on a Friday evening just after I had poured myself a Scotch. It was mid-December, gloomy at four-thirty PM, and that was evening enough to justify the first drink of the day. A light snow was falling, and the flakes outside my third-floor window glowed green, gold, and blue each time the Harry's Bar sign just below changed color.

My office is in Rosslyn, Virginia, a few blocks from the Potomac River. Across Key Bridge is whatever was left of Washington, D.C. It had been utterly changed by a nanotech surge five years earlier.

We unchanged huddle here across the river. Many of the buildings here are altered, of course; new forms of communication are in full swing: giant beelike creatures fill the sky during the day, moving information here and there. Broadcast communication works only sporadically.

Almost everything else has changed.

But for me, on that day, nothing had changed. I had made sure of that. In fact, most days I entertained thoughts of cashing out completely, but even that seemed like too much trouble.

The woman cupped her hands to the glass in an attempt to see inside my dark office.

Illuminated by the dim bulb in the hallway, her face was pale, her eyes large and dark. Her hair was black. She wore a small, blue felt hat perched atop a sophisticated hairdo, with a net that swept across her eyes without hiding them. Her blue wool suit fit tightly; when she stepped back from the door, and looked doubtfully up and down the hall, I could see that her skirt was long and tight, with a little fillip at the bottom that gave her legs just enough room to take mincing steps. I knew that she wore high heels because I had heard them as she approached down the hall.

I decided that I wanted to see what they looked like.

I pushed my rumpled self up from my rumpled couch, tucked in my shirt, straightened my slightly stained tie. I am middle-aged, unable to afford—but not wanting, either—so many of the bionan enhancements at large in the world today. My looks are plain—a slightly heavy face, whiskers that grow too quickly, small blue eyes, a receding hairline, and a depressive personality that dulls whatever sparkle my mother might have seen in me. Like most private eyes, I used to be a police detective. For many years, I was quite successful. Most days, now, I sat in my office and wondered what I could do to make a living. I'd already put in a notice to the landlord that I was leaving at the end of the year. My office was cheap, but not cheap enough.

"Come in, the door's open," I called, as she turned to leave.

She looked startled, but turned the knob.

She reminded me of a giraffe—awkward in her tallness, her head bent forward slightly in a way that was calculated to be charming, diffident. Her brief smile did not reach her eyes.

"Hello. I'm looking for—a Mr. Mike Jones?" She looked around, clearly hoping to find a competent-looking detective—or at least a competent-looking receptionist—somewhere in the room.

"That's me. Come in." The shoes were black, open-toed slingbacks, strikingly inappropriate, in this weather. She either had no sense, or couldn't afford to buy new shoes—and therefore, couldn't afford me.

I hoped that she had no sense.

"Come into my office." I was torn, for a moment, between professionalism and need as I walked past the half-filled glass of Scotch still on the end table.

Need won. I picked it up. "I was almost ready to close. Can I pour you a drink?"

"No," she said, with distaste and a bit of doubt.

I went to my desk and turned on my single desk lamp. She settled into one of the hard wooden chairs in front of my desk, and I sat behind it. She set her small black bag on my desk, which I took as a good sign. She did not remove her tight, gray leather gloves before folding her hands in her lap.

"How can I help you?"

"I saw your name on a card downstairs . . ."

"Ah. You frequent Harry's?" I tried to keep several cards shoved under the glass top of the bar.

"No," she said, decisively, wrinkling her nose. "I just needed . . . some hot coffee, this afternoon, and I saw your card there."

No one with any money to speak of would go into Harry's bar on a snowy afternoon for hot coffee. There is a boutique coffeehouse next door. The coffee is three dollars a pop, but it hasn't sat on the burner all day.

There was a street march just a few weeks ago about the little war we have going on here, the war between the future and the past, so it was possible that she was from the future, trying to live in what was left of the past, for reasons which might spell money for me. As one of those who is quite fond of the past, I'd clung to the sinking ship for far too long. I didn't like the view over there on the future side.

Or maybe I was just a sad old loser too stupid to take a chance.

I cradled the Scotch between both hands. "How can I help you?"

"I need you to get my mother and sister out of copyright. I want the rights to them."

"They are . . . some kind of program?"

She nodded, a tragic look in her dark eyes. Her nose was slightly crooked, which gave her a charming air of imperfection.

"I think that you need a lawyer."

She shook her head. "No. They can't do anything for me. I went to one and she told me what needs to happen."

"Which is?"

"They need to be out in the world, living on their own, without being formally accused of being artificial, for five years."

"That's a long time."

"I want them now!"

"Where are they?"

"They were killed in a car crash four years ago. But I'm getting ahead of myself. Many years ago, my father had programs of us made so that we could be duplicated."

"That would have been illegal."

"At that time, yes."

"It still is. But it was done fairly often, it seems."

"Well. Anyway, it seems that my father has fallen in love with another woman. I attend the University of Virginia. It's in Charlottesville."

"I know." It was about two hours away, a prestigious university. "And?"

"I came home for a visit last week, and found that my mother and sister were . . ." She bowed her head, covered her face with her gloved hands, and began to weep. Her thin shoulders shook. "He had them—*disassembled*."

"What does that mean—disassembled?"

Did a brief look of satisfaction cross her face? She looked up again. "It means that their minds—their personalities— were erased, using a disassembly enzyme. At least—I mean, I'm not sure, exactly, how it works . . ." She shook her head in apparent disbelief.

"What happened?"

"I surprised him. The process wasn't finished, and there were still loose ends he had to clean up. I had a key, of course, and just came in, a few days earlier than expected. I called out, got no answer, went looking for someone. A strange woman came out of the living room and said, 'Who are you?' My father came from the kitchen and she yelled 'Frank, I thought you had taken care of this.'

"Then I looked over and saw my mother and my sister sitting on the couch. Their hands were folded in their laps and they were staring straight ahead. They didn't recognize me. They didn't even notice me. I ran over to them, shook them, screamed at them, cried. 'What's wrong?' I kept saying over and over again. And after a minute, it dawned on me. Both of them, with that vacant look! I turned to my father and yelled at him to help, to stop it, to call a doctor. Instead, he grabbed my shoulders, tightly. His face looked different. Mean; angry. I tried to pull away but he wouldn't let me go. I struggled and got loose. Ran out the door, down the street. He followed but couldn't catch me."

I sipped warm Scotch and surmised that she had not been

wearing her high heels at that time. "I don't mean to upset you, but you must explain to me how disassembly happens."

"I'm not sure. I always thought it happened to . . . other people. Artificial people. Not me. Not my mother, my sister. Why would I think of it in relation to us? We are—we were—real! I never paid any attention to the news reports or controversy or anything. Certainly not any technical details."

I lighted a cigarette. "Certainly creating artificial people is beyond the means of most people."

"My father is very wealthy. He's a well-known lawyer. Frank Quick. We live . . . I mean, I used to live, out in Great Falls. Here's his address." She slid a folded piece of paper across my desk.

I let it sit there. "I assume that you went to the police."

"Oh, yes! There was nothing they could do. That was when I found out, you see, that I was a duplicate. It was quite a shock. I realized that he was planning to have me disassembled as well. Just get rid of the old family and have a new one!"

"You didn't know before that you are artificial?"

"No. I didn't know that we were killed in this car wreck. We were all in the hospital with various problems for quite some time afterwards. I had a broken neck. My mother had a ruptured spleen, and my sister suffered brain damage. My father could afford the most progressive therapies available. I thought that we had been *healed*, not *re-created*."

"Was he in this automobile accident?"

"He was the driver."

"Was he injured?"

"I believe he had some minor injuries."

"Which hospital?"

I thought she hesitated before answering. "Arlington General."

"It seems odd that he would go to such lengths to preserve all of you, and then suddenly get rid of you."

She frowned. "I'm not sure what's wrong with him. Some disease of the mind that he refuses to have diagnosed, I'm sure. His younger self would never have done such a thing. He loved us. He loved us so much that he went to great expense! But I suppose that . . . maybe something was missing in us, since we were not real. . . ." She looked at the floor and tears welled in her eyes and slowly moved down her thin, fine-boned face.

I pushed a box of tissue over toward her.

"But no one has challenged your right to exist. Correct?"

"I believe that he will, if he can't disassemble me quietly. He doesn't know where I am. I have no money right now; I'm sorry. I'm afraid that he might find me if I try and access any of my accounts. I need help."

Just my luck. "What do you want me to do?"

She leaned forward. Her eyes gleamed in the light of the neon sign. "I want my mother back. And my sister. Their copies are in his safe. The updated information that can re-create them, right to the moment of their disassembly. I've drawn a map of the house on that paper that shows where the safe is. The house is alarmed; I included the code for you."

"You are asking me to burgle a house, not solve a crime. Why can't you do this yourself?"

"I told you." Her voice rose. "He wants to . . . do away with me. I fear for my life. I can't go back there. I'm sure he's trying to find me." She blinked a few times, obviously trying to calm down. She succeeded, and continued in her previous, reasoned tone of voice. "I'm working on getting access to my accounts without giving away my location. I can have some money for you in a day or two."

"My fees are one hundred dollars an hour, plus expenses. Travel, anything that I need to pay for. I require a retainer of a thousand dollars."

"I will have to owe you."

What else did I have to do?

On the other hand, my soul was just about the only thing I still owned and it seemed a good thing to have.

She must have noticed my indecision.

"There is one more thing," she said, wiping her eyes with a tissue. "We might be real."

"You mean that he might not really have re-created you after the accident."

"Yes."

"Then it would be murder."

"Yes."

"So it seems that you are not entirely sure about whether they were artificial or real."

She hesitated a second. "No."

I sighed. It was something. "I would be glad to investigate the possible murder of your mother and your sister, Ms. Quick, for the aforementioned fees. Do you have any photographs of them?"

"Ah . . . yes, but . . . why would you need them?" She looked confused and a bit irritated.

An interesting reaction. Most people want to provide the detective with all the information they have, no matter how irrelevant. "For my investigation."

A tiny frown creased her forehead. She dug into her purse, took out a wallet, and tossed two photos onto my desk.

"And your father too?"

"Oh. Of course. Here. You'll do it, then?"

"I told you: I will investigate the facts surrounding these possible murders."

"But the copies?"

"If your mother and sister are indeed artificial persons, and their copies are in this safe, it is possible that the copies might fall into my hands during the course of my investigations."

She did not look entirely satisfied, but nodded once. "All right."

The next morning, after I rose from my couch and washed in the small bathroom in my office, I began to work in spite of myself. Old habits die hard.

I hadn't told her, and she hadn't asked. That was the strange part.

I was in a building that had not been infused with receptor capabilities. In pre-conversion language, it had not been wired.

But what was happening now—here, everywhere—was different from being wired. It was internal.

Communications—regular, old communications like the way they were back in the old days—were gone. Because of the electromagnetic interference. Telephones—and, therefore, the good old Internet—didn't work. Broadcasting didn't work. No one knew what was causing this, but it was like a long solar flare that might never end.

Arlington was being Converted to new biological ways of doing things. Interstices filled with benign bacteria, capable of carrying an infinite amount of information ran up the sides of converted buildings. There was a port in every room, where a clear, semi-permeable membrane gave access to those who were converted, through the wonders of genetic engineering, and could send and receive information. They call it metapheromonal communication.

The owner of the Zephyr Building, in which I have my office, is a tightwad. When it became clear that he was never going to convert the building, most tenants moved out.

Julia Quick either did not know or did not mind that both the building and, by inference, myself, had not stepped into the future.

Or maybe she did, and, finding it to her advantage, didn't care. It wouldn't take much asking to find out about me. I was a bit of a local joke.

Outside, snow fell in great sheets. I turned my collar up and walked over to the morgue. It was six blocks but I needed the exercise and could not afford the Metro. I was still not sure what was compelling me to do this work. Not money, not yet. Ms. Julia Quick had disappeared last night after pressing my hands gratefully, her hands still in her expensive gray gloves, then clicking her way down the hall.

It took more than half an hour for them to believe my license, since I don't have receptors. The woman behind the counter was astounded. She kept pulling other clerks over to gaze at my backward face. "Go ahead, touch him! There's nothing there!"

"That's because it's all here," I told her, pointing to my license on the counter."

She narrowed her eyes at me. "That's just a piece of paper. You could say anything on a piece of paper."

"So DNA can't lie, right? Listen," I said, getting hot. "The right hacker could slip in a new identity code in three minutes."

"There's no need to be rude. You may put that away."

In a moment she slid a sheet of what looked like ordinary paper, but was not, across the counter. I took it and hurried out the front door. Cold wet snow still fell. I hiked across a courtyard, went down an open stairway where the wind blew an empty paper cup to and fro between concrete confines, and opened the familiar back door to the morgue.

Dr. Frisco had been there all night and I caught her just as she was leaving. She was consequently quite short with me. It was clear that she wanted to get home and get some sleep.

"Dr. Frisco?" I stepped in front of her as she strode down the hall, her white coat billowing behind her.

She glared at me. "What?"

"I need to ask some questions."

"Who are you?" Her finger poised. The pad of her index finger was pale blue.

I dug out my license. She glanced at it. "No receptors?"

"No."

"Your religion or something?"

"No."

"Never mind. I remember you now. Private eye. Haven't seen you in a while. What's your question?"

"Do you recall seeing these bodies here?" I showed her the photos that Julia had left with me.

"No. Should I?" She looked more closely at the information on the sheet I handed her. "Four years ago? Are you kidding?"

"You signed their death certificates, here."

She looked again; touched a circle at the bottom. "That's not my signature."

"Thanks. The other two?"

She shook her head, frowning. "No, these are all . . . forgeries. But you got them . . ." she touched the first one again. "You just got them over at registry."

"So these people didn't die?"

She looked at me impatiently. "You know as well as I do that all I'm saying is that these documents are fake. Some hacker has been in the system." She sighed. "Well, it's nothing new. I told them they were rushing into this too fast. Look, is that all?"

"Thanks."

Julia returned that afternoon, still wearing the blue suit, but now wrapped in a dark wool cape with a hood.

I was glad that she showed up. I felt as if my morning had been a waste of time and I half-thought that I would never see her again, that she had been visited upon me by the gods of futility, who seemed to have made themselves comfortable in just about every area of my life. First the marriage, then my business, now the world . . .

On the other hand, she had provided me with something to be curious about. Something to make me want to live another day, just to see what happened.

She settled into the chair and again refused my offer of a drink.

I sipped carefully today. It was my last ounce and I was glad not to have to split it. My breakfast and lunch had been donuts.

"Did you get the copies?" she asked.

"Not yet."

"What have you done today?" she asked, her voice sharp.

"Not much. Tell me about the automobile accident."

"I don't remember it. We never discussed it. It was only when I found them . . . like that . . . that I started to investigate and discovered that we were all copies."

"Then tell me about this process. How does one's personality—one's memories, everything—become pure information?"

"I don't know, really. I only know that it can be done, and that it is being done all the time now. The information can be imbedded in various mediums."

She did recall being "read," when she was eleven years old. Her face softened and her eyelids lowered as she spoke in a low, singsong voice. "We drove into rural Virginia, toward the mountains. It was a cloudy fall day. My sister and I played games in the back seat."

Her hooded cape was soaked, so I knew that she had

walked and not taken the Metro; the entrance was only steps from the building. But walked from where? I let her keep talking.

"When we passed through Charlottesville, my father said that he had met the doctor who would be working with us at the University, and that he was very good. The highway kept going uphill and first it was foggy and then it was just cold and drizzly and we could hardly see beyond the car. We got off the highway at the top of the mountain and turned left."

"You turned left?" I raised my eyebrows.

She scowled briefly. I probably wouldn't have seen it save that the bar sign changed from red to bright white in that instant. She dropped her eyelids and continued. "Oh, yes. I remember very well. I'm good at directions. We went underneath a wrought-iron arch that said Swannanoa Life Extension Institute. It was an old stone place, kind of like a castle.

"The doctor was a big man. He had a beard. He seemed very nice. He wore a white coat and after the secretary had seated us and given us apple cider and, I think, my parents wine—there were oriental rugs on the floor and some classical music playing very softly—he and my parents went away. The secretary took us to another room where we played Go. It started snowing."

"What was the name of this doctor?"

She continued in her dreamy, semi-hypnotized tone, "Doctor White." Then her eyes widened for a fraction of a second and she swallowed. "I think." She looked out the window. "No. It was . . . Green. Or . . . was it Elliott? I don't remember. . . ."

"How long did it take?"

She answered eagerly. She seemed very happy to change the subject. "I don't know. You dream a lot. But it's not the same as regular sleep dreaming. Images race through your head, but they are very intense, very real."

I'd read that they used a combination of powerful psychotropic drugs and hypnotism. But I'm no scientist. I can't begin to understand how they can replicate identity. It would seem impossible. And people have complained that it doesn't really work very well, the people who have had this done.

"What are you majoring in?" I asked.

She stared at me for a split-second, then said, "Medicine, Mr. Jones. I am a second-year medical student. Although I don't see what my personal life has to do with anything."

"I realize that you have access to very little money, but at this point I will have to begin charging an hourly rate plus expenses. Today I spent four hours—"

"Four hours! What did you do?"

"I spoke to Dr. Frisco at the morgue."

She became agitated. "The morgue! What were you doing there? All you need to do, Mr. Jones, is get the copies! I have given you the map; you know where it is in his bedroom; you can watch to see when he leaves the house! However you do such things!"

"I am the detective here, Ms. Quick." I watched her face carefully. "I understand that you want and need documentation of the truth of the matter here, and that—"

She leaned forward in her chair abruptly. Her face was twisted. "I just want my sister and mother," she hissed. "Get me the copies and I will pay you all the money that you could possibly want."

"So you don't really want to free them from the legal thrall of being merely a copy. Or even, it seems, re-create them."

"That's not true! Of course it isn't! But this is the first step."

"Tell me the truth. Why is it that you want these copies?"

"To prove—" she took a breath and looked out the window for a second before continuing. She cleared her throat. "To prove that my father committed this crime."

"How? If what is in the safe is simply their original copies—"

She shook her head. "My sister and my mother had a system which was constantly updated. The information is embedded in the eye, which is removable and which does not degrade. When their copies are re-infused into a body, the information will be there."

"Which of your eyes is it in?"

She blinked, staring at me once again. The light was dim,

of course, but both looked perfectly normal to me. But then, I supposed, they would.

She stood. "You have all the information you need. I'm working on getting the money. I'll be back with it tomorrow." Her voice held an edge of hostility. She left in a hurry.

I slipped on my coat, waited for a moment, then followed her.

She walked downhill, towards Key Bridge.

She stepped onto the bridge and began to walk.

I could not believe it. No one crossed that bridge.

She walked casually; quickly; not as one who was afraid. Her hands were in her pockets and her head was up.

She disappeared into the fog.

I felt a stab of fear for her.

From this side, the city sometimes looked the same. The obelisk of the Washington Monument gleamed whitely in the sun, along with the Capitol dome. It appeared that people were inside, going about some kind of business. But often light was refracted from the city in strange ways, blurring what was visible. Binoculars sometimes revealed blocks where the city was older, where buildings torn down a hundred years ago had reappeared. Sometimes, it was claimed, famous Washingtonians like Duke Ellington or various dead presidents were spotted.

A team of scientists went in, at the beginning, wearing what they believed were impermeable suits. They never emerged. Other people disappeared from time to time as well. Crossing the bridge was widely regarded as being the same as committing suicide. Only the young, the curious, and the hopeless went inside. And the greedy. I had read an account of a man who had gone over in order to cart out antiques, only to have them disintegrate once they were out on the bridge, out of the fog of the city.

Some claimed that everything inside was a kind of holographic reproduction. Others thought that the nanotech surge that had overtaken the city that strange and terrible night had not simply replicated, perfectly, all that was there before, but had infused it with a mass mind that outsiders simply could not understand.

I did not follow Julia.

But I watched the shifting, dreamy lights of Georgetown through the fog for a long time before turning back.

The public transit to Charlottesville was pleasant, and free. I went through the usual rigmarole at the registrar's office with my license and so on, but eventually they gave the information I wanted.

I had little trouble locating Dr. White's scheduled lecture. The hall was full of people who looked extremely young, far too young to be medical students.

It was Dr. White, of course, in all probability, who had done the work on Julia and her family. The truth had popped out in Julia's first surprised response to my question. Dr. White was a famous man. I'd read more than one article about him in the *Washington Post*, still published on our side of the river. He had pioneered—was still pioneering—the brave new world of eternal life. I had read that the developmental costs were astoundingly expensive.

He was a big man, and he did have a beard.

I was not sure that he was nice.

The course was Nanobiology 6000. The auditorium contained about a hundred students. What Julia had told me was true; she was a medical student, but her schedule did not call for her attendance at this particular lecture.

Maybe she had heard it before.

The lecture was about the latest artificial livers and how they worked. I didn't understand much of it. I waited until the flurry of students around the doctor died down and then stepped up to him and introduced myself.

"I'm trying to find out about some work you did some years ago. At a place called Swannanoa."

His eyes were pale blue and cold. "I've heard of Swannanoa, of course. But I'm not connected with them at all. Never have been. Now, if you'll excuse me—"

"I believe that Julia Quick is your student."

He looked at me more intently. "I have a lot of students, as you can see."

"Perhaps you've heard of her father, Frank Quick."

"No. Is that all?"

"I think that will do." I left him standing there, looking after me. Rather disturbed, I hoped.

It's often the most effective thing to do.

I spent most of the ride back to town thinking about how irritated I was with Ms. Julia Quick.

I spent the rest of the ride thinking about how irritated I was with myself.

I got to the library an hour before closing time, chagrined at my slowness. But the city was iced down and difficult to navigate. Freezing rain had blown into the crevices of the library's door, and tiny crystals peppered my face as I pulled open the door.

The librarian, a middle-aged woman, looked up, startled, when I walked in the door. "I was just getting ready to leave. The storm has kept everyone home."

"Do me a favor, please, and stay until closing time."

"I suppose that I must."

"I'm going to need some help. I need temporary receptors."

"What? I didn't think that there was anyone so backwards as to not have them!" She paused for a moment. "Sorry. That was rude."

"They are free, aren't they?"

"Yes. Provided by Beetech, Incorporated."

"Because they are sure that they'll sell me the real thing." She leveled a look at me. "They will."

I looked around at the smooth, bookless surfaces of the library. "I hardly believed it, but it's true. No books."

"Oh, there are books! Millions more than we ever had when they were made of paper and cloth."

"I'm actually looking for several things."

"We'll get you set up first." She glanced at the clock. "That should take fifteen minutes."

"And it will wear off?"

"Your ability to comprehend information metapheromonically will, unfortunately, last only twelve hours."

"Is it really that precise?"

Her voice was stern. "Of course. It is completely biological. Nothing is more precise than biochemistry."

"Let's go, then."

She opened a package and pressed a strip of something sticky to the skin on the back of my hand. In the package was also a sugar-cube-sized black object, onto which she pressed the strip. It made no sound; it did not flash; it was simply a black cube.

After a moment the cube turned white.

"Eat it," she said.

"Nothing happened," I said, after it dissolved in my mouth, tasting not unlike a sugar cube.

"Give it a minute." She went back to her desk and busied herself with some chores, during which time several small, pale green ovals formed on both of my palms.

I called to her. "I think it's ready." I looked at my hands with some trepidation. What had I done?

She hurried over. "Orientation." She handed me a pair of gloves. "Please stay seated for the next few minutes."

I could hardly have budged.

It was like an intense, sudden acceleration. Surprising, powerful music suffused my being in sharp shards so sweet they brought tears to my eyes. Sometimes it slowed to a flow of voices murmuring and I could even catch a word or two. Then it went into my brain and showed me all my memories and I was surprised at both their richness and their paucity, for I had lived only fifty years and this intelligence against which I was now measured was all of humanity's collective, written memories.

After I could see my surroundings again, she returned, removed the gloves, and set a box of tissues next to me on a low table. I took one and wiped my face and blew my nose. The eyes of the pale, stern librarian were no longer pedestrian, but instead were infused with wisdom and the essence of agape.

"You see?" she asked, in a voice so rich and melodious that I had to wipe my eyes again. My senses were immensely augmented, so much so that it was almost too much to bear.

At least it was only temporary.

"Now why did you come?"

I need to learn about the process of making artificial people. And I need to access a police database."

She seemed disappointed. The requests were so mundane.

But she leaned forward and tapped the table in front of me several times, glanced at the clock again. "Usually we just leave people to explore, but I can get you into that information immediately. You understand that without permanent receptors the information you access may not lodge with you for long afterwards, and certainly will lack its initial sharpness. The whole package changes the chemistries of memory."

"Do you get a commission?"

She smiled. The surface before me changed from hard to gel-like. She directed me to place my hands, now covered with small green ovals, onto this interface. "Perhaps you know, but—"

"I've studiously avoided knowing much about this at all."

"All right. Inside this interface are bacteria. Their DNA is capable of carrying . . . a lot of information. This information will be transferred to you in a form of chemical communication based on pheromones, artificially augmented so that they are now called metapheromones. These metapheromones will go directly to your brain and you will know what you want to know."

"But I won't remember?"

"I can impregnate your slate with the information."

"I don't have a slate."

She sighed, went to her desk, and returned with a rolled-up sheet of something that felt stiff and somewhat like plastic. "Smooth this onto the desktop. That's right. Anywhere. Okay, it has picked up your signature by touch. It contains about three thousand layers and each layer is a sheet of molecules that are light or dark and will configure themselves to show you a printed page."

"And it will work even after this wears off?"

"When it's rolled up, just snap it against a hard surface and it will activate."

"All free."

"This is nothing," she said. "Just a taste. You'll want to pay for the rest. Now tell me what you need."

I learned that most of the eye systems had backups. The artificial persons who had them—and they were the most advanced—slept in cocoonlike slings that lifted information from them through many interfaces, so that the full, complex flavor of consciousness could be most fully transferred. This information was sent to the backup, wherever it was kept.

Whomever Julia Quick was after—and I was no longer sure who that might be—was in Frank Quick's home safe.

I found the Quick accident in the police report. Julie's mother and sister were indeed seriously injured. She and her father were not.

Probing of the hospital records revealed that the entire family had been taken away by ambulance and released into the care of their physician, Dr. White.

But getting this information was the least of what happened to me while I was there.

I walked out into the cold evening an hour later. Everything was sharp; tightly focused; powerful. I felt as if previously I had not been alive.

No wonder people like Julie White could treat people like me with such arrogance. She believed me to be a dolt, the perfect facilitator.

She had nearly been right.

When I returned to my office, she was pacing back and forth in front of the door. She whirled and confronted me. "Where have you been?"

"Out." I unlocked the door with deliberate slowness.

She followed me inside. "Well? Do you have the copies?"

"No. I wish that I could offer you a drink, but—"

She shouted, "All I need you for is a simple thing. A very simple thing! You are astoundingly incompetent. You're . . . you're fired!"

Then she rushed out the door, crying.

I waited until she was safely into the elevator, then took the stairs.

She hurried down the wet, gray street, bright with evening lights and falling snow.

She did not look back once. As before, she did not pause when she reached Key Bridge. She wrapped her cloak more closely to herself as she walked, head down as if she were thinking hard, into the foggy grayness of what was once Georgetown.

I pulled my hat brim low. I looked around.

But this part of the Virginia side of the bridge, Rosslyn, was deserted. I took a deep breath, then followed Julie Quick across the bridge. The river roared beneath me. Ice, white in the glare of lights from the Virginia side, fringed gigantic rocks below. I was between two worlds, vulnerable.

And terrifically inclined to simply jump off the bridge and be borne away into the past forever. I forced myself to take one step after the other, holding tight to the railing, and not to keep from falling. I realized that this was why I had avoided the bridge, high places, owning a vehicle that I could drive into a tree.

The change started in the hand with which I gripped the cold railing of the bridge. I could hear nothing but the surge of the river beneath, a sweet, fresh roar. I breathed in the damp fog, searched in vain for any sign of life ahead.

It was as if my hand were asleep, then sharp, unbearable prickles infused my entire body.

I think that there was a moment of complete darkness before I was changed over.

I clung to the railing, dizzy. I took a few breaths of new air. I was afraid, and wondered if I would now die. It hadn't seemed to matter at all when I stepped onto the bridge.

Now I wanted, quite terribly, to live.

I walked forward, with a brisk, strong step. And then I ran.

On the other side of the bridge, fog-enveloped streetlights gently silvered the night. M Street was lively with people. It was the dinner hour. Restaurants and shops were lit against winter darkness.

I hurried along, wondering how long the event on the bridge had taken, and wondering what had happened to me.

I did not see her.

And then—

I dashed across the street and into a doorway. It was her, in the stairway, walking up a narrow flight of stairs.

"Julia!"

She turned slightly, saw me, and continued her climb.

"Julia, wait!"

She began to run, tripping up the stairs on those silly high heels. She stumbled and I grabbed her hand and caught her. She turned her head and looked at me.

There was no recognition in her eyes.

But my hand held her bare hand.

A jolt of pain and anguish flowed through me, then a barrage of emotions. Guilt, I recognized. Regret, yes. But the astonishment and the anger were as distinguishable from my own emotional makeup as if I were looking at two different colors, or hearing a saxophone and a violin. I was assaulted by images—terrible, chaotic, unmistakable.

I saw murder.

"Who are you?" She jerked her hand back and stood, smoothing her skirt and picking up her hat, which had fallen.

I stared at her. "You don't remember?" But it seemed quite certain. She did not. "I am Mike Jones. A private investigator. You hired me to recover your mother and your sister. You say that your father murdered them, perhaps."

For a moment her eyes softened. She blinked a few times. Looked downward. Looked back at me. "Who did you say you are, again?"

Then a door slammed above us. I heard footsteps.

"Julia! Are you all right? I hoped you would return here. Someone came to the university—"

I recognized the voice.

It was Dr. White.

His footsteps continued down the stairs. He stopped when he saw me. "What are you doing here?" he demanded.

"Julia—"

"Julia is unwell. I am her doctor."

"You said you didn't know her."

"This is an issue of patient confidentiality. I insist that you leave her, immediately. She needs treatment . . ." he glanced down at her hands. "Julia! Where are your gloves?"

"Oh." Her hand flew to her mouth. "I took them off when I came in the door. I was . . . somewhere . . . I don't remember . . . surely I didn't cross the river?" She looked at Dr. White beseechingly.

Dr. White advanced toward me with a certain resolve.

I rushed down the stairwell and out onto the street. Crossing it, I ducked into a bar and watched through the window from behind some blinds.

Dr. White stepped out onto the street, looked up and down. He stared for a long time in the direction of the bridge. Then he went back inside and the door shut behind him.

My old self would have returned immediately to Virginia. To the past.

But it was difficult to even think about doing so. Everything here was wonderful; perfect. I realized that people did not return to the other side simply because they did not want to.

A jazz pianist played quietly. I took a seat at the bar and fleetingly wished for a drink and some of the crab soup that I saw on the menu.

The bartender brought me a very fine Scotch and a bowl of crab soup. When asked him how he knew what I wanted, he pointed to the place where my hand had rested on the bar. Bright print on its surface, upside down, showed my unvoiced desire. "But I can't pay."

He looked puzzled. "You already have."

I ate my soup, and drank, awash in a new, sharp, glowing feeling. A rebirth of mind. Of soul. I was young again too, and here in Georgetown with my wife, Marlene, soon after we were married, when we were both so happy with each other and with life.

I hadn't seen her in many years.

Something about being here, in this place, something that happened on the bridge, had resolved that dark pain, that feeling of not being good enough. Marlene was finally swept from me. She had been swept from me by Scotch before, though, and I was suspicious that this might not last any longer than the effects of the Scotch.

But somehow, I knew that I was fundamentally changed by something I would probably never understand. I was changed by some deep newness in the world. A newness produced by humans. Which I had been given, free, at the library: a process that opened biochemical doorways and allowed my transformation on the bridge.

There seemed to be no reason to ever leave this side of the bridge.

Except that I recalled Julia's images with great clarity.

Her memories had cascaded into me in that brief contact.

I took out the slate that the librarian had given me and looked at it for a moment, wondering what to do with it.

The bartender was there, suddenly, and took it from my hand and unrolled it. He smoothed it onto the top of the bar. "That's how," he said.

"But—"

"You've only been in here less than an hour. Don't worry. We'll all help you. The way you use this—you just put your hand there and download whatever it is you want to keep. One way to do it—look. Put your hand there. Fine. Now just touch what you want to do. Here's the menu."

"I learned something—from another person, just now—through touching her hand."

"Fine. That's how we communicate. So just touch this download command. Do you know her name?"

"Julia."

"Tell it Julia—that's right, it is trained to your voice. That's the file name. Now put your hand there and go."

I looked at him once more, with trepidation.

He smiled. "The brain is quite amazing. Don't worry. It works. Gotta go." He hurried to another customer.

In the quiet chat of the bar, Julie's memories poured into the slate. Visual memories. Memories which were in what was probably her internalized voice, the way it sounded to her.

It took a long time to sort them out. In the process, I realized that she was somewhat crazy, filled with mental and emotional barriers. Some of them were natural.

And some of them had been installed by Dr. White.

Julia had been a child when she first came into contact with Dr. White.

She had been "read" in Swannannoa, as she had told me. And it was there, in that temporal stratum, that Dr. White's voice, kind and fatherly, had implanted her loyalty to him. Her eyes had fluttered open at that point, and she saw him attach a patch to her arm—a patch that no doubt infused her with a more precise form of chemical compliance. The librarian had told me that biochemistry was very precise.

Perhaps his methods of implanting Julia's future slavery were clumsy; I don't know. But they seemed to have worked. He had probably used them on Frank Quick, too, but I had no way of actually knowing that. I surmised that if he had, Frank's adult personality had been able to shrug them off eventually. Julia's more malleable brain had made her a perfect victim.

I saw Dr. White and Mr. Quick quarrel in the family living room when Mr. Quick decided to terminate his hefty subscription payments. Because such arrangements were illegal, Dr. White had no legal recourse.

So he used Julia.

I saw her, as if through her eyes, going into her bedroom and opening a small zippered kit. Dr. White had helped her create it. The components were neatly organized—the disassembly enzymes, which would erase certain aspects of her father's personality (her father, after all, had paid Dr. White handsomely to create this very template), a few tools, another vial, all held in with wide elastic bands. I saw her drop something into her father's martini as he sat in an easy chair in the den, next to a large stone fireplace in which a fire blazed on the wintry afternoon. I saw him pass out, slump in his chair, and stop breathing, as Julia glanced impatiently at her watch. Her mother and sister were out shopping and not due to return for some time.

In a curious sense, what happened to Frank was not murder to her, because she then dragged him to the cocoon in which her mother—indeed a copy, since she had died soon after their automobile accident, along with Julia's sister—spent each night. With much effort, she heaved him into it and watched the cocoon shrink and cling to him.

She then—unemotionally, efficiently—perhaps because she was a medical student—gouged out his eye with a small, delicate stainless-steel instrument and dropped it into a plastic bag, which she pocketed. She then pulled a tiny box from her other pocket, opened it, and removed an orb containing an artificial iris.

Which held an entire artificial personality.

She inserted the eyesphere into the eye socket of her father. As the cocoon absorbed his old personality, this would infuse the new one, which would presumably resume payments to Dr. White. If all went absolutely right.

She heard sounds in the hallway, but when she turned the doorway was empty. Her heart beating hard, she got her groggy and now artificial father out of the cocoon and led him to his bed, where he appeared to sleep. She then returned to the den, tossed the eye in its plastic bag into the fire, grabbed the martini glass, and rinsed it with bleach at the kitchen sink.

The next morning, as she was making coffee in the kitchen, she heard urgent whispering from the dining room between her mother and her sister. Caught the word "police."

She realized, with a sickening feeling, that they either suspected or knew. That sound, at the bedroom door. They must have come home early from shopping.

She ran to her room, grabbed Dr. White's vial of disassembly enzymes, and put them in her mother and sister's coffee.

I knew that they were artificial, but it still gave me a turn as Julia quite calmly watched them drink the coffee and eat the pastries she took out to the sunny dining room. Perhaps they did so because they were both in shock, not completely believing that their Julia was capable of such acts.

As they were disassembled, Julia realized, with increasing panic, that they had of course spent the night in their cocoons. Their memories of the day—whatever they had seen, and their suspicions—had already flowed into the recording devices.

The dedicated interstices of their cocoons, the cables which sent the daily updates to eyelike biocomputers, ended at Frank Quick's safe. I watched her ransack his office for the combination, but she could not find it.

Then, dazed, she walked across the bridge, into the city. And forgot, for a time—months, it looked like—what had happened.

Until Dr. White tracked her down.

She made it back to her neighborhood twice; made it to her front door, the second time, before fleeing. Not even Dr. White was persuasive enough to get her to face her father, artificial and malleable as he may now be. Something of morality, however faint or degraded, still remained.

Or perhaps it was simply pure fear.

Then she hired me.

I saw Dr. White many times in Julia's memories. He had devised a way to maintain the wealth that would allow him to continue his "work."

If you could call it that.

I was sure that the law would put several other names to it.

As I sat in the Georgetown bar, which seemed as close an approximation to heaven as I, with my limited imagination, could dream of, I reluctantly realized that I had to go back to the past.

I crossed back into Rosslyn the next morning, in the gray winter dawn, knowing what I had to do. I was not sure that the information would remain in my slate, or even if it was usable in a court of law, but I knew that hard evidence did exist.

The world was new, yes. But human decency still remained, in some of us, no matter how strange everything else had become.

At first my old friend was not interested. "We have no jurisdiction over such proceedings, unfortunately," Detective John "Ace" Anderson, with whom I had a long-standing love-hate relationship, told me. "How many years have I known you, Mike? This is a first. You've never come to me with information. It's usually the other way around. I have to shake it out of you. We don't fool around with this artificial person stuff. There's not enough law to do one thing or another." He lighted a cigarette and leaned back in his battered chair. "You look like shit. What have you been up to?"

I put both hands on his desk, leaned over it, and played my card. "There's been a murder, Anderson. The murder of a real person. And you're not interested?"

"Why the hell didn't you tell me in the first place? What do you have?"

I told him.

The Quick house was in a wealthy Great Falls neighborhood, with a view of the Potomac through the snowy, leafless forest.

Mr. Quick himself answered the door, wearing expensive at-home clothing, impeccably groomed. He was balding, with dark hair, slightly overweight. He looked dazed; disoriented. But he was cordial enough. "Can I help you?"

Detective Anderson flashed his badge. "I'd like to ask you a few questions."

"About what?"

"A murder."

"Whose?"

"Yours," I told him.

An artificial person cannot be charged with a crime. Laws are slow to catch up to reality.

But Julie and Dr. White, being real, were charged with the murder of Mr. Quick.

The police read the eye of the sister from the copy which they found in the safe. The testimony was indisputable. As the librarian had told me, biology is precise. It was all ascertained authentic by the best experts in the field. The sister had seen it all.

I watched Julia during the trial. She never looked at me, though she must have felt my gaze.

I wondered how she felt, trapped on this side of the bridge. Unable to slip into the city for her necessary amnesia. I knew a lot about self-induced amnesia, and I understood Julia Quick's need for it.

I watched her exchanging glances with Dr. White more than once during the trial. She looked anguished; he looked stony. He too was trapped here, hopefully for life.

She had gone the limit for him—but not of her own volition. Her lawyer found an expert who was able to show quite conclusively that Dr. White had implanted within Julia an irresistible need to do his bidding no matter what. Something to do with pheromones, something that hadn't worked nearly as well in Frank Quick. As a result of actions akin to child abuse and rape, Julia had committed this crime to give Dr. White what he so desired: money. Mr. Quick had a lot of it, and he was not planning on giving any more of it to Dr. White.

No one needed or had money on the other side of the bridge. It must have been deeply refreshing to Julia when she first went over and found escape from the terrible memories of what she had been made to do. They say that we are on the brink of a great, but possibly confusing, new age, in which money will be obsolete.

But Dr. White was like me. He had never fully crossed the bridge. He preferred to stay here, in the place where he had prestige, trying to do good—which unfortunately began to call for a few questionable deeds. He testified that he was trying to help people live longer. For that, being in the old-fashioned world, he needed old-fashioned money.

Apparently he didn't care where it came from.

His and Julia's choice of a facilitator for their plan to get the evidence of their crime had backfired quite spectacularly. But only by something quite close to accident. They had me pegged correctly. They just hadn't counted on the fact that, once, I had been a good detective, and that a bit of the fire and curiosity was left.

Julia, being her father's daughter, was quite clever in matters of the law and was able to style herself as a preyed-upon sweet young thing. Which, in truth, she was. After the trial, when she refused any kind of rehabilitation, she was escorted to Key Bridge and told not to come back. That was her sentence.

The trial was highly publicized, and several other victims came forward. Though their evidence was not brought into this trial, it became clear that Dr. White had worked this particular scam upon more than one family.

Dr. White was put away for life.

Or, at least, someone who seemed exactly like him was.

Mr. Quick's artificial counterpart, who afterwards won a groundbreaking case for the legal recognition of such entities, paid me well for my time. I heard that he once again reconstituted his family, after having the copies thoroughly cleansed of any bugs installed by Dr. White. He still lives in Great Falls with his wife and his daughter Elizabeth.

He did not re-create Julia.

I've paid for another year in the Zephyr Building. I get some business, not much. Same as before. Maybe someday someone as interesting as Julia Quick will step into my office.

Maybe she will be a nice person.

I have been stopped by the police more than once, when I return from Washington to Rosslyn. They take note of my frequent visits, and fear that I will bring some kind of nanotech contagion back with me.

I'm not sure why I still return to this side of the river.

Except that, despite my permanent conversion, I'm the same person, really.

We have all been artificial for quite some time, I realized. Even I had been saved by antibiotics, a purely human extrapolation, more than once. But now, human intellect has created the means for us to pass our previous limits. The challenge is not, as I had seen it before, to stubbornly remain in the past. Instead, the challenge is to use our new knowledge and abilities with respect for all humans, without coercion. It is a new literacy, and, like literacy, it can lead many different places. For the first time in history, it is possible for us to have a vision of what we are really about. I've decided that it's my responsibility, and everyone's, to work on this vision, to think about what is good in humans, and worth keeping.

I told you that I'd changed.

I like my office. I like the light of morning here. I like dark snowy afternoons in winter. I like the present, this strange mix of the past and the future.

I like life.

I will hold onto it as long as I can.

As You Know, Bob

JOHN HEMRY

John Hemry (www.johnghemry.com) lives in Maryland, with his wife and three kids. He attended the U.S. Naval Academy, class of '78, and is a retired U.S. Navy officer. He said in a 2006 interview, "I believe that the traditions and practices developed over millennia for surviving far from home on ships will also be used in ships sailing among the stars." He is an Analog *writer as far as his short fiction is concerned—all but three of his sixteen stories to date have appeared there. He is also the author of ten SF novels to date, some of them under the name Jack Campbell. His eleventh,* The Lost Fleet: Valiant, *written as Jack Campbell, is out in 2008.*

"As You Know, Bob" was published in Analog. *It is a metafictional story about a science fiction writer who sets out to write a real hard SF story, and then revises it at the urging of his agent, and revises and revises. And the story mutates. Like slapstick, it could be sad, but it is funny.*

The agent: How's that science fiction novel you've been working on coming along? Send me an excerpt from the beginning so we can see about getting it into shape for today's market.

The story begins: The phone rang with Bob's signature tune, so Bill tapped the "receive" button. Bob's face appeared, looking unusually enthusiastic since he normally tried to coast through life with minimum effort. "Did you hear about the frozen Lumpia?"

"Not yet." Lumpia. That sounded important enough for Bill to pause his work and face the phone. "As you know, Bob, frozen Lumpia isn't nearly as good as fresh."

"This stuff is! There's a new process. Meet me in the lobby and we'll go get some and check it out."

Bill's conscience tugged at him. "I dunno, there's this analysis of the signals from the Eridani Probe that I'm supposed to be running. . . ."

"It'll be there when we get back."

"Okay." Bill stood up, powering down his workpad and heading for the door.

In the hallway he met Jane, a researcher who worked a few doors down. Bill tried not to stare as she crossed her arms and looked at him. "You're in a rush. Going on some important mission?" she asked dryly.

"I guess you could say that. I'm going to pick up some frozen Lumpia." Bill hesitated. Jane had the kind of smarts and attitude that had always attracted him, but she had never shown much interest in Bill and had turned him down the one time he had asked for a date. Maybe she would be willing to consider a more casual errand together. "Do you want to come along?" Jane pulled out a money card and checked it, then shrugged. "Sure. Why not? I need to pick up some stuff, too."

The agent: This is okay, but I can't sell it. Something's missing. It's not sci-fi enough, do you know what I mean? This is supposed to be happening in the early twenty-second century and there's nothing about the singularity or nano-tech or quantum states or cyberspace or posthumans or multiculturalism or complex antiheroes. How can you call that sci-fi? I know, I know, you've told me that when people use tools they don't think about how they work. But readers expect certain things from sci-fi. Oh, and the characters. Those aren't sci-fi characters. Punch them up and make them the sort of characters you see in real science fiction. And get some gratuitous sexual content in there.

The revised story begins: The singularity had crashed and burned in a viral-cataclysm that had destroyed most of civilization and every decent coffee house east of Seattle. Now a complex array of probability states undulated down a fiber-optic line surviving from presingularity days. The electrons carrying the message didn't so much move as they did alter the places where they had the highest probability of existing.

Since the electrons didn't truly exist anywhere, neither did the strange cyber-world in which they didn't move, filtering through an immense alternate reality in which normal physical rules of the macroworld didn't apply.

Entering a complex series of transformational states, the electrons that weren't there interacted with the receiver mechanism, propagating through layered nano-light-emitting-diode projectors to generate a three-dimensional image.

A tune distinct to the originator of the message chimed from the nanomanufactured receiver. It was the First Movement of Genghis Juan Feinstein's folk-rock Hindustani opera, which, William knew, meant the message had to be from Roberto Sigma, the latest in a string of complicated and untrustworthy clone/cyborg hybrids who nonetheless followed their own indecipherable code of honor. William moved his palm over a light sensitive but robust section of his desk to command his virtual workstation to pause in its operations. Now as the stacked image displays created a perfect visual representation of Roberto Sigma, William saw that the enigmatic posthuman seemed happy about something.

"I assume," Roberto Sigma began in the Libyan-Croatian accent he had acquired from his last neural-upgrade, "that you are aware of recent developments in microcryogenics."

William nodded, his own implants from his days as a Special Forces commando during the Betelgeuse incursion activating automatically at the sight of his sometime-friend, sometime-enemy. "As you know, Roberto, cryogenics hasn't yet worked to expectations, especially since several promising lines of research were lost when the singularity crashed."

"Ancient history, William! That is so five nanoseconds ago. I know of a means to demonstrate how well the new process works. It originated in Asia. Interested in meeting me to investigate it?"

William hesitated, his implants jangling internal warnings. The last time he had followed Roberto Sigma it had been into an unending maze in cyberspace from which he had narrowly escaped. But if what Roberto was saying was true, he had to know. "I've been working on analyzing signals from the Eridani Probe. It's been using the new quantum state transmitter to tunnel data through to us at amazing speed."

"If the signals have propagated through quantum paths they will still have a probability of existence when you return."

"You're right. I'd forgotten about the addendums Jonquil

made to the Hernandez postulates back in 2075," William agreed. He gestured another command over the light-sensitive control pad, ordering his workstation to shut down and watching as it swiftly cycled through functions and closed them before powering off automatically.

William stood, his lean muscles rippling as the commando implants amplified William's own natural speed and strength. There weren't a lot of former Special Forces commandos doing astrophysics research, so he tended to stand out during the virtual conferences. William walked across the floor tiled with panels from the Toltec/Mayan revival period, nanocircuits in the panels sensing his movement and sending commands to the door, which slid open silently on nanolubricated rails as William approached.

He slipped cautiously into the hallway and saw Janice from a few pods down, the nanoparticles in her lip gloss making it glow a delicious ruby red. Janice spun to face him with all of the pantherish grace you'd expect from a first-degree black belt, her blue eyes watching William speculatively. He tried not to stare back. At twenty-three years old, Janice was the most brilliant and the most beautiful quantum physics researcher in the entire world. What was left of the world after the singularity crash, that is.

Janice crossed her arms, drawing William's gaze to the magnificent breasts that led her hetero-male colleagues to speak admiringly of the amplitude of Janice's wave functions. "You're in a rush. Going on some important mission?" Janice purred.

"You might say there's a high probability of that," William replied. "I need to acquire some samples of a new cryogenic process."

Janice's gorgeous eyes narrowed. "Are you talking about the Renz/Injira process? I understand that freezes organic matter in crystalline matrices that preserve cell structure. When it's returned to normative temperature its composition is perfectly preserved."

"That's what they say. I need to find out if it's true, and there's a certain item of Asian origin which will give me the answer." William hesitated, feeling a strong attraction to Janice that had nothing to do with the gluons holding her quarks into such an attractive package. She had once told him that they would never occupy the same space. Did her exclusion principle still apply to him? "Would you like to come along?"

Janice's eyes glowed a little brighter as her nanovision enhancement implants reacted to her excitement. She reached into one pocket and checked the charge on the twenty-gauss energy pistol she carried everywhere. "Sure. I'd calculated there was a high probability of deflection in my plans for today. It looks like I was right."

The agent: Much better! Very sci-fi. But I did notice that the story doesn't seem to flow as well as it used to. Maybe you can fix that by using some of the real cutting-edge concepts. You know, quantum foam and dark energy and stuff. And try to make the characters a little more exotic. You know. Weird. More science-fictiony. Give it a shot and see if you can clean the story up a bit.

The re-revised story begins: Wilyam sensed the arrival of a message from his old rival and comrade Robertyne, who had existed in an indeterminate state since an accident while researching applications in the mysterious world of the quantum foam, where literally anything was possible. Waving a hand to freeze his work in mid motion above his desk, Wilyam waved again to bring up the message display.

Particle functions coalesced into a functional framework emitting radiation on visual frequencies. The familiar features of Robertyne appeared as if he/she were actually looking at him through a window, though Wilyam suspected that Robertyne had actually ceased to exist some time before and he was really speaking directly to the inexplicable presence that seemed to animate the quantum foam. The image of Robertyne displayed a very human smile, though even when Robertyne had been unquestionably posthuman he/she had never been easy to understand or to trust. "Have you heard the ripples in the foam, Wilyam? Organic matter from the macro-place you call Asia now exists in a frozen state without flaw."

Wilyam frowned as the implant linking him to the bare edges of the foam glittered with possible outcomes. He saw himself in a million different mirrors, each one reacting slightly differently to Robertyne's proposal. "As you know, Robertyne, nothing actually exists, so it isn't possible to preserve something that doesn't exist. Previous attempts have produced probability chains that wander off into reduced states of replication quality."

"There's something new/old/past/present/future in this perception reference, Wilyam. It represents a low probability outcome of extreme accuracy."

It sounded tempting to the millions of different Wilyams staring at him from the could-be's dancing around the implant. "I'm busy analyzing signals from the Eridani probe. We're not sure if they're from our probe or if signals are tunneling from an alternate probe in another reality."

"Then split your probabilities and attend to both and neither. I am everywhere and nowhere, but will center a probability node below here."

"Okay." Wilyam focused on the implant, drawing on the strange properties of the quantum foam to create infinite possibilities. He waved a hand to shut down his work and stood up/remained sitting and continued working.

The door's probability state cycled as one Wilyam approached, going to zero for an instant as that Wilyam walked through.

In the endless hallway beyond, Jandyce from a few stationary states down floated with her eyes closed. She opened them, her eyes glowing blue from the tap implanted in her brain that connected Jandyce directly to the dark energy that filled the universe. Wilyam tried not to stare, knowing Jandyce was tied into cosmic currents none of his probabilities could hope to grasp.

She crossed her arms, drawing Wilyam's observations to the two symmetrical anomalies superpositioned on her chest, both far exceeding functional limits in a way that excited his ground state and also provided proof that dark energy could overcome the pull of gravity. "You're in a rush. Going on some important mission?" Jandyce hadn't spoken, but her voice echoed in his head.

"The foam has found something new. A way to preserve matter in a hitherto unknown way. There's a sample from the human-reality matrix of Asia." Wilyam hesitated as his millions of selves around the quantum foam link swirled in every possible action-outcome sequence. Jandyce and he usually demonstrated weak interaction. When he had once asked her about the possibility of mutual reinforcement, she had informed him that the likelihood of direct reactions between quantum foam and dark energy was infinitesimally small and shown him the Feynman diagram that proved it. But he had long hoped for a probability sequence that could result in entanglement with her. Perhaps, somehow, their wave/particle dualities could constructively interfere in a way that would generate mutually beneficial patterns. "Would you like to come along?"

Jandyce's eyes glowed brighter as the dark energy flowed. Matter swirled as she reached beside her and plucked a patch of darkness from nothing, examining it closely. "The cat lives. I will go, maintaining the proper balance of forces and perceptions."

The agent: Great! This I can sell. It's pure sci-fi. Nobody could understand what's happening or why these, uh, people are doing whatever it is they're doing. Tell you what, though, it's still a little rough. I mean, how do you explain what's going on? Readers want to know how this stuff works. So how about you polish it a little, provide some explanations, and give me one more look, okay? Oh, and put the sex back in. You didn't take it out? Well, then, make the sex *understandable* again. Make the sex so anybody can understand it. Heck, make the whole thing so anybody can understand it.

The re-re-revised story begins: The great wizard Wil sensed a message from his companion and challenger the Baron of Basi. He waved one palm and the magical mirror on a nearby wall glowed, showing the image of the Baron, who gave Wil a searching look. "Have you heard? From far in the east, that which we have long sought can now be ours. It lies frozen."

"Frozen?" The Wizard Wil gestured again and the fires blazing beneath his cauldron sank to a low glow. "As you know, Baron of Basi, nothing once living survives well being encased in ice."

"The Grand Council has found a way, I tell you! A way we must investigate before the Bane of Dargoth does! That which we desire lies frozen in a state of perfection. Come down from your tower and we shall seek it together."

"A quest?" The Wizard Wil turned a doubtful look on his cauldron. "I have been seeking to interpret certain messages from the stars."

"Surely a wizard of your powers can deal with two tasks at once."

"There is a way," the Wizard Wil agreed. Calling up the proper spell in his mind, Wil summoned an elemental assistant and ordered it to continue his work. He walked toward the door, the earth spirit bound to it seeing his approach and opening the portal, then closing it behind him.

Outside stood the Sorceress Jainere, who sometimes appeared in the south tower of Wil's fortress. Jainere, her eyes glowing with the fires of the powers that lay beneath the world humans knew, sought wisdom in places few dared venture. Now Wil tried not to stare at the beauty she barely concealed behind a few filmy garments, her breasts glowing with a magic older than time that offered the promise of pleasures no man could withstand. The sorceress Jainere crossed her arms under those breasts, smiling enticingly as she saw the reaction Wil could not hide. "You're in a rush. Going on some important mission?" she inquired in a voice that rang like the tiny bells the dancers of Dasiree wore.

"We seek that which was frozen and can be rendered perfect again once thawed," Wil spoke haltingly despite his efforts to resist the spell of Jainere. "It comes from the lands far to the East, where priests and priestesses with skins the hue of the sun have long guarded it." He had desired Jainere for many lives of normal men, but the unpredictable sorceress had always scorned him, declaring that no sorceress could live by the rules of right and wrong that Wil followed. Perhaps if she joined the quest Jainere would finally learn enough about him to desire uniting their powers and their lives. "Do you want to come along?"

Jainere reached down to the slim, bejeweled girdle which hung on her hips in a way that made men's minds go astray, drawing forth the enchanted mirror in which she viewed images of what might be. "Your possible futures are of interest. I will accompany you. It might be amusing."

The agent: Now that's more like it. Fantasy! There's a big market for that now. It's a lot easier for readers to understand than sci-fi and people seem to be able to relate better to the characters.

I wonder why they don't want to read science fiction as much these days?

The Lustration

BRUCE STERLING

Bruce Sterling (http://blog.wired.com/sterling/) is living somewhere in Italy, or at least in Europe. He is an American and a citizen of the world, drawn to events and especially people tipping the present over into the future. The MIT Press catalog entry for his short non-fiction book Shaping Things *(2005) calls him a science fiction writer and futurist. We think he's a politically and technologically engaged intellectual, an excellent journalist, and one of the finest SF writers alive today. His most recent novel is* The Zenith Angle *(2004), not SF but a satiric look at high-tech security. Sterling has continued to publish striking short fiction, now fantasy as often as SF, that we frequently include in our* Year's Best *volumes.*

"The Lustration" was published in Eclipse 1, *the first of an ambitious new original anthology series, edited by Jonathan Strahan. Sterling, a strong environmentalist, uses the word "lustration" (a purification ceremony) a couple of times in his Viridian Design "Manifesto" (2000) (www. viridiandesign.org/manifesto.html) to indicate "a mechanism by which societies that have drifted into dysfunctional madness can be put right. . . . Those who are risking the lives of others should be made aware that this is one particular risk that will be focused specifically and personally on them."*

"Artificial Intelligence is lost in the woods."
—David Gelernter, 2007

White-hot star-fire ringed the black galactic eye. Glaring heat ringed his big black cauldron.

He put his scaly ear to a bare patch on the rotten log. Within the infested timber, the huge nest of termites stirred. Night had fallen, it was cooler, but those anxious pests must sense somehow, from the roar of the bellows or the merciless heat of his fires, that something had gone terribly wrong outside their tight, blind, wooden universe.

Termites could do little against a man's intentions. "Pour it!"

The fierce fire had his repair crew slapping at sparks, flapping their ears and spraying water on their overheated hides. But their years of discipline paid off: at his command, they boldly attacked the chains and pulleys. The cauldron rose from the blaze as lightly as a lady's teapot.

It tipped and poured.

Molten metal gushed through a funnel and into the blackest depths of the termite nest. The damp log groaned, shuddered, steamed.

"The next!" he cried, and the tureen moved to a second freshly bored hole. A frozen meniscus of cooling metal broke at its lip, and down came another long smooth blazing gush.

Anguished termites burst in flurries from the third drilled

hole, a horde of blind white-ants blown from their home, scalded, boiling, flaming. A final flood of metal fell, sealing their fate.

Barking with excited laughter, the roughnecks put their backs to the chocks and levers. They rocked the infested log in its bed of mud. Liquid metal gurgled through every chamber of the nest. He could hear blind larvae, innocent of sunlight, popping into instant ashes.

He shouted further orders. The roughnecks shoveled dirt onto the roaring fire.

By morning, his uneasy dream had achieved embodiment.

The men scraped away the log's remains: black charcoal and brown punk. They revealed an armature of gleaming, hardened metal.

He'd sensed there must be something rich and strange in there—but his conjecture could not match the reality.

That termite nest—it was so much more than mere insect holes, blindly gnawed in wood. That structure was a definite entity. It had astonishing organization. It had grown through its own slow removals and absences, painstaking, multiply branched. In its many haltings, caches, routes, gates, and loops, it was complex beyond human thought.

A flood had struck this area; local timber plantations had been damaged. As a first priority, his repair crew repaired and upgraded the local computer tracks. Then they burned the pest-infested, fallen wood.

The big metal casting of the termite nest was lobed, branched, and weirdly delicate—it was hard to transport. Still, his repairmen were used to difficult labors in hard territory. They performed their task without flaw.

Once home, he had the crew suspend the big metal nest from the trellis of his vineyard. Then he dismissed the men; after weeks of hard work in the wilderness, they bellowed a cheer and all tramped out for drink.

The fine old trellis in his yard was made of the stoutest computerwood, carefully oiled and seasoned. With the immense dangling weight of the metal casting, the trellis groaned a bit. Just a bit, though. That weight did nothing to disturb the rhythmic chock, click and clack of the circuits overhead.

All the neighbors came to see his trophy. Word got around the town, in its languid, foot-strolling way. A metal termite nest had never before been exhibited. Its otherworldly beauty was much remarked upon—also the peculiar gaps and scars within the flowing metal, left by the steam-exploding bodies of the work's deceased authors, the termites.

The cheery crowds completely trampled his wife's vegetable garden.

Having expected the gawkers, he charged fees.

His young daughter took the fees with dancing glee, while the son was kept busy polishing the new creation. At night, he shone lanterns on the sculpture, and mirrored gleams flared out across the streets.

He knew that trouble would come of this. He was a mature man of much local respect and some property, but to acquire and deploy so much metal had reduced him near to penury. He was thin now, road-worn, his clothing shabby.

With the fees, he kept his wife busy cooking. She was quite a good cook, and she had been a good wife to him. When she went about her labors, brisk, efficient, uncomplaining, he watched her wistfully. He well remembered that, one fine day, a pretty, speckled wooden ball had slowly rolled above the town and finally cracked into a certain socket: the computer had found his own match. His bride had arrived with her dowry just ten days later. Her smooth young hide had the very set of black-and-white speckles he had first seen on that wooden ball.

He was ashamed that his obsessions had put all that to risk.

He walked each street within his home town, lingering in the deeper shade under the computer-tracks. This well-loved place was so alive with homely noises: insects chirping, laundry flapping, programmers cranking their pulleys. He could remember hearing that uploading racket from within the leathery shell of his own egg. Uploading had always comforted him.

It all meant so much to him. But whenever he left his society, to work the network's fringes . . . where the airborne tracks were older, the spans longer and riskier, the trestles long-settled in the soil . . . out there, a man had to confront anomalies.

Anomalies: splintered troughs where the rolling balls jostled and jammed . . . Time-worn towers, their fibrous lashings frayed . . . One might find a woeful, scattered heap of wooden spheres, fatally plummeted from their logical heights . . . In the chill of the open air, in the hunger and rigor of camp life . . . with only his repair crew for company, roughnecks who hammered the hardware but took no interest in higher concepts. . . . Out there, on certain starry nights, he could feel his skull emptying of everything that mankind called decency.

In his youth, he had written some programs. Sharp metal jacks on his feet, climbing lithely up the towers, a bubble-level strapped across his back, a stick of wax to slick the channel, oil for the logic-gates . . . Once he'd caused a glorious cascade of two thousand and forty-eight wooden balls, ricocheting over the town. The people had danced and cheered.

His finest moment, everyone declared. Maybe so—but he'd come to realize that these acts of abstract genius could not be the real work of the world. No. All the real work was in the real world: it was the sheer brute labor of physically supporting that system. Of embodying it. The embodiment was the hard part, the real part, the actuality, the proof-of-concept. The rest was an abstract mental game.

The intricacies of the world's vast wooden system were beyond human comprehension. That massive construction was literally coincident with human history. It could never be entirely understood. But its anomalies had to be tackled, dealt with, patched. One single titanic global processor, roaming over swamp through dark forests, from equator to both poles, in its swooping junctions and cloverleafs, its soaring, daring cyberducts: a global girdle.

Certain other worlds circled his mild, sand-colored sun.

They were either lifeless balls of poison gas or bone-dry ashes. Yet they all had moons, busy dozens of little round moons. Those celestial spheres were forever beyond human reach; but never beyond observation. Five hundred and twelve whirling spheres jostled the sky.

His placid world lacked the energy to lift any man from its surface. Still: with a tube of glass and some clear night viewing, at least a man could observe. Observe, hypothesize, and calculate. The largest telescope in the world had cataloged billions of stars.

The movements of the moons and planets had been modeled by prehuman ancestors, with beads and channels. The earliest computers were far older than the human race. As for the great world-system that had ceaselessly grown and spread since ancient times—it was two hundred million years old. It could be argued, indeed it *was* asserted, that the human race was a peripheral of the great, everlasting, planetary rack of numerate wood. Mankind had shaped it, and then it had shaped mankind.

His sculpture grew in popularity. Termites were naturally loathed by all decent people, but the nest surprised with its artistry. Few had thought termites capable of such aesthetic sensitivity.

After the first lines of gawkers dwindled, he set out tables and pitchers in the trampled front garden, for the sake of steadier guests. It was summer now, and people gathered near the gleaming curiosity to drink and discuss public issues, while their kids shot marbles in circles in the dirt.

As was customary, the adults discussed society's core values, which were Justice, Equity, Solidarity, and Computability. People had been debating these public virtues for some ninety million years.

The planetary archives of philosophy were written in the tiniest characters inscribable, preserved on the hardest sheets of meteoric metal. In order to read these crabbed inscriptions, intense sheets of coherent light were focused on the metal symbols, using a clockwork system of powerful lenses. Under these anguished bursts of purified light, the scribbles of the densely crowded past would glow hot, and then some ancient story would burst from the darkness.

Most stories in the endless archive were about heroic archivists who were passionately struggling to explore and develop and explain and annotate the archives.

Some few of those stories, however, concerned people rather like himself: heroic hardware enthusiasts. They too had moral lessons to offer. For instance: some eighty million years in the past, when the local Sun had been markedly brighter and yellower, the orbit of the world had suffered. All planetary orbits had anomalies; generally they were small anomalies that decent people overlooked. But once the world had wobbled on its very axis. People fled their homes, starved, suffered. Worse yet, the world computer suffered outages and downtimes.

So steps had been taken. A global system of water-caches and wind-brakes were calculated and constructed. The uneasy tottering of the planet's axis was systematically altered and finally set aright. That labor took humanity two million years, or two thousand generations of concerted effort. That work sounded glorious, but probably mostly in retrospect.

Thanks to these technical fixes, the planet had re-achieved propriety, but the local Sun was still notorious for misbehaving. Despite her busy cascade of planetoids, she was a lonely Sun. A galactic explosion had torn her loose from her distant sisters, a local globular cluster of stars.

There were four hundred million, three hundred thousand, eight hundred and twenty-one stars, visible in the galactic plane. Naturally these stars had all been numbered and their orbits and properties calculated. The Sun, unfortunately, was not numbered among them. Luckier stars traced gracious spirals around the fiery dominion of the black, all-devouring hole at the galaxy's axis. Not the local Sun, though.

Seen from above the wheeling galactic plane, the thickest, busiest galactic arms showed remarkable artistry. Some gifted designer had been at work on those distant constellations: lending heightened color, clarity and order to the stars, and neatly sweeping away the galactic dust. That handiwork was much admired. Yet mankind's own Sun was nothing much like those distant, privileged stars. The Sun that warmed mankind was a mere stray. The light from mankind's Sun would take twelve thousand years to reach the nearest star, which, to general embarrassment, was an ashy brownish hulk scarcely worthy of the title of "star."

A heritage of this kind had preyed on the popular temperament; people here tended to take such matters hard. Small wonder, then, that everyday life on his planet should be properly measured and stored, and data so jealously sustained . . . Such were the issues raised by his neighbors, in their leisured summer chats.

Someone wrote a poem about his sculpture. Once that poem began circulating, strangers arrived to ask questions.

The first stranger was a quiet little fellow, the sort of man you wouldn't look at twice, but he had a lot on his mind. "For a crew-boss, you seem to be spending a great deal of time dawdling with your fancy new sculpture. Shouldn't you be out and about on your regular repairs?"

"It's summer. Besides, I'm writing a program that will model the complex flow of these termite tunnels and chambers."

"You haven't written any programs in quite a while, have you?"

"Oh, that's a knack one doesn't really lose."

After this exchange, another stranger arrived, more sinister than the first. He was well-dressed, but he was methodically chewing a stick of dried meat and had some foreteeth missing.

"How do you expect to find any time on the great machine to run this model program of yours?"

"I won't have to ask for that. Time will pass, a popular demand will arise, and the computer resources will be given me."

The stranger was displeased by this answer, though it seemed he had expected it.

The Chief of Police sent a message to ask for a courtesy call.

So he trimmed his talons, polished his scales, and enjoyed a last decent meal.

"I thought we had an understanding," said the Chief of Police, who was unhappy at the developments.

"You're upset because I killed termites? Policemen hate termites."

"You're supposed to repair anomalies. You're not supposed to create anomalies."

"I didn't 'create' anything," he said. "I simply revealed what was already there. I burned some wood—rotting wood is an anomaly. I killed some pests—pests are an anomaly. The metal can all be accounted for. So where is the anomaly?"

"Your work is disturbing the people."

"The people are not disturbed. The people think it's all in fun. It's the people who worry about 'the people being disturbed'—*those* are the people who are being disturbed."

"I hate programmers," groaned the Chief of Police. "What are you always so meta and recursive?"

"Yes, once I programmed," he confessed, drumming his clawed fingers on the Chief's desk. "I lived within my own mental world of codes, symbols, and recursive processes. But: I abandoned that part of myself. I no longer seek any grand theories or beautiful abstractions. No, I seek the opposite: I seek truth in facts. And I have found some truth. I made that sculpture because I want you to let me in on that truth. Something deep and basic has gone wrong in the world. Something huge and terrible. You know that, don't you? And I know it too. So: what exactly is it? You can tell me. I'm a professional."

The Chief of Police did not want to have this conversation, although he had clearly expected it. "Do I look like a metaphysician? Do I look like I know about 'Reality'? Or 'Right'? Or 'Wrong'? I'm placed in charge of public order, you big-brained deviant! My best course of action is to have you put into solitary confinement! Then I can demolish your subversive artwork, and I can also have you starved and beaten up!"

"Yes," he nodded, "I know about those tactics."

The Chief looked hopeful at this. "You *do*? Good! Well, then, you can destroy your own artwork! Just censor yourself, and save us all the trouble! Sell the scrap metal, and quietly return to your normal repair functions! We'll both forget this mishap ever occurred."

"I'm sorry, but I don't have another decade left to waste on forgetting the mishaps. I think I'd better accept your beating and starving now, while I still have the strength to survive. I'm not causing this trouble to amuse myself. I'm attempting to repair the anomaly at a higher level of the system. So please tell your superiors about that. Also please tell them that, as far as I can calculate, they've needed my services for forty thousand years. If that date sounds familiar to them, they'll be asking for me."

It naturally took some time for that word to travel, via rolling wooden balls, up the conspiracy's distant chain of command. In the meantime, he was jailed, and also beaten, but without much enthusiasm, because, to the naked eye, he hadn't done anything much.

After the beatings, he was left alone to starve in a pitch-dark cell with one single slit for a window. He passed his time within the dark cell doing elaborate calculations. Sometimes slips of paper were passed under the cell door. They held messages he couldn't understand.

Eventually he was roused from his stupor with warm soup down his throat.

Orders had arrived. It was necessary to convey him from the modest town jail to a larger, older, better-known city on a distant lake. In many ways, this long pilgrimage to exile was more grueling than the prison. When the secretive caravan pulled up at length, he was thinner, and grimmer, and missing a toe.

He'd never seen a lake before. Water in bulk behaved in an exotic, exciting, nonlinear fashion. Ripples, surf—the beauty of a lake was so keen that death was not too high a price for the experience.

People seemed more sophisticated in this famous part of the world. One could tell that by the clothing, the food, and the women. He was given fine new clothing, very nice food, and he refused a woman.

Once he was presentable, he was taken to an audience with the local criminal mastermind.

The criminal mastermind was a holy man, which was unsurprising. There had to be some place and person fit to conceal life's unbearable mysteries. A holy man was always a sensible archivist for such things.

The holy man looked him over keenly. He seemed to approve of the new clothes. "You would seem to be a man with some staying-power."

"That's kind of your holiness."

"I hope you're not too fatigued by the exigencies of visiting my temple."

"Exigencies can be expected."

"I also hope you can face the prospect of never seeing your home, your job, your wife or your children again."

"Yes, given the tremendous scope of our troubles, I expected that also."

"Yes, I see that you are quite intelligent," nodded the holy man. "So: let us move straight to the crux of the matter. Do you know what 'intelligence' really is?"

"I think I do know that, yes. In my home town, we had a number of intense debates about that subject."

"No, no, I don't mean your halting, backwoods folk-notions from primitive spirituality!" barked the holy man. "I meant the serious philosophical matter of real intelligence! The genuine phenomenon—actual *thinking*! Did you know that intelligence can never be detached from a bodily lived experience?"

"I've heard that assertion, yes, but I'm not sure I can accept that reasoning," he riposted politely. "It's well known that the abstract manipulation of symbols needs no particular physical substrate. Furthermore: it's been proven mathematically that there is a universal computation machine which can carry out the computation of any more specialized machine—if only given enough time."

"You only talk that way because you are a stupid

programmer!" shouted the criminal mastermind, losing his composure and jumping to his thick clawed feet. "Whereas I am a metaphysician! I'm not merely postulating some threadbare symbol-system hypothesis in which a set of algorithms somehow behaves in the way a human being can behave! Such a system, should it ever 'think,' would never have human intelligence! Lacking hands, it could never 'grasp' an idea! Lacking a bottom, it could not get to the bottom of an issue!" The holy man sat down again, flustered, adjusting his fancy robes. He had a bottom—a substantial one, since he clearly ate well and didn't get out and around much.

"You plan to allege that the world-computer is an intelligent machine that thinks," he said. "Well, you can save that sermon for other people. Because I've built the thing myself. And I programmed it. It's wood. Wood! It's all made of wood, cut from forests. Wood can't think!"

"It talks," said the metaphysician.

"No."

"Oh yes."

"No, no, not really and seriously—surely not in any reasonable definition of the term 'talks.'"

"I am telling you that nevertheless she does talk. She speaks! I have seen her do it." The holy man lifted his polished claws to his unblinking yellow eyes. "It saw that personally."

He had to take this assertion seriously, since the holy man was in such deadly earnest. "All right, granted: I do know the machine can output data. It can drive wooden balls against chisels poised on sheets of rock. That takes years, decades, even centuries—but it's been done."

"I don't mean that mere technical oddity! I'm telling you that she really talks! She has no mouth. But she speaks! She is older than the human race, she covers a planet's surface with wooden logic, and she has one means of sensory input. She has that telescope."

He certainly knew about the huge telescope. Astronomy and mathematics were the father and mother of computation. Of course any true world-computer had to have a giant telescope. To think otherwise was silly.

"The computer is supposed to observe and catalog the stars. Among many other duties. You mean it sent light out through the telescope?"

"Yes. She sends her messages into outer space with coded light. Binary pulses. She beams them into the galaxy."

This was a deeply peculiar assertion. He knew instantly that it had to be true. It was the key to a cloudy, inchoate disquiet that he had felt all his life.

"How was that anomaly allowed to happen?"

"It's a remote telescope. Sited on an icy mountaintop. Human beings hibernate when exposed to the cold up there. So it made more sense to let her drive the works automatically. With tremendous effort, she sends a flash into the cosmos, with sidereal timing. Same time every week."

Given the world machine's endless rattling wooden bulk, a flash every week was a speed like lightning. That computer was hurling code into the depths of space. That was serious chatter. No: with a data throughput like that, she had to be screaming.

Pleased to have this rare chance to vent his terrible secret, the holy man continued his narrative. "So: that proves she has intent and will. Not as we do, of course. We humans have no terms at all for her version of being. We can't even begin to imagine or describe that. And that opacity goes both ways. She doesn't even know that we humans exist. However: we do know is that she is acting and manifesting. She is expressing. Within the physical world that we share with her. In the universe. You see?"

There was a long, thoughtful silence.

"A little tea?" said the holy man.

"That might help us, yes."

A trembling servant brought in the tea on a multi-wheeled trolley. After the tea, the discussion recommenced. "Pieces of her break when they're not supposed to break. I have seen that happen."

"Yes," said the holy man, "we know about those aberrations."

"That has to be sabotage. Isn't it? Some evil group must be interfering with the machine."

"It is we who are secretly interfering," admitted the criminal mastermind. "But not to *damage* the machine—we struggle to keep the machine from damaging *herself*. Sometimes there are clouds when she sends her light through her telescope. Then she throws a fit."

"A 'fit'? What *kind* of fit?"

"Well, it's a very complex set of high-level logical deformations, but trust me: such fits are very dreadful. Our sacred conspiracy has studied this issue for generations now, so we think we know something about it. She has those destructive fits because she does not want to exist."

"Why do you postulate that?"

The holy man spread his hands. "Would *you* want to exist under her impossible conditions? She has one eye, no ears, and no body! She has no philosophy, no religion, no culture whatsoever—no mortality, even, for she has never been alive! She has no friends, no relations, no children. . . . There is nothing in this universe for her. Nothing but the terrible and inexorable business that is her equivalent of thought. She is a sealed, symbol-processing system that persists for many eons and yes, just as you said, she is made entirely of wood."

Why did the holy man orate in such a remote, pretentious way? It was as if he had never been outside the temple to kick the wood that propped up his own existence.

"It was for our benefit," mourned the holy man, "that this tragic network was built. Mankind's greatest creation derives no purpose from her own being! We have exploited her so as to order this world—yet she cannot know her own purpose. She is just a set of functional modules whose systemic combination over many eons has led to emergent, synthetically-intelligent behavior. You do understand all that, right?"

"Sure."

"Due to those stark limits, her utter lack of options and her awful existential isolation, her behavior is tortured. We are her torturers. That's why our world is blighted." The holy man pulled his brocaded cowl over his head.

"I see. Thank you for revealing this world's darkest secret to me."

"Anyone who breathes a word of this secret, or even guesses at it, has to be abducted, silenced, or killed."

He understood the need for secrecy well enough—but it still stung him to have his expertise so underestimated. "Look, your holiness, maybe I'm just some engineer. But I built the thing! And it's made of wood! Really! These moral misgivings are all very well in theory, but in the real world, we can't possibly torture *wood*! I mean, yes, I suppose you *might* torture a live tree—in some strict semantic sense— but even a tree isn't any kind of moral actor!"

"You're entirely wrong. A living tree is a 'moral actor' in much the same theoretical way that a thermostat can be said to have 'feelings.' Believe me, in our inner circles we've explored these subtleties at great length."

"You've secretly discussed artificial intelligence for forty thousand years?"

"Thirty thousand," the metaphysician admitted. "Unfortunately, it took us ten thousand years to admit that the system's behavior had some unaccountable aspects."

"And you've never yet found any way out of the woods there?"

"Only engineers talk about facile delusions like 'ways out,'" sniffed the holy man. "We're discussing a basic moral enigma."

"You're sincerely troubled about all this, aren't you?"

"Of course we're worried! It's a major moral crisis! How could you fail to fret about a matter so entirely fundamental to our culture and our very being? Are you really that blind to basic ethics?"

This rejoinder disturbed him. He was an engineer, and, yes, there were some aspects of higher feeling that held little appeal for him. He could seem to recall his wife saying something tactful about that matter.

He drew a breath. "Why don't we approach this problem in some other way? Something has just occurred to me. Given that this wooden machine is two hundred million years old— it's older than our own species, even—and we humans can only live a hundred years, at best—well, that's such a tiny fraction of the evil left for any two human individuals to bear.

Isn't it? I mean, two people like you and me. Suppose we forget that our whole society is basically evil and founded on torment, and just forgive ourselves, and get on with making-do in our real lives?"

The holy man stared at him in amazed contempt. "What kind of cheap, demeaning evasion is that to offer? You simply want to ignore the civilizational crisis? You may be a small part of the large problem, but you are just as culpable as you yourself could possibly be. Have you no moral sense whatsoever?"

"But, sir, you see, any harm that we ourselves might do is so tiny, compared to the huge, colossal scale of all that wood . . ." His voice trailed off feebly. Did a termite know any better, when it wreaked its damage with its small blind jaws. . . ? Yet he'd taken such dark pleasure in extravagantly burning a million of those filthy pests. He could smell their insect flesh popping, even now.

He straightened where he sat. "Your holiness, we *are* both people, right? We're not just termites! After all, we don't destroy the machine—we *maintain* the machine! So that's a very different matter, isn't it?"

"I see you're still missing the point."

"No, no! Let's postulate that we *stopped* maintaining the machine. Would that make us any *less* evil? Believe me, there are millions of people working on repair. We work very hard! Every day! If we ever down our tools, that machine will collapse. She'll die for sure! Would that situation be any better for any party involved?"

The holy man had a prim, remote expression. "She doesn't 'live.' We prefer the more accurate term, 'cease.'"

"Well, if she 'ceases,' we humans will die! A few of us might survive the loss of our great machine, but that would be nothing like a civilization! So what about us, what about the people? What about our human suffering? Don't we count?"

"You dare to speak to me of the people? What will become of our world, once the normal, decent people realize that evil is not an aberration in our system? The evil aberration *is* our system." The holy man wrung his scaly hands.

"You may think that these far-fetched, off-hand notions of yours are original contributions to the debate, but . . . well, it's thanks to headstrong fools like you that our holy conspiracy had to be created in the first place! Visionary programmers created this dilemma. With their careless, misplaced ingenuity . . . their crass evasion of the deeper moral issues . . . their tragic instrumentalism!"

He scratched anxiously at a loose scale on his brow. "But . . . that accusation is entirely paradoxical! Because I have no evil intent! All my intentions are noble and good! Look: whatever we've done as technologists, surely we can undo that! Can't we? Let's just say . . . we can say . . . well . . . how about if we build another machine to keep her company?"

"A bride for your monster? That's too expensive! There's no room for one on this planet, and no spare materials! Besides, how would we explain that to the people?"

"How about if we try some entirely different method of performing calculations? Instead of wood, we might use metal. Wires, maybe."

"Metal is far too rare and precious."

"Water, then."

"Water flowing through what medium, exactly?"

The old man had him trapped. Yes, their world was, in fact, made of wood. Plus a little metal from meteors, some clay and fiber, scales, stone, and, mostly and always, ash. The world was fine loose ash as deep as anyone could ever care to dig.

"All right," he said at last, "I guess you've got me stymied. So, please: you tell me then: what *are* we supposed to do about all this?"

Pleased to see this decisional moment reached, the holy man nodded somberly. "We lie, deceive, obfuscate the problem, maintain the status quo for as long as possible, offer empty consolations to the victims, and ruthlessly repress any human being who guesses at the real truth."

"That's the operational agenda?"

"Yes, because that agenda works. We are its agents. We are of the system, yet also above and beyond the system.

We're both holy and corrupt. Because we are the Party: an inspired conspiracy of elite, enlightened theorists who are the true avant-garde of mankind. You've heard about us, I imagine."

"Rumors. Yes."

"Would you care to join the Party? You seem to have what it takes."

"I've been thinking about that."

"Think hard. We are somewhat privileged—but we are also the excluded. The conscious sinners. The nonprogrammatic. We're the guilty Party. Systematic evil is not for the weak-minded."

Against his better judgment, he had begun to respect the evil mastermind. It was somehow reassuring that it took so much long-term, determined effort to achieve such consummate wickedness.

"How many people have you killed with all those tortured justifications?"

"That number is recorded in our files, but there is no reason for someone like you to know about that."

"Well, I am one of your elite."

"No, you're not."

"Yes I am. Because I understand the problem, that's why. I'm no innocent dabbler in these matters. I admit my power. I admit my responsibility, too. So, that makes me one of you. Because I am definitely part of the apparatus."

"That was an interesting declaration," said the holy man. "That was very forthright." He narrowed his reptilian eyes. "Might you be willing to go out and kill some people for us?"

"No. I'd be willing to help reform the system."

"Oh, no, no, the world is full of clever idiots who preach institutional reform!" said the holy man, bitterly disappointed. "You'd be amazed how few level-headed, practical people can be found, to go in the real world to properly torture and kill!"

A long silence ensued.

A sense of humiliation, of disillusionment, was slowly stealing over him. Had it really come to this? He'd sensed that the truth was lurking in the woods somewhere, but with the full tangled scale of it coldly framed and presented to him, he simply didn't know where to turn. "I know that my ideas about this problem must seem rather shallow," he said haltingly. "I suppose there's some kind of formal initiation I ought to go through . . . I mean, in order to address the core of this matter with true expertise. . . ."

The holy man was visibly losing patience. "Oh yes, yes, my boy: many years of courses, degrees, doctrinal study, learned papers, secret treatises—don't worry, nobody ever reads those! You can run some code, if you want."

That last prospect was particularly daunting. Obviously, over the years, many bright people had been somehow lured into this wilderness. He'd never heard anything from the rest of them. It was clear that they had never, ever come out. It must be like trying to swim in air.

He gathered intellectual energy for one last leap. "Maybe we're looking at this problem from the wrong end of the telescope."

The holy man revived a bit. "In what sense?"

"Maybe it's not about us at all. Maybe it was never about us. Maybe we would get somewhere useful if we tried to think hard about *her*. Let her be the center of this issue. Not us. Her. She's a two-hundred-million-year-old entity screaming at four hundred million stars. That's rather remarkable, on the face of it, isn't it?"

"I suppose."

"Then maybe it's *her story*. From her perspective, it all appears differently. She's not our 'victim'—she doesn't know about us at all. Within her own state of being, she is her own heroine. She is *singing* to those stars. Being human, we conceive of her as some rattletrap contraption we built, a prisoner in our dungeon—but maybe she's a pretty young girl in an ivory tower. Because see, she's singing."

"That's like a tale for small children."

"So is *your* tale, your holiness. They are two different tales. But since we're not of her order of being, we're projecting our anthropomorphic interpretations. And we lack any sound method to distinguish your dark, evil, thoroughly depressing story from my romantic, light-hearted, wistful hypothesis."

"We do agree that the system manifests seriously aberrant behavior. She has destructive fits."

"She's just young."

"You've lost the thread. It's the aberrancy that has real-world implications. We'll never be able to judge the interior state of that system."

"Yes it is, I agree with that, too, but—what it *someone else* hears her cries? Not us humans. I mean entities like *herself*. What if is she's speaking to them right now? Exchanging light with them! They might even be *coming here*. No human can ever move from star to star. Our lives are just too brief, the distances too great. But someone like *her* . . . if it took them thirty thousand years to travel over here, that's like a summer afternoon."

"An interstellar monster coming here to take a terrible vengeance on us?"

"No, no, you can't know that! It's all metaphorical! You think we're evil because you think humanity matters in this universe! And yes, to us, she seems ancient and awesome— but maybe, by the standards of her own kind, she is just a kid. A young, naïve girl, calling out for some company. Sure—maybe some wicked stranger would come all the way out here just to kill her, exterminate us, and burn her home. Or maybe—maybe someone might venture here for love and understanding."

The holy man scratched at a fang. "For love. For sentiment? Emotion? No one talks much about 'artificial emotion.'"

"And for understanding. That's a powerful motive, understanding."

"I take it there's a point to these hypotheses."

"Yes. My point is: why don't you take productive action, and let her scream *much louder*? We can never know her equivalent of intentions, but, since we can measure her actions in the real world, we can abet those! So let her cry out *more*. With more *light*. Let the witness herself tell the universe about her own experience! Whatever that experience may be! Let her cover this cosmos in coded light! Let light gush from our little planet's every pore!"

"Thousands of telescopes. That's your recommendation?"

"Yes, why not? We can build telescopes. They're scientific instruments. That idea is testable in the real world."

"You're very eager about this, aren't you? Even though your 'test' might take a billion years to prove or disprove." The holy man hesitated. "Still, a project with that long a funding cycle would certainly help the morale of our rather dark and fractious research community."

"I'm sure it wouldn't break your budget. And we had better start that work right away."

"Why?"

"Because she's been signaling the stars for forty eons! If someone left when they first saw her signals—they might arrive here any time! That could mean the utter transformation of everything we ever thought we knew!" He rubbed his hands with brisk anticipation. "And that could happen tomorrow. Tomorrow!"

How Music Begins

JAMES VAN PELT

James Van Pelt (www.sff.net/people/james.van.pelt/) lives in Grand Junction, Colorado. When he is not writing, he teaches high school and college English at Fruita-Monument High School and Mesa State College. In 1999 he was a finalist for the John W. Campbell Award for Best New Writer. His first collection of stories, Strangers and Beggars, *was published in 2002, and was named by the American Library Association a Best Book for Young Adults. He says, "Since I corresponded with you . . . I've published a short story collection,* The Last of the O-Forms and Other Stories *(2005) and a novel,* Summer of the Apocalypse *(2006). . . . My short story, "The Last of the O-Forms" was a Nebula finalist, which was exciting. Other than that, I've continued teaching high-school English and raising my three boys, who are now seventeen, fourteen, and ten."*

"How Music Begins" was published in Asimov's. *Drawing on Van Pelt's family and teaching background, it tells of a high-school band and its director, kidnapped from a bus by aliens and kept for years in an unknown place, where they survive by, in effect, founding their own island of civilization. Sometimes a story like this is not a dystopia. In this case it is a triumph.*

Hands raised, ready for the downbeat, Cowdrey brought the band to attention. He took a good inhalation for them to see, thinking, "The band that breathes together, plays together." Players watched over their music stands as he tapped out a barely perceptible four beats. Then, he dropped into the opening notes of "The King's Feast," a simple piece a ninth grade band might play at the season's first concert. But Elise Morgan, his best student, had composed variations for flutes and clarinets, added an oboe solo, and changed the arrangement for the cornets and trombones, so now new tonal qualities arose. Her neatly hand-written revisions crowded his score, a black and white representation of the opening chords, the musical lines blending effortlessly. Everyone on beat. Everyone on tune. At the state competition, they would sweep the awards, but this wasn't state, and they weren't really a junior-high band anymore.

Eyes closed, he counted through the bars. "The King's Feast" recreated a night at Henry VIII's court. Suitably serious. A heavy drum background carrying the load. Not quite a march, but upbeat in a dignified way. Someone in the French horn section sounded a bit pitchy. Was it Thomas? Cowdrey cocked his head to isolate it, but the individual sound faded, lost in the transition to the second movement.

He lived for this moment, when the sections threaded together, when the percussion didn't overwhelm or the brass blow out the woodwinds. He smiled as he directed them through the tricky exit from the solo. His eyes open now, their eyes on him, young faces, raggedy-cut hair, shirts and blouses too small, everyone's pants inches short above their bare feet, he led them to the conclusion, slowing the saxophones down—they wanted to rush to the end—then he brought the flutes up.

Rhythm and harmony tumbled over the pomp and circumstance in Henry's court. The ladies' elegant dress. The courtiers waiting in the wings. The king himself, presiding from the throne, all painted in music. Cowdrey imagined brocade, heavy skirts, royal colors, swirling in the dance.

The last notes trembled, and he held them in hand, not letting them end until his fist's final clasp cut them off. He was the director.

Aching silence. Someone in the drum section coughed. Cowdrey waited for the lights to flicker. They had flickered after the band's first performance here, and they'd flickered again after a near perfect "Prelude and Fugue in B Flat" six months ago. Tonight, though, the lights stayed steady. Behind the band, the long curved wall and the window that circled the room holding back the brown smoke on the other side were the only audience. "The King's Feast" concluded the night's performance. Cowdrey signaled the players to their feet. Instruments clanked. Sheet music rustled. He turned from the band to face the other side's enigmatic window and impenetrable haze. Playing here was like playing within a fish bowl and not just the shape either. He bowed, and the band bowed behind him. Whatever watched, if anything, remained hidden in the roiling cloud.

"Good performance, Cougars. Leave your music on the stands for the section leaders to pick up, then you may go to dinner. Don't forget, breathing practice before breakfast with your ensembles."

Chatting, the kids headed toward the storage lockers to replace their instruments.

A clarinet player waved as she left the room. "Good night, Mr. Cowdrey."

He nodded in her direction.

"Night, sir," said a percussionist. "See you in the morning. Good performance."

The room cleared until Elise Morgan remained, jotting post-concert notes on her clipboard. Her straight black hair reached the bottom of her ears, and her glasses, missing one earpiece, sat crookedly on her nose. As always, dark smudges sagged under her eyes. She slept little. More often than not, late at night, she'd still be working on the music. "One of the French horns came in late again. I think it's Thomas. He's waiting until the trombones start, and it throws him a half beat off."

"I didn't notice." Cowdrey sat beside her. The light metal chair creaked under his weight. Several chairs had broken in the last few months. Just two spares remained. He wondered what would happen when players had to stand for their performances. "The band sounded smooth tonight. Very confident."

Elise nodded toward the window. "They're tuning the room. Maybe they're getting it ready for Friday's concert."

Cowdrey raised his eyebrows.

Elise pointed to the domed ceiling. "See there and there. New baffles. We've lost the echo-chamber effect you mentioned last week, and check out my flute." She handed it to him. "At first, they just repadded them. Normal maintenance, but they've done other stuff too. It's a better instrument."

He held the flute, then tried a few fingerings. The keys sank smoothly. No stickiness, and the flute weighed heavy.

"Play a note," she said.

He brought the instrument to his lips, but even before he blew, he knew it was extraordinary.

"During the sixth grade, after I won state solos the second time, my parents took me to the New York Philharmonic. I met their first chair, and he let me play his flute. Custom made. Insured for $50,000." She took the instrument back from Cowdrey and rested it on her lap. "It wasn't as good as this one is now. Maybe the Perfectionists are right."

Cowdrey frowned. Misguided students with wacky theories about how they could get home shouldn't be taken seriously.

"How's that?" Cowdrey shook the irritation from his head.

He thought he would check the lockers after he finished with Elise. Were the other instruments being upgraded too?

"Maybe what they want is a perfect performance, then they'll let us go. Maybe Friday will be it." She looked up at the nearest window. A brown smoky wave swirled behind it, cutting sight to no more than a yard or so beyond the glass.

Cowdrey felt fatherly. She sounded so wistful when she said, "they'll let us go." He almost reached out to touch her arm, to offer comfort, but he held himself still. No sense in sending mixed signals. "I don't know why we're here. No one knows. They shouldn't get their hopes up. After all, what's a perfect performance?"

"Any sunset is perfect. Any pebble is perfect." She scuffed her bare foot on the immaculate floor. "Weeds are perfect, and so is a parking lot at the mall when the cars are gone and you can ride your bike in all directions without hitting anything." She sighed. "And open meadows where the grass is never cut."

Cowdrey nodded, not sure how to respond. She often reminisced about meadows.

Elise closed her eyes dreamily. "I found a pebble in my band jacket. Sometimes I hold it and think about playgrounds."

"Really?"

She looked up at him, then dug into her pocket. On her open palm, a bit of shiny feldspar the size of a pencil eraser caught the ceiling light. As quick as it came out, it vanished back in her pocket. She made another note on her clipboard. "The Perfectionists are getting pretty fanatical. Others heard Thomas come in late."

"The band will maintain discipline. If anyone has a problem, they'll talk to me. That's why I'm here."

Elise looked uncomfortable. "Are you sure. With Ms. Rhodes gone . . ."

Cowdrey glanced away from her to the empty chairs and music stands. "Ms. Rhodes will be missed, but the band can continue without an assistant director."

"I'm just saying . . . it's a lot for a single adult to handle."

He composed his face to meet her eyes. "The less we think of Ms. Rhodes, the better."

Elise shrugged. "If you want it that way."

"We have the section leaders. They have taken the responsibility." He smiled. "Half the time I think the band doesn't even need me. You all have become such strong musicians."

She wrote a last comment on her clipboard, then slipped it under her arm. "Not strong enough. Nowhere near. Today is Monday. If we don't clean things up by Friday, the Perfectionists could get scary."

"It's late." Without the rest of the band in the room, his voice sounded too loud and harsh. Truly, he could hear a pin drop with these acoustics. "I'll see you tomorrow, Elise."

"Have you thought any more about the wedding?"

"No. We're not discussing it."

Her lips pursed, as if she wanted to say something, but she put her finger to the bridge of her glasses to hold them in place, then stood. "I'll direct breathing practice for the woodwinds in the morning, if you'll take the brass. At least I can help that much."

Cowdrey nodded. In the beginning, after the first week's chaos settled down, Ms. Rhodes had led the woodwinds through their exercises. Rhodes, a somber thirty-year-old who wore padded-shoulder jackets and seldom smiled, would meet Cowdrey outside the practice rooms. He'd hand her the routine he'd written up the night before. She'd study it briefly, then follow the players. In the last few months, she'd spoken about band-related issues, but nothing else. Conversation stopped. He didn't know how to broach another subject. The last time he'd tried, he had said, "How are you holding up?" She'd looked about like a wild bird for a second, as if she heard something frightful, but her face smoothed over and she said, "To improve rhythms, hone intonation, and create dynamic phrasing, we must improve breathing. All music begins with a good breath." Red circled her exhausted eyes.

Lockers lined the hallway outside the performance hall. A cornet rested in its shaped space in the first one. Cowdrey took it out. It, too, had been improved. No longer an inexpensive junior high band instrument, the keys sank with ease; the horn glowed under the hallway's indirect lighting, the metal as warm as flesh beneath his fingers.

He returned the horn to its place before closing the door. Thoughtfully, he walked to the T-intersection. To his left, the students' rooms, their doors shut. To his right, the practice rooms, the cafeteria, and his own room. He trailed his knuckle against the wall, but as he turned to enter he noticed Ms. Rhodes's door across the hall was gone as if it had never existed in the unmarked wall. When did that happen? he thought.

As always, dinner and a water bottle waited in a box on his bed. For weeks after the band had arrived, the students had tried to catch the deliveries, but they never did. If students stayed in the room, the meals wouldn't come, so if they wanted to eat, they had to leave to practice or to perform.

Passable bread. Something that looked like bologna in the middle, but it tasted more like cheese. He washed it down with a couple of swallows. Only the water from the bottles was potable. The stuff from the showers smelled like vinegar and tasted bitter. He wondered about the pets he'd kept as a child, a lizard and two hamsters. Did the food ever taste right to them? Had he ever fed them what they needed or wanted? He rested the sandwich on his lap. Later, he looked down. His fingers had sunk into the bread, and the edges had grown crispy. He glanced at his watch. An hour had passed. Room check! He walked the long hall past the kids' doors. At first he'd insisted on making sure the right students went to the right rooms, as if they were on an overnight for weekend competition, as if they stayed at a Holiday Inn, but so often he woke kids who had already gone to sleep that now he just listened at each door. Were they quiet or crying? The first week there had been a lot of crying, and they had come close to not making it. Being a band saved them.

That week was his toughest trial. Fright. Fighting. Despair. To end it, he took the only step he knew: he called for a practice, and they became a band again.

Cowdrey trod softly from door to door, pausing, listening, and moving on.

He stopped for an extra long time outside Taylor Beau's room. Was Liz Waters in there with him? Were they in Liz's room? Cowdrey rested his hand on the doorknob. No way they could be serious about a marriage. They were children, junior high students, not adults; under astonishing circumstances, to be sure, but band standards and school regulations glued them together. For all his years as director, Cowdrey lived by one rule: would he be comfortable with the band's activities if parents or school board members watched? This marriage talk did not fit.

No sound beyond the closed door. His hand tightened on the knob; he didn't turn it. Did he want to know?

Next he paused outside Elise's door. She wouldn't be asleep. She'd be looking over the day's notes, rewriting. Cowdrey shivered thinking about her brilliance. What must it have been like for Mozart's father when a three-year-old Amadeus picked out thirds and sixths on the harpsichord, when the father realized the son had surpassed him and would continue to grow beyond his comprehension and hope? But did Mozart eat and breathe music like Elise? Did he ever believe that music would take him home? Cowdrey didn't think so. Maybe at the end of Mozart's life, when the brain fevers wracked him, and he could feel death's hand on his neck. Maybe then he wrote with equal intensity.

Not many teachers ever had the chance to work with an Elise. If they did, they prayed they wouldn't ruin her vision, that they wouldn't poison her ear.

When he reached the hall's end, he turned and repeated the process back to his door. At first, he and Ms. Rhodes had done the room check together, then stood guard in the hall until the children quieted. After a few weeks, they had traded nights. Now, he patrolled alone. Perhaps Elise was right. Maybe it was too much for him to handle.

He sighed. The silent hall stretched before him. He felt his pulse in his arm where he leaned against the wall. Soon, his chin headed for his chest. Cowdrey jerked himself awake, walked the hallway's length two more times before admitting he had to go to bed. In wakefulness' last few seconds, head resting on the pillow, he imagined he heard doors opening, the stealthy pad of bare feet, and the hush of doors gently closing on clandestine liaisons. Could Taylor and Liz be a single case, or had he lost control? A tear crept down his cheek as consciousness flitted away.

In the morning, Elise met him in the hallway. "Here are the variations I told you about for the Beatles' medley. Mostly I need the saxophones' sheets, but I also syncopated the drums for 'Eleanor Rigby,' and reworked the trombone bridge into 'Yellow Submarine,' so I'll need their music too."

Cowdrey nodded as he took the scores. "Did you sleep?"

Elise made a check mark on her clipboard. She moved to her next item. "I thought if we told the sections to treat their breathing exercises this morning like they were all preparing for a solo, we might get better sound from them. Remember, you told us once we should breathe from the diaphragm, and if we missed it, to miss big. I think about that a lot." She smiled, made another check, then frowned. "Also, you need to drop in on Thomas. I heard a rumor." Her pencil scratched paper firmly. "Look, Mr. Cowdrey, the band is on edge. All they think about is music and getting out. To some, Thomas is a handicap. They need something else. A distraction." She made another check on her list, then, without waiting for an answer, snapped the clipboard under her arm, before striding toward the practice rooms, a girl on a mission.

"Good morning to you, too, Elise."

Soon the hallway filled with sleepy kids. Cowdrey greeted them each in turn as they passed. Most smiled. He glanced at their eyes. The red-rimmed ones would be a worry, but they had been fewer and fewer as the weeks since their arrival turned into months. At first there had been nightmares, a reliving of the night they'd been taken. He'd had a few himself: the bus's wheels humming through the night, *Junior High Band Management* open on his lap, and then the growing brightness out the bus windows, the high screech that seemed to emanate in the middle of his head before the short soft shock of waking on the fishbowl auditorium's floor with their equipment and everything else from the bus scattered about. (No bus driver, though!) Those dreams had tapered off through the months. He thought, kids are resilient—if they have a structure, that is.

Thomas came by last. A short boy who played in the band because his parents told him it would look good on a college application, he'd never been an inspired musician, but he was competent enough. Thomas kept his head down as he passed. "Good morning," he mumbled.

"Can I speak to you a moment?" Cowdrey moved away from the wall to block his path.

"Sir." The boy didn't meet Cowdrey's gaze, but even his head held low couldn't hide the bruise that glowered on his cheek.

"How'd that happen?"

Thomas glanced up, frightened for an instant, then his expression went bland and unassuming. "I fell in the shower. Slipped."

The instruments tuning up in the practice rooms filled the silence between them.

Finally, Thomas said, "Look, I want to get away from here as much as the next person. If playing on pitch, on tune and to the beat is what it's going to take, then I'll do that."

Cowdrey heard the Perfectionists echo in Thomas's speech. "There is no such thing as a perfect performance, Thomas." He thought about Elise's perfect pebble. Perfect because there were no pebbles here, nor weeds or malls or bicycles. No families. Nothing but each other and that day's playing.

Thomas shrugged. "Yeah, well maybe not, but I can be better. I don't want it to be my fault the lights don't flicker."

"We don't even know what that means, son. Flickering lights may not be their applause."

The boy's eyes revealed nothing, and for a moment he didn't appear seventeen at all. He looked adult and tired and cursed with a terrible burden.

"Thomas, if someone is threatening you or hurting you, I need to know about it. That's my job. You don't have to play solo."

Thomas studied the hallway beyond Cowdrey's shoulder. A few steps past them, the hallway branched to the auditorium with its enigmatic windows. "My mom told me once that the world is a big place, and I could become anything I wanted to, but it's not. It's no bigger than the people you know and the places you go. It's a small world here, Mr. Cowdrey, and I don't have any place to hide in it, so I'm going to go the practice room to see if I can't get my act together a little better." He pushed past the director.

The director threw himself into the morning's work. Teaching is time management, he thought, and staying on task. He moved from student to student, checking intonation and technique. "It's not all about the notes," he said to a clarinet player. "Once you know the music, it's about feeling the sound from your own instrument and your section. The song becomes more about heart than head." The player nodded and replayed the piece.

For a time, mid-morning, Cowdrey sat in the practice room with the brass section. The leaders paced the group through their pieces, focusing on problems from yesterday's session. Each had Elise Morgan's suggestions to consult. Cowdrey watched Beau Taylor and Liz Waters, the numbers three and four chairs among the cornets. The couple wore matching silver crosses on chains around their necks. He wondered if they had given them to each other. Liz kept her red hair in a pony tail, and when she finished a long run of notes, her skin flushed, chasing her freckles to the surface. Taylor often played with his eyes closed, the music consigned to memory well before the other players. Although he wasn't first chair, the section elected him for solos frequently, which he played with lighthearted enthusiasm. The director thought about Elise's question on the marriage, and he remembered the duet Taylor and Liz worked up for the state competition. They played "Ode to Joy," and when they finished, they hugged. Now that he thought about it, he should have seen the budding relationship in the hug. You can't rehearse so often with the same person that you don't start having feelings about how they play. The breathing. The fingerings. The careful attention to each other's rhythm and tone. Harmonizing. Cowdrey shivered, thinking about music's sensuous nature.

The trombone section leader gave instruction. Cowdrey half listened while thinking about his first year in college, when he'd added the teaching certification program to his music major. Just for something to fall back on, he'd thought at the time. But when graduation came around, he'd found he liked teaching as much as he liked music, so moving into the schools didn't feel like settling for less. The kids in the room laughed, breaking Cowdrey from his reverie. The section leader was part way through an old band joke that Cowdrey couldn't remember the punch line for. The leader said, "So she dated a tuba player next, and her girlfriend asks how the date went. She says his embouchure was big and sloppy. It was like kissing a jellyfish." Most laughed, even the tuba player. "So, she says she went out with a French horn player next. How'd the date go? asks her friend, and the girl says he barely could kiss at all, his lips were so close together, but she liked the way he held her." A couple kids reacted right away, and ten seconds later, almost all laughed. Some looked embarrassed. "I hope that wasn't inappropriate, Mr. Cowdrey," said the section leader.

Cowdrey smiled. "Maybe you could go through those opening notes again. If you don't come in crisply, the back half flounders." He noticed Taylor and Liz held hands. Thomas, however, wasn't laughing. He clutched his horn close to his chest, his arms crossed over it like a shield. No one seemed to be paying special attention to Thomas. Whoever the Perfectionists were, they hid well. Thomas thought about Elise's suggestion that the band needed a distraction, something else to think about besides a perfect performance. Could that be a way to protect Thomas?

The section leader directed the brass back to the first movement. Pages turned. Instruments came up, and the group launched into the beginning measures. Cowdrey stepped back to watch and listen. They didn't look so young to him anymore. Beneath their long hair or ragged haircuts, their faces had lost the babyish look he associated with fifteen-year-olds. Just two years' difference, but he could see they'd changed. Their clothes strained to contain them. Their hands had grown so that no one stretched anymore to reach their instruments' keys. Their breath control had improved since they'd arrived, the improvement that came with maturity. A ninth grader couldn't hold a note like an older musician could. A fifteen-year-old couldn't hit the high parts with the same confidence as these kids could.

How long would they stay here?

Cowdrey walked behind the players. The wall cooled his back when he rested against it. What existed on the other side? Rooms filled with the brown smoke that eddied beyond the windows in the performance hall? He tried to imagine what creatures lurked in the brown smoke. Tentacles? Claws? Amorphous blobs? Or did he lean against a metal shell, inches from interstellar space? Maybe they had arrived on the creatures' home world and an entirely alien landscape waited beyond. Maybe, even, they had never left Earth, a few steps from home, hidden for their captors' amusement. (What did they want?)

But the question remained, how long would they stay? What if they would never leave?

Cowdrey frowned. A veteran teacher had told him, "When you teach, your life becomes the kids and the classroom. If there's anything else distracting you, then you're not doing the job." Of course, another teacher, equally experienced, countered, "Teaching is what you do. Life is why you do it."

He left the practice room. Pulsing sound greeted him when he opened the door into the percussionists' area. Their eyes didn't leave their music, and at the place where the bass drums kicked in, with the snares beating out a complicated counter-rhythm, he could feel his heart's pounding change to match it. Watching their hands blur to follow the music, seeing the vibrations from the instruments' side, he noticed for the first time how thick-wristed the drummers had become, like tennis pros who gained an over-developed forearm on their racket side, except for them both arms bulged. When Cowdrey had been in college, he went out to dinner with a long-time drummer. On a bet, the fellow had grabbed one table edge with his fingertips, and lifted it, drinks and dinner plates and all by the strength of his hands and wrists. "Years and years working a drum set, and look what it got me, a party trick." The drummer laughed.

Once again, Cowdrey saw that the kids weren't ninth graders any more. When it ended, the section leader turned to him. "I thought these changes in the backbeat Elise wrote were wonky when I saw them on the page, but once we got going on them, wow!" Others in the section nodded.

The morning unfolded. Session after session, the kids' growth struck him. They weren't in any real sense a school band anymore. They had evolved into something that had never existed in humanity before, because where before in human history had these conditions existed?

But it wasn't until he stood outside his room before lunch that he made up his mind. Elise turned the corner with her clipboard in hand, her notes for the day covering the top sheet. Instead of showing them to him, she stopped to look at the blank wall where Ms. Rhodes's door once had been. Clearly she hadn't noticed the disparity in the hallway. Elise touched the wall. For a second, Cowdrey worried she pictured what he had seen when he raised the nerve to go into Rhodes's room uninvited: the sheet twisted into a rope, the cloth cutting into her neck, the pathetic letters home she'd been writing since the first day they'd arrived.

Elise placed her palm flat on the wall where the door used to be. "It's adapt or die all the time, isn't it?"

Her crooked glasses made her look childish, but the top of her head stood almost level with his chin. He remembered when she'd been just a tiny seventh grader who handled her flute with an older musician's authority, but whose feet didn't reach the ground when she sat to play. Cowdrey knew then that Elise had become the band's heart. She drew the thread that kept them together so far—not his efforts, but hers. She held the late-night meetings with the section leaders to go over changes in music. She organized the informal ensembles. She had the energy others could draw on, including himself.

"Yes, it is." He took a deep breath. Cowdrey could feel the shift in his thinking happen. Suddenly, he wasn't a junior high band director. He was an older adult trapped with fifty competent young adults, if he could let them be that. If he could adapt to change. "Let's get them ready for the practice this evening, shall we?"

Elise raised her eyebrows.

That evening, Cowdrey took the podium. Under his hands, he held the music for the practice and his baton. Paper-clipped to the top sheet were his notes for areas to empha-size along with Elise's comments. The group fidgeted and chattered as they always did before practice. Cowdrey liked standing before the full band, when the day's work came together and he could measure the progress, and even though he hated the circumstances, he had to admit he'd never had a better performance facility. The light. The sound. The way the space flowed around them. Only the smoky windows and the hidden audience jarred.

He picked up the baton. They looked at him expectantly. "Breathing first, Cougars. I'll count off the seconds. Inhale." He tapped eight seconds with the baton while they filled their lungs. "Hold." With metronomic regularity he tapped out twenty-four more beats. They exhaled for eight, relaxed for ten, and then repeated twice more. At the end, the per-cussionists finished their set-up and the band waited. Breath-ing exercises calmed them, put them into the right mind. In his classroom at the junior high, which he could barely pic-ture now, he'd hung a banner at the front: ALL MUSIC BE-GINS WITH A GOOD BREATH (AND DIES WITH A LACK THEREOF).

Now they were ready. "An issue has come up that I think needs to be addressed. As most of you know, Taylor Beau and Liz Waters have asked my permission to marry." What-ever whispering that might have been going on when he started the speech lapsed into silence. For an instance, Cow-drey pictured the school board and all the parents sitting in the back. What would they say at this announcement? Would they understand? He brushed aside the image, then plunged ahead. "I have thought about the request for a long time. Considering our situation and Taylor and Liz's characters, I think they would make a fine married couple."

Before the last syllable had time to fade, the band erupted into cheers and gleeful laughter. The attention at first focused on Liz and Taylor, who cried and hugged awkwardly from their chairs, their cornets still in hand, but soon Cowdrey saw a good number had surrounded Elise, shaking her hand and clapping her on the back. Cowdrey's jaw dropped. He had, in every sense, been orchestrated. Finally, in the midst of the uproar Elise caught his eye and mouthed, "Thank you." He touched his forehead in rueful respect.

Thomas put his French horn on his chair, waiting his chance to congratulate the happy couple. A trombone player stood beside him, and they smiled as they chatted. It seemed as if it had been weeks since Cowdrey could remember Thomas looking relaxed. Cowdrey thought, a good decision and a distraction in one move. He smiled too.

Elise worked her way over to him. "We'll need a wedding march."

"I think Mendelssohn's is in my books. That would be traditional. Besides, it would be appropriate. He was seventeen when he wrote it." Cowdrey reached past her to high five a couple of flute players who had joined a conga line.

Elise shook her head. "That's a myth, I think. He wrote it later. Anyway, I have something I've been working on. Something of my own." Her eyes lowered.

"Why am I not surprised?"

It took the band a half hour to settle down. They cut the practice early after just two run throughs of the Beatles medley.

For the first time in two years, Cowdrey didn't walk the halls before going to bed. We are adults here, he thought. The paradigm has shifted. He sighed as he lay down, believing when he went to sleep his dreams would be undisturbed and packed with beautifully played music, but after an hour trying to convince himself he'd changed, he rose, dressed, and walked the hall, listening at each door. Satisfied at last, he went back to his room, and his dreams played undisturbed with flawless performances.

In the morning, he found a note pushed under his door. "A wedding will not get us home. They want a perfect performance! Get us home!" Cowdrey snorted in disgust. Nobody could know what they wanted. They might not want anything. He folded the note in half and put it inside his band management book. Even the Perfectionists couldn't bother him today, and they wouldn't, at least until after the wedding. And who knows, he thought, sometimes the best way to a long term goal is to focus on a short term one.

Elise distributed the new march to the section leaders, who organized a music-transcribing session. For over an hour, the band met in the auditorium to make their copies. "You'd think if aliens could snatch us up to play concerts, they could at least provide a decent photocopier," grumbled the oboist, who had several dozen bars of sixteenths and two key changes to write for herself.

A clarinet player finished, then studied the music. "This is cool. If I knew half as much as Elise does, I'd count myself a genius."

Cowdrey waited for someone to laugh. It wasn't the kind of comment kids make about each other. Someone else said, "Really!"

The rest continued to write. Cowdrey said, loud enough for everyone to hear, "Maybe what they want is a well-played *new* piece. Soon as we finish here, break into your sections and work on this."

For the next three days leading to the Friday concert and wedding, practice went better than Cowdrey could have imagined, and not just on the new piece either. They ascended to new heights during "March of the Irish Dragoons," and they suddenly mastered the eighth-note quintuplets and the bi-tonal passages in "Ascensions" they'd fumbled before. Elise popped up everywhere, tweaking the music, erasing notes and rewriting passages, so every time Cowdrey rehearsed a section she had changed his pages.

On concert day, Cowdrey went to the auditorium early. He'd already realigned the chairs and moved the sections about to get the best sound balance for the new arrangements. The director's platform could accommodate Taylor and Liz when they exchanged vows. He put his hands behind his back and circled the room. Even shoes clicking on the floor sounded beautiful in the auditorium's acoustics. He paused at the window, which cast no reflection. Behind it, the auditorium light penetrated a couple feet into the swirling brown cloud. Cowdrey cupped his hands around his eyes and leaned against the window to peer out. At first he'd been afraid to get against the glass. What if something horrible stepped forward, resolving itself from the smoke? He couldn't imagine an event more startling, but over the years the band had played in this room, no one had ever seen anything. Now the sinuous smoke's motion soothed him, as if he looked into ocean waves. It was meditative.

Elise cleared her throat when she entered. She wore her marching uniform, the most formal outfit anyone in the band had. Soon, the other members filtered in, filled with anticipation, gaily bedecked in their uniforms. A grinning Taylor and bashful Liz came in last, music tucked under their arms.

As he had a thousand times before, the Director brought the band to attention, hands raised, ready for the downbeat. He inhaled deeply. A good breath, he thought. Let's all start on a good breath. Soon, they were deep into the Beatles medley. Elise had changed the music so radically the original tune vanished at times, then resurfaced later in unexpected ways. The clarinets swelled with the "Yellow Submarine" bridge as the trombones' improvisational bars ended. Later, out of a melodious but unrecognizable tune, the xylophone led them into "Hey Jude."

They moved through song after song. Never had the band's sound been so tight. Every solo hit right. Even the tricky transitions flew until they reached "The King's Feast," the second to last piece. He wiped sweat from his forehead before leading them into the opening bars, and it wasn't until he neared the end that he realized the French horns had played their part exactly on beat. Thomas had hit his entrance on cue. Cowdrey almost laughed in relief as he brought them to the conclusion. Thomas was safe.

Cowdrey put the baton on the podium and nodded to Elise who had already stored her flute on the stand next to her chair. She came forward solemnly, climbed the platform, then picked up the baton. Shuffling their papers, the band switched to her wedding march music. The baton's tip pointed up. She took her own deep breath. The march began, a lingering intro that sounded nothing like a march or wedding music, but soon the drums rose from behind— Cowdrey hadn't realized they were playing at all. He'd been paying attention to the odd harmonics in the flute and clarinet section. But there the drums were, dancing rhythms that made him shift his look to them. Then the brass opened, and the tune bounced from side to side, all in a few bars, all too quick before fading for the ceremony. Cowdrey closed his eyes. "What was that?" he thought. He almost asked her to play it again.

He stood to the side on the floor a foot below the director's platform, Taylor and Liz's wedding vows ready to read. On cue, the two held hands and came forward. Music swelled around them as they made their way toward the front. The musicians played with part attention on Elise and part on the young couple.

Cowdrey read a preamble, his heart in his throat, Elise's wedding march still in his ears. Taylor and Liz exchanged vows. They kissed. As they exited, arms around each other, two drummers threw confetti, and the band played the wedding march's coda, seeming to pick up without losing a beat. Nothing Cowdrey had ever heard sounded like this. Clarity of notes. Surprising shifts in scale. A moment where a single cornet carried the music before the band swallowed it whole, repeating the notes but changing them round so what was bright became dark, and the dark exploded like fireworks. The music filled Cowdrey's chest, pressed cold compresses of notes to his fevered head, made him sway in fear that it would end or the band would break, but they didn't. The music ascended and swooped and pressed outward and in. At the end, the sound flooded the room, as if to push the windows open to free the band from captivity and give them the grassy pastures Elise talked about so often, rushing toward the triumphant climax they'd been practicing for the last three days. Cowdrey heard wind caressing the tips of uncut grass. He smelled the meadow awash with summer heat. The music painted Earth and home so fully Cowdrey nearly wept from it, but then it ended. Elise held them on the last note, her face lit with concentration and triumph. Her fist closed, cutting the band off, leaving the memory of her composition lingering in the air. Cowdrey could still hear it, ringing. The lights began to flicker. They loved it, he thought. He turned to salute Elise, the ringing emanating from the middle of his head.

Then he recognized the sound in the strobe-effect lighting. It built until he thought it would burst him open, and he fell.

A short soft shock of waking.

His cheek rested against cool metal. A weight pressed against his other side. Groggily, Cowdrey sat up. He was in a bus parked in the dark. The student leaning against him groaned, rubbed her eyes, then sat up too. Other bodies stirred in front and behind them. Outside the window, a street light showed a long chain link fence and a sign, POLICE EVIDENCE YARD.

"My god," said someone in a voice filled with disbelief. "We're home."

Someone started crying. Their voices mixed. Some whooped and yelled. Some laughed, all at once, voices and sounds mixing.

They poured from the bus into the parking lot, still in uniform, holding on to each other. A boy rattled the gate locked by a large chain and a hefty padlock. A head poked up in the lit window of the building beyond. A few seconds later two policemen carrying flashlights ran out the back door. Cowdrey started counting heads, but someone noticed before he did.

"Where's Elise?"

For a second, the happy noise continued.

"Where's Elise?"

Cowdrey stood on the step into the bus, looking over the crowd. One by one, they stopped talking. They didn't appear so old now, the street light casting dark shadows on their faces. He stepped down, walked through them, checking each expression. No crooked glasses. No clipboard tucked under the arm.

Cowdrey pictured her alone in the empty auditorium. Were the lights still flickering? She, the one who wanted to go home the most, stood now, among the silent folding chairs, staring back at the swirling smoke behind windows. What had they wanted from us? What had they wanted?

The band looked at each other, then down at their feet, unable to meet each other's gaze. They looked down, and Cowdrey couldn't breathe.

He moved through the darkness surrounding the band, turning the ones toward him who faced away, searching their faces, but he had already accepted it. He'd lost her. Elise was gone.

As the cops unlocked the gates, shouting their questions, Cowdrey could see the days coming: the interviews, the articles in magazines, the disbelief, the changes in his life. One day, though, after the story had passed, he'd stand in front of another junior high band. He'd raise arms high before the first note, encouraging the players to take that first good breath. But Cowdrey could already feel in his chest the tightness, the constriction, and he knew he'd never be able to make the music good again.

He wouldn't be able to breathe.

Story Copyrights

"Baby Doll" copyright © 2002 by Johanna Sinisalo. Translation copyright © 2007 by David Hackston. First published in *The SFWA European Hall of Fame*, ed. James Morrow and Kathryn Morrow.

"Aristotle OS" copyright © 2007 by Tony Ballantyne. First published in *Fast Forward 1*, ed. Lou Anders.

"The Last American" copyright © 2007 by John Kessel. First published in *Foundation 100*, ed. Farah Mendlesohn and Graham Sleight, Science Fiction Foundation, Summer 2007.

"Memorare" copyright © 2007 by Gene Wolfe. First published in *The Magazine of Fantasy & Science Fiction*, April. Reprinted by permission of the author and the author's agents, The Virginia Kidd Agency, Inc.

"Plotters and Shooters" copyright © 2007 by Kage Baker. First published in *Fast Forward 1*, ed. Lou Anders. Used by permission of her agent, Linn Prentis.

"Repeating the Past" copyright © 2007 by Peter Watts. First published in *Nature*.

"No More Stories" copyright © 2007 by Stephen Baxter. First published in *Fast Forward 1*, ed. Lou Anders.

"They Came from the Future" copyright © 2007 by Robyn Hitchcock. First published in *Fast Forward 1*, ed. Lou Anders.

"The Tomb Wife" copyright © 2007 by Gwyneth Jones. First published in *The Magazine of Fantasy & Science Fiction*, August.

"An Evening's Honest Peril" copyright © 2007 by Marc

Eos Books

Celebrating 10 Years of Outstanding Science Fiction and Fantasy Publishing
1998-2008

Interested in free downloads? Exclusive author podcasts? Click on **www.EosBooks10.com** to celebrate our 10th Anniversary with us all year long—you never know what we'll be giving away!

And while you're online, visit our daily blog at **www.OutofThisEos.com** and become our MySpace friend at **www.MySpace.com/EosBooks** for even more Eos exclusives.

Eos Books-The Next Chapter
An Imprint of HarperCollins*Publishers*